Dragons!

Orson Scott Card presents all new stories
about these fabulous creatures, written by
some of the finest writers in the field, each
illustrated by an outstanding artist.

ORSON SCOTT CARD

DRAGONS OF DARKNESS

BART

NEW YORK

TABLE OF CONTENTS

INTRODUCTION

This book is a companion volume of *Dragons of Light,* but that doesn't mean that the other book is cheerful, while this one is depressing. In fact, there is as much comedy in this volume as in the other, and as many happy endings. In *Dragons of Darkness,* however, the dragons generally come from or strike at a darker place in the human heart; they are, on the whole, crueller and more dangerous. And yet this only serves to make victory over them all the more exalting; defeat by them all the more tragic; and comedy about them all the funnier. For pain is at the heart of all powerful stories, whether happy or sad. What would *A Christmas Carol* be without Tiny Tim's agony, Scrooge's loneliness, the ghoulish thieves? What would be funny about Charlie Chaplin or Woody Allen if we did not share their woes? The majesty of cathedrals cries out for gargoyles and dark corners; Oedipus must tear out his eyes to vindicate himself; even Frank Capra's cheerfulest films rest upon a foundation of fear and suffering. Pity and terror—Aristotle said they were at the heart of tragedy. He overlooked them in comedy, hidden as they were in all those raucous belly laughs of comedy. *Dragons of Darkness*—they'll take you by surprise, make you laugh, make you rejoice in the nobility of the characters who oppose or fulfill them. And then they'll take you by surprise again, for they have distant cousins dwelling in an unsuspected place, closer to your neighborhood than you might have thought at first.

When Michael Goodwin and I began this project sometime in the nineteenth century (or does it only feel that ancient?), one worry was that we would not have enough variety to make a really viable anthology. After all, how many possible stories can there be about dragons? You hold half the answer in your hands. There are as many dragons as there are writers, just as each artist has brought his own interpretation to the dragons in this book, and our problem was not variety but simply fitting all the excellent stories into a book small enough to bear a reasonable price. (And the cover price on this book *is* reasonable. A few hundred years ago, only the very rich could afford to own books, and a dozen volumes made up an impressive library. Now even people who can't read own books by the hundreds; if you don't believe me, glance at a few book review columns and you'll see what I mean.)

Another problem we faced was answering the question, "When is a dragon not a dragon?" Our solution was that if by any stretch of the imagination a story could be said to include a dragon, we would stretch our imaginations to fit. As a result you will find that the dragon in "The Thermals of August" doesn't shed scales in the summer; the dragon in "Fear of Fly" does not breathe fire; and the dragons in "A Plague of Butterflies" are really another sort of creature entirely. But most of the dragons here are of a familiar species, the wyrm that has fascinated storytellers from China to Europe, from the Quetzelcoatl serpents of Mesoamerica to the Satan figure in the Apocalypse of St. John. You know what he looks like. But what the dragon will do next—that you do not know, until you turn the pages.

DRAGONS
OF
DARKNESS

All four held ornate silver daggers.

FILED TEETH

GLEN COOK

ILLUSTRATIONS BY
MICHAEL WHELAN

I

Our first glimpse of the plain was one of Heaven. The
snow and treacherous passes had claimed two men and
five animals.

Two days later we all wished we were back in the
mountains.

The ice storm came by night. An inch covered the
ground. And still it came down, stinging my face, frosting
the heads and shoulders of my companions . The footing
was impossible. We had to finish two broken-legged mules
before noon.

Lord Hammer remained unperturbed, unvanquishable.
He remained stiffly upright on that red-eyed stallion, im-
placably drawing us northeastward. Ice clung to his cowl,
shoulders, and the tail of his robe where it lay across his
beast's rump. Seldom did even Nature break the total
blackness of his apparel.

The wind hurtled against us, biting and clawing like a
million mocking imps. It burned sliding into the lungs.

The inalterable, horizon-to-horizon bleakness of the
world gnawed the roots of our souls. Even Fetch and

1

irrepressible Chenyth dogged Lord Hammer in a desperate silence.

"We're becoming an army of ghosts," I muttered at my brother. "Hammer is rubbing off on us. How're the Harish taking this?" I didn't glance back. My concentration was devoted to taking each next step forward.

Chenyth muttered something I didn't hear. The kid was starting to understand that adventures were more fun when you were looking back and telling tall tales.

A mule slipped. She went down kicking and braying. She caught old Toamas a couple of good ones. He skittered across the ice and down an embankment into a shallow pool not yet frozen.

Lord Hammer stopped. He didn't look back, but he knew exactly what had happened. Fetch fluttered round him nervously. Then she scooted toward Toamas.

"Better help, Will," Chenyth muttered.

I was after him already.

Why Toamas joined Lord Hammer's expedition I don't know. He was over sixty. Men his age are supposed to spend winter telling the grandkids lies about the El Murid, Civil, and Great Eastern Wars. But Toamas was telling us his stories and trying to prove something to himself.

He was a tough buzzard. He had taken the Dragon's Teeth more easily than most, and those are the roughest mountains the gods ever raised.

"Toamas. You okay?" I asked. Chenyth hunkered down beside me. Fetch scooted up, laid a hand on each of our shoulders. Brandy and Russ and the other Kaveliners came over too. Our little army clumped itself into national groups.

"Think it's my ribs, Will. She got me in the ribs." He spoke in little gasps. I checked his mouth.

"No blood. Good. Lungs should be okay."

"You clowns going to talk about it all week?" Fetch

snapped. "Help the man, Will."

"You got such a sweet-talking way, Fetch. We should get married. Let's get him up, Chenyth. Maybe he's just winded."

"It's my ribs, Will. They're broke, sure."

"Maybe. Come on, you old woods-runner. Let's try."

"Lord Hammer says carry him if you have to. We've still got to cover eight miles today. More, if the circle isn't alive." Fetch's voice went squeaky and dull, like an old iron hinge that hadn't been oiled for a lifetime. She scurried back to her master.

"I think I'm in love," Chenyth chirped.

"Eight miles," Brandy grumbled. "What the hell? Bastard's trying to kill us."

Chenyth laughed. It was a ghost of his normal tinkle. "You didn't have to sign up, Brandy. He warned us it would be tough."

Brandy wandered away.

"Go easy, Chenyth. He's the kind of guy you got to worry when he stops bitching."

"Wish he'd give it a rest, Will. I haven't heard him say one good word since we met him."

"You meet all kinds in this business. Okay, Toamas?" I asked. We had the old man on his feet. Chenyth brushed water off him. It froze on his hand.

"I'll manage. We got to get moving. I'll freeze." He stumbled toward the column. Chenyth stayed close, ready to catch him if he fell.

The non-Kaveliners watched apathetically. Not that they didn't care. Toamas was a favorite, a confidant, adviser, and teacher to most. They were just too tired to move except when they had to. Men and animals looked vague and slumped through the ice rain.

Brandy gave Toamas a spear to lean on. We lined up. Fetch took her place at Lord Hammer's left stirrup. Our ragged little army of thirty-eight homeless bits of war-flotsam started moving again.

II

Lord Hammer was a little spooky . . . What am I saying? He scared hell out of us. He was damned near seven feet tall. His stallion was a monster. He never spoke. He had Fetch do all his talking.

The stallion was jet. Even its hooves were black. Lord Hammer dressed to match. His hands remained gloved all the time. None of us ever saw an inch of skin. He wore no trinkets. His very colorlessness inspired dread.

Even his face he kept concealed. Or, perhaps, especially his face . . .

He always rode point, staring ahead. Opportunities to peek into his cowl were scant. All you would see, anyway, was a blackened iron mask resembling a handsome man with strong features. For all we knew, there was no one inside. The mask had almost imperceptible eye, nose, and mouth slits. You couldn't see a thing through them.

Sometimes the mask broke the colorless boredom of Lord Hammer. Some mornings, before leaving his tent, he or Fetch decorated it. The few designs I saw were never repeated.

Lord Hammer was a mystery. We knew nothing of his origins and were ignorant of his goals. He wouldn't talk, and Fetch wouldn't say. But he paid well, and a lot up front. He took care of us. Our real bitch was the time of year chosen for his journey.

Fetch said winter was the best time. She wouldn't expand.

She claimed Lord Hammer was a mighty, famous sorcerer.

So why hadn't any of us heard of him?

Fetch was a curiosity herself. She was small, cranky, long-haired, homely. She walked more mannish than a man. She was totally devoted to Hammer despite being inclined to curse him constantly. Guessing her age was impossible. For all I could tell, she could have been anywhere between twenty and two hundred.

She wouldn't mess with the men.

By then that little gnome was looking good.

Sigurd Ormson, our half-tame Trolledyngjan, was the only guy who had had nerve enough to really go after her. The rest of us followed his suit with a mixture of shame and hope.

The night Ormson tried his big move Lord Hammer strolled from his tent and just stood behind Fetch. Sigurd seemed to shrivel to about half normal size.

You couldn't see Lord Hammer's eyes, but when his gaze turned your way the whole universe ground to a halt. You felt whole new dimensions of cold. They made winter seem balmy.

Trudge. Trudge. Trudge. The wind giggled and bit. Chenyth and I supported Toamas between us. He kept muttering, "It's my ribs, boys. My ribs." Maybe the mule had scrambled his head, too.

"Holy Hagard's Golden Turds!" Sigurd bellowed. The northman had ice in his hair and beard. He looked like one of the frost giants of his native legends.

He thrust an arm eastward.

The rainfall masked them momentarily. But they were coming closer. Nearly two hundred horsemen. The nearer they got, the nastier they looked. They carried heads on lances. They wore necklaces of human fingerbones. They had rings in their ears and noses. Their faces were painted. They looked grimy and mean.

They weren't planning a friendly visit.

Lord Hammer faced them. For the first time that morning I glimpsed his mask paint.

White. Stylized. Undeniably the skullface of Death.

He stared. Then, slowly, his stallion paced toward the nomads.

Bellweather, the Itaskian commanding us, started yelling. We grabbed weapons and shields and formed a ragged-assed line. The nomads probably laughed. We were scruffier than they were.

"Gonna go through us like salts through a goose," Toamas complained. He couldn't get his shield up. His spear seemed too heavy. But he took his place in the line.

Fetch and the Harish collected the animals behind us.

Lord Hammer plodded toward the nomads, head high, as if there were nothing in the universe he feared. He lifted his left hand, palm toward the riders.

A nimbus formed round him. It was like a shadow cast every way at once.

The nomads reined in abruptly.

I had seen high sorcery during the Great Eastern Wars. I had witnessed both the thaumaturgies of the Brotherhood and the Tervola of Shinsan. Most of us had. Lord Hammer's act didn't overwhelm us. But it did dispel doubts about his being what Fetch claimed.

"Oh!" Chenyth gasped. "Will. Look."

"I see."

Chenyth was disappointed by my reaction. But he was only seventeen. He had spent the Great Eastern Wars with our mother, hiding in the forests while the legions of the Dread Empire rolled across our land. This was his first venture at arms.

The nomads decided not to bother us after all. They milled around briefly, then rode away.

Soon Chenyth asked, "Will, if he can do that, why'd he bring us?"

He lifted his left hand, palm towards the riders.

"Been wondering myself. But you can't do everything with the Power."

We were helping Toamas again. He was getting weaker. He croaked, "Don't get no wrong notions, Chenyth lad. They didn't have to leave. They could've took us slicker than greased owl shit. They just didn't want to pay the price Lord Hammer would've made them pay."

III

Lord Hammer stopped.

We had come to a forest. Scattered, ice-rimed trees stood across our path. They were gnarled, stunted things that looked a little like old apple trees.

Fetch came down the line, speaking to each little band in its own language. She told us Kaveliners, "Don't ever leave the trail once we pass the first tree. It could be worth your life. This's a fey, fell land." Her dusky little face was as somber as ever I had seen it.

"Why? Where are we? What's happening?" Chenyth asked.

She frowned. Then a smile broke through. "Don't you ever stop asking?" She was almost pretty when she smiled.

"Give him a break," I said. "He's a kid."

She smiled a little at me, then, before turning back to Chenyth. I think she liked the kid. Everybody did. Even the Harish tolerated him. They hardly acknowledged the existence of anyone else but Fetch, and she only as the mouth of the man who paid them.

Fetch was a sorceress in her own right. She knew how to use the magic of her smiles. The genuine article just sort of melted you inside.

"The forest isn't what it seems," she explained. "Those

trees haven't died for the winter. They're alive, Chenyth. They're wicked, and they're waiting for you to make a mistake. All you have to do is wander past one and you'll be lost. Unless Lord Hammer can save you. He might let you go. As an object lesson."

"Come on, Fetch. How'd you get that name, anyway? That's not a real name. Look. The trees are fifty feet apart . . ."

"Chenyth." I tapped his shoulder. He subsided. Lord Hammer was always right. When Fetch gave us a glimmer of fact, we listened.

"Bellweather named me Fetch. Because I run for Lord Hammer. And maybe because he thinks I'm a little spooky. He's clever that way. You couldn't pronounce my real name, anyway."

"Which you'd never reveal," I remarked.

She smiled. "That's right. One man with a hold on me is enough."

"What about Lord Hammer?" Chenyth demanded. When one of his questions was answered, he always found another.

"Oh, he chose his own name. It's a joke. But you'll never understand it. You're too young." She moved on down the line.

Chenyth smiled to himself. He had won a little more.

His value to us all was his ability to charm Fetch into revealing just a little more than she had been instructed. Maybe Chenyth could have gotten into her.

His charm came of youth and innocence. He was four-teen years younger than Jamal, child of the Harish and youngest veteran. We were all into our thirties and forties. Soldiering had been our way of life for so long we had forgotten there were others. Some of us had been enemies back when. The Harish bore their defeat like the banner of a holy martyr . . .

Chenyth had come after the wars. Chenyth was a baby. He had no hatreds, no prejudices. He retained that bubbling, youthful optimism that had been burned from the rest of us in the crucible of war. We both loved and envied him for it, and tried to get a little to rub off. Chenyth was a talisman. One last hope that the world wasn't inalterably cruel.

Fetch returned to Lord Hammer's stirrup. The man in black proceeded.

I studied the trees.

There was something repulsive about them. Something frightening. They were so widely spaced it seemed they couldn't stand one another. There were no saplings. Most were half dead, hollow, or down and rotting. They were arranged in neat, long rows, a stark orchard of death . . .

The day was about to die without a whimper when Lord Hammer halted again.

It hadn't seemed possible that our morale could sink. Not after the mountains and the ice storm. But that weird forest depressed us till we scarcely cared if we lived or died. The band would have disintegrated had it not become so much an extension of Lord Hammer's will.

We massed behind our fell captain.

Before him lay a meadow circumscribed by a tumbled wall of field stone. The wall hadn't been mended in ages. And yet . . .

It still performed its function.

"Sorcery!" Brandy hissed.

Others took it up.

"What'd you expect?" Chenyth countered. He nodded toward Lord Hammer.

It took no training to sense the wizardry.

Ice-free, lush grass crowded the circle of stone. Wildflowers fluttered their petals in the breeze.

We Kaveliners crowded Fetch. Chenyth tickled her sides. She yelped. "Stop it!" She was extremely ticklish. Anyone else she would have slapped silly. She told him, "It's still alive. Lord Hammer was afraid it might have died."

Remarkable. She said nothing conversational to anyone else, ever.

Lord Hammer turned slightly. Fetch devoted her attention to him. He moved an elbow, twitched a finger. I didn't see anything else pass between them.

Fetch turned to us. "Listen up! These are the rules for guys who want to stay healthy. Follow Lord Hammer like his shadow. Don't climb over the wall. Don't even touch it. You'll get dead if you do."

The black horseman circled the ragged wall to a gap where a gate might once have stood. He turned in and rode to the heart of the meadow.

Fetch scampered after him, her big brown eyes locked on him.

How Lord Hammer communicated with her I don't know. A finger-twitch, a slight movement of hand or head, and she would talk-talk-talk. We didn't speculate much aloud. He was a sorcerer. You avoid things that might irritate his kind.

She proclaimed, "We need a tent behind each fire pit. Five on the outer circle, five on the inner. The rest here in the middle. Keep your fires burning all night. Sentinels will be posted."

"Yeah?" Brandy grumbled. "What the hell do we do for wood? Plant acorns and wait?"

"Out there are two trees that are down. Take wood off them. Pick up any fallen branches this side of the others. It'll be wet, but it's the best we can do. *Do not* go past a live tree. Lord Hammer isn't sure he can project his protection that far."

I didn't pay much attention. Nobody did. It was *warm* there. I shed my pack and flung myself to the ground. I rolled around on the grass, grabbing handfuls and inhaling the newly mown hay scent.

There had to be some dread sorceries animating that circle. Nobody cared. The place was as cozy as journey's end.

There is always a price. That's how magic works.

Old Toamas lay back on his pack and smiled in pure joy. He closed his eyes and slept. Even Brandy said nothing about making him do his share.

Lord Hammer let the euphoria bubble for ten minutes.

Fetch started round the troop. "Brandy. You and Russ and Little, put your tent on that point. Will, Chenyth, Toamas, yours goes here. Kelpie . . ." And so on. When everyone was assigned, she erected her master's black tent. All the while Lord Hammer sat his ruby-eyed stallion and stared northeastward. He showed the intensity of deep concentration. Was he reading the trail?

Nothing seemed to catch him off guard.

Where was he leading us? Why? What for? We didn't know. Not a whit. Maybe even Fetch didn't. Chenyth couldn't charm a hint from her.

We knew two things. Lord Hammer paid well. And, within restrictions known only to himself, he took care of his followers. In a way I can't articulate, he had won our loyalties.

His being what he was was ample proof we faced something grim, yet he had won us to the point where we felt we had a stake in it too. We wanted him to succeed. We wanted to help him succeed.

Odd. Very odd.

I have taken his gold, I thought, briefly remembering a man I had known a long time ago. He had been a member of the White Company of the Mercenaries Guild. They were a monastic order of soldiers with what, then, I had thought of as the strangest concept of honor . . .

What made me think of Mikhail? I wondered.

IV

Lord Hammer suddenly dismounted and strode toward Chenyth and me. I thought, thunderhead! Huge, black, irresistible.

I'm no coward. I endured the slaughterhouse battles of the Great Eastern Wars without flinching. I stood fast at Second Baxendala while the Tervola sent the *savan dalage* ravening amongst us night after night. I maintained my courage after Dichiara, which was our worst defeat. And I persevered at Palmisano, though the bodies piled into little mountains and so many men died that the savants later declared there could be no more war for generations. For three years I had faced the majestic, terrible hammer of Shinsan's might without quelling.

But when Lord Hammer bore down on me, that grim death mask coming like an arrowhead engraved with my name, I slunk aside like a whipped dog.

He had that air. You *knew* he was as mighty as any force of Nature, as cruel as Death Herself. Cowering was instinctive.

He looked me in the eye. I couldn't see anything through his mask. But a coldness hit me. It made the cold of that land seem summery.

He looked at Chenyth, too. Baby brother didn't flinch.

I guess he was too innocent. He didn't know when to be scared.

Lord Hammer dropped to one knee beside Toamas.

Gloved hands probed the old man's ribs. Toamas cringed. Then his terror gave way to a beatific smile.

Lord Hammer strode back to where Fetch pursued her regular evening ritual of battling to erect their tent.

"You're a damned idiot, girl," she muttered. "You could've picked something you could handle. But no, you had to have a canvas palace. You knew the boys would just fall in love and stumble all over themselves to help. Then you hired lunks with the chivalry of tomcats. You're a real genius, you are, girl."

The euphoria had reached her too. Usually she was louder and crustier.

Chenyth volunteered. Leaving me to battle with ours.

That little woman could shame or cajole a man into doing anything.

I checked Toamas. He was sleeping. His smile said he was feeling no pain. "Thanks," I threw Lord Hammer's way, softly. No one heard, but he probably knew. Nothing escaped him.

When the tents were up Fetch chose wood-gathers. I was one of the losers.

"Goddamned, ain't fair, Brandy," I muttered as we hit the ice. "Them sumbitches get to sit on their asses back there . . ."

He laughed at me. He was that kind of guy. No empathy. And no sympathy even for himself.

Some lessons have to be learned the hard way.

The circle had turned me lazy. Malingering is a fine art among veterans. I decided to get the wood-gathering over with.

What I did was go after a prime-looking dead branch laying just past the first standing tree. I mean, how hard could it be to find your way back when all you had to do was turn around?

I whacked and hacked the branch out of the ice. All the while Brandy and the others were cussing and fussing behind me as they wooled a dead tree.

I turned to go back.

Nothing.

I couldn't see a damned thing but ice, those gnarled old trees, and more ice. No circle. No woodcutters.

The only sound was the ice cracking on branches as the wind teased through the forest.

I yelled.

Chips of ice tinkled off the nearest tree. The damned thing was laughing! I could feel it. It was telling me that it had me, but it was going to play with me a while.

I even felt the envy of neighboring trees, the hatred of a brother, who had scored . . .

I didn't panic. I whirled this way and that, moving a few steps each direction, without surrendering to terror. Once a man has faced the legions of the Dread Empire, and has survived nights haunted by the unkillable *savan dalage*, there isn't much left to fear.

I could hear the others perfectly when I turned my back. They were yelling at me, each other, and Lord Hammer. They thought I had gone crazy.

"Will," Brandy called. "How come you're jumping around like that?"

"Tree," I said, "you're going to lose this round."

It laughed in my mind.

I started backing up. Dragging my branch. Feeling for any trace of footsteps I had left coming here.

Good thinking. But not good enough. The tree hadn't exhausted its arsenal.

A branch fell. A big one. I dodged. My feet slipped on the ice. I cracked my head good. I wasn't thinking when I got up. I started walking. Probably the wrong way.

I heard Brandy yelling. "Will, you stupid bastard, stand still!"

And Russ, "Get a rope, somebody. We'll lasso him."

I didn't understand. My feet kept shuffling.

Then came the crackle of flames and stench of oily smoke. It caught my attention. I stopped, turned.

My captor had become a pillar of fire. It screamed in my mind.

Nothing should burn that fast, that hot. Not in that weather. But the damned thing went up like an explosion.

The smell of sorcery fouled the air.

The flames peaked, began dying. I could see through.

The circle and my friends glimmered before me. Facing the tree, a few yards beyond, stood Lord Hammer. He held one arm outstretched, fingers in a King's X.

He stared at me. I peered into his eye slots and felt him calling. I took a step.

It was a long, long journey. I had to round some kink in the corridor of time before I got my feet onto the straight line path to safety.

I made it.

Still dragging that damned branch.

I stumbled. Lord Hammer's arm fell. He caught me. His touch was as gentle as a lover's caress, yet I felt it to my bones. I had the feeling that there was nothing more absolute.

I got hold of myself. He released me.

His shoulders slumped slightly as he wheeled and stalked back to the circle. It was the first sign of weariness he had ever shown.

I glanced back.

That damned tree stood there looking like it hadn't been touched. I felt its bitterness, its rage, its loss . . . And its siren call.

I scooted back inside the circle like a kid running home after getting caught pulling a prank.

V

"Chenyth, it was on fire. I saw it with my own eyes."

"I saw what happened, Will. Lord Hammer just stood there with his arm out. You stopped acting goofy and came back."

The campfires cast enough light to limn the nearest trees. I glanced at the one that had had me. I shuddered. "Chenyth, I couldn't get back."

"Will . . ."

"You listen to me. When Lord Hammer says do something, do it. Mom would kill me if I didn't bring you home."

She was going to get nasty anyway. I had taken Chenyth off after she had sworn seven ways from Sunday that he wasn't going to go. It had been a brutal scene. Chenyth pleading, Mom screaming, me ducking epithets and pots.

My mother had had a husband and eight sons. When the dust of the Great Eastern Wars settled, she had me and little Chenyth, and she hadn't seen me but once since then.

Then I came back with my story about signing on with Lord Hammer. And Chenyth, who had been feeding on her stories about Dad and the rest of us being heroes in the wars, decided he wanted to go too.

She told him no, and meant it. It was too late to do anything about me, but her last child wasn't going to be a soldier.

Sometimes I was ashamed of sneaking him out. She

would be dying still, in tiny bits each day. But Chenyth had
to grow up sometime . . .

"Hey! Listen up!" Fetch yelled. "Hey! I said knock off
the tongue music. Got a little proclamation from the
boss."

"Here it comes. All time ass-chewing for doing a
stupid," I said.

She used Itaskian first. Most of us understood it. She
changed languages for the Harish and a few others who
didn't. We drifted toward the black tent.

From the heart of the meadow I could see the pattern of
the fire pits. Each lay in one of the angles of a five-pointed
star. A pentagram. This meadow was a live magical symbol.

"It'll only be a couple days till we get where we're
heading. Maybe sooner. The boss says it time to let you
know what's happening. Just so you'll stay on your toes.
The name of the place is Kammengarn." She grinned,
exposing dirty teeth.

It took a while. The legend was old, and didn't get much
notice outside Itaskia's northern provinces, where
Rainheart is a folk hero.

Bellweather popped first. "You mean like the Kammengam in the story about Rainheart slaying the Kammengarn Dragon?"

"You got it, Captain."

Most of us just put on stupid looks, the southerners more
so than those of us who shared cultural roots with Itaskia. I
don't think the Harish ever understood.

"Why? What's there?" Bellweather asked.

Fetch laughed. The sound was hard to describe. A little
bit of cackle, of bray, and of tinkle all rolled into one
astonishing noise. "The Kammengarn Dragon, idiot. Silcroscuar. Father of All Dragons. The big guy of the dragon

world. The one who makes the ones you saw in the wars look like crippled chickens beside eagles."

"You're not making sense," Chenyth responded. "What's there? Bones? Rainheart killed the monster three or four hundred years ago."

Lord Hammer came from his tent. He stood behind Fetch, his arms folded. He remained as still, as lifeless, as a statue in clothes. We became less restive.

He was one spooky character. I felt my arm where he had caught me. It still tingled.

"Rainheart's successes were exaggerated," Fetch told us. She used her sarcastic tone. The one that blistered obstinate rocks and mules. "Mostly by Rainheart. The dragon lives. No mortal man can kill it. The gods willed that it be. It shall be, so long as the world endures. It is the Father of All Dragons. If it perishes, dragons perish. The world must have its dragons."

It was weird, the way she changed while she was talking. All of a sudden she wasn't Fetch anymore. I think we all sneaked peeks at Lord Hammer to see if he were doing some ventriloquist trick.

Maybe he was. He could be doing anything behind that iron mask.

I wasn't sure Lord Hammer was human anymore. He might be some unbanished devil left over from the great thaumaturgic confrontations of the wars.

"Lord Hammer is going to Kammengarn to obtain a cup of the immortal Dragon's blood."

Hammer ducked into his tent. Fetch was right behind him.

"What the hell?" Brandy demanded. "What kind of crap is this?"

"Hammer don't lie," I replied.

"Not that we know of," Chenyth said.

"He's a plainspoken man, even if Fetch does his talking. He says the Kammengarn Dragon is alive, I believe him. He says we're going to kype a cup of its blood, there it is. I reckon we're going to try."

"Will . . ."

I went and squatted by our fire. I needed a little more warming. The dead wood of the forest burned pretty ordinarily.

The men were quiet for a long time.

What was there to say?

We had taken Hammer's gold.

Even professional griper Brandy didn't say much by way of complaint.

Mikhail had been right. You went on even when the cause was a loser. It became a matter of honor.

Ormson killed the silence. His action was minor thing, characteristic of his race, but it divided the journey into different phases, now and then, and inspired the resolution of the rest of us.

He drew his sword, began whetting it.

The stone made a *shing-shing* sound along his blade. For an instant it was the only sound to be heard.

We were old warriors. That sound spoke eloquently of battles beyond the dawn. I drew my sword . . .

I had taken the gold. I was Lord Hammer's man.

VI

A metallic symphony played as stones sharpened swords and spearheads. Men tested bowstrings and thumped weathered shields. Old greaves clanked. Leather armor, too long unoiled, squeaked.

Lord Hammer stepped from his tent. His mask bore no paint now. Only chance flickers of firelight revealed the existence of anything within his cowl.

When his gaze met mine I felt I was looking at a man who was smiling.

Chenyth fidgeted with his gear. Then, "I'm going to see what Jamal's doing."

He sheathed the battered sword I had given him and wandered off. He didn't cut much of a figure as a warrior. He was just a skinny blond kid who looked like a gust of wind would blow him away, or a willing woman turn him to jelly.

Eyes followed him. Pain filled some. We had all been there once. Now we were here.

He was our talisman against our mortality.

I started wondering what the Harish were up to myself. I followed Chenyth. They were almost civil while he was around.

They were ships without compasses, those four, more lost than the rest of us. They were religious fanatics who had sworn themselves to a dead cause. They were El Murid's Chosen Ones, his most devoted followers, a dedicated cult of assassins. The Great Eastern Wars had thrown their master into eclipse. His once vast empire had collapsed. Now, according to rumor, El Murid was nothing but a fat, decrepit opium addict commanding a few bandits in the south desert hills of Hammad al Nakir. He spent his days pulling on his pipe and dreaming about an impossible restoration. These four brother assassins were refugees from the vengeance of the new order . . .

Defeat had left them with nothing but one another and their blades. About what victory had given us.

Harish took no wives. They devoted themselves totally to the mysteries of their brotherhood, and to fulfilling the commands of their master.

No one gave them orders anymore. Yet they had sworn to devote their lives to their master's needs.

They were waiting. And while they waited, they survived by selling what they had given El Murid freely.

Like the rest of us, they were what history had made them. Bladesmen.

They formed a cross, facing their fire. Chenyth knelt beside Jamal. They talked in low tones. The others watched with stony faces partially concealed by thin veils and long, heavy black beards. Foud, the oldest, dyed his to keep the color. They were all solid, tough men. Killers unfamiliar with remorse.

All four held ornate silver daggers.

I stopped, amazed.

They were permitting Chenyth to watch the consecration of Harish kill-daggers. It was one of the high mysteries of their cult.

They sensed my presence, but went on removing the enameled names of their last victims from amidst the engraved symbols on the flats of their blades. Those blades were a quarter inch thick near the hilt. The flat ran half the twelve inch length. Each blade was an inch wide at its base.

They seemed heavy, clumsy, but the Harish used them with terrifying efficiency.

One by one, oldest to youngest, they thrust their daggers into the fire to extinguish the last gossamer of past victims' souls still clinging to the deadly engraving. Then they laid their blades across their hearts, beneath the palms of their left hand. Foud spoke a word.

Chenyth later told me the ritual was coached in the language of ancient Ilkazar. It was an odd tongue they used, like nothing else I've heard.

Foud chanted. The others answered.

Fifteen minutes passed. When they finished even a

dullard like myself could feel the Power hovering round the Harish fire.

Lord Hammer came out of his tent. He peered our way briefly, then returned.

The four plunged their blades into the fire again.

Then they joined the ritual everyone else had been pursuing. They produced their whetstones.

I considered Foud's blade. Nearly two inches were missing from its length. It had been honed till it had narrowed a quarter. The engraving was almost invisible. He had served El Murid long and effectively.

His gaze met mine. For an instant a smile flickered behind his veil.

That was the first any of them had even admitted my existence.

A moment later Jamal said something to Chenyth. The younger Harish was the only one who admitted to understanding Itaskian, though we all knew the others did too. Chenyth nodded and rose.

"They're going to name their daggers. We have to go."

Times change. Only a few years ago men like these had tried to kill Kavelin's Queen. Now we were allies.

The glint in Foud's eye told me that things might be different now if he had been the man sent then.

The Harish believed. In their master, in themselves. Every assassin who consecrated blade was as sure of himself as was Foud.

"What're they doing here?" I muttered at Chenyth. I knew. The same as me. Doing what they knew. Surviving the only way they knew. Still . . . The Harish revered their Cause, even though it was lost .

They wanted to bring The Disciple's salvation to the whole world, using every means at their disposal.

Toamas was awake and chipper when we got back. "I

ever tell about the time I was with King Bragi, during the El
Murid Wars, when he was just another blank shield? It was
a town in Altea . . .''

I guess that kept us going, too. Maybe one mercenary in
fifty thousand made it big. I guess we all had some core of
hope, or belief in ourselves, too.

VII

"All right, you goat-lovers! Drag your dead asses out.
We got some hiking to do today.''

Fetch had a way with words like no lady I've ever
known. I slithered out of my blankets, scuttled to the fire,
tumbled some wood on, and slid back into the wool. That
circle may have been springish, but there was a nip in the
air.

Chenyth rolled over. He muttered something about
eyes in the night.

"Come on. Roll out. We got a long walk ahead.''

Chenyth sat up. "Phew! One of these days we've got to
take time off for baths. Hey. Toamas. Wake up.'' He shook
the old man. "Oh!''

"What's the matter?''

"I think he's dead, Will.''

"Toamas? Nah. He just don't want to get up.'' I shook
him.

Chenyth was right.

I jumped out of there so fast I knocked the tent down on
Chenyth. "Fetch. The old man's dead. Toamas.''

She kicked a foot sticking out of another tent, gave me a
puzzled look. Then she scurried into the black tent.

I tried to get a look inside. But there were inside flaps too.

Lord Hammer appeared a moment later. His mask was paintless. His gaze swept the horizon, then the camp. Fetch popped out as he started toward our tent.

Chenyth came up cussing. "Damnit, Will, what the hell you . . ." His jaw drooped. He scrambled out of Lord Hammer's path.

Fetch whipped past and started hauling tent away. Lord Hammer knelt, hand over Toamas's heart. He moved it to the grass. Then he walked to the gap we thought of as a gate.

"What's he doing?" Chenyth asked.

"Wait," Fetch told him.

Lord Hammer halted, faced left, began pacing the perimeter. He paused several times. We resumed our morning chores. Brandy cussed the gods both on Toamas's behalf and because he faced another miserable breakfast. You couldn't tell which mattered more to him. Brandy bitched about everything equally.

His true feelings surfaced when he was the first to volunteer to dig the old man's grave.

Toamas had saved his life in the mountains.

"We Kaveliners got to stick together," he muttered to me. "Way it's always been. Way it'll always be."

"Yeah."

His family and Toamas's lived in the same area. They had been on opposite sides in the civil war with which Kavelin had amused itself in the interim between the El Murid and Great Eastern Wars.

It was one of the few serious remarks I had ever heard from Brandy.

Lord Hammer chose the grave site. It butted against the wall. Toamas went down sitting upright, facing the forest.

"That's where I saw the thing last night," Chenyth told me.

"What thing?"

"When I had guard duty. All I could see was its eyes." He dropped a handful of dirt into the old man's lap. The others did the same. Except Foud. The Harish Elder lowered himself to his belly, placed a small silver dagger under Toamas's folded hands.

We Kaveliners bowed to Foud. This was a major gesture by the Harish. Their second highest honor, given a man who had been their enemy all his life.

I wondered why Foud had done it.

"Why did he die?" Chenyth asked Fetch. "I thought Lord Hammer fixed him."

"He did. Chenyth, the circle took Toamas."

"I don't understand."

"Neither do I."

I wondered some more. Ignorance and Lord Hammer seemed poles apart.

Maybe he had known. But I couldn't hate him. The way Fetch talked, thirty-seven of us were alive because Toamas had died. The circle certainly was more merciful than the forest.

Lord Hammer gestured. Fetch ran to him. Then he ducked into his tent while she talked.

"Get with it. We've got a long way to go. We'll have to travel fast. Lord Hammer doesn't want to spend any more lives. He wants to leave the forest before nightfall."

We moved. Our packs were trailing odds and ends when we started. Our stomachs weren't full. But those were considerations less important than enduring the protection of another circle.

As we were leaving I noticed a flower blooming in the soft earth where we had put Toamas down. There were

dozens of flowers along the wall. The few places where
they were missing were the spots where Lord Hammer
had paused in his circuit of the wall.

What would happen when all the grave sites were full?

Maybe Lord Hammer knew. But Hammer didn't have
much to say.

We passed another circle about noon. It was dead.

The day was warmer, the sky clear. The ice began
melting. We made good time. Lord Hammer seemed
pleased.

I stared straight ahead, at Russ's back, all morning. If I
looked at a tree I could hear it calling. The pull was terrifying.

Chenyth seized my arm. "Stop!"

I almost trampled Russ. "What's up?" Lord Hammer
had stopped.

"I don't know."

Fetch was dancing around like a barefoot burglar on a
floor covered with tacks. Lord Hammer and his steed
might have been some parkland pigeon roost, so still were
they. We shuffled round so we could see without leaving
the safety of the trail.

We had come to a clearing. It was a quarter mile across.
What looked like a mud-dauber's nest, the kind with just
one hole, lay at the middle of the clearing. It was big. Like
two hundred yards long, fifty feet wide, and thirty feet high.
A sense of immense menace radiated from it.

"What is it?" we asked one another. Neither Lord
Hammer nor Fetch answered us.

Lord Hammer slowly raised his left arm till it thrust
straight out from his shoulder. He lifted his forearm vertically, turning the edge of a stiffened hand toward the
structure. Then he raised his right arm, laying his forearm
parallel with his eyeslits. Again he stiffened his hand, facing
the structure with its edge.

"Let's go!" Fetch snapped. "Follow me." She started running.

We whipped the mules into a trot, ran. We weren't gentle with the balky ones.

We had to go right along the side of that thing. As we approached, I glanced back. Lord Hammer was coming, his mount pacing slowly. Hammer himself remained frozen in the position he had assumed. He was almost indiscernible inside a black nimbus.

His mask glowed like the sun. The face of an animal seemed to peep through the golden light.

I glanced into the dark entry to that mound. Menace, backed by rage and frustration, slammed into me.

Lord Hammer halted directly in front of the hole. The rest of us raced for the forest behind the barrow.

Fetch was scared, but not scared enough to pass the first tree. She stopped. We waited.

And Lord Hammer came.

Never have I seen a horse run as beautifully, or as fast. It may have been my imagination, or the way the sun hit its breath in the cold, but fire seemed to play round its nostrils. Lord Hammer rode as if he were part of the beast.

The earth shuddered. A basso profundo rumble came from the mound.

Lord Hammer swept past, slowing, and we pursued him. No one thought to look back, to see what the earth brought forth. It was too late once we passed that first tree.

"Will," Chenyth panted. "Did you see that horse run? What kind of horse runs like that, Will?"

What could I tell him? "Sorcerer's horse, Chenyth. Hell horse. But we knew that already, didn't we?"

Some of us did. Chenyth never really believed it till then. He figured we were giving him more war stories.

He never understood that we couldn't exaggerate what had happened during the Great Eastern Wars. That we told toned-down stories because there was so much we wanted to forget.

Chenyth couldn't take anything at face value. He worked his way up the column so he could pump Fetch. He didn't get anything from her, either. Lord Hammer led. We followed. For Fetch that was the natural order of life.

VIII

We passed another dead circle in the afternoon. Lord Hammer glanced at the sun and increased the pace.

An hour later Fetch passed the word that we would have to stop at the next circle—unless it were dead.

Dread sandpapered the ends of our nerves. The men who had stood sentry last night had seen too much of the things that roamed the forest by dark. And Hammer's reluctance to face the night . . . It made the price of a circle almost attractive.

Even thirty-seven to one aren't good odds when my life is on the line. I've been risking it since I was Chenyth's age, but I like having some choice, some control . . .

The next circle was alive.

Darkness was close when we reached it. We could hear big things moving behind us, beyond the trees. Hungry things. We zipped into the circle and pitched camp in record time.

I stood sentry that night. I saw what Chenyth had seen. It didn't bother me much. I was a veteran of the Great Eastern Wars.

I kept reminding myself.

Lord Hammer didn't sleep at all. He spent the night pacing the perimeter. He paused frequently to make cabalistic passes. Sometimes the air glowed where his fingers passed.

He took care of us. Not a man perished. Instead, the circle took a mule.

"Butcher it up," Fetch growled. "Save the good cuts. Couple of you guys dig a hole over there where I left the shovel."

So we had mule for breakfast. It was tough, but good, our first fresh meat in weeks.

We were about to march when Fetch announced, "We'll be there tomorrow. That means goof-off time's over. Respond to orders instantly if you know what's good for you."

Brandy mumbled and cussed. Chenyth wasn't any happier. "I swear, I'm going to smack him, Will."

"Take it easy. He was in the Breidenbacher Light. I owe him."

"So? They got you out at Lake Turntine. That was then. What's that got to do with today?"

"What it's got to do with is, he'll kick your ass up around your ears."

"Kid wants to duke it out, let him, Will. He's getting on my nerves too."

"Stow it," Fetch snarled. "Save it for the other guys. It's time to start worrying about getting out alive."

"What? Then we'd have to walk all the way back." Brandy cackled.

"Fetch, what's this all about?" Chenyth asked.

"I already told you, question man."

"Not why."

She scowled, shook her head. I asked, "Weren't you ever young, Fetch? Hey! Whoa! I didn't mean it like that."

She settled for the one shin-kick. Everybody laughed. I winked. She grinned nastily.

Brandy and Chenyth had forgotten their quarrel.

Chenyth hadn't forgotten his question. He pressed.

"All I know is, he wants the blood of the Father of Dragons. We came now because the monster is sluggish during the winter. Now why the hell don't you just jingle the money in your pocket and do what you're told?"

"Where'd you meet him, Fetch? When?"

She shook her head again. "You don't hear so good, do you? Long ago and far away. He's been like a father. Now get your ass ready to hike." She tramped off to her position beside Lord Hammer's stallion.

The woman had the least feminine walk I've ever seen. She took long, rolling steps, and kind of leaned into them.

"You ask too many questions, Chenyth."

"Can it, will you?"

We were getting close. Not knowing, except that we were going to go up against a dragon, frayed tempers. Chenyth's trouble was that he hadn't had enough practice at keeping his mouth shut.

Noon. Another barrow blocked our trail. We repeated our previous performance. The feeling of menace wasn't as strong. The thing in the earth let us pass with only token protest.

The weather grew warmer. The ice melted quickly, turning the trail to mud.

Occasionally, from ridgetops, we saw the land beyond the forest. Mountains lay ahead. Brandy moaned his heart out till Fetch told him our destination lay at their feet. Then he bitched about everything happening too fast.

Several of those peaks trailed dark smoke. There wasn't much snow on their flanks.

"Funny," I remarked to Chenyth. "Heading north into warmer country."

We passed a living circle. It called to us the way the trees called to me.

An end to the weird, wide forest came. We entered grasslands that, within a few hours, gave way to rapidly steepening hills. The peaks loomed higher. The air grew warmer. The hills became taller and more barren. Shadows gathered in the valleys as the sun settled toward the Dragon's Teeth.

Lord Hammer ordered us to pitch camp. He doubled the sentries.

We weren't bothered, but still it was a disturbing night. The earth shuddered. The mountains rumbled. I couldn't help but envision some gargantuan monster resting uneasily beneath the range.

IX

The dawn gods were heaving buckets of blood up over the eastern horizon. Fetch formed us up for a pep talk. "Queen of the dwarves," Brandy mumbled. She *was* comical, so tiny was she when standing before a mounted Lord Hammer.

"Lord Hammer believes we are about three miles from the Gate of Kammengarn. The valley behind me will lead us there. From the Gate those who accompany Lord Hammer will descend into the earth almost a mile. Captain Bellweather and thirty men will stay at the Gate. Six men will accompany Lord Hammer and myself.

Her style had changed radically. I had never seen her so subdued.

Fetch was scared.

"Bellweather, your job will be the hardest. It's almost certain that you will be attacked. The people of these hills believe Kammengarn to be a holy place. They know we're here. They suspect our mission. They'll try to destroy us once we prove we intend to profane their shrine. You'll have to hold them most of the day, without Lord Hammer's help."

"Now we know," Brandy muttered. "Needed us to fight his battles for him."

"Why the hell else did he hire us?" Chenyth demanded.

"Knock it off back there!" Fetch yelled.

Lord Hammer's steed pranced impatiently. Hammer's gaze swept over us. It quelled all emotion.

"Lord Hammer has appointed the following men to accompany him. Foud, of the Harish. Aboud, of the Harish. Sigurd Ormson, the Trolledyngjan. Dunklin Hanneker, the Itaskian. Willem Clarig Potter, of Kavelin. Pavlo della Contini-Marcusco, of Dunno Scuttari." She made a small motion with her fingers, like someone folding a piece of paper.

"Fetch! . . ."

"Shut up, Chenyth!" I growled.

Fetch responded, "Lord Hammer has spoken. The men named, please come to the head of the column."

I hoisted my pack, patted Chenyth's shoulder, said, "Do a good job. And stay healthy. I've got to take you back to Mom."

"Will . . ."

"Hey. You wanted to be a soldier. Be a soldier."

He stared at the ground, kicked a pebble.

"Good luck, Will." Brandy extended a hand. I shook. "We'll look out for him."

"All right. Thanks. Russ. Aral. You guys take care." It was a ritual of parting undertaken before times got tough.

The red-eyed horse started moving. We followed in single file. Fetch walked with Bellweather for a while. After

half an hour she scampered forward to her place beside
Lord Hammer. She was nervous. She couldn't keep her
head or hands still.

I glanced back, past Ormson. "Fight coming," I told the
Trolledyngjan. Bellweather was getting ready right now.

"Did you ever doubt it?"

"No. Not really."

The mountains crowded in. The valley narrowed till it
became a steep-sided canyon. That led to a place where
two canyons collided and became one. It had a flat bottom
perhaps fifty yards across.

It was the most barren place I had ever seen. The
boulders were dark browns. The little soil came in lighter
browns. A few tufts of dessicated grass added sere browns.
Even the sky took on an ochre hue . . .

The blackness of a crack in the mountainside ahead
relieved the monochromism.

It was a natural cleft, but there were tailings everywhere,
several feet deep, as if the cleft had been mined. The
tailings had filled the canyon bottom, creating the little flat.

I searched the hillsides. It seemed I could feel eyes
boring holes in my back. I looked everywhere but at that
cavern mouth.

The darkness it contained seemed the deepest I had
ever known.

Lord Hammer rode directly to it.

"Packs off," Fetch ordered. "Weapons ready." She
twitched and scratched nervously. "We're going down.
Do exactly as I do."

Bellweather brought the others onto the flat. He
searched the mountainsides too. "They're here," he announced.

War howls responded immediately. Here, there, a
painted face flashed amongst the rocks.

Arrows and spears wobbled through the air.

There were a lot of them, I reflected as I got myself between my shield and a boulder. The odds didn't look good at all.

Bellweather shouted. His men vanished behind their shields . . .

All but my baby brother, who just stood there with a stupefied look.

"Chenyth!" I started toward him.

"Will!" Fetch snapped. She grabbed my arm. "Stay here."

Brandy and Russ took care of him. They exploded from behind their shields, tackled the kid, covered him before he got hurt. That got his attention. He started doing the things I had been teaching the past several months.

An arrow hummed close to me, clattered on rock. Then another. I had been chosen somebody's favorite target. Time to worry about me.

The savages concentrated on Lord Hammer. Their luck was poor. Missiles found him repulsive. In fact, they seemed to loath making contact with any of us.

Not so the arrows of Bellweather's Itaskian bows.

The Itaskian bow and bowman are the best in the world. Bellweather's men wasted no arrows. Virtually every shaft brought a cry of pain.

Then Lord Hammer reached up and caught an arrow in flight.

The canyon fell silent in sheer awe.

Lord Hammer extended an arm. A falling spear became a streak of smoke.

The hillmen didn't give up. Instead, they started rolling boulders down the slopes.

"Eyes down!" Fetch screamed. "Stare at the ground."

Lord Hammer swept first his right hand, then his left, round himself. He clapped them together once.

A sheet of fire, of lightning, obscured the sky. Thunder tortured my ears. My hearing recovered only to be tormented anew by the screams of men in pain.

It had been much nastier above. Dozens of savages were staggering around with hands clasped over their eyes or ears. Several fell down the slope.

Bellweathers archers went to work.

"Let's go," Fetch said. "Remember. Do exactly what I do."

The little woman was scared pale. She didn't want to enter that cavern. But she took her place beside Lord Hammer, who laid a hand atop her disheveled head.

His touch seemed fond. His fingers toyed with her stringy hair. She shivered, looked at the ground, then stalked into that black crack.

He only touched the rest of us for a second. The feeling was similar to that when he had caught me after my run-in with the siren tree. But this time the tingle coursed through my whole body.

He finished with Foud. Once more he swept hands round the mountainsides, clapped. Lightning flashed. Thunder rolled. Bellweather's archers plied their bows.

The savages were determined not to be intimidated.

Lord Hammer dismounted, strode into the darkness. The red-eyed stallion turned round, backed in after us, stopping only when its bulk nearly blocked the narrow passage. Hammer wound his way through our press, proceeded into darkness.

Fetch followed. Single file, we did the same.

X

"Holy Hagard's Golden Turds!" Sigurd exploded. "They're on fire."

Lord Hammer and Fetch glowed. They shed enough light to reveal the crack's walls.

"So are you," I told him.

"Eh. You too."

I couldn't see it in myself. Sigurd said he couldn't, either. I glanced back. The others glowed too. They became quite bright once they got away from the cavern mouth. It was spooky.

The Harish didn't like it. They were unusually vocal, and what I caught of their gabble made it sound like they were mad because a heresy had been practiced upon them.

The light seemed to come from way down inside the body. I could see Sigurd's bones. And Fetch's, and the others' when I glanced back. But Lord Hammer remained an enigma. An absence. Once more I wondered if he were truly human, or if anything at all inhabited that black clothing.

After a hundred yards the walls became shaped stone set with mortar. That explained the tailings above. The blocks had been shaped *in situ*.

"Why would they do that?" I asked Sigurd.

He shrugged. "Don't try to understand a man's religion, Kaveliner. Just drive you crazy."

A hundred yards farther along the masons had narrowed the passage to little more than a foot. A man had to go through sideways.

Fetch stopped us. Lord Hammer started doing something with his fingers.

I told Sigurd, "Looks like the dragon god isn't too popular with the people who worship him."

"Eh?"

"The tunnel. It's zig-zagged. And the narrow place looks like it was built to keep the dragon in."

"They don't worship the dragon," Fetch said. "They worship Kammengarn, the Hidden City. Silcroscuar is blocking their path to their shrines. So they blocked him in in hopes he would starve."

"Didn't it work, eh?"

"No. Silcroscuar subsists. On visitors. He has guardians. Descendants of the people who lived in Kammengarn. They hunt for him."

"What's happening?"

Lord Hammer had a ball of fire in his hands. It was nearly a foot in diameter. He shifted it to his right hand, rolled it along the tunnel floor, through the narrow passage.

"Let's go!" Fetch shrieked. "Will! Sigurd! Get in there!"

I charged ahead without thinking. The passage was twenty feet long. I was halfway through when the screams started.

Such pain and terror I hadn't heard since the wars. I froze.

Sigurd plowed into me. "Go, man."

An instant later we broke into wider tunnel.

A dozen savages awaited us. Half were down, burning like torches. The stench of charred flesh fouled the air. The others flitted about trying to extinguish themselves or their comrades.

We took them before the Harish got through.

Panting, I asked Sigurd, "How did he know?"

Sigurd shrugged. "He always knows. Almost. That first barrow . . ."

"He smelled their torches," Foud said. The Harish elder wore a sarcastic smile.

"You're killing the mystery."

"There is no mystery to Lord Hammer."

"Maybe not to you." I turned to Sigurd. "Hope he's on his toes. We don't need any surprises down here."

Lord Hammer stepped in. He surveyed the carnage. He seemed satisfied.

Several of the savages still burned.

Fetch lost her breakfast.

I think that startled all of us. Perhaps even Lord Hammer. It seemed so out of character. And yet . . . What did we know about Fetch? Only what we had seen. And most of that had been show. This might be the first time she had witnessed the grim side of her master's profession.

I don't think, despite her apparent agelessness, that she was much older than Chenyth. Say twenty. She might have missed the Great Eastern Wars too.

We went on, warriors in the lead. The tunnel's slope steepened. Twice we descended spiraling stairs hanging in the sides of wide shafts. Twice we encountered narrow places with ambushes like that we had already faced. We broke through each. Sigurd took our only wound, a slight cut on his forearm. We left a lot of dead men on our backtrail.

The final attack was more cunning. It came from behind, from a side tunnel, and took us by surprise. Even Lord Hammer was taken off guard.

His mystique just cracked a little more, I thought as I whirled.

There was sorcery in it this time.

The hillmen witch-doctors had saved themselves for the final defense. They had used their command of the Power passively, to conceal themselves and their men. Our only warning was a premature warwhoop.

Lord Hammer whirled. His hands flew in frenetic

passes. The rest of us struggled to interpose ourselves between the attackers and Lord Hammer and Fetch.

Sorceries scarred the tunnel walls. The shamen threw everything they had at the man in black.

Their success was a wan one. They devoured Lord Hammer's complete attention for no more than a minute.

We soldiers fought. Sigurd and I locked shields with Contini-Marcusco and the Itaskian. The Harish, who disdained and reviled shields, remained behind us. They rained scimitar strokes over our heads.

The savages forced us back by sheer weight. But we held the wall even against suicide charges.

They hadn't the training to handle professional soldiers who couldn't be flanked. We crouched behind our shields and let them come to their deaths.

But they did get their licks in before Lord Hammer finished their witch-doctors and turned on them.

It lasted no longer than three minutes. We beat them again. But when the clang and screaming faded, we had little reason to cheer.

Hanneker was mortally wounded. Contini-Marcusco had a spearhead in his thigh. Sigurd had taken a deep cut on his left shoulder.

Fetch was down.

Me and the Harish, we were fine. Tired and drained, but unharmed.

I dropped to my knees beside Fetch's still little form. Tears filled my eyes. She had become one of my favorite people.

She had been last in line, walking behind Lord Hammer. We hadn't been able to get to her.

She was alive. She opened her eyes once, when I touched her, and bravely tried one of her smiles.

Lord Hammer knelt opposite me. He touched her

cheeks, her hair, tenderly. The tension in him proclaimed his feeling. His gaze crossed mine. For an instant I could feel his pain.

Lord, I thought, your mystique is dying. You care.

Fetch opened her eyes again. She lifted a feeble hand, clasped Lord Hammer's for an instant. "I'm sorry," she whispered.

"Don't be," he said, and it felt like an order from a god. The fingers of his left hand twitched.

I gasped, so startling was his voice, so suddenly did the Power gather. He did something to Fetch's wounds, then to Sigurd's, then to Contini-Marcusco's. Hanneker was beyond help.

He turned, faced downhill, stared. He started walking.

We who could do so followed.

"What did he do?" I whispered to Sigurd.

The big man shrugged. "It don't hurt anymore."

"Did you hear him? He talked. To Fetch."

"No."

Had I imagined it?

I glanced back. The Harish were two steps behind us. They came with the same self-certainty they always showed. Only a tiny tick at the corner of Aboud's eye betrayed any internal feeling.

Foud smiled his little smile. Once again I wondered what they were doing here.

And I wondered about Lord Hammer, whose long process of creating a mythic image seemed to be unraveling.

A mile down into the earth is one hell of a long way. Ignoring the problem of surviving the dragon, I worried about climbing back out. And about my little brother, up there getting his blooding . . .

I should have stayed with Chenyth. Somebody had to look out for him . . . .

"I have taken the gold," I muttered, and turned to thoughts of poor Fetch.

Now I would never learn what had brought her here. I was sure we wouldn't find her alive when we returned.

If we returned.

Then I worried about how we would know what Lord Hammer wanted of us.

I needn't have.

XI

The home hall of the Father of All Dragons was more vast than any stadium. It was one of the great caverns that, before Silcroscuar's coming, had housed the eldritch city Kammengam.

The cavern's walls glowed. The ruins of the homes of Kammengam lay in mounds across the floor. As legends proclaimed, that floor was strewn with gold and jewels. The great dragon snored atop a precious hillock.

The place was just as Rainheart had described. With one exception.

The dragon lived.

We heard the monster's stentorian snores long before we reached his den. Our spines had become jelly before we came to that cavern.

Lord Hammer paused before we got there. He spoke. "There are guardians."

"I wasn't wrong," I whispered.

The others seemed petrified.

The voice came from everywhere at once. It was in keeping with Lord Hammer's style. Deep. Loud. Terrifying. Like the crash of icebergs breaking off glaciers into arctic seas. Huge. Bottomless. Cold.

Something stepped into the tunnel ahead. It was tall, lean, and awkward in appearance. Its skin had the pallor of death. It glistened with an ichorous fluid. It had the form of a man, but I don't think it was human.

Fetch had said there would be guardians who were the descendants of the people of Kammengarn. Had the Kammengarners been human? I didn't know.

The guardian bore a long, wicked sword.

An identical twin appeared behind it. Then another. And another.

Lord Hammer raised his hands in one of those mystic signs. The things halted. But they would not retreat.

For a moment I feared Lord Hammer had no power over them.

I didn't want to fight. Something told me there would be no contest. I am good. Sigurd was good. The Harish were superb. But I knew they would slaughter us as if we were children.

"Salt," Lord Hammer said.

"What the hell?" Sigurd muttered. "Who carries salt around? . . ."

He shut up. Because Foud had leaned past him to drop a small leather bag into the palm of Lord Hammer's glove.

"Ah!" I murmured. "Sigurd, salt is precious in Hammad al Nakir. It's a measure of wealth. El Murid's true devotees always carry some. Because the Disciple's father was a salt caravaneer."

Foud smiled the smile and nodded at Sigurd. Proving he wasn't ignorant of Itaskian, he added, "El Murid received his revelation after bandits attacked his father's caravan. They left the child Micah al Rhami to die of thirst in the desert. But the love of the Lord descended, a glorious angel, and the child was saved, and made whole, and given to look upon the earth. And, Lo! The womb of the desert brought forth not Death, but the Son of Heaven, El Murid, whom you call the Disciple.''

For a moment Foud seemed almost as embarrassed as Sigurd and I. Like sex, faith was a force not to be mocked.

Lord Hammer emptied the bag into his hand.

Foud flinched, but did not protest. Aboud leaned past Sigurd and me, offering his own salt should it be needed.

Lord Hammer said no more. The guardians flinched, but did not withdraw.

Hammer flung the salt with quick little jerks of his hand, a few grains this way, a few that.

Liverish, mottled cankers appeared on the slimy skin of the guardians. Ther mouths yawned in silent screams.

They melted. Like slugs in a garden, salted.

Like slugs, they had no bones.

It took minutes. We watched in true fascination, unable to look away, while the four puddled, pooled, became lost in one lake of twitching slime.

Foud and Aboud shared out the remaining salt.

Lord Hammer went forward, avoiding the remains of the guardians. We followed.

I looked down once.

Eyes stared back from the lake. Knowledgeable, hating eyes. I shuddered.

They were the final barrier. We went into the Place of the Dragon, the glowing hall that once had been a cavern of the city Kammengarn.

I began to think that, despite the barriers, it was too easy.

I don't know why. It couldn't have been accomplished without Lord Hammer. Mortal men would never have reached Kammengarn.

"Gods preserve us," I muttered.

The Kammengam Dragon was the hugest living thing
I've ever seen. I had seen Shinsan's dragons during the
wars. I had seen whales beached on the coast . . .

The dragons I had seen were like chicks compared to
roosters. The flesh of a whale might have made up Silcroscuar's tail. His head alone massed as much as an elephant.

"Reckon he'd miss a cup of blood?" Sigurd whispered.

The northmen and their gallows humor. A strange race.

The dragon kept on snoring.

We had come in winter, according to Fetch, because
that was the best time of year. I suppose she meant that
dragons were more sluggish then, or even hibernated.

But at that depth the chill of winter meant nothing. The
place was as hot as an August noon in the desert.

We flanked Lord Hammer, Sigurd and I to his right, the
Harish to his left. Hammer started toward the dragon.

The monster opened an eye. Its snakelike tongue
speared toward Lord Hammer.

I interposed my shield, chopped with my sword. The
tongue caroomed away. My blade cut nothing but air.

A mightly laugh surrounded us. It came from no detect-
able source.

"You made it, fugitive. Ah. Yes. I know you, Lord
Hammer. I know who you are. I know what you are. I
know more than you know. All tidings come to me here.
There are no secrets from me. Even the future is mine to
behold. And yours is a cosmic jest."

Lord Hammer reacted only by beginning a series of
gestures, the first of which was the arm cross he had used at
the barrows in the forest.

The dragon chuckled. "You'll have your way. And be
the poorer for it." It yawned.

My jaw sagged. The teeth in that cavernous mouth! Like
the waving scimitars of a horde of desert horsemen . . .

Laughter assailed the air. "I have been intimate with the future, refugee. I know the vanity of the course you have chosen. Your hope is futile. I know the joke the Fates have prepared. But come. Take what you want. I'll not thwart you, nor deny the Fates their amusement."

The dragon closed his eye. He shifted his bulk slightly, as if into a more comfortable position.

Lord Hammer advanced.

We stayed with him.

And again I thought it was too easy. The monster wasn't making even a token attempt to stop us.

That matter about the Fates and a cosmic joke. It reminded me of all those tales in which men achieved their goals only to discover that the price of success was more dear than that of failure.

Lord Hammer clambered up the mound of gold and jewels, boldly seizing a gargantuan canine to maintain his balance.

My stomach flipped.

The dragon snored on.

Sigurd started grabbing things small enough to carry away. I selected a few souvenirs myself. Then I saw the contempt in Foud's eyes.

He seemed to be thinking that there were issues at stake far greater than greed.

It was an unguarded thought, breaking through onto his face. It put me on guard.

"Sigurd," I hissed. "Be ready. It's not over."

"I know," he whispered. "Just grabbing while I can."

Lord Hammer beckoned. I scrambled across the treacherous pile. "Cut here." He tapped the dragon's lip where scaly armor gave way to the soft flesh of the mouth. "Gently."

Terror froze me. He wanted me to cut that monster?

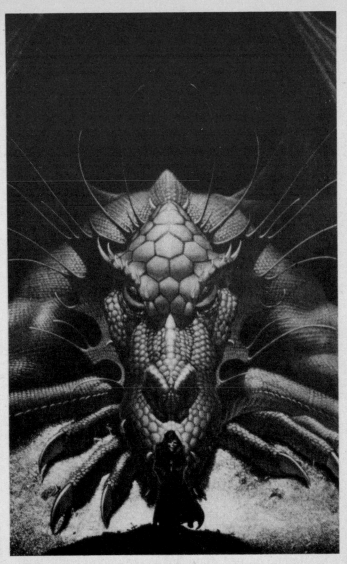

Lord Hammer screwed a top onto his container, satisfied.

When it might wake up? What chance would we have? . . .

"Cut!"

Lord Hammer's command made the cavern walls shudder. I could not deny it. I drew the tip of my blade across dragon flesh.

Blood welled up, dribbled down the monster's jaw.

It was as red as any man's. I saw nothing remarkable about it, save that men had died for it. Slowly, drop by drop, it filled the ebony container Lord Hammer held.

We waited tensely, anticipating an explosion from the monster. Dragons had foul and cunning reputations, and that of the Kammengarn Dragon outstripped them all.

I caught a smile toying with Aboud's lips. It was gone in an instant, but it left me more disturbed, more uncertain than ever.

I searched the cavern, wondering if more guardians might not be creeping our way. I saw nothing.

Sigurd bent to secure one more prize jewel . . .

And Lord Hammer screwed a top onto his container, satisfied.

Foud and Aboud surged toward him. Silver Harish kill-daggers whined through the air.

I managed to skewer Aboud and kick Foud in one wild movement. Then my impetus carried me down the mountain of treasure to the cavern floor. Golden baubles gnawed at my flesh.

Sigurd roared as he hurled himself at Foud, who was after Lord Hammer again. I regained my feet and charged up the pile.

A gargantuan laughter filled the caverns of Kammengarn.

Foud struck Lord Hammer's left arm, and killed Sigurd, before he perished, strangling in the grip of Lord Hammer's right hand.

Aboud, though dying, regained his feet. Again he tried to plant his kill-dagger in Lord Hammer's back.

I reached him in time. We tumbled back down the pile.

Lord Hammer flung Foud after us.

Aboud sat up. He had lost his dagger. I saw it lying about five feet behind him. Tears filled his eyes as he awaited the doom descending upon him.

"Why?" I asked.

"For the Master. For the blood of the dragon that would have made him immortal, that would have given him time to carry the truth. And for what was done to him during the wars."

"I don't understand, Aboud."

"You wouldn't. You haven't recognized him as your enemy."

Lord Hammer loomed over us. His left arm hung slackly. The kill-dagger had had that much success.

Lord Hammer reached with his right, seizing Aboud's throat.

The Harish fought back. Vainly.

I recovered his dagger during the struggle. Quietly, carefully, I concealed it inside my shirt. Why I don't know, except that the genuine article was more valuable than anything in the dragon's hoard.

"Come," Lord Hammer told me. Almost conversationally, he added, "The dragon will be pleased. He's hungry. These three will repay him for his blood." He strode to the gap where the guardians had perished. Their hating eyes watched us pass.

I had to strain to keep pace with him. By the time we reached Fetch I was exhausted. Hanneker had expired in our absence.

"We rest here," Lord Hammer told me. "We will carry these two, and there may be ambushes." He sat down with his back against one wall. He massaged his lifeless arm.

The image had slipped even more. He seemed quite human at that moment.

"Who are you?" I asked after a while.

The iron mask turned my way. I couldn't meet his gaze. The power was still there.

"Better that you don't know, soldier. For both our sakes."

"I have taken the gold," I replied.

I expect he understood. Maybe he didn't. He said nothing more till he decided to go.

"It's time. Carry Fetch. Be wary."

I hoisted the little woman. She seemed awfully heavy. My strength had suffered. The mountains. The forest. The fighting. The tension, always. They had ground me down.

We met no resistance. Only once did we hear what might have been men. They avoided us.

We rested often. Lord Hammer seemed to be weakening faster than I, though his resources were more vast. Maybe the Harish kill-dagger had bitten more deeply than he let on.

"Stop," he gasped. We were close to the end of the tunnel. I dropped Fetch.

Men's voices, muted, echoed along the shaft. "Chenyth." I started on.

"Stay." The command in Hammer's voice was weak, but compelling.

He moved slowly, had trouble keeping his feet. But he negated the spells that made us glow. "We must rest here."

"My brother . . ."

"We will rest, Willem Potter."

We rested.

XII

Outside ambushed us.

The sun had set. No moon had risen. The stars didn't cast much light. Bellweather had lighted no fires. We were suddenly there, beside Lord Hammer's stallion.

The last dozen yards we had to step over and around the dead and wounded. There were a lot of them. I kept whispering Chenyth's name. The only man I could find was Brandy. The griper had been dead for hours.

"They've killed or captured most of the animals," Bellweather reported. Lord Hammer grunted noncommittally. "We've killed hundreds of them, but they keep coming. They'll finish us in the morning. This's serious business to them."

"Chenyth!" I called.

"Will? Will! Over here."

I hurried over. He was doing sentry duty. His post was an open-topped bunker built of the corpses of savages.

"You all right?" I demanded.

"So far. Brandy and Russ and Aral are dead, Will. I'm sorry I came. I'm tired. So tired, Will."

"Yeah. I know."

"What happened down there?"

"It was bad." I told him the story.

"The other Harish. Will they? . . ."

"I'm sure their daggers are consecrated to the same name."

"Then they'll try again?"

"They made it? Then we'd better warn . . ."

A shriek ripped the air.

I hurled myself back toward Lord Hammer. I arrived at the same time as the Harish. Blades flashed. Men

screamed. Lord Hammer slew one. I took the other.
Bellweather and the others watched in dull-eyed disbelief.

Before Jamal died he cursed me. "You have given the
Hammer his life," he croaked. "May that sin haunt you all
the ages of earth. May his return be quickened, and fall
upon you heavily. I speak it in the Name of the Disciple."

"What did he mean, Will?" Chenyth asked.

"I don't know." I was too tired to think. "They knew
him. They knew his mission. They came to abort it. And to
capture the dragon's blood for El Murid." I glanced at Lord
Hammer. He had begun a sorcery. His voice sounded
terribly weak. He seemed the least superhuman of us all.
My awe of him had evaporated completely.

He was but a man.

"Maybe they were right," Chenyth suggested. "Maybe
the world would be better without him. Without his kind."

"I don't know. His kind are like the dragon. And we
have taken the gold, Chenyth. It doesn't matter who or
what he is."

Sleep soon ambushed me. The last thing I saw was a ball
of blue light drifting into the rocks where the savages
lurked. I think there were screams, but they might have
come in my dreams.

They took me back to the wars. To the screams of entire
kingdoms crushed beneath the boots of legions led by men
of Lord Hammer's profession. Those had been brutal,
bitter days, and the saddest part of it was that we hadn't
won, we had merely stopped it for a while.

My subconscious mind added the clues my conscious
mind had overlooked.

I awakened understanding the Harish.

"His name is a joke," Fetch had said.

It wasn't a funny one. It was pure arrogance.

One of the arch-villians of the Great Eastern Wars had

been a sorcerer named Ko Feng. He had commanded the
legions of the Dread Empire briefly. But his fellow wizards
on the Council of Tervola had ousted him because of his
unsubtle, straightforward, expensive, pounding military
tactics. For reasons no one understood he had been ordered into exile.

His nickname, on both sides of the battle line, had been
The Hammer.

Aboud had told me he was my enemy . . .

The savages bothered us no more. Lord Hammer's
sorcery had sufficed.

Only a dozen men were fit to travel. Chenyth and I were
the only surviving Kaveliners . . .

Kavelin had borne the brunt of the Great Eastern Wars.
The legions of the Dread Empire knew no mercy. The
nation might never recover . . .

I was sitting on a rock, fighting my conscience. Chenyth
came to me. "Want something to eat?"

"I don't think so."

"What's that?"

"Kill-dagger. Aboud's." I had been staring at it, and had
hidden it at his approach. I showed him.

"What's the matter, Will?"

"I think I know who he is. What he's doing. Why."

"Who?"

"Lord Hammer."

"I meant, who is he?"

"Lord Ko Feng. The Tervola. The one we called The
Hammer during the wars. They banished him from Shinsan after it was over. They took his immortality and drove
him into exile. He came for the dragon's blood to win the
immortality back. To get the time he needed to make his
return."

"Oh, Gods. Will, we've got to do something."

"What? What's the right thing? I don't *know* that he's really Ko Feng. I do know that we've taken his gold. He's treated us honorably. He even saved my life when there was no demand that he do so. I know that Fetch thinks the world of him, and I think well enough of Fetch for that to matter. So. You see what's eating me."

My life wasn't usually that complicated. A soldier takes his orders, does what he must, and doesn't much worry about tomorrow or vast issues. He takes from life what he can when he can, for there may be no future opportunity. He seldom moralizes, or becomes caught in a crisis of conscience.

"Will, we can't turn an evil like Ko Feng loose on the world again. Not if it's in our power to stop it."

"Chenyth. Chenyth. Who said he was evil? His real sin is that he was the enemy. Some of our own were as violent and bloody."

I glanced toward the split in the mountain. The giant black stallion stood within a yard of where Lord Hammer had posted him yesterday. Hammer slept on the ground beneath the animal.

Easy pickings, I thought. Walk over, slip the dagger in him, and have done.

If the horse would let me. He was a factor I couldn't fathom. But somehow I knew he would block me.

My own well-being wasn't a matter of concern. Like the Harish, it hadn't occurred to me to worry about whether or not I got out alive.

I saw no way any of us could get home without Lord Hammer's protection.

Fetch dragged herself to a sitting position.

"Come with me," I told Chenyth.

We went to her. She greeted us with a weak smile. "I wasn't good for much down there, was I?"

"How you feeling?" I asked.

"Better."

"Good. I'd hate to think I lugged you all the way up here for nothing."

"It was you?"

"Lord Hammer carried the Scuttarian."

"The others?"

"Still down there, Love."

"It was bad?"

"Worse than anybody expected. Except the dragon."

"You got the blood?"

"We did. Was it worth it?"

She glanced at me sharply. "You knew there would be risks. You were paid to take them."

"I know. I wonder if that's enough."

"What?"

"I know who Lord Hammer is, Fetch. The Harish knew all along. It's why they came. I killed two of them. Lord Hammer slew two. Foud killed Sigurd. That's five of the company gone fighting one another. I want to know what reason there might be for me not to make it six and have the world rid of an old evil."

Fetch wasn't herself. Healthy she would have screeched and argued like a whole flock of hens at feeding time. Instead she just glanced at Lord Hammer and shrugged. "I'm too tired and sick to care much, Will. But don't. It won't change the past. It won't change the future, either. He's chasing a dead dream. And it won't do you any good now." She leaned back and closed her eyes. "I hated him for a while, too. I lost people in the wars."

"I'm sorry."

"Don't be. He lost people, too, you know. Friends and relatives. All the pain and dying weren't on our side. And he lost everything he had, except his knowledge."

"Oh." I saw what she was trying to say. Lord Hammer was no different than the rest of us leftovers, going on being what he had learned to be.

"Is there anything to eat?"

"Chenyth. See if you can get her something. Fetch, I know all the arguments. I've been wrestling them all morning. And I can't make up my mind. I was hoping you'd help me figure where I've got to stand."

"Don't put it on me, Willem Potter. It's a thing between you and Lord Hammer."

Chenyth brought soup that was mostly mule. He spooned it into Fetch's mouth. She ate it like it was good.

I decided, but on the basis of none of the arguments that had gone before.

I had promised myself that I would take my little brother home to his mother. To do that I needed Lord Hammer's protection.

I often wonder, now, if many of the most fateful decisions aren't made in response to similarly oblique considerations.

XIII

I need not have put myself through the misery. The Fates had their own plans.

When Lord Hammer woke, I went to him. He was weak. He barely had the strength to sit up. I squatted on my hams, facing him, intimidated by the stallion's baleful stare. Carefully, I drew the Harish kill-dagger from within my shirt. I offered it to him atop my open palms.

The earth shook. There was a suggestion of gargantuan mirth in it.

"The Dragon mocks us." Lord Hammer took the dagger. "Thank you, Willem Potter. I'd say there are no debts between us now."

"There are, Lord. Old ones. I lost a father and several brothers in the wars."

"And I lost sons and friends. Will we fight old battles here in the cupped hands of doom? Will we cross swords even as the filed teeth of Fate rip at us? I lost my homeland, and more than any non-Tervola could comprehend. I have nothing left but hope, and that too wan to credit. The Dragon laughs with cause, Willem Potter. Summon Bellweather. A journey looms before us."

"As you say, Lord."

I think we left too soon, with too many wounded. Some survived the forest. Some survived the plains. Some survived the snows and precipices of the Dragon's Teeth. But we left men's bones beside the way. Only eight of us lived to see the plains of Shara, west of the mountains, and even then we were a long way from home.

It was in Shara that Lord Hammer's saga ended.

We were riding ponies he had bought from a Sharan tribe. Our faces were south, bent into a spring rain.

Lord Hammer's big stallion stumbled.

The sorcerer fell.

He had been weakening steadily. Fetch claimed only his will was driving him toward the laboratories where he would make use of the dragon's blood . . .

He lay in the mud and grass of a foreign land, dying, and there was nothing any of us could do. The Harish dagger still gnawed at his soul.

Immortality rested in his saddlebags, in that black jar, and we couldn't do a thing. We didn't know how. Even Fetch was ignorant of the secret.

He was a strong man, Lord Hammer, but in the end no different than any other. He died, and we buried him in alien soil. The once mightiest man on earth had come to no more than the least of the soldiers who had followed him in his prime.

I was sad. It's painful to watch something magnificent and mighty brought low, even when you loath what it stands for.

He went holding Fetch's hand.

She removed the iron mask before we put him into the earth. "He should wear his own." She obtained a Tervola mask from his gear. It was golden and hideous, and at one time had terrorized half a world. I'm not sure what it represented. An animal head of some sort. Its eyes were rubies that glowed like the eyes of Lord Hammer's stallion. But their inner light was fading.

A very old man lay behind the iron mask. The last of his mystique perished when I finally saw his wizened face.

And yet I did him honor as we replaced the soil above him.

I had taken his gold. He had been my captain.

"You can come with us, Fetch," Chenyth said. And I agreed. There would be a place for her with the Potters.

Chenyth kept the iron mask. It hangs in my mother's house even now. Nobody believes him when he tells the story of Lord Hammer and the Kammengarn Dragon. They prefer Rainheart's heroics.

No matter. The world goes on whether geared by truth or fiction.

The last shovelful of earth fell on Lord Hammer's resting place. And Chenyth, as always, had a question. "Will, what happened to his horse?"

The great fire-eyed stallion had vanished.

Even Fetch didn't know the answer to that one.

VINCE'S DRAGON

BEN BOVA

ILLUSTRATIONS BY
TIM KIRK

The thing that worried Vince about the dragon, of course, was that he was scared that it was out to capture his soul.

Vince was a typical young Family man. He had dropped out of South Philadelphia High School to start his career with the Family. He boosted cars, pilfered suits from local stores, even spent grueling and terrifying hours learning how to drive a big trailer rig so he could help out on hijackings.

But they wouldn't let him in on the big stuff.

"You can run numbers for me, kid," said Louie Bananas, the one-armed policy king of South Philly.

"I wanna do somethin' big," Vince said, with ill-disguised impatience. "I wanna make somethin' outta myself."

Louie shook his bald, bullet-shaped head. "I dunno, kid. You don't look like you got th' guts."

"Try me! Lemme in on th' sharks."

So Louie let Vince follow Big Balls Falcone, the loan sharks' enforcer, for one day. After watching Big Balls systematically break a guy's fingers, one by one, because he was ten days late with his payment, Vince agreed that loan sharking was not the business for him.

Armed robbery? Vince had never held a gun, much less fired one. Besides, armed robbery was for the heads and zanies, the stupids and desperate ones. *Organized* crime didn't go in for armed robbery. There was no need to. And a guy could get hurt.

After months of wheedling and groveling around Louie Bananas' favorite restaurant, Vince finally got the break he wanted.

"Okay, kid, okay," Louie said one evening as Vince stood in a corner of the restaurant watching him devour linguine with clams (white sauce). "I got an openin' for you. Come here."

Vince could scarcely believe his ears.

"What is it, *Padrone?* What? I'll do anything!"

Burping politely into his checkered napkin, Louie leaned back in his chair and grabbed a handful of Vince's curly dark hair, pulling Vince's ear close to his mouth.

Vince, who had an unfortunate allergy to garlic, fought hard to suppress a sneeze as he listened to Louie whisper, "You know that ol' B&O warehouse down aroun' Front an' Washington?"

"Yeah." Vince nodded as vigorously as he could, considering his hair was still in Louie's iron grip.

"Torch it."

"Burn it down?" Vince squeaked.

"Not so loud, *chidrool!*"

"Yeah."

"But that's arson."

Louie laughed. "It's a growth industry nowadays. Good opportunity for a kid who ain't afraid t' play with fire."

Vince sneezed.

It wasn't so much of a trick to burn down the rickety old warehouse, Vince knew. The place was ripe for the torch. But to burn it down without getting caught, that was different.

The Fire Department and Police and, worst of all, the insurance companies all had special arson squads who would be sniffing over the charred remains of the warehouse even before the smoke had cleared.

Vince didn't know anything at all about arson. But, desperate for his big chance, he was willing to learn.

He tried to get in touch with Johnnie the Torch, the leading local expert. But Johnnie was too busy to see him, and besides Johnnie worked for a rival Family, 'way up in Manayunk. The two other guys that Vince knew who had something of a reputation in the field had mysteriously disappeared within the past two nights.

Vince didn't think the library would have any books on the subject that would help him. Besides, he didn't read too good.

So, feeling very shaky about the whole business, very late the next night he drove a stolen station wagon filled with jerry cans of gasoline and big drums of industrial paint thinner out to Front Street.

He pushed his way through the loosely-nailed boards that covered the old warehouse's main entrance, feeling little and scared in the darkness. The warehouse was empty and dusty, but as far as the insurance company knew, Louie's fruit and vegetable firm had stocked the place up to the ceiling just a week ago.

Vince felt his hands shaking. *If I don't do a good job, Louie'll send Big Balls Falcone after me.*

Then he heard a snuffling sound.

He froze, trying to make himself invisible in the shadows.

Somebody was breathing. And it wasn't Vince.

Kee-rist, they didn't tell me there was a night watchman here!

"I am not a night watchman."

Vince nearly jumped out of his jockey shorts.

"And I'm not a policeman, either, so relax."

"Who . . ." His voice cracked. He swallowed and said again, deeper, "Who are you?"

"I am trying to get some sleep, but this place is getting to be a regular Stonehenge. People coming and going all the time!"

A bum, Vince thought. *A bum who's using this warehouse to flop . . .*

"And I am not a bum!" the voice said, sternly.

"I didn't say you was!" Vince answered. Then he shuddered, because he realized he had only thought it.

A glow appeared, across the vast darkness of the empty warehouse. Vince stared at it, then realized it was an eye. A single glowing, baleful eye with a slit of a pupil, just like a cat's. But this eye was the size of a bowling ball!

"Wh . . . wha . . ."

Another eye opened beside it. In the light from their twin smolderings, Vince could just make out a scaly head with a huge jaw full of fangs.

He did what any man would do. He fainted.

When he opened his eyes he wanted to faint again. In the eerie moonlight that was now filtering through the old warehouse's broken windowpanes, he saw a dragon standing over him.

It had a long, sinuous body covered with glittering green and bluish scales, four big paws with talons on them the size of lumberjacks' saws. Its tail coiled around and around, the end twitching slightly all the way over on the other side of the warehouse.

". . . I could show you some very fascinating exhibits . . ."

And right over him, grinning down toothily at him, was this huge fanged head with the giant glowing cat's eyes.

"You're cute," the dragon said.

"Huh?"

"Not at all like those other bozos Louie sent over here the past couple of nights. They were older. Fat, blubbery men."

"Other guys . . .?"

The dragon flicked a forked tongue out between its glistening white fangs. "Do you think you're the first arsonist Louie's sent here? I mean, they've been clumping around here for the past several nights."

Still flat on his back, Vince asked, "Wh . . . wh . . . what happened to them?"

The dragon hunkered down on its belly and seemed, incredibly, to *smile* at him. "Oh, don't worry about them. They won't bother us." The tongue flicked out again and brushed Vince's face. "Yes, you are *cute!*"

Little by little, Vince's scant supply of courage returned to him. He kept speaking with the dragon, still not believing this was really happening, and slowly got up to a sitting position.

"I can read your mind," the dragon was saying. "So you might as well forget about trying to run away."

"I . . . uh, I'm supposed to torch this place," Vince confessed.

"I know," said the dragon. Somehow, it sounded like a female dragon.

"Yes, you're right," she admitted. "I am a female dragon. As a matter of fact, all the dragons that you humans have ever had trouble with have been females."

"You mean like St. George?" Vince blurted.

"That pansy! Him and his silly armor. Aunt Ssrishha could have broiled him alive inside that pressure cooker he was wearing. As it was, she got to laughing so hard at him that her flame went out."

"And he killed her."

"He did not!" She sounded really incensed, and a little wisp of smoke trickled out of her left nostril. "Aunt Ssrishha just made herself invisible and flew away. She was laughing so hard she got the hiccups."

"But the legend . . ."

"A human legend. More like a human public relations story. Kill a dragon! The human who can kill a dragon hasn't been born yet!"

"Hey, don't get sore. I didn't do nuthin."

"No. Of course not." Her voice softened. "You're cute, Vince."

His mind was racing. Either he was crazy or he was talking with a real, fire-breathing dragon.

"Uh . . . what's your name?"

"Ssrzzha," she said. "I'm from the Polish branch of the dragon family."

"Shh . . . zz . . ." Vince tried to pronounce.

"You may call me 'Sizzle,' " the dragon said, grandly.

"Sizzle. Hey, that's a cute name."

"I knew you'd like it."

If I'm crazy, they'll come and wake me up sooner or later, Vince thought, and decided to at least keep the conversation going.

"You say all the dragons my people have ever fought were broads . . . I mean, females?"

"That's right, Vince. So you can see how silly it is, all those human lies about our eating young virgins."

"Uh, yeah. I guess so."

"And the bigger lies they tell about slaying dragons. Utter falsehoods."

"Really?"

"Have you ever seen a stuffed dragon in a museum? Or dragon bones? Or a dragon's head mounted on a wall?"

"Well . . . I don't go to museums much."

"Whereas *I* could show you some very fascinating exhibits in certain caves, if you want to see bones and heads and . . ."

"Ah, no, thanks. I don't think I really wanna see that," Vince said hurriedly.

"No, you probably wouldn't."

"Where's all the male dragons? They must be *really* big."

Sizzle huffed haughtily and a double set of smoke-rings wafted past Vince's ear.

"The males of our species are tiny! Hardly bigger than you are. They all live out on some islands in the Indian Ocean. We have to fly there every hundred years or so for mating, or else our race would die out."

"Every hundred years! You only get laid once a century?"

"Sex is not much fun for us, I'm afraid. Not as much as it is for you, but then you're descended from monkeys, of course. Disgusting little things. Always chattering and making messes."

"Uh, look . . . Sizzle. This's been fun and it was great meetin' you and all, but it's gettin' late and I gotta go now, and besides . . ."

"But aren't you forgetting why you came here?"

Truth to tell, Vince had forgotten. But now he recalled, "I'm supposed t' torch this warehouse."

"That's right. And from what I can see bubbling inside your cute little head, if you don't burn this place down tonight, Louie's going to be very upset with you."

"Yeah, well, that's my problem, right? I mean, you wanna stay here an' get back t' sleep, right? I don't wanna bother you like them other guys did, ya know? I mean, like, I can come back when you go off to th' Indian Ocean or somethin' . . ."

"Don't be silly, Vince," Sizzle said, lifting herself ponderously to her four paws. "I can sleep anywhere. And I'm not due for another mating for several decades, thank the gods. As for those other fellows . . . well, they annoyed me. But you're cute!"

Vince slowly got to his feet, surprised that his quaking knees held him upright. But Sizzle coiled her long, glittering body around him, and with a grin that looked like a forest made of sharp butcher knives, she said:

"I'm getting kind of tired of this old place, anyway. What do you say we belt it out?"

"Huh?"

"I can do a much better job of torching this firetrap than you can, Vince cutie," said Sizzle. "And I won't leave any telltale gasoline fumes behind me."

"But . . ."

"You'll be completely in the clear. Anytime the police come near, I can always make myself invisible."

"Invisible?"

"Sure. See?" And Sizzle disappeared.

"Hey, where are ya?"

"Right here, Vince." The dragon reappeared in all its glittering hugeness.

Vince stared, his mind churning underneath his curly dark hair.

Sizzle smiled at him. "What do you say, cutie? A life of crime together? You and I could do wonderful things together, Vince. I could get you to the top of the Family in no time."

A terrible thought oozed up to the surface of Vince's slowly-simmering mind. "Uh, wait a minute. This is like I

"What do you say, cutie?"

seen on TV, ain't it? You help me, but you want me to sell my soul to you, right?"

"Your *soul*? What would I do with your soul?"

"You're workin' for th' devil, an' you gimme three wishes or somethin' but in return I gotta let you take my soul down t' hell when I die."

Sizzle shook her ponderous head and managed to look slightly affronted. "Vince—I admit that dragons and humans haven't been the best of friends over the millennia, but we do *not* work for the devil. I'm not even sure that he exists. I've never seen a devil, have you?"

"No, but . . ."

"And I'm not after your soul, silly boy."

"You don' want me t' sign nuthin?"

"Of course not."

"An' you'll help me torch this dump for free?"

"More than that, Vince. I'll help you climb right up to the top of the Family. We'll be partners in crime! It'll be the most fun I've had since Aunt Hsspss started the Chicago Fire."

"Hey, I just wanna torch this one warehouse!"

"Yes, of course."

"No Chicago Fires or nuthin like that."

"I promise."

It took several minutes for Vince to finally make up his mind and say, "Okay, let's do it."

Sizzle cocked her head slightly to one side. "Shouldn't you get out of the warehouse first, Vince?"

"Huh? Oh yeah, sure."

"And maybe drive back to your house, or—better yet—over to that restaurant where your friends are."

"Whaddaya mean? We gotta torch this place first."

"I'll take care of that, Vince dearie. But wouldn't it look better if you had plenty of witnesses around to tell the police they were with you when the warehouse went up?"

"Yeah . . ." he said, feeling a little suspicious.

"All right, then," said Sizzle. "You just get your cute little body over to the restaurant and once you're safely there I'll light this place up like an Inquisition pyre."

"How'll you know . . .?"

"When you get to the restaurant? I'm telepathic, Vince."

"But how'll I know . . ."

"When this claptrap gets belted out? Don't worry, you'll see the flames in the sky!" Sizzle sounded genuinely excited by the prospect.

Vince couldn't think of any other objections. Slowly, reluctantly, he headed for the warehouse door. He had to step over one of Sizzle's saber-long talons on the way.

At the doorway, he turned and asked plaintively, "You sure you ain't after my soul?"

Sizzle smiled at him. "I'm not after your soul, Vince. You can depend on that."

The warehouse fire was the most spectacular anyone had seen in a long time, and the police were totally stymied about its cause. They questioned Vince at length, especially since he had forgotten to get rid of the gasoline and paint thinner in the back of the stolen station wagon. But they couldn't pin a thing on him, not even car theft, once Louie had Big Balls Falcone explain the situation to the unhappy wagon's owner.

Vince's position in the Family started to rise. Spectacularly.

Arson became his specialty. Louie gave him tougher and tougher assignments and Vince would wander off a night later and the job would be done. Perfectly.

He met Sizzle regularly, sometimes in abandoned buildings, sometimes in empty lots. The dragon remained invisible then, of course, and the occasional passerby got the impression that a young, sharply-dressed man was standing in the middle of a weed-choked, bottle-strewn empty lot talking to thin air.

More than once they could have heard him asking, "You really ain't interested in my soul?"

But only Vince could hear Sizzle's amused reply, "No, Vince. I have no use for souls, yours or anyone else's."

As the months went by, Vince's rapid rise to Family stardom naturally attracted some antagonism from other young men attempting to get ahead in the organization. Antagonism sometimes led to animosity, threats, even attempts at violence.

But strangely, wondrously, anyone who got angry at Vince disappeared. Without a trace, except once when a single charred shoe of Fats Lombardi was found in the middle of Tasker Street, between Twelfth and Thirteenth.

Louie and the other elders of the Family nodded knowingly. Vince was not only ambitious and talented. He was smart. No bodies could be laid at his doorstep.

From arson, Vince branched into loan-sharking, which was still the heart of the Family's operation. But he didn't need Big Balls Falcone to terrify his customers into paying on time. Customers who didn't pay found their cars turned into smoking wrecks. Right before their eyes, an automobile parked at the curb would burst into flame.

"Gee, too bad," Vince would say. "Next time it might be your house," he'd hint darkly, seeming to wink at somebody who wasn't there. At least, somebody no one else could see. Somebody very tall, from the angle of his head when he winked.

The day came when Big Balls Falcone himself, understandably put out by the decline in his business, let it be known that he was coming after Vince. Big Balls disappeared in a cloud of smoke, literally.

The years rolled by. Vince became quite prosperous. He was no longer the skinny, scared kid he had been when he first met Sizzle. Now he dressed conservatively, with a carefully-tailored vest buttoned neatly over his growing paunch, and lunched on steak and lobster tails with bankers and brokers.

Although he moved out of the old neighborhood row house into a palatial ranch-style single near Cherry Hill, over in Jersey, Vince still came back to the Epiphany Church every Sunday morning for Mass. He sponsored the church's Little League baseball team and donated a free Toyota every year for the church's annual raffle.

He looked upon these charities, he often told his colleagues, as a form of insurance. He would lift his eyes at such moments. Those around him thought he was looking toward heaven. But Vince was really searching for Sizzle, who was usually not far away.

"Really Vince," the dragon told him, chuckling, "you still don't trust me. After all these years. I don't want your soul. Honestly I don't."

Vince still attended church and poured money into charities.

Finally Louie himself, old and frail, bequeathed the Family fortunes to Vince and then died peacefully in his sleep, unassisted by members of his own or any other Family. Somewhat of a rarity in Family annals.

Vince was now *Capo* of the Family. He was not yet forty, sleek, hair still dark, heavier than he wanted to be, but in possession of his own personal tailor, his own barber, and more women than he had ever dreamed of having.

His ascension to *Capo* was challenged, of course, by some of Louie's other lieutenants. But after the first few of them disappeared without a trace, the others quickly made their peace with Vince.

He never married. But he enjoyed life to the full.

"You're getting awfully overweight, Vince," Sizzle warned him one night, as they strolled together along the dark and empty waterfront where they had first met. "Shouldn't you be worrying about the possibility of a heart attack?"

"Naw," said Vince. "I don't get heart attacks, I give 'em!" He laughed uproariously at his own joke.

"You're getting older, Vince. You're not as cute as you once were, you know."

"I don't hafta be *cute,* Sizzle. I got the power now. I can look any way I wanna look, and act any way I wanna act. Who's gonna get in my way?"

Sizzle nodded, a bit ruefully. But Vince paid no attention to her mood.

"I can do anything I want!" he shouted to the watching heavens. "I got th' power and the rest of those dummies are scared to death of me. Scared to death!" He laughed and laughed.

"But Vince," Sizzle said, "I helped you to get that power."

"Sure, sure. But I got it now, an' I don't really need your help anymore. I can get anybody in th' Family to do whatever I want!"

Dragons don't cry, of course, but the expression on Sizzle's face would have melted the heart of anyone who saw it.

"Listen," Vince went on, in a slightly less bombastic tone, "I know you done a lot to help me, an' I ain't gonna forget that. You'll still be part of my organization, Sizzle old girl. Don't worry about that."

But the months spun along and lengthened into years, and Vince saw Sizzle less and less. He didn't need to. And secretly, down inside him, he was glad that he didn't have to.

I don't need her no more, and I never signed nuthin about givin' away my soul or nuthin. I'm free and clear!

Dragons, of course, are telepathic.

Vince's big mistake came when he noticed that a gorgeous young redhead he was interested in seemed to have eyes only for a certain slick-looking young punk. Vince thought about the problem mightily, and then decided to solve two problems with one stroke.

He called the young punk to his presence, at the very same restaurant where Louie had given Vince his first big break.

The punk looked scared. He had heard that Vince was after the redhead.

"Listen kid," Vince said gruffly, laying a heavily be-ringed hand on the kid's thin shoulder. "You know the old clothing factory up on Twenty-Eighth and Arch?"

"Y . . . yessir," said the punk, in a whisper that Vince could barely hear.

"It's a very flammable building, dontcha think?"

The punk blinked, gulped, then nodded. "Yeah. It is. But . . ."

"But what?"

His voice trembling, the kid said, "I heard that two-three different guys tried beltin' out that place. An' they . . . they never came back!"

"The place is still standin', ain't it?" Vince asked severely.

"Yeah."

"Well, by tomorrow morning, either *it* ain't standin' or *you* ain't standin'. *Capisce?*"

The kid nodded and fairly raced out of the restaurant. Vince grinned. One way or the other, he had solved a problem, he thought.

The old factory burned cheerfully for a day and a half before the Fire Department could get the blaze under control. Vince laughed and phoned his insurance broker.

But that night, as he stepped from his limousine onto the driveway of his Cherry Hill home, he saw long coils of glittering scales wrapped halfway around the house.

Looking up, he saw Sizzle smiling at him.

"Hello, Vince. Long time no see."

"Oh, hi Sizzle ol' girl. What's new?" With his left hand, Vince impatiently waved his driver off. The man backed the limousine down the driveway and headed for the garage back in the city, goggle-eyed that The Boss was talking to himself.

"That was a real cute fellow you sent to knock off the factory two nights ago," Sizzle said, her voice almost purring.

"Him? He's a punk."

"I thought he was really cute."

"So you were there, huh? I figured you was after those other guys never came back."

"Oh Vince, you're not cute anymore. You're just soft and fat and ugly."

"You ain't gonna win no beauty contests yourself, Sizzle."

He started for the front door, but Sizzle planted a huge taloned paw in his path. Vince had just enough time to look up, see the expression on her face, and scream.

Sizzle's forked tongue licked her lips as the smoke cleared.

"Delicious," she said. "Just the right amount of fat on him. And the poor boy thought I was after his *soul!*"

THE THERMALS OF
AUGUST

EDWARD BRYANT

ILLUSTRATIONS BY
ROGER STINE

I see the woman die, and the initial beauty of the event takes away my breath. Later I will feel the sickness of pain, the weakness of sorrow. But for the moment I sit transfixed, face tilted toward the irregular checkerboard of cumulus. The drama of death has always seemed to me the truest element in life.

The other diners see what I had detected a moment before: a tiny irregularity in the smooth sweep of the newly launched kite. The kite is cobalt blue and dart-shaped, apparently a modified Rogallo wing—not one of the Dragons we'll all be flying later in the week.

Having come to the outdoor cafe by Bear Creek for a late breakfast, I'd hoped simply to satisfy a necessary but unwanted need. Now, however, the bite of croissant lies dry in my mouth and the cup of coffee cools undrunk. Perhaps I did not really see the minute lurch in the kite's path. I allow myself that one brief luxuriant hope, staring at the kite and its pilot more than two thousand feet above the valley floor. The kite is a vivid midge against the lighter blue of the sky.

Then the kite falls.

I see the craft first slip into a stall, then nose downward—no problem for even a moderately experienced pilot. But suddenly half the wing folds back at an unnatural angle. In a little more than a second, we on the ground hear the twang and snap of breaking control wires and twisting aluminum frame.

The kite tumbles.

I am surrounded by babble and one of the other diners begins to whimper.

It seems to take forever to fall.

My brain coolly goes to work and I know that the descent is far more rapid in terms of feet per second than appears to our eyes.

At first the kite fell like a single piece of confetti pitched from a Wall Street window. Now the collapsed portion of the wing has wrapped around pilot and harness, and the warped mass rotates as it appears to us to grow larger.

The crippled kite twists and spins, flutters and falls like a leaf of aspen. I think I see the shrouded form of the pilot, a pendulum flung outward by centripetal force.

The kite's fall seems to accelerate as it nears ground, but that also is illusion. Someone screams at us to take cover, evidently thinking that the kite will plunge into the midst of the outdoor diners. It doesn't. The kite makes half a final revolution and spins into the corner of the Conoco Building. The cocooned pilot slams into the brick with the flat smack of a beef roast dropped onto kitchen tile. The wreckage drapes over the temporary barbed wire fence protecting this building under perpetual reconstruction.

The bit of croissant still lies on my tongue. I feel every sharp edge. I gag and taste bitterness coat my throat.

The dead moth corpse of the kite is not more than fifty feet away, and the crowd slowly begins to close the distance. I am among them. The others grant me a wide path because most recognize that I too am a pilot. "Let the woman through." Gingerly I approach my fallen comrade.

Her body is almost totally swathed in the cobalt fabric of the kite. I can see her face; her eyes stare open and unpeacefully. The concealed contours of her body are smooth. I suspect most of the bones of her body are splintered.

When I softly touch one of her shoulders, I inadvertently drag one tightly folded flap of kitewing against a steel barb. Pooled blood bursts forth in a brief cataract. Mixed with the scent of her blood is the odor of urine.

This is not death; it is indignity.

My nylon windbreaker is composed of my colors: gold and black. I take it off and cover the dead woman's face. Then I glare around the circle of onlookers. Most of them stare at the ground and mumble, then turn and leave.

I draw back the jacket for a moment and lightly kiss the dead woman's lips.

*   *   *

I love this town between festivals. Living among the stable population of two thousand refreshes me after months of engulfment in the cities of the coasts. I am pleased by the ambivalent socialness of friendly greetings on the street, but without anyone pushing me to respond further. Warm people who hold a fetish of privacy are an impossible paradox elsewhere. This town prides itself on paradox.

The rules do not always hold true in the public downtown, particularly during the festivals. The outsiders flood in at various times of the year for their chamber music and jazz festivals, art symposiums, video circus, and other, more esoteric gatherings.

Although the present festival will not begin until tomorrow at dawn, the town is crowded with both participants and spectators. Tonight people fill the bars downtown and spill out onto the sidewalks along both sides of Main. Though August is not yet ended, the cold crisps the night. The town is at nearly nine thousand feet, and chill is to be expected; but the plumes of breath billow more than one would expect. The stars are clear and icy tonight; I see clouds scudding up the valley from the west.

There is a shifting, vibrant energy in the crowds that runs like quicksilver. I can feel it. The moon tonight is new, so I can't ascribe anything to lunar influence. The magic must generate from the gestalt interaction of the flyers and the watchers. Or, more likely, from the ancient mountains that ring us on three sides.

The air seems most charged in the Club Troposphere, the street-front bar on the ground floor of the Ionic Hotel. I have a table in one of the Trope's raised bay display windows overlooking the sidewalk. The crowd flux continually alters, but at any given moment, at least a dozen others share the table with me. Some stand, some sit, and in the crowd din, body language communicates at least as much as words. I'm stacking empties of imported beers in front of my glass. This early in the evening, my pyramid looks more Aztec than Egyptian.

I continue to taste blood; the thick, dark ale won't wash it away. Before I truly realize what I'm doing, I grasp the latest empty by the neck and slam it down on the hardwood. "God *damn!*" Amber glass sprays across the table and I raise the jagged edges of the neck to the level of my eyes.

"Mairin!" Across the table I see Lark look up from nuzzling Haley's throat. "Mairin, are you all right?" he says. Haley stares at me as well. Everyone at the table is staring at me.

"I dropped it," I say. I set the severed neck down beside my glass.

Lark gets up from Haley's lap and comes around the table to me. I stare from one to the other of the vertices of my present triangle. Lark is small, compact and dark, with the sense of spatial orientation and imagination and the steel muscles, all of which make him a better Dragon pilot than anyone else here. With the probable exception of me. Haley is tall and light, a woman of the winter with silky hair to her waist and eyes like ice chipped from inaccessible glaciers. But when she smiles, the ice burns.

"Are you okay?" Lark places his fingers lightly on the hand with which I smashed the bottle. I move the hand and pick up my glass. A barmaid hovers beside us, wiping shards into a paper towel.

I nod. "It was an accident."

Lark puts his face very close to mine. "The rookie who died today—you saw the whole thing, right?"

"I saw her get into the truck for the ride up to the point. She was very young. I didn't know her."

"She was good," Lark says. "I know people who flew with her in the midwest. Today she was very unlucky."

"Obviously."

"That's not what I meant," Lark smiles in the way I've learned to interpret during the long years of competition as all teeth and no mirth. "After the medics took her body away from you practically at gun point, I went over her equipment with the officials. She committed a beginner's error, you know—dipped a wingtip when she went off. Clipped an outcropping."

"I saw," I say. "She recovered."

"We did X-rays. There was a flaw in the metal. That's why the one wing buckled."

"God." I feel sick, dizzy, as though I'm whirling around in that bright cobalt body-bag, waiting for the ground to smash out my life.

"Whoever," Lark says. "Just bad luck." He hesitates. "I keep thinking about all the times I've inspected my own equipment. You can only check so much."

Haley has come around the table too and stands close to Lark. "I wonder what it felt like."

"I know," I say. I look at Lark's face and realize he knows too. Haley is an artist and photographer who sticks close to her gallery here in town. She has never flown. She can never know.

I'm really not sure how many beers I've drunk tonight. It must be more than I think I've counted, because I do and say what is uncharacteristic of me. With Lark and Haley both standing there, I look into Haley's winter eyes and say, "I need to be with someone tonight."

"I—Mairin—" Haley almost stutters. She gentles her voice. "Lark asked me already . . ."

"Lark could un-ask you," I say. I know that's unfair, but I also know my need. Lark is staring studiously out the window, pretending to ignore us both.

Haley says, "Lark was there too. He needs—"

"*I* need." They both stare at me uncomfortably now without speaking. Individually I know how stubborn each can be. Three springs tauten. I want to reach out and be held, to thaw and exhaust myself with body warmth. I want to reach out with the shattered bottle-neck and rip both of them until I bathe in steaming blood. Then it all goes out from me and I sink back in my chair. I am so goddamned suspicious of the word *need* and I have heard it too many times.

"I'm sorry," I say. "I'm behaving badly."

"Mairin—" both start to say. Lark touched my shoulder. Haley reached out.

I shove back my chair and get up unsteadily. My head pounds. Nausea wracks my belly and I am glad there is no competition for me tomorrow. "I'm going to my room. I don't feel . . ." I let the words trail off.

"Do you need help?"

"No, Haley. No, love. I can make it." I push past and leave them at the table. I hope I'm leaving my self-pity there too. The lobby of the Ionic is another zoo of milling humans. I make it to the lone elevator where luck has brought the cage to the first floor. As I enter the car, a bearded flyer-groupie in a yellow down jacket unwisely reaches in from the lobby and grabs my wrist.

"Lady, would you like a drink?" he says.

The spring, still taut, ratchets loose. Luckily for him my knee catches him only in the upper thigh and he flails backward into the lobby as spectators gape. The doors close and the elevator climbs noisily toward my floor. Two young men stand nervously in the opposite corner, just as far from me as four feet will allow.

I'll regret all this tomorrow.

*   *   *

I know the woman who comes to me that night.

I am she.

The cotton sheet slides coolly, rustling, as I restlessly change position. I've pushed the down comforter to my knees. It's too hot for that. The cold will come later, past midnight when the hotel lowers all the thermostats.

Finally I despair of sleeping, lie still, lie on my back with my hands beside me. I can see dimly in the light from the frosted glass transom, as well as the white glow from the hotel neon outside the single window. I hear the muffled sounds of celebration from the street below.

Then I see the woman standing silently at the foot of the bed. I know her. She is short—five-four without shoes. Her body is slender and muscular. The shadows shift as she moves around to the side of my bed. Darkness glides across her eyes, her neck, between her breasts, on her belly and below. Her breasts are small with dark, prominent nipples. Her muscles, when she moves, are not obtrusive but are clearly delineated.

She steps into the light from the street. There are no crowsfeet visible in chiaroscuro. Her face is delicately boned, heart-shaped with a chin that misses sharpness by only a degree. Her eyes are wide and as dark as her close-cut hair. In the semi-darkness I know I am seeing her as she was when she was twenty and as she will be when she is forty.

I slip the sheet aside as she silently lies in my bed. Slowly, delicately, I slide the fingers of one hand along the side of her face, down the jawline, across her lips. Her lips part slightly and one fingertip touches the firm, moist cushion of her tongue.

Then even more gently I cup her breasts, my palms feeling their warmth long before the skin touches the tips of each erect nipple.

It takes a thousand years.

My hands slide down her flanks and touch all that is moist and warm between her legs. I know what to seek out and I find it. The warmth builds.

I think of Haley. I think of Lark. I blink him out. Haley leaves of her own accord and abandons me pleading. My pleading, her leaving.

My finger orbits and touches, touches and orbits, touches. The warmth builds and builds, is more than warmth, builds and heats, the heat— The heat coils and expands, ripples outward, ripples across my belly, down my thighs. For a moment, just a bare moment, something flickers like heat lightning on the horizon—

—but it is not sufficient. I am not warm enough.

Heat radiates and is lost, spent. I see Lark and Haley again in my mind and blink away the man. But Haley leaves too.

Only I am left.

I wish the woman would sleep, but I know her too well. I wish I could sleep, but I know me so well.

*   *   *

Dragon Festival.

It is nearly dawn and the roar of dragons splits the chilly air. The tongues of propane burners lick the hearts of twenty great balloons. The ungainly shapes bulk in the near darkness and slowly come erect. The crews hold tight to nylon lines.

As the sun starts to rise above the peaks beyond the two waterfalls, I see that snow dusted the San Juans sometime past midnight. The mountains are topped with were-snow—a sifting that came in the night and will shortly vanish with morning sun. The real storms are yet to come with the autumn.

Mythic creatures rear up in the dawn. These are nothing so simple as the spherical balloons of my childhood. Laboratory-bred synthetics have been sculpted and molded to suggest the shapes of legend. A great golden gargoyle hunches to the east. To the west, a hundred-foot tall gryphon strains at its handlers' lines. The roaring, rushing propane flames animate a sphynx, a satyr, a kra-ken with basket suspended from its drooping tentacles, a Cheshire cat and chimera of every combination. The giants bob and dip as they distend, but it is a perfect morning with no wind.

I find a perverse delight in not feeling as wretched as I anticipated last night. My mind is clear. My eyes do not ache. Though I was not able to cope with breakfast food, I did manage to drink tea. I realize I'm being caught up in the exhilaration of the first festival day. I know that within the hour I will be flowing with the wind, floating with the clouds.

"How do you feel this morning?" A familiar voice.

"Did you get any rest?" Another familiar voice.

I turn to greet Haley and Lark. "I feel fine. I got some sleep." I determine to leave any qualifications behind.

"I'll see you on the ground," says Lark.

Haley looks at me steadily for several seconds, a time that seems much longer. Finally she draws me close and says, "Good luck. Have a fine flight." Her lips are cool and they touch my cheek briefly.

Lark and she walk toward the balloon called *Cheshire*. I hear fragmented words from a portable public address system that tell me all flyers should be linking their craft to their respective balloons. I walk across the meadow to *Negwenya*. *Negwenya* is the Zulu word for dragon. *Negwenya* is a towering black and scarlet balloon owned by a man named Robert Simms. Robert's eight-times-removed grandparents were Zulu. Robert is a great believer in the mystique of dragons and sees an occult affinity between *Negwenya* and the Dragon V flyers he ferries up to the sky.

I walk between the serpentine legs of *Negwenya* and feel the sudden chill of entering shadow. The people holding *Negwenya*'s lines, mostly local volunteers, greet me and I answer them back. From where he waits beside my Dragon V, Robert raises a broad hand in welcome. My gold and black glider looks as fragile on the wet grass as it did in the electric glow when I left to watch the coming dawn.

"You ready?" Robert's voice is permanently hoarse from a long-ago accident when a mooring line snapped and lashed around his throat.

"I'm ready," I check the tough lightweight lines that will
allow my Dragon to dangle below *Negwenya* as the balloon takes us up to twelve thousand feet. The ends of the
lines tuck into safety pressure catches both on the underside of *Negwenya*'s gondola and on my craft's keel tube
and wing braces. Either Robert or I can elect at any time to
release the catches. Once that happens, *Negwenya* will go
on about its own business and I will describe the great
descending spiral that eventually brings me back to earth.

More orders blare from the bullhorn across the field. It
doesn't matter that none of us can understand the words;
we all know what happens next.

"Let's link up," says Robert.

I nod and climb into my harness under the Five as
Robert and a helper hold the wings steady on the support
stands. It isn't like getting ready to fly a 767; just a few
metallic clicks and the appropriate straps are secured. I pull
on my helmet and check the instrumentation: the mi-
croprocessor-based unit in the liner records air speed,
ground speed, and altitude. The figures appear on a narrow band along the inside of the transparent visor. There is
an audible stall warning, but I rarely activate that; I'd rather
gauge stability directly from the air flutter on the wing-
fabric.

"Okay, just a few more minutes," says Robert.

I'm glad the Five is resting on the supports. The entire
craft may only weigh sixty pounds, but that's half what I
weigh. My flight suit feels sticky along the small of my back;
I'm sweating. I hear the amplified words of the pageant
director continue to fragment on the leading edge of the
mountain.

"Time to do it," says Robert. He climbs up to the launch
ladder and steps into the gondola. Then he looks back
over the edge—I see the reflection in the bulge of my

visor—and grins. "Good luck, lady." He displays an erect thumb. "Break a leg."

*   *   *

With a rush and a roar, the twenty lighter than air craft embark. The paradox is that with all the fury and commotion, the score of balloons rises so slowly. Our ascension is stately.

Excited as ever by the sight, I watch the images of ground things diminish. I see the takeoff field swarm with video people; the insect eyes of cameras glitter. From beyond the ropes, the sustained note of the crowd swells with the balloons' first rising.

Harpies, genies, furies all, we soar toward a morning clear but for high cirrus. I fill my lungs with chill clean air and feel the exuberance, the climactic anticipation of that moment when each of us cuts loose the tether from our respective balloon and glides into free flight.

Free is the word, free is the key. I know I'm smiling; and then I feel the broad, loose grin. My teeth ache with the cold, but it doesn't matter. I want to laugh madly and I restrain myself only because I know I can afford to waste none of the precious oxygen at this altitude.

The weather's fine!

I raise a gloved hand to Lark as *Cheshire* slowly rises past *Negwenya*. His brown and yellow wings bob slightly as he waves back. The grin on *Cheshire*'s cat doesn't seem nearly so wide as mine.

The valley town is a parti-colored patchwork. I glance up and scan the line of red figures along my visor. I'm a thousand feet above the meadow. I look from the comfortable brick and frame of the old town to the newer, wooden, fake Victorian homes rising from the mountain's skirts. Now I'm level with the end of the trees and the beginning of bare rock. To the east I look beyond the old

Pandora Mill and see sun catch the spray from Ingram Falls and Bridal Veil. The waterfalls have not yet been turned off for the winter.

Toward the top of the canyon, light crosswinds buffet the balloons slightly as I expected they would. *Negwenya* rotates slowly and I concentrate on feeling no vertigo. We sweep past a sheer rock face to the waves and shouted greetings of a party of climbers strung like colored beads from their ropes. The balloon pilots yell back.

I can intellectually understand the attraction of technical climbing, but I was never able to appreciate it on a gut level. And I tried. Perhaps the only level on which it communicates to me is: *because it's there. Haley.* I wonder if I should desire Haley so intensely if she were more accessible. Even the anticipation of the coming long flight cannot erase the chill and heat of her from my mind,

"Mairin!"

I hear Robert's shout above the rushing-wind sound of the burner.

"Mairin, are you watching your gauge?"

I hadn't been. *Negwenya*'s at twelve-seven and it won't be long before we're thirteen thousand feet above sea level. While I was thinking about sapphire eyes, like a rank amateur, the other flyers had been cutting loose from their balloons. Below me I see the looping, swarming flight of Dragons.

I glance at the readouts again. Robert has assured my wind-direction. I drop.

My Dragon V drops away from the gondola and *Negwenya*'s roar grows faint; then is gone. The silence of my flight enfolds me. I lie prone in my harness, nothing else between me and the valley but air.

I fly for this moment.

The microprocessor's electronic senses tell me hard information: I am two thousand, nine hundred and sixty-two feet above the valley floor. My air speed is twenty-two miles per hour, only slightly less than my ground speed. My Dragon V presently travels nearly twelve feet horizontally for every foot it drops. In a minute I will lose about two hundred feet. Without searching out the thermal currents, I'll reach the ground in about fifteen minutes.

I pay no attention to the readouts. For the moment, the silence and openness, the caress of air on my face, all stir a complex reaction in my mind and body. I feel the throbbing start, far inside.

The slight shift of my body affects the attitude of my flight. The Dragon responds and I sweep into a wide, shallow turn.

No women or men have given me this feeling so fully as has the sky. I spiral down above the land and desire this to last forever. Gravity is the enemy of my love. As well I remind myself that I am part of the pageant; that just as the balloons are now drifting eastward, engaged in their slow-motion behemoth race, so it's demanded of the flyers that all land at about the same time in a live simulation of wide-screen spectacle. The cameras whir. The broadcasts fan out from microwave towers. The spectators watch.

But I want to make it last.

And I realize, first shocked, then amused, how many minutes it's been since I've held Haley's image in my mind.

I wheel the Dragon around in a descending spiral, as silent and graceful as any gull. Catching up with the other Dragons, I hear the mutter of wind rippling the fabric ever closer to the wing's trailing edge. I recognize the proximity of a stall and moderate slightly the angle of the warperons.

There are times when I have thought of gently and irrevocably slipping into the tightest of spirals and hurling myself blackly through the heart of the air. I cannot count the times I have skirted that final edge. Always I've refrained.

The air touches my cheekbones with the soft, tickling touch of Haley's cloudy hair.

There are times . . .

* * *

Death in triplicate stands by my elbow at the bar. Three tall shapes in black hooded robes have stepped to the brass rail. Skull faces, obviously sculpted with care, grin from cowled shadows. They say nothing. The trio reminds me of participants in a Mexican holy day parade.

Two deaths stare around the crowded Trope. The other looks at me. With my beer, I toast it back silently.

"Hey! You people want anything?" The barman tonight is one of the Trope's owners. With the Dragon Festival now started, all possible personnel are needed to service the crowds.

Three bony grins turn to smile at him. There are no words.

After a pause the owner says, "Listen, this is for paying customers. You want something?"

Three shrouded figures lean across the bar toward him. The owner draws back. "Drink," he says, "or get out."

Dead silence.

He apparently decides he's outnumbered. "Shit," the owner mutters, and goes off to wait on newcomers at the end of the bar. I think I hear a giggle from the death figure farthest from me. The nearest turns again to face me. Again I raise a glass in toast.

The figure reaches, hand ivory with makeup, into a pocket beneath the robes and withdraws an object. Then it extends the hand toward me. I accept a small skull made of spun sugar, another relic of Mexican religious celebrations. I incline my head gravely and set the candy skull beside my glass.

Death in triplicate stands by my elbow at the bar.

The nearest figure turns back to its fellows. I hear a whispered consultation. Then all three leave the bar together. As they reach the door, the barman shouts, "Good goddamn riddance!" He walks past me on the way to the cash register and I hear him say in a lower voice, "Give me the creeps."

"Friends of yours?"

I turn to face Haley and Lark. I hadn't seen them coming. "Friends of ours." I shrug.

"Spooky," says Haley.

"Striking masks," says Lark.

"Want a beer?"

"We're already set," says Lark. "We've got a table back behind the grove of rubber plants. Do you want to join us?"

I toss down the final swallow of beer. "Thanks, no. Not yet. I'm going to get some fresh air before I do any more drinking. You want to come along?"

Lark shakes his head. "We've got to do some drinking before we get some more fresh air."

"Then I'll see you both later. I need the air." I pick up the spun-sugar skull and gnaw on the jaw region as I push through the crowd.

Outside it's warmer than it was last night. There is cloud cover; I suspect the San Juans will be solidly snowcapped by morning. I zip the front of my flight jacket and stick my balled fists into the pockets. Turning right, I head along Main toward the landing meadow. I see the amber lights of trucks still bringing in and unloading the deflated forms of the racing balloons. I heard earlier that Robert Simms and *Negwenya* won. I decide that's a good omen.

"Girl? Hey, stop a moment, girl."

I turn and look toward the source of the voice. I'm in front of the Teller House, the town's lone real department store. I look into the display window and see the life-sized image of an elderly ragged woman staring back at me. It's an argee screen—the name comes from the initials of the people who started setting up these synchronous video arrangements back in the late 'seventies. One enormous complex of electronic art, the argee screens are spotted in cities and towns around the globe. Each screen shows a live, life-sized, simultaneous transmission of a street scene somewhere else in the world. Sound and video equipment beam my voice and image back to the linked screen. A computer randomly changes the linkages.

Right now the old woman sees and hears me. I see and hear her. I have no idea where she really is. The scene behind her is dark and obviously urban. It could be any night-time city.

"I'm in Baltimore," she says. "Where are you?"

I tell her.

"Oh yeah," she says. "I heard about you people. Saw you on the news. Bunch of fools who jump off cliffs on kites."

I laugh. "Condors launch from cliffs."

"Birds aren't too smart."

"But they fly."

"Yeah." She inspects me seriously. "You one of them?"

"Do I fly?" I nod. "Not exactly on a kite, though."

Her voice is thirsty. "Tell me about it."

For some reason I cannot ignore the imperative in her voice. I tell her about flying. I describe my Dragon Five as the combination of a high-winged monoplane and a bat. I talk of tomorrow's competition. I paint with words the colors of the long, gliding dragon kite I will tow behind my Five. I tell her of the *manjha,* the razor-sharp cutting line with which I will attempt to sever the tow-line of my opponent's kite. And with which he or she will try to sever mine. But most of all, I describe the flying. I talk religiously of fighting maneuvers in the sky.

And when I pause for breath, she says, "Girl, God bless you." Her image flickers.

The argee screen re-links. I blink a moment at the light. I see a daylight scene under bright sun. In the background is something that looks vaguely like the Taj Mahal. A man in a white linen suit looks out of the screen at me. He inspects me and stares at the colors of my jacket. Slowly he nods his head as though comprehending something. He says, *"Woh kata hai?"*

I smile, spread my hands helplessly, and walk on.

Woh kata hai. I believe that's an Indian kite fighter's challenge.

* * *

Dreaming.

It's called a *pench* and I love it more than either soccer or skiing. Each of us stands in a circle about three yards in diameter; the circles are approximately twenty feet apart. The officials have limed the circles on the grass as they would stripe the yardlines for a football game. The breeze is light this morning, but it may kick up. I have brought several different sizes of fighting kites. When I look around at my competition, I generally have to tilt my head back. I am eleven years old.

My gear litters the close-cropped grass around my feet: kites, extra lines, a spare spool. My little brother, eight, sits boredly reading a science fiction paperback just inside my circle. If I need it, he'll help with the launching.

I love Saturday mornings in general, but this particular one is the Michael Collins Annual Kite Fly. It's the second Saturday in September and it delights everyone except the high school football coach who wanted to use this field for a practice scrimmage. Luckily the principal has an auto-graphed picture of the Apollo 11 crew and is an old kite fighter himself, so that was that.

The kite fighting contest isn't the only event today, but it's the only one that interests me. The *pench* should start in a few minutes, at nine, and will continue until noon. Since I've got some sort of reputation, I'm one of the flyers who gets to start. Anyone who wants can take a turn standing in the opponent circle. If he loses, someone else takes his place. And if I lose, I'm out. Then I get to stand in line, waiting to challenge the current champions. I don't plan to spend a lot of time waiting in line.

This is an average Indian summer morning. It's cool now, but I'm guessing it's going to get very hot by midday. The nearest referee—Mr. Schindler, the junior high shop teacher—tells us through his bullhorn that each contestant should be ready. My first opponent steps into the next circle. I don't know his last name, but his first name is Ken and he's really sure of himself. I tell him I wish him luck. Ken snickers. He's in at least eight grade.

"You want help launching?" says my little brother.

"I can do the first one myself." I adjust the bridle on a middle-sized kite. The breeze is gentle but steady.

"Okay." His attention returns to his Robert Heinlein novel.

Ken's kite looks fourteen inches by a foot—too small. He's over-estimating the wind velocity. Too bad.

"Launch 'em," says the referee.

I lightly throw my gold-and-black fighter into the air and pump the cotton string with my right hand: pull in, let out, pull in, let out, until the diamond-shaped kite gains lift in the breeze and begins to climb. I sneak a glance at Ken. His fighter autumnleafs into the ground. I catch his eye and smile. He glares before picking up his kite to launch again.

My kite is solidly airborne. I continue the rhythm of launch; now the pumping motions are longer, smoother, slower. With one handle of the spool anchored at my feet, I stand at an angle to the nine-pound control line. String sings between thumb and forefinger of my left hand at shoulder level. I brake with right hand at right hip. My fighting kite soars. My mind goes with it and, for a moment, I look down at the field and see myself distantly below. I recognize me because of the colors of my jacket.

Ken has finally launched his kite, and is trying to gain altitude with brute force rather than subtlety. I pay out another hundred feet of line and feel the knot that signals I'm at the pre-agreed altitude. I practice wind-current turns with my kite and look bored. I know Ken's looking at me, but I studiously ignore him.

"Okay," says the referee. "You both got the altitude? Go to it."

The strategy is fairly simple. Each of us has a flying line of five hundred feet. Then there's one hundred feet of cutting line between that and the kite. The cutting line is *manjha*, ordinary four-stranded string coated with a mixture of egg, starch, and powdered glass. I mixed mine myself. The rules allow us to double-coat the line so that when it's dry, it can slice an opponent's line either from above or below. The winner of the competition is the flyer who has cut loose the greatest number of opponents' kites.

Ken opens the battle ferociously and heavy-handedly, diving his fighter at cross-angles to my string. I dive mine to compensate and am slightly faster. Ken cancels the tactic. That's a mistake too. I see his kite lurch sluggishly for just a moment. I pay out line and let my string rise into his. My index finger detects the slight vibration as the lines touch. I pull in and my fighter rises, tugging the cutting line against Ken's. His kite, severed, spins down with the wind while he reels in loose string. He does not look happy as my next competitor steps up to replace him.

"Good flight," says my little brother, and I'm not sure whether he's being sarcastic to Ken or to me.

My new opponent is a girl in the seventh grade who has just taken up fighting. She has promise, but very little experience. Her kite doesn't fly long after reaching fighting altitude.

It keeps going like that. In the first hour, I destroy five opponents. Next hour, six more. I let the competition keep their defeated kites if they can find them. Where would I store them all in my room?

Each hour we're allowed fifteen minutes out of competition. I use my time to change lines on my kite. Every time I cut someone else's line, my string loses some of its abrasive. I also adjust the bridle angle because the breeze continues to pick up.

The third and final hour gives me some better competition, but no one all that challenging. Not until Lark steps into the circle. He's even smaller than I am, but he's really tough. He's my age. We've grown up in the same small town and gone to school together from the first grade. We both started flying kites about the same time. Lark is the only one whose fighting ability I respect.

He nods to me and smiles, but says nothing as he launches his fighter. Even my little brother is interested in this contest so he puts his paperback down for the while. "Mairin hasn't lost yet," he says to Lark.

"I'd hate to spoil her morning," Lark says, "but I'm feeling pretty good."

His kite soars on the late morning heat. Lark's fighter is brown with bright yellow bird-wings inset. "Okay," says Mr. Schindler, the referee. "This is the last one. It's almost noon."

At first Lark fights conservatively, not actively counter-ing my spectacular strategies. The trouble is that my kite is all color. I dive on him like a falcon, swoop up from beneath, twirl my fighter across his like the blade of a buzz saw. Nothing happens. I know that much of the abrasive has been scraped from my cutting line by the seven com-petitions of the past hour. But I'm sure that at least a few feet of cutting edge remain on the line. It's a matter of finding it.

Lark realizes my problem and bides his time.

"Hey," says Mr. Schindler. "I want to go to lunch."

Lark makes his move. His brown and yellow fighter crosses the angle of my own string, then drops. My index finger feels the slight vibration as his line touches mine. Lark starts rolling his kite sideways. I compensate by letting out more string and somehow neither line cuts. What does happen, though, each of us discovers simultaneously through fingertips. Our lines have become entangled. Lark's expression is grim.

"Don't worry," I call. I pay out more string as I simul-taneously give the line a series of small tugs. Instead of rotating my kite so as to unwind our lines, I rotate to wrap them tighter. Then I pull.

I cut Lark's string; and capture his kite because the upper line is still entwined with mine; all at the same time.

"Mairin!" He sounds furious. My eyes are on the two fighters.

"What?"

His voice moderates as I begin to reel in the kites. "It was a good contest."

I'll keep his kite in my room. For now, I lower my gaze to him and say, "Yes, it was very good." Unaccountably I want to run across to his circle and hug him. I would like to kiss him.

Hug Lark? Kiss him? I sit upright suddenly, supported on my elbows, and stare confusedly at the curtained light. My room in the Ionic Hotel takes on a dawn reality. I glance to the side. Beside me, a humped form snores beneath the comforter. It's not Lark; I know that.

Lark? I didn't grow up with him; we come from opposite sides of the continent. We did not match our kites in childhood. My disorientation causes me to touch my face gently with my fingers to see if I am still who I think I am.

I try to recapture something of the dream. There is an elusive truth I'm missing.

* * *

Skyfighters.

We spend our lives riding the thermals, those great columns of heated air that lend lift to our machines and spirits. The thermals rise because they are warmer than the surrounding air. We look for the clues and seek them out, using them as elevators to the sky.

The best thermals generate in this valley from mid to late afternoon. Since there are two competitors remaining in the Dragon Festival contests, that time has been reserved for them. The sun has begun its descent into the open western end of the valley and the colors are, as always, spectacular. Crimson tongues lick through the cumulus.

Lark is one competitor; I am the other. All but we have seen our towed dragon kites spin down the long drop into mountainside, forest, or town, where the children vie to find the many-colored dragons and rip them to shreds.

Our duel will climax the festival.

Negwenya and *Cheshire* are waiting to ferry us both to a minimal fighting altitude. Then we will ride the thermals. Today Haley walks with me across the staging meadow. Her hand is in mine.

"You do talk in your sleep, you know," Haley says. "Do you know that?" Without an answer, she continues, "Some of the time the words are clear. Sometimes you simply make sounds and your body moves. You're a restless sleeper. I sleep like a lizard on a hot rock." She laughs. "Did you notice?"

I nod.

Her expression turns serious. "I know last night was important to you—at least it was before last night." Her smile is indecipherable. "Now isn't the time to ask you things, I suppose." She hesitates, and her grip tightens in mine. "People don't work well as goals for you. That's my game." Now I see sadness in her face. "You love the sky more."

We have reached *Negwenya.* Robert Simms waits with his assistants by my Dragon V. Haley enfolds me in her arms and kisses me a long time on the lips. "Fly well," she whispers, then turns and walks across the field toward *Cheshire.*

I realize I'm crying, and I'm not sure yet why.

"Time to link up," says Robert, and his harsh, rope-scarred voice sounds to me softer than usual. I fasten myself into the harness of the Dragon V. I check to make sure the bridle of my fighting kite is securely fastened to the winch-post projecting downward from the Five's keel tube, just behind the point to which my legs extend. The fighting kite is a long, serpentine dragon of mylar, painted in my colors. It has the oval face and trailing, snake-like body characteristic of dragon kites. The only differences are the additional lifting surfaces and stabilizing fins.

The flight is ready to begin. I look across to *Cheshire.* Lark gives me a thumbs-up sign and Haley waves. At *Negwenya,* Robert offers me a brilliant smile and his ritual. "Break a leg, lady." And we launch.

* * *

At twelve thousand feet, *Negwenya* floats almost directly above the immense tailings pond of the moribund Pandora Mine. The bright white tailings heap looks like some malignant thing beached between creek and trees. I think of kids singing their technological jingles when the wind rises and sifts white dust from the tailings down across the town: "Hexa, hexa, hexa-valent chromium!"

I notice that the aspen on the steep sides of the valley are starting to turn prematurely. Great slashes of golden yellow have suddenly appeared within twenty-four hours. No aspen is an island. The root systems of groves are interconnected. When the chlorophyll breaks down in one tree's leaves in the autumn, so goes its extended family.

I had seen broken cumulus above the valley when I linked up to *Negwenya*. Scattered puffy formations are the giveaway signs of thermals, since condensation forms atop the pillars of warm air. The problem is that clouds move with the wind and usually only indicate where the thermals *were*. Extrapolation and a few good guesses should gain my ride up.

At twelve-five. I release the pressure catches and the Five drops away from *Negwenya*. I crane my neck and see that Lark has also dropped. In terms of radiated heat, both of us are more likely to find thermals over the tailings pond or the rooftops of town than above the darker fields or forest. Lark seems to be making for the pond. I stretch my body, feel the muscles loosen, and wheel my Dragon toward the center of town.

The scarlet sunset momentarily dazzles my eyes. I guessed correctly. I feel the left wing rise slightly indicating I am skirting a thermal. I bring the nose down and turn into it; then feel the mild confirming bump that I am all the way in. Now what I have to do is stay inside the current in a gentle ascending spiral until I've reached the prearranged

Lark and I stalked each other like soaring birds.

altitude. In this case, that is fifteen thousand feet. Neither Lark nor I want to try for altitude records today, though kite pilots here have gone above eighteen thousand without oxygen.

Up, up, and the readout on my visor lists off the numbers. As I rise in the thermal column, I touch the button on my control bar that unreels the line tethering my fighter. The black and gold dragon shape drops below and behind my Five. The lift ratio of the kite with its fins is excellent, so it takes only a few moments before it is gliding behind the Dragon. I pay out the entire hundred feet of line. Dragon follows Dragon like an offspring trailing the parent.

I am allowed fifty feet, half the tether, to be cutting line. But where the abrasive lengths are placed, and indeed, *what* lengths are made abrasive, are up to me. Equipment officials carefully checked before launch to ensure that no more than fifty percent of the dragon's two-line is a cutting surface. Like shagreen, the surface cuts only in one direction.

As I swing back across the town, I see that Lark is ascending above the tailings pond. I see his Dragon followed by the brown and yellow fledgling that is his fighter.

At fifteen thousand feet, the air is thin and painfully crisp. The sunlight feels like it's striking my eyes with sharp edges until I polarize my visor. Now that it's time to leave the thermal, I exit on the upwind side to minimize altitude loss in the cooler surrounding air.

Lark and I stalk each other like soaring birds. These Dragons are not the Indian fighting kites of childhood. There are no sudden moves—or rarely. Maneuvers tend to be graceful and conservative, to minimize loss of altitude.

We sweep by each other in a wide pass and I estimate I'm about one hundred feet higher than Lark. From one point of view, we might seem to be tracing arabesques across the sky. From a more realistic referent, we circle each other like hungry, cautious predators.

Lark loops back in a figure-eight and sails along still below, but parallel to me. I assume he is offering bait and try to guess how many moves ahead he's thinking. My craft and I are slightly heavier than he and his; my sink rate is higher and so I'm gradually descending to his altitude. I'm in a position to wing over and pounce, but that's the expectable thing. Lark doesn't expect me to do the expected; so I do it.

I hit the warperons hard; the ends of my wings deform and peel me into a steep, descending bank. I'm losing vertical advantage fast, but my Dragon is cutting down hard behind Lark's tail. It should have been an easy victory except that Lark reacts as though anticipating me—and I have the bemused thought that he probably was. The brown and yellow Dragon matches me move for move. If he's not duplicating the exact angle of bank and degree of dive, I can't tell the difference.

Damn it! Frustration moderates my caution as I slam the Dragon into a reverse-angle bank. Stablizied fabric crackles like firecrackers; the aluminum skeleton groans.

Lark predicted that one too. I know the long lenses on the ground are taking all this in. I hope the viewers are enjoying it.

The hell with this. I tighten my downward spiral, knowing that sooner or later I'll suck him out of the tactic. Either that or we'll hit the ground together.

Anyone else would have pulled out of this falling moth spiral in some sort of sane maneuver that should have allowed me to use the slim remaining margin of altitude and cross their fighter's tether with my cutting line. At times I must remind myself that Lark is no saner than I. One

moment I'm aware that I'm still sinking closer to Lark and
in a relatively short time am going to be right on top of him.
The next moment Lark reverses the pitch of his spiral in an
aching, crushing maneuver that neither rips off his wings
nor puts him into a stall. I see brown fabric rush past my
right eye, so close that I recoil slightly. *Jesus!* One track of
my mind wonders how close his cutting line came to
severing my wing—or my head.

I don't know what he's planning, but I won't equal his
suicide maneuver. As I level off less precipitously, I see
Lark to my right, apparently fleeing. I look beyond his
Dragon and know this is not an abdication of the field. Lark
is making for what appears to be a great funnel of birds
soaring upward. They're in a thermal.

Rather than seek out my own thermal, I pursue Lark,
hoping to catch him before he reaches the elevator. The
epinephrine surge from Lark's spectacular maneuver
starts to abate, leaving tingling in my chest and hands. I will
the Dragon to fly faster; other than that I can do nothing
but let the craft sail serenely along. I enjoy the silence. I
remember the network coverage of a previous Dragon
tourney in which, as a novelty, audio technicians had
dubbed in the wasp-buzz sounds of old, piston-engined
fighter planes. It was amusing at first, but ultimately offen-
sive.

I am close to Lark, but not close enough as he enters the
thermal and begins his ascent. I glance at my altimeter
readout: ten-seven. That means we were about a
thousand feet above the town when Lark pulled out of the
spiral. I trust all the groundlings were suitably thrilled. At a
thousand feet, people truly *do* look like ants.

The gentle bump of entering the warmer air rocks the
Dragon's nose and I start to follow Lark vertically. As I go
into the ascending bank, I sneak a look behind and see that

my black and gold fighter is still trailing. Good. It hasn't occurred to me in these past minutes to check. It's an article of faith that I won't lose the dragon kite through mechanical accident or chance.

Again because he's lighter, Lark rises faster in the thermal than I. I resign myself fatalistically to the ride up and start to think like a tourist. I never, *never* think like a tourist. But now I look at the aspen, or I stare down at the checkerboard town, or I think about the act of flight rather than feeling it. Or something.

Something!

I look up and stare and react—try to do all those things at once. Lark hasn't done as I anticipated. He has not waited until achieving the fighting altitude. No need—no rule that says he must. Instead he swoops upon me like a hawk at prey.

His Dragon grows in my vision. I watch. I know I must choose a maneuver, but something else bids me wait. By now I should be reacting unconsciously. If my conscious is at work, it's now too late. There are several possible defensive maneuvers. So far today, Lark has correctly anticipated my every movement.

—large, so large. Brown and—

I must choose, I must— I do nothing.

That is my choice.

Lark does not anticipate it. Our vectors merge. His Dragon slams into mine with a force I could probably calculate, except—except I cannot think. I don't know if I'm hurt or if I'm in shock. I feel nothing. I simply know a buffeting like a great wind has seized us. I realize we are flying a ragged craft composited of bits and pieces of our two Dragons: snapped, flailing wires, twisted tubing, rent fabric. Lark hangs in his harness only a few feet from me, but he doesn't look up.

My vision skips like the frames in a badly spliced film. I see the golden aspen and the town spread out in the valley below us. I see Lark start to raise his head. Blood covers one side of his face. Droplets fly backward from his head like a fan.

I see the truth in that scarlet spray.

It is a long moment suspended in time.

Then it falls.

We fall—as bits of shattered Dragon spin away from us like colored confetti. I try to reach out toward Lark, but I can move only one arm. He stares back at me and I think he's alive. The sky, I try to tell him. At least we're in the sky. There could have been so many other ways. But the sky— those who fly there are more important than any others.

Wind sucks the breath from my lungs. Lark, I try to say. Friend. I was wrong. I think Haley knows. Lovers. I should have—

I see green fields below.

Lark, it should have been us. We know the sky—

And the ground rises up like a fist.

The light disappeared and Clyde shifted into high gear.

THE DRAGONS' CLUBS

STEPHEN KIMMEL

ILLUSTRATIONS BY
TOM MILLER

I was the pilot on the 82 Epsilon Eridani 2 expedition. My duties involved piloting the landing craft safely to the planet's surface, take off and coking with the ship and general ferrying work. My damned hibernation pod woke me a full month earlier than was necessary. A whole month! I've never been so bored. When we landed, it wasn't much better. There I was stuck on Eridani 2 . . . I'm sorry. You know it as Tralmaf. There I was with nothing to do. No one to play cards with but Jones and his idea of a card game was Old Maid. Nothing. That's boredom.

"Why don't you study—what do you call that lizard that's always following you?" the commander asked me.

"Clyde. And I think of him as a dragon."

"Right. Why don't you study Clyde? Write up a report," the commander said.

"Well . . ." It could have been worse.

"Good," the commander said. He turned and walked back to the cluster of inflated buildings and tents that surrounded the base of the ship.

I walked up the incline to my favorite spot . . . a sandy patch at the top of the hill. It had a spectacular view.

Endless sand to the east and west. The ship to the north. To the south was a line of rocky cliffs. It was quiet and peaceful. It was the only place where I could play cards without being in someone's way. I heard the nearly silent scraping behind me. Tiny daggers touched my shoulder.

"Hi, Clyde," I said.

The dragon released my shoulder. It waved its tail as it danced around me on its rear legs. The dragon, standing upright, looked me right in the eye. Its head was easily a third of its body.

"Hi, hi," the dragon said. I laughed at the sight of Clyde panting with its tongue hanging over a row of razor sharp teeth. I used to have a dog that looked like Clyde. Except he wasn't covered with brown scales. Also, he didn't dance around on two feet and talk to me.

"Hi, hi."

I shuffled the cards. The dragon stared at me, tilting its head.

"Want to play cards, Clyde?"

"Hi, hi."

The dragon reached out a claw for the cards. I flipped one over. Clyde pulled back, his curiosity apparently satisfied. The dragon tilted its head to the other side. Its foot long tongue shot out between the scaled sides of its mouth, flicked at me and then withdrew. I've seen them do that a hundred times—at least—and it still makes me uncomfortable.

"Solitare," I said, more to the cards than to Clyde. "You've seen me play it a million times . . . at least . . . Not a bad game. But its better to play with someone else."

"Play with Clyde," the dragon said. Just like that. No one had ever heard them say anything but "Hi, hi." There was no doubt in my mind that someone was playing a joke on me. I looked but no one was there.

"Play with Clyde."

"Did you say that, Clyde?" I watched its mouth closely. I wanted to be absolutely certain.

"Play with Clyde."

It was the dragon!

"Ho, ho. A new word. Three of them. That will give the commander a thrill," I said. I cursed myself for not bringing a notebook. Well, no loss. I can remember three words. A complete sentence. It reminded me of a fellow who had a talking dog and would get people to bet on whether the dog could answer a question.

"Play with Clyde."

"What do you want to play? Poker?"

"Poker. Poker. Play poker with Clyde."

"Poker isn't any good with just two," I said. The conversation was getting out of hand. I would have bet even money that if anyone heard me it would land me in some home. I felt like an idiot talking to Clyde as though he could talk back.

Clyde screeched like a strangled cat. Clyde did what could only be called a smile with enough teeth to chop off a leg in a heartbeat. I shuddered when a second dragon popped over the rise and sat next to Clyde. Then a third. Then another. And another. Before I could catch my breath, I was sitting in circle with seven dragons. The dragons chattered noisily as I mumbled a quick explanation of the game.

"You aren't suppose to talk while you play," I said. The dragons were silent. The only sound was that of the cards hitting the sand. That was the first time it actually occurred to me that they might understand what I was saying. I know that sounds funny to you now. You have to remember that you've always talked to dragons. We assumed they were overgrown, scaly parrots. But if they could understand what I said, then perhaps they could play cards and maybe . . . I pushed the thought from my head. No one relishes a long visit to the psychiatrist.

"I'll bet."

I paused. Now I've gambled on each of the forty-seven planets. Gambling is life itself. It takes you out of the ordinary and plunges you into a world where only wits, skill and your ability to concentrate will save you from disaster. I've wagered with asteroid miners and I've played for friendlier stakes with ladies from Marsport. But what do you bet when you're playing with a dragon? I looked up at all those teeth. Sharp ripping teeth and claws imply a carnivore. I tried to swallow but my throat had suddenly turned dry.

"Uh, you guys like ham sandwiches, don't you?"

Seven long dragon tongues licked seven dragon faces. I knew these fellows weren't the sort you wanted to meet alone on unfriendly terms.

"All right, then. I'll bet a ham sandwich."

"I'll bet Tralglor," the dragon next to me said. I looked at him closely. It showed no emotion. Hell, I wasn't even sure if they had emotions. It had a natural poker face.

"What's a Tralglor?" I said.

"Tralglor is all the territory from here to the cliffs," Clyde said. "Will you accept that as being equal to a ham sandwich?"

"Sure, sure," I said. You're a gambler. You understand the concentration that's required. I was relieved that they weren't playing for my right leg. Tralglor is almost a thousand square kilometers. Then I realized what was happening.

"Wait a minute!"

The dragons began laughing raucously.

"Don't worry, Bert," Clyde said. "They're laughing at you. A ham sandwich is worth much more than Tralglor.

Nothing is better than Tralglor and a ham sandwich is better than nothing. Still, the wager was accepted.''

"That's not it. Ten minutes ago, you never said anything but 'Hi, hi.' Now you're using complex sentences and bad jokes."

A creeping fear began to take over as I realized that there was much more to these dragons than we had believed. I croaked out one more word.

"How?"

"We're quick learners.''

As though that explained anything. Before I could open my mouth, the dragons started the game again. Each one wagered a major piece of real estate. I was too shocked to protest. My concentration was shattered. The magic of the game was gone. I was too scared to run. I just gulped.

None of the dragons wanted any more cards.

"All right then, what do you have?"

The dragon next to me laid down a club flush. I smiled. The thrill of winning is always there. My full house had a club flush beaten. Clyde screeched and squalled. Simultaneously, the six dragons each laid down a club flush. I knew something was wrong as I laid down my full house. Something . . .

"You win. You win," Clyde said. The dragons jumped and pranced in a circle apparently gleeful at having lost. "We'll play more tomorrow. Bye. Bye. Bye."

"You just lost half the planet's surface. You played thirty-five clubs! There are only thirteen! Hey. Come back!"

And each dragon disappeared over the rise. All I could do was gather my shredded cards and wonder how come there were thirty five clubs.

I knew they wouldn't believe me back at camp. Still, I had to try. There was more to this than met the eye.

"The dragons were talking to you? You mean more than just 'Hi'?" the commander said. He stared at me. And then up at the doctor as though waiting for my certification and then back at me.

"Yes, sir. And telling bad jokes."

"Telling bad jokes. And playing cards. With you?"

"Poker, sir," I said. I tried very hard to look sane and I wondered if I looked as bad as I sounded. What could I do? I had to tell them the truth. The commander smiled that horrible benevolent smile.

"Poker."

"Yes, sir. I think they're intelligent."

"Because they played poker with you?"

When the commander said it that way, it did sound awfully dumb. I looked to the doctor for help. He was busy stifling his laughter.

"Maybe gambling is their chief form of interaction," I said. My stomach told me I was better off being quiet.

"And you won half of Tralmaf. Right, Bert," the commander said. "Confine yourself to quarters. Relax. Take it easy. This whole expedition is meaningless if you can't land us safely. I won't lose my pilot to sunstroke. Just get a good rest."

I walked back to my tent. There was something I was missing and it bothered me. I slumped in my bunk and began to study the remains of my cards. I tried to piece them back together a dozen times. There was no escaping the fact that there were thirty-five clubs. But how? Why? How could there possibly be that many clubs? I fell asleep that night and dreamed about dragons operating casinos. There were hundreds of tables each with a card game. The walls were lined with stuffed heads of strange creatures. One of them was mine.

I woke in a sweat. I jumped from my bunk when I saw Clyde staring at me.

"How did you get in here?"

"No time for that, chief. Time to play poker," Clyde said. "Come. Come."

"But . . ."

Clyde pulled my arm and grinned at me. With those teeth and that grip on my arm, there was no refusing. None of Tralmaf's four moons were up when we stepped onto the sand. The darkness wrapped itself around me like a scratchy blanket. Clyde insisted on running across the sand. The scraping of his claws stopped abruptly as a light danced across my face. I stopped breathing.

"That you, Bert?" The voice was familiar and my heart started beating again. It was definitely human and that was comfort enough. The light walked closer and swung from me to Clyde. The dragon seemed nearly black blending into the darkness. Clyde hissed softly like a demon waiting to spring.

"What are you doing out here at this hour, Bert?"

"I was . . . couldn't sleep." I raised my arm to shield my eyes.

"Yeah. I know what you mean. This place gives me the creeps too," the sentry said. "I can't shake the feeling that I'm being watched. You know what I mean? Like playing cards with you. Like you've got eyes on you all the time."

Jones!

"Yeah."

The sharp stabs on my wrist grew much worse. The cool air chilled my sweat.

"What are you doing with Clyde? Got a game going?" He laughed softly.

"Yeah. Clyde! Be seeing you, Jones."

The light disappeared and Clyde shifted into high gear. I had to strain to keep up with the meter tall dragon. Clyde led me through a sea of unseen eyes. We didn't stop until we reached a cave in the cliffs. I refused to go further. The darkness of the cave was much deeper than the black of the night. I looked up a hundred meters of unbroken granite silhouetted by stars. There was something irresistible about the bottomless blackness of the cave. I couldn't take my eyes away from the leering maw. I knew that it was the mouth of hell.

"Home sweet home."

"Underground?"

"Right. Right. Come. Come."

"How—how many of you?" The words came with difficulty.

"Whole cities. Zillions. Can we cut the gab?"

"Clyde, I don't think this is a very good idea," I said. I tried to turn back but the claws refused to release their grip.

"Don't be a dummy."

Clyde dragged me into the cave. Worries about running into something drove all other thoughts from my mind. I was completely blind. My pupils kept trying to open farther, and couldn't. The only things I could hear were my breath and the scratching of Clyde's claws. We twisted and turned constantly going deeper. I held on for sweet life. Then there were new sounds. A high pitched whistle that grew from a disquieting whisper to a menacing roar. Suddenly the passageway took another turn and opened wide. The dim light was blinding. I had never seen anything like it anywhere in the galaxy. Diamond buildings with yellow trim towered hundreds of meters. Dragons of all sizes and shapes were everywhere. It was an underground crystalline city. The longer I stared, the more complex the city seemed to become. A huge bird caught my attention. It had a huge cranium. I expected it to move. It didn't.

"What's that?" I asked pointing at the bird.

"A loser and a dummy. Don't worry. It's been stuffed."

"I don't understand how you can do all this. Architecture. Taxidermy. You don't even have an opposed thumb."

"Kidneys, Boss," Clyde said, tapping his head with a claw. "Kidneys."

I started to protest, but Clyde was pulling on my arm. Marsport is nice. New Boston is magnificent. But they don't even come close to the splendor of the draconian city. I didn't even notice when Clyde dragged into a building. There were hundreds of tables and thousands of dragons. Most of them were playing cards. It was unbelievable.

The room became silent and the dragons turned to stare at me with their lidless eyes. My heart was roaring as I watched the millions of razor teeth smiling at me.

"You're a big celebrity, Bert," Clyde said. I glanced at him. "Poker is now the number one game on Tralmaf . . . Next to eating, of course."

"Of course. Eating what?"

"Dummies. Have a seat," Clyde said. I felt myself shoved to the nearest chair. Seven dragons quickly sat around the table. I could feel the breath of hundreds of dragons on my neck. I turned and saw one dragon who seemed to be concentrating on my arm. I looked away quickly. "Would you like a drink?"

"Well . . ."

The drink was in front of me before I could close my mouth. I smelled the silver liquid in the crystal glass. It had a sickly smell like too much perfume. I set it down without tasting it. The dragons began to chatter. Along the crystalline walls were heads of animals with multifaceted eyes. There were heads with horns and heads that were grotesque mockeries of men. Clyde dealt cards that clanged as they hit the table. The cards were cool and smooth. I was only too glad to look away from the heads."

"Metal cards?"

"Very practical when you have claws. Hmmm . . . I need a manicure. Do you open?" Clyde said. I'm certain that Clyde's claws got shorter as I watched. I concentrated on my cards. Only the game counted, I told myself. It was difficult to concentrate. It was as though they had designed this place just to make it hard to concentrate.

"Clyde. Those heads and the bird. Those are dummies. Meaning unintelligent?"

"Right," Clyde said. My arm jerked reflexively at the wet touch of the large dragon's tongue. Clyde screeched at the dragon behind me and it backed away. I hate kibitzers and I hate dragon kibitzers most of all.

"How do you tell if they're dummies?"

"They don't play."

Only the game counted, I told myself.

"I'll open with a ham sandwich."

"Or they play badly."

"Two ham sandwiches?"

"Listen, Bert. I know you and your friends aren't just more dummies from above but the fellow behind you doesn't. Wager a piece of territory unless you want there to be a big picnic tonight," Clyde said. I turned and looked at the dragon behind me. It looked as though it was drawing a menu.

"Bet three ham sandwiches," the large dragon hissed. I shuddered.

"I'll open with Tralglor." I choked out the words. The dragons shrieked and clattered. My hands were shaking. I stared at the cards. Only the game counted, I told myself. My cards were all clubs. That wouldn't look too bad if I lost. Just as long as it was good enough to keep me and the expedition from becoming breakfast, I didn't care.

The betting went around the table several times. One dragon wagered Tral, the star. Others wagered things that were beyond my comprehension. There was a pattern to

"Bet three ham sandwiches," the large dragon hissed.

the betting. Maybe the game didn't count. Maybe all that mattered was the betting. I wagered huge when they wagered huge. When the dragons wagered small, I wagered small. When they didn't take any more cards, I decided to stand too. Sweat began to run down my face as I laid down a jack high straight club flush. My heart stopped as the seven dragons laid down seven queen high straight club flushes.

"You lose. You lose. You lose," Clyde said as he jumped on the table. The noise inside the club was deafening as all the dragons began to screech and squall. The large dragon grabbed my arm and licked.

"Our Father which art in heaven, hallowed be thy name," I said. Clyde yanked my arm away from the larger dragon and pulled me through the doorway. Screaming dragons joined the dragons behind us. I felt myself hoisted onto rough shoulders. The dragons carried me through alleys and corridors. Dragons dropped foul smelling garbage on me from higher levels. The draconian mob grew until I couldn't hear anything except the screams and screeches. Through streets, around a corner and into the tunnel. My hands were tight knots holding onto the scales of the dragons carrying me. Suddenly we were outside. They set me on the ground and were silent. I knew it was the end. They were going to eat me. Make a regular picnic of it.

"No we aren't," Clyde said.

"But I thought . . ."

"I know what you thought. Dummies we eat. Not losers. Unless the losers are also dummies."

"Oh," I said. My mouth hung slightly open. My mind refused to work.

"You played very well and that's all that counts. Do you think we should have dancing girls in the clubs?"

"Dancing girls?" The only thing I could think was a girl named Lola who had shown me quite a night as part of my winnings. I smiled.

"That's what I thought," Clyde said. His scaly paw grabbed my hand and began to shake it vigorously. "First contact with you has been a real pleasure. Much more rewarding than some of those dummies. We'll let you know what we decide to do with you folks. You're the first group that wasn't just a free meal from heaven. But you can tell your friend that we've decided to call off the barbeque. Once your gambling convinced us you were intelligent."

"They're never going to believe this. The commander thinks I'm crazy as it is," I said. "Maybe he's right."

"An easily corrected problem. Just so you don't go away empty handed. Take a deck of cards," Clyde said. The dragon reached behind his back and produced one. "That should convince your commander."

"Thanks. You know, after you sliced up my cards, I—I've got it! You do that with your mind."

"Of course. Gold is all right, isn't it?"

I looked at the cards. "These cards are gold!"

"That's what we like about you, Bert. You catch on quick."

"But these cards are gold!"

"You want us to reconsider the barbeque?"

"No!"

"You'd rather have platinum?"

"Maybe later."

"Then take, enjoy. Be sure to tell all your friends." Clyde said. Without a sound the horde of dragons disappeared into the cave. I found myself alone in the desert like a piece of driftwood washed ashore. I listened to the lonely wind echo my relief and my doubts. I glanced at the cards. They didn't disappear.

"And that's why they treat you like a king around here?" she said. I've always loved the Martian accent and hers was especially nice. I raised my deck of cards and the waiter brought us new drinks.

"Yeah. The work's not bad. I like being a technical consultant at the casino. Still, I'm kind of sorry I started all this."

"Bert Miller, I don't think I believe a word you've said," she said. The laughter of a human female is sheer music compared to the draconian shrieking. "That would mean that the dragons cheat!"

"Ask the waiter if you don't believe me."

"I think I will." She turned to our waiter. "Clyde, is there any truth in Mr. Miller's story?"

"Right. Right, Boss. If Bert says it, it must be true. He's no dummy."

©1981 T·O·M

NEGWENYA

JANET GLUCKMAN

ILLUSTRATIONS BY
RICHARD HULL

1.

Tom Sibanda lay sweating in the tall Zeekoevlei grass.
His eyes were closed but he was not asleep. He was
concentrating. Blocking out the day so that he could feel
the dandelion fluff being carried to him by the summer
wind. He had to be able to feel it against his skin or his
game didn't work; it was hard enough to convince himself that they were snowflakes when he'd never seen any.
With his eyes open, it was impossible. Riena was lucky, he
thought. It had snowed once in Johannesburg when she
was two. Not in December, of course. No matter how
many times they played Jingle Bells, December would still
be the middle of summer. Maybe if those dumb announcers played it in June, he thought, it would snow in Cape
Town too. Still, the game helped, when it was very hot.
Like today.

"Come on, Tom. Building this house was your idea and
now you're not helping.

"Coming," Tom said. But he didn't move. It was his
twelfth birthday. He had the right to lie around and do

nothing. Not that he expected Riena to understand. What did ten year old girls know, anyway? It was Alfred who should have understood. Kept her off his back. His half-brother was even dumber than the radio announcers, Tom decided. And cocky too. Strutting around like a bantam just because some Whitey had told him he was a Zulu and could live with their father while Tom had to stay with his mother. How could someone else tell you what you were!

He opened his eyes and lifted his arm. Inspecting it. Turning it around the way his mother examined a piece of meat at the corner store. It's at least as dark as Alfred's, he thought. Not olive at all. Not like Riena's or his mother's. They were Colored for sure.

Closing his eyes again, Tom remembered the first time the man came to the house to tell them they couldn't live together anymore. How could they have been a family one day and not the next? He still didn't understand. In the beginning he'd kept asking his mother to explain. And she'd tried. It hadn't made any sense to him then and it didn't now. Then Riena had come to live with them and his mother had asked him not to talk about it any more.

"Tom. I can't carry this all by myself. It's too heavy."

"I'm coming, Riena," Tom said again. A summer day's for doing nothing, he though resentfully, forgetting that the hideout had been his idea. It was for planning all of the things he was going to do when he was grown up; the books he was going to write. He pictured himself six foot tall, instead of only five and a bit. Maybe he would grow up to be a witchdoctor, he thought. Like Nkolosi. Then if people ordered him around, he could punish them the way Nkolosi did. He would be the one giving orders. And he'd have a secret helper. Like Nkolosi. One that obeyed his every command. Only maybe it wouldn't be a dragon; he'd think of something else.

Tom stood up and grinned. The first thing he'd do was order his helper to turn Alfred into a Whitey. Serve him right. "See if you'd run around boasting about being a purebred then, Alfred Mtshali," he said. He picked a small bug off his leg and squished it between his fingers. "Thomas Mtshali. Thomas Sibanda." He repeated the two names a few times. He was beginning to get used to his new name, the one they'd given him after his father and Alfred had moved away.

Staring out over the vlei, Tom imagined himself being quoted, the way people always repeated Nkolosi's words. "Sibanda says . . ." He liked the sound of it. He'd do good things, too, he thought, the way Nkolosi did sometimes. Cure people. Help them get food. Make them send their children to school . . .

"Tom!"

This time there was no way Tom could ignore Riena. Something was wrong, something much more important than the fact that he wasn't pulling his weight with their project.

"Where are you?"

"Over here. Under the bush."

Under which bush, Tom thought, hearing the hysteria in her voice. Yanking at his shorts, he ran in the direction he hoped was right. He found her by almost tripping over the leg that she was clutching with both hands. She was crying.

"What happened? What's wrong?" He knelt down beside her.

"It was a *boomslang,* Tom. You said they didn't bite but they do. They do."

"Get your hands away so I can see." Tom's voice was patient, the way his mother's was when she was afraid something really bad might have happened. She's probably just scared, he thought hopefully. He'd never heard of a treesnake biting anyone before.

"I can't let go. I can't. It hurts too much."

"Come on, Riena," Tom said, wondering where Alfred had disappeared to. He always managed to disappear when things went wrong.

Slowly, Riena released her hold on her leg. She was right. There it was, swelling like crazy and red and puffy.

"We're going over to the vlei," Tom said. "When we get there, I'm going to use my knife and . . ."

Riena clutched her leg again and started to wail.

"You wanna die, or you going to do what I tell you?" He sounded much surer of himself than he felt. "Where the hell is Alfred?"

"He said . . . he said he was going to get Nkolosi. I told him to call you but he said I would die if Nkolosi didn't come. He said treesnakes only bit Colored people who've been bad and had a spell put on them. He said . . ."

She began to cry again but allowed Tom to help her up. Damn Alfred, Tom thought. Always acting like a big shot. Shooting off his mouth and saying things like that so he didn't have to stick around when the going got rough. Oh well. It didn't really matter. He was used to taking care of Riena. He'd been doing it ever since his mother had found her wandering around the streets and taken her in.

"Come on, Riena," he said, helping her hobble toward the water. "Hey, if you could live through Sharpeville, guns going off and blood and all that stuff, you can live through a little old snake bite."

When they reached the edge of the bracken water, Tom helped Riena sit down. Taking out the old pocket knife his father had given him, he opened it and flashed it through the dirty water. It was only a pretense at hygiene but it was the best he could do. Before either of them had time for second thoughts, he slid the blade into Riena's flesh and put his lips to the geyser that rose instantly from the wound. It wasn't until he could no longer stand Riena's screams that he stopped sucking and spitting. Sucking and spitting.

"Shouldn't we tie something around it? I'm going to bleed to death," Riena said, between sobs.

Tom rinsed his mouth several times to try to get rid of the metallic taste of her blood in his mouth. Then he reluctantly examined his surgery. The blood that was running down her leg was showing no sign of stopping. He looked down at the shirt he was wearing. His birthday shirt. The new one his mother had made for him and given him that morning. Alfred's wearing an old one, he thought, willing his half-brother's return but knowing it wasn't going to happen. Cursing, he took off his shirt, removed one of the sleeves with his blood stained knife, and bound Riena's leg.

"Think it's okay now," he said, flopping down next to her. She had stopped crying but every once in a while she took two or three quick breaths involuntarily, the way everyone did after they'd been crying that hard. She's pretty gutsy, Tom thought, finding it difficult to admit that about a girl—even one who had been orphaned at Sharpeville. He felt a little bad about having reminded her of that and wondered again how she'd ended up a thousand miles away from home. All the way from Johannesburg to Cape Town. A journey like that and she refused to talk about it. If he ever had an adventure like that he'd want to talk about it to anyone who'd listen. His mother had told him that Riena used to live in the *location*. At Sharpeville. Until a policeman shot her mother in the back during the riot. His mother said that she didn't have anyone left to take care of her, except the relative who'd brought her to Observatory and dumped her there. Too much trouble for some people to have a kid hanging around, his mother said.

Suddenly, lying there in the sun, Tom felt a peculiar sensation. It had nothing to do with fear that he hadn't done the right thing, nor was it pride that he had. Whatever it was, it made him forget that he wasn't supposed to like girls and he reached for Riena's hand.

"Don't worry, Riena," he said. "I'll take care of you. I'll always take care of you."

2.

"That sonofabitching Zulu's dropping out of school. Stop him, Nkolosi," Tom Sibanda said. He stared at the back of Alfred Mtshali's charcoal neck until it blended into the trees at the edge of De Waal Drive.

"Aren't you overreacting?" Nkolosi said, tilting his head to catch the last rays of the afternoon sun before the Atlantic devoured it.

Tom tried to analyze the complexities of his hatred for his half brother. It had been ten years since the day Alfred had run out on Riena, the day the treesnake had bitten her. She had almost lost her leg because of the time lapse between the bite and Tom's first aid. Not that he'd been wild about Alfred before that day, Tom admitted to himself, but somehow that had been the seed of what he felt now.

He released a pine cone from his grip and watched it do an adagio against the slope that led to the university entrance. "Alfred's the first Black man they've let into this engineering school," he said, examining the indentations the cone's scales had left on his palm. "He was opening doors for all of us."

"Quit whining, Sibanda. Maybe Mtshali's just tired of playing guinea pig. Or maybe he's bored with going hungry to pay for books. Isn't it his prerogative to give up his potential to fill his belly?"

"Selling out is one thing. Joining the South African police force is another. With help like his . . ."

" . . . Have you ever considered helping yourself? At least he's learned to make bombs. All you ever do is cover pages with useless words that end up in the rubbish. You complain and assume everyone else will do the dirty work."

"So he's learned to make bombs! That's just what the Nationalists expected. You can be sure they'll use it as their rationale for refusing to allow another Black man into this place. And the Liberals will pat themselves on the back and tell each other how hard they tried."

"What exactly is it you want me to do, Sibanda?" Nkolosi asked.

"You're the witchdoctor. You think of something."

Nkolosi smiled. "It's my Negwenya's services you want, isn't it? Neither of us come cheap, you know."

"I can pay your price. And your Mata Hari's."

"Can you? Our price may not be money."

"What then?"

"You'll know when it's demanded of you."

"If you'll order the Negwenya to go to Mtshali I'll pay your price. No matter what it is."

"I can order her into his dreams to seek the source of his fears," Nkolosi said. "He'll know why she's there . . ."

" . . . Will you order her to take him as her lover?"

"I can't dictate the form of his discipline, Sibanda. My Negwenya makes that decision herself. Once she's taken possession of Mtshali, his actions will determine his punishment."

Tom watched the Negwenya take shape.

Nkolosi knelt and drew in the sand and Tom watched the Negwenya take shape, her dragon ears pointed, her tail curled, her wings in repose.

"You know she can be a passionate and consuming mistress. You must hate Mtshali very much," Nkolosi said.

Tom Sibanda tried to recollect the time before he had hated his half-brother. It was so long ago, it was ancient history. Before the hue of his palms and the color of the quick of his nails condemned him to a mulatto no-man's land between White ritual hatred and the Black struggle; before they told him he was a *kaffir* and he found out it meant "man without a soul." Not like Alfred Mtshali, whose parents were both Zulus. *His* palms had no trouble passing the closest scrutiny.

"What's Riena doing these days?" Nkolosi asked, trimming the dirt from the tips of the Negwenya's wings.

"I haven't seen her for a while."

"Don't lie to me Sibanda, not even about something that trivial," the witchdoctor said. He dug his long nail into the sand to complete the Negwenya's eye.

"Since you know I'm lying, you must know that she spends her time down at the docks, sleeping with sailors." Tom found it almost as difficult to think the words as he did to say them.

"White sailors?"

"How the hell would I know."

"I thought she was a history teacher." Nkolosi was enjoying Tom's discomfort.

"She was. Until some bounty hunter reported her for including slavery and civil rights in her American History courses," Tom said. He had last seen Riena in that damn corrugated iron shanty down near the water. A broken down shack. Rented to her by a righteous Afrikaner minister whose Sunday sermons rarely failed to touch on the evils of prostitution.

Nkolosi stood up and cleaned his hands on the sides of his trousers.

"Will you send the Negwenya?" Tom asked. He was staring at the dragon as if he expected it to move.

"Does Mtshali believe?"

Tom nodded.

"Do you?"

Tom nodded again, surprised that Nkolosi needed to ask the question. No one who had grown up the way Tom had would dare entertain doubts about the witchdoctor's power. Or the Negwenya's. Nkolosi had demonstrated his knowledge of the ancient arts, had succeeded too often, for anyone to question them. He commanded no less fear and respect than his father before him. And his father's father.

"Then it is done," Nkolosi said. "I'll gather the Ligewaan, the lizards, for Mtshali's pillow. They will let him know the Negwenya is courting him. I promise you he won't sleep much."

But he will live, Tom thought. At least for now.

"The payment?" he asked, as Nkolosi began to move away.

Nkolosi only laughed and kept on walking.

Tom waited a week before he went to see Alfred. In his cop's uniform, his half-brother looked like any other sell-out.

"You seem tired. Haven't you been sleeping well?" Tom asked. Alfred's puzzled look told him his half-brother had not made the connection between Tom and the lizard carcasses that had forced him out of his bed and onto the floor. "I heard you were lonely," Tom went on. "I thought I'd provide you with some companionship."

Light dawned on Alfred's face.

"Did you think the lizards were an accident? Didn't it occur to you that you'd earned yourself a courtesan?"

"You can't mean that, Tom."

"Oh, I mean it all right."

Alfred was beginning to look frightened. "Make her stay away," he said.

Tom laughed. "You know I don't have control over her," he said. "Take care. I hear she's a most demanding mistress."

"I'll go to Nkolosi."

"You have to find him first. And for that he has to want to be found."

"You know where he is. I'll follow you till you lead me to him."

"You stupid *kaffir*. A few weeks on the force and you think you're Sam Spade." Tom grinned at his choice of detectives. Then he turned to leave. There was nothing more Alfred could say to interest him.

Alfred, not about to submit that easily, followed.

At first Tom enjoyed the sport of leading his half-brother from shebeens to churches, through alleyways, on trains and buses, but after a few days he tired of the game. Deciding Alfred would eventually tire of it, too, he picked up the threads of his normal life. Though he'd tried to lie about it to Nkolosi, part of his routine was a weekly visit with Riena. He saw no reason to cancel because Alfred was dogging his trail; no matter what Riena had become, he looked forward to seeing her.

They met, as ususal, under the town hall clock. Hugging each other affectionately, they dodged Cape Town's morning traffic and went across the street to the parade grounds.

The parking lot had given way to a flea market. "Let me buy you something," Tom said, holding up a piece of cheap costume jewelry. She shook her head and walked on. Stepping over the discarded gift boxes and ribbons that littered the sidewalk, she mingled with the Whites and Coloreds, Malays and Indians, Zulus and Xosas, homogenized by their bargain hunting and rubbing shoulders if they were all equals. That was probably what drew Riena there every week, Tom thought, watching her tug at the hem of her short cotton skirt and swing her hips with practiced carelessness. She was beginning to look like a tart.

"I'm not going with you to see Ma today," she said when he caught up with her.

"Why?"

"I'm tired of lying to her and telling her stories about the kids in my class. Besides, I have a date."

"Anyone I know?"

"No."

Before Tom could question her further, Riena veered off to the left, between two fruit stands and away from the flea market.

"Where are you taking me?"

"There is something I want to buy. But not here," Riena said.

"What?"

"Violets," she said.

It was a long time since Tom had been to the flower market. It was flanked at one end by the general post office and at the other by Adderley Street's constant traffic. Masses of flowers in wooden tubs seemed to grow out of the concrete. Roses. Gladioli. Carnations so perfect that Tom's sense that none of them were real didn't dissipate until Riena had bought her violets and he saw her shiver as their moisture penetrated the paper wrapping and dripped down her arm.

Riena leaned slightly backwards against the wind as they exited the alley. Tom, thinking she was about to fall, darted forward to catch her. The sudden movement allowed him a glimpse of Alfred and he considered saying something to Riena. She had interacted so little with him, however, that it seemed pointless to involve her in their quarrel.

"Are you meeting him down there?" Tom asked, realizing he was being led down the Heerengracht toward the docks.

"Yes, I'm meeting him 'down there,' " Riena said, imitating Tom's contemptuous tone. She said no more until they reached the shanty. It wasn't until she had raised her hand to knock at the door and said: "Come in and meet Jake," that Tom became aware of her degree of apprehension.

"Is he a customer?"

"Jake's my lover, Tom," Riena said. Softly. "I'm going to have his child." She put her hands over her ears as if to block out the sound of his anger.

"You goddamned whore!" Tom shouted with no regard for anything but his own feeling of betrayal. The door was open and his words, bouncing off the shanty's walls, echoed back at him. They were punctuated by a tug, bellowing as it guided a clumsy ward into the shelter of Duncan Dock.

"I love him," Riena said. "He's an American. He's going to send me a passport."

Tom Sibanda turned from the look in her eyes and stood in the doorway, watching a cable car sway up Table Mountain. The edges of a late southeaster whipped his face, and he felt fear for Riena settle like a permanent deposit between his skin and the air. Crossing the classification lines "for the purposes of miscegenation" was illegal. She was risking jail. And for what? Love him, my ass, Tom thought, stepping forward and kicking the door shut behind him. She wants to get out of here, like the rest of us.

She always did. Even .when they were children she'd
sworn to leave South Africa.

The whirring of an electric motor somewhere out of sight
triggered an assault wave of memory. It reminded him of
the incessant hum of his mother's sewing machine and of
Riena, ten year old hands clutched over her ears to deaden
the sound. It was a gesture that had become habitual; she
did it still when faced with something beyond her control.
Like a few minutes ago, standing at the door. She'd done it
then.

Tom tried not to think about Riena in bed with that
White man, his body pressing down on hers. Instead he
remembered Riena the child, lying under the yellow and
orange weave of her Bantu blanket, staring at the vibrating
kerosene lamp that stood next to his mother's Singer and
chanting: "I won't be like her. I won't stay here forever."
Over and over again. Not knowing that she was shouting
beneath the protection of her hands.

That damn house of ours, Tom thought. It was enough
to corrupt anybody. Ma's compulsive cleanliness—
sending her to the bottle of Dettol like an alcoholic. The
pine smell mixing with machine oil. The machine her God,
taking precedence over his needs and Riena's.

Furiously, Tom pushed the memories aside. He was not
ready yet to have his anger diluted. Nor did he wish to
speak to Riena, now or any time in the future. He had
managed to come to terms with her prostitution but this
was a different kind of betrayal. Grinding his teeth, he
stalked up the Heerengracht. It did not occur to him to look
around for Alfred. Had he done so, he might have seen his
half-brother step out of the shadow of a storage shed,
buttoning his uniform jacket as he moved toward the door
of Riena's shanty.

3.

Tom wasted no time getting to a liquor store. He took his purchases home and spent the rest of the day getting progressively drunker. When he woke up the next morning, he opened a new bottle and started all over again. His supply lasted for the better part of two months.

Sobering up at last, Tom found himself with no job. Worse than that, he had nothing left of the novel he'd been working on for a year. He retained a vague memory of having sacrificed it to some goddess of the water, imploring her to regurgitate it as a bound best seller. Which body of water eluded him completely. The hurt caused by Riena's love affair had dulled to a steady ache. Not so his hatred for Alfred; that had, if anything, intensified.

That night Tom went to see his half-brother.

"Did you find Nkolosi?"

"I found Riena instead," Mtshali said.

The look on Alfred's face filled Tom with a nameless terror. "What did you do to her?"

"I arrested her. Fucking White man got away."

"You did what?"

"My patriotic duty."

"Why?"

"Why?" Mtshali laughed. "That's easy. You punished me with the Negwenya. I saw a way to hurt you."

"By punishing Riena? Doesn't your conscience keep you awake at night?"

Mtshali shrugged. "The Negwenya keeps me awake."

"Riena's been your friend since we were children."

"To me she's just a woman. I'm a Zulu, remember." Mtshali grinned. "I didn't grow up with her the way you did." He paused. "How do you think it will feel to have a

White relative? You did know she was pregnant, didn't you?''

Tom's first instinct was to drive his fist through his half-brother's grin. The trouble was, he had never been much of a fighter. Besides, a cut lip would heal.

Once again, Tom went to see Nkolosi.

"I was expecting you," the witchdoctor said, without looking up from his cross-legged position on the ground. This time, the Negwenya was already clearly drawn in the soft earth.

"I want him to die," Tom said, without preliminaries.

"That decision was made some time ago."

"How? When? Order the Negwenya . . ."

" . . . I told you, I can't make demands. She's decided he's to die; the means, too, must be her choice."

Forgetting the respect he owed Nkolosi, Tom cursed roundly. He expected to be reprimanded but Nkolosi's eyes simply hardened.

"Riena's belly was filled with child when Mtshali arrested her," the witchdoctor said.

"You knew that?"

"There is nothing I don't know."

"And the Negwenya?"

Nkolosi nodded.

"Then she must also know how he deserves to die."

"I know what you want, Sibanda. Now I must ask the Negwenya what it is she wants. Come back tonight and I'll tell you if her desires match yours."

"I'll wait here."

"You will do as I tell you," Nkolosi said quietly.

Tom retreated. When he returned, Nkolosi was ready. "The Negwenya says Mtshali dreams of hunger and sweats when he thinks of Riena in labor," he said. "She has determined to make sure Mtshali's belly is never empty again. She will take him as her lover tonight."

"Will she plant her seed in him?"

"In seven months his belly will have swollen like a pregnant cow's. By then the young Negwenya's scales will have hardened inside him and Alfred Mtshali will be ready to breathe fire."

"Will the fire kill him?"

"Would it not kill you?"

"And my payment?"

Nkolosi laughed. "I promise you that will come. Now go and inform Mtshali."

Tom found his half-brother at the local shebeen. Savoring the responses to each carefully chosen word, Tom told him of the Negwenya's decision. "Her son will grow a little more each day, until you will no longer be able to button your jacket. In seven months the scales will have hardened, and he will be ready to breathe fire," he said, repeating Nkolosi's prediction.

Mtshali, his hand unconsciously rubbing his stomach, swayed and leaned against the wall.

"You'll be able to feel the scales, Mtshali. The tail will uncurl, and you'll watch it push out your flesh like . . ."

The Zulu's knees buckled. With a look of contempt, Tom spat on the floor and left.

For three months Tom tried repeatedly to see Riena. He was no less angry at her betrayal but the memories that came to him at night had softened him enough that he wanted to see her. The authorities' refusal to allow him visiting privileges was consistent and did not include an explanation. He made no effort, however, to see Alfred, even when he heard that his half-brother had left the force and moved into their old hideout. He told himself it was intelligent to avoid an unpleasant confrontation but in truth, he was scared. And it wasn't only Alfred's anger he feared; he wanted to avoid contact with the Negwenya

who was surely watching over her son as he became visible
under Alfred's stretching belly.

After half a year had gone by, six months of wondering
when Nkolosi would exact payment and what that payment would be, Tom sought out the witchdoctor.

"You have not been to visit Mtshali. Why?" Nkolosi
began, as if they had not been apart for six months.

"I am afraid of the Negwenya," Tom said, admitting his
fear because he was sure Nkolosi knew of it anyway.
"How is Alfred?"

"How would you be? Your half-brother is big and growing bigger. And he is in great pain."

"What does he do out there at the vlei?"

"Talks to the frogs. Makes bombs. He has made one for
you."

Tom stepped back as if he had been struck. He stumbled over an exposed root and barely saved himself from
an undignified fall. Nkolosi threw back his head and
laughed.

"The bomb is for you to *use*," he said. "I instructed him
to make it."

"Has it anything to do with my payment?"

"It is *my* fee." Nkolosi was no longer laughing. His eyes
were expressionless but the corners of his mouth showed
renewed amusement. "Go to Mtshali and get the bomb.
Seven months from the eve of the day the Negwenya
entered Mtshali's body, you are to blow up the women's
section of Roeland Street Gaol."

"But Riena is there," Tom said.

It was not Nkolosi the witchdoctor who responded; it
was Nkolosi the reactionary. The political activist. Tom had
never seen him play that role before, though he'd heard it
rumored that the witchdoctor was also the leader of Afri-
cans For Independence. As a dedicated believer in the pen

being mightier than the sword, he had stayed away from the AFI.

"I warned you payment would not be easy," Nkolosi said. "Dead women make good publicity."

"And if I refuse?"

Apparently assuming his command to be stronger as magician rather than as soldier, Nkolosi resumed the mantle of witchdoctor. Crouching, he directed his right hand in the design that was becoming all too familiar to Tom. When he reached the tail, he drew it lovingly, his long nail creating intricate patterns with a circular, flowing motion.

"Stop!" Tom said. His eye caught the silhouette of a *Ligewaan,* sunning itself behind a rock. He felt a chill, despite the summer heat.

"I knew I could rely on you," Nkolosi said. He put the finishing touches on the Negwenya's tail, then slowly and gently erased the image.

Tom delayed going to see Alfred until his fear of Nkolosi outweighed his revulsion at the idea of what he had to do. Three weeks after his visit to the witchdoctor, he finally drove around the mountain to Zeekoevlei. To the shack where the three of them—he, Alfred and Riena—had talked of growing up and going to college and getting married. Pretending they could be anything they wanted to be. Like real people. White people.

"Get the hell out of here, Sibanda," Alfred screamed when he saw Tom. He was in bed. A sheet, strung across the window, protected him from the sunlight and kept his face in shadow. Tom couldn't see his half-brother's face, but the voice was that of a very old man.

"Since you don't appear to be leaving," Mtshali said, when he had calmed down, "would you care to see beneath this blanket?"

Tom shook his head, knowing full well Mtshali would take no notice. "Nkolosi sent me for the bomb."

"You'll look at your handiwork before I show you mine," Mtshali said, throwing off the covers.

His belly was enormous. Even in the dim light, Tom could see that the flesh was taut, its black surface patterned by waves and ridges. He watched, fascinated, as a large protrusion moved back and forth, a centimeter at a time, pulling the flesh along with it in a pendulum motion that synchronized with Tom's heartbeat.

"Is that . . ."

" . . . The tail. It is never still." Mtshali sat up with extreme difficulty. "The bomb's in the corner."

He might as well have been talking to himself. Tom was gone. In the garden. Retching as if he were trying to expel some evil being from his own body.

A week later, with only a few hours to go before the job had to be done, Tom went back to collect the bomb. Then unable to rid himself of the image of Riena's body splattered against the walls of her cell, he dialed the number of Roeland Street Gaol and asked to speak to warden Piet Barnard.

"Empty the cells," Tom warned. "The jail's going to be bombed."

"You and who else. You're the tenth caller this week."

"This call's for real," Tom said. Insisting.

"Where would you suggest we put all the prisoners, man? Out on the streets?"

"I don't care where you put them. Just get them out of there."

"What can you hope to achieve by killing your own people? You must know they won't let me empty the cells."

There it is again, that anonymous "they," Tom thought. The world's scapegoat. And his, too. "I've warned you warden. That makes it your choice as much as mine. If you do nothing, you'll be as responsible as I—we—are for their deaths. And they will die, you know."

"There have been too many false alarms. No one will listen to me," Barnard's voice held a note of pleading. "Don't those lives mean anything to you?"

"They're expendable," Tom said coldly. "Just as you and I are."

The harsher he sounded, Tom thought, the more likely Barnard would be to believe him. He was already convinced that the man cared and he wanted to say something more, something that would strike whatever chord it was that would make the warden take the risk of offending "them." He waited for a moment before replacing the receiver. Hoping. Praying to a God he'd thought he'd long since abandoned.

That God had, apparently, abandoned him. He heard a click at the other end of the line. Forgive me, Riena, he thought. For what I am about to do—forgive me.

4.

Dynamite is non-discriminatory.

Mtshali's bomb caught even the rats by surprise and mingled their remains with black flesh and brown limbs and grey blankets.

It also blew a jagged, body-sized hole in the south wall of a corner cell.

Tom knew he had no business staying so close to the prison but he crouched in the shadows, watching the area around the service gates turn into a bizarre discotheque. Sirens wailed. Sentries danced a grotesque Watusi between their posts and gyrating strobes bounced in a crazy kaleidoscope off the thousands of glass fragments embedded in the top surface of the prison wall. When the khaki-clad guard at the gate slicked back his hair and raised himself lightly on his toes, Tom half expected him to use his rifle as a cane and break into a soft-shoe.

"A boiler accident," a voice said close to him.

Tom recognized the warden's voice and froze. The man was standing at the outer edge of a concrete yard that separated the service gates from the burning building.

"Any survivors?" a second voice asked.

"I don't think so."

"Could this happen again?"

"Probably," the warden said. Tom could hear the same hesitation he had heard before in the man's voice. Then something drew his attention away from the conversation, and he watched a figure emerge from the hole he had blown in the wall.

"Come with me," the warden said loudly to his hidden companion. "I'll see if I can get you a list of the dead."

The deliberate way in which he moved out of the path of the survivor told Tom he had surely seen the figure too. He watched it come closer. It was wrapped in a prison blanket and looked more like a moving rock than a human being.

Forgetting the pain she had caused him, Tom willed the figure to be Riena. His mouth filled with the metallic memory of the blood he had sucked from her ten year old leg and he smiled, remembering how she hated being called "stokkies" by all of the boys because of her skinny legs. By the time she was fourteen and her legs stopped resembling sticks, the nickname had stopped bothering her.

The figure was more than halfway across the concrete before Tom dared to look closely at its face. When he recognized its contours, it was all he could do to restrain himself from calling out to Riena. He dug his nails into his palm and concentrated on the pain, forcing himself to remain silent.

"Where the hell d'you think you're going lady?"

Tom couldn't see the questioner but he assumed it to be one of the guards.

"Home," Riena said.

"You work in there?"

By craning his neck, Tom could see the guard's face. He watched Riena relax her hold on the blanket and imagined the man's eyes sliding from the curve of her breast to her bare toes and ankles. Clever, Riena. Very clever, Tom thought, waiting to hear the guard's reaction to her nudity. If there was anything that could get her out of there, it was the promise of her body.

"Where are your clothes, woman?" The man's tone was relatively gentle.

"In there," Riena said. "Lucky I got out with my bloody life."

"If you're hurt I can get the ambulance boys to take a look at you," the man said. "If not . . ." He took a step forward.

"I'm fine. All I need is a hot bath," Riena said.

She let the man fondle her for a moment. Satisfied, he opened the gates for two ambulances and waved her through. She stumbled into the dimly lit parking lot, and Tom caught a side view of her pregnancy. He had hoped she might have lost the baby in prison, but the white thing was still growing inside her; the sight brought on a surge of the old contempt. Then, seeing her collapse against the nearest car, instinct took over.

"Riena!"

She moved her head slightly.

"Riena. It's Tom."

As if her adrenalin had stopped flowing after her charade with the guard, Riena allowed herself to be led to

Tom's car. She didn't react at all until she felt the movement of the wheels, and even then all she did was cross her
hands over her breasts to warm her hands in her armpits
and cover her nakedness.

The gesture touched Tom. He leaned sideways and
pulled the blanket over her. "It won't do to get arrested
now for obscenity," he said lightly.

"Where are we going?" Riena asked, speaking for the
first time.

"Zeekoevlei. To visit Mtshali."

"Alfred? What for?"

The two of you can help each other give birth, Tom
thought. "Go to sleep. It's a long drive," he said offering
no explanation.

Like a child used to obeying orders, Riena settled herself
against the seat and closed her eyes. She held her hands
around her extended belly, as if protecting the infant inside. Seeing her do that, Tom felt his anger at her returning. He concentrated on keeping the wheels of the car as
far away as possible from the edge of the cliff.

Executing De Waal Drive's convolutions made the sand
road to the hideout seem like an easy ride, despite the
familiar potholes which jerked Riena awake.

"Is Alfred allowed to live here now?" she asked. "Have
things improved that much?"

"Allowed?" Tom laughed. "No. He's not allowed to live
here. But the animals and the weeds don't give a damn.
This is still White territory but no one cares."

He stopped the car and told Riena to wait while he got
out and opened the trunk to remove a small kerosene
lamp. "Alfred won't allow anything resembling fire in the
place, but I can't stand that perpetual darkness," he said
helping her out.

"Damn mosquitoes. Don't they know they're supposed
to sleep at night," Riena said, brushing her face as they

approached the shack. The screeching of the gulls, whose sleep they had also disturbed, followed them inside.

"The place stinks," Tom said. He fumbled in his pocket for matches. "He's turned it into a giant womb."

He lit the lamp. As it flared, Riena doubled over. "I'm in labor, Tom," she said.

Tom ignored her until she straightened up. He was about to speak, to tell her about Alfred, but his half-brother's voice preempted him.

"Negwenya!"

The word was barely intelligible, the fear unmistakable.

"Alfred's in labor, too," Tom said, as Riena doubled over again.

When the pain had subsided she straightened up, though with difficulty. Tom could see by the look on her face that she understood what was happening.

"The young Negwenya is ready to breathe fire with the coming dawn," he said.

Picking up the kerosene lamp, he led the way into Alfred's room. Riena followed. The room was littered with stacks of unwashed dishes and with the paraphernalia of making bombs. Underwear—dirty judging by the odor—covered the chair next to Alfred's bed.

Riena sat down on the bed and stretched out her hand to touch Mtshali, her face torn between disgust and pity.

"Why haven't you taken him to a hospital, Tom?" she asked quietly. Her right hand was resting on the Zulu's pregnant belly, her left anticipating the next pain from her own womb.

The figure on the bed shook and turned to face the wall. "Go away; it's no use. Leave me alone. If I'm alone she'll come for the child and it will all be over."

"Can't we get him to a hospital? Show him x-rays? Convince him there's nothing there?"

"The Negwenya's child is in there. Can't you see him?" Tom said. He leaned over and tugged at the light blanket that covered the Black man's swollen belly.

"In God's name force him to get medical attention," Riena shouted, recoiling from the sight of Alfred Mtshali's undulating skin. She could see a shape, moving gently, first from side to side and then up and down, like a watersnake caught in the weeds.

Her own child demanded attention and she bent over. When the pain passed, she lifted her head and wiped her face on one of Alfred's undershirts. "I'm not going to sit here and watch him die," she said. "If I can forgive him for what he did to me, you can surely do the same."

Tom didn't move. There was no way he was going to help that bastard, he thought.

"I'm not having my baby in this place," Riena said, standing up.

"The fire," Alfred croaked. "Get it out of here. The Negwenya doesn't like it."

Tom glanced out of the window at the lightening sky. He didn't care about Riena's White bastard. As far as he was concerned, it could burn with his half-brother. He did care about himself; he wasn't ready to let the Negwenya take him. Nor, he admitted to himself, did he want to be responsible for hurting Riena. He had risked that once, and once was more than enough.

Holding the lamp in one hand, Tom half-carried Riena out of the house. When they were some distance away, he released his hold on her and she sank to the ground.

"I won't be the first woman to give birth here," she said, drawing her knees toward her chin. "Help him, Tom. Get him out of there before the Negwenya takes him."

Allowing himself a split-second of doubt, Tom turned to face the house.

Suddenly the Negwenya began to move. Sensuously. Lazily.

149

"Now, Tom. Please.

She checked to see if the head of her child had appeared. Tom, who had turned to look at her, averted his eyes. Rising slowly from his haunches, he stepped forward, moving into the sun's first rays.

He didn't have time for a second step. With a roar that muffled the cry of a newborn generation, the shanty burst into flames.

Tom, near enough to feel the heat, watched their hideout burn as if a giant match had ignited the world's largest junkpile. Flames licked the sky and he stared awestruck as they formed themselves into the shape Nkolosi had drawn in the dirt—the pointed ears, the curling tail, the wings ready to unfurl.

Suddenly the Negwenya began to move. Sensuously. Lazily. Dancing to the tune of Nkolosi's laughter.

"Run, Tom," Riena yelled, placing her son on her stomach so that she could cover him with her prison blanket. "Run. We'll be all right till someone comes."

Though he wanted desperately to take Riena at her word and run, he knelt in the grass and stroked her hair. "I'll carry you to the car and take you with me," he said.

"They prepared me for natural childbirth in prison," Riena said, "not for the Grand Prix."

Tom looked up at the sky, where the Negwenya hovered over them. Nkolosi, he thought. He had to get to Nkolosi. In a futile last gesture, he tucked the blanket around Riena. Then he was in the car, flooring the accelerator, bumping his way off the dusty road and onto De Waal Drive.

With fear running a marathon in his head, Tom took De Waal Drive's curves at reckless speed. For three miles he refused to look in his rear view mirror. When he did, the Negwenya was so close that he could read the affection in her eyes. She was floating, keeping the distance between them constant, her wings only half-extended.

Forgetting about everything except the need to outrun his pursuer, Tom sped through town, over High Level Road, and onto Marine Drive. He wound past miles of ocean at sea level, past deserted beaches waiting for Cape Town's sleeping sun worshipers to assume their positions on the sand, then up again, over a mountain pass, the sea dropping further and further below, and back down, thousands of feet, until he was at sea level once more. And driving. Still driving, toward a harbor now, fishing boats coming closer, rocking violently in the curve and splash of water rebounding from a long wooden pier. Enticing the car closer. Closer. Daring him to plunge between the whipping masts and the rough quay that held the waves at bay.

Tom's foot jammed the brake.

The perfume of seaweed mingled with salt. Fishermen, drawing their nets up against the wind, looked curiously at him and two teenagers, astride their bicycles, turned away disappointed that he hadn't driven into the water. Sorry to let you down kids, Tom thought, clutching the steering wheel and breathing hard. Then, jumping out of the car, he ran onto a stretch of beach that was protected from the intrusion of the open sea by a semi-circular barrier of rocks.

As a shadow overhead cut out the sun, he saw Nkolosi, cross-legged, drawing with slow, semi-circular movements.

"I paid the asking price, Nkolosi," Tom said, panting. He dropped onto his knees.

"You paid my price," the witchdoctor said. He laughed, erasing the image in the sand. "The Negwenya will be lonely without your half brother. It seems she finds you attractive. She has already bought your services, so perhaps this time she will be a less demanding mistress. I trust you will be an attentive gigolo, Sibanda."

Tom felt the shadow of the Negwenya protecting his neck from the sun. He watched Nkolosi unfurl himself and stand up to his full height. He wore no shirt and his muscles rippled under a shiny layer of sweat.

"We'll be seeing you, Sibanda," he said evenly. "Now go."

Go, Tom thought. Go where? No matter where he went, Nkolosi and his Negwenya would find him.

"Go, Sibanda!"

When Tom stood up he was taller than Nkolosi, yet he felt infinitesimally small. He looked down at the sand crab that had moved slowly over his shoe and clung there now, seeking refuge from the burning sand in the shadow of his trouser cuff.

"Negwenya?" he said, afraid to look up, sure he would be greeted by the avaricious eyes of a courtesan.

"She's long gone you fool," Nkolosi said. He turned on his heel and padded across the sand away from Tom, his hardened soles barely leaving an indentation to prove he had been there at all.

Suddenly Tom was aware of the sun, beating mercilessly into the back of his neck where the Negwenya's shadow had protected him. With a slow, tentative motion, he looked up. The sky was clear. A few wisps of clouds, a seagull, a kite spinning its tail on a downward spiral. There was nothing else.

MIDDLE WOMAN
BYRON WALLEY

ILLUSTRATION BY
LYNNE ANNE GOODWIN

Ah-Cheu was a woman of the great kingdom of Ch'in, a land of hills and valleys, a land of great wealth and dire poverty. But Ah-Cheu was a middle person, neither rich nor poor, neither old nor young, and her husband's farm was half in the valley and half on the hill. Ah-Cheu had a sister older than her, and a sister younger than her, and one lived thirty leagues to the north, and the other thirty leagues to the south. "I am a middle woman," Ah-Cheu boasted once, but her husband's mother rebuked her, saying, "Evil comes to the middle, and good goes out to the edges."

Every year Ah-Cheu put a pack on her back and journeyed for a visit either to the sister to the north or to the sister to the south. It took her three days to make the journey, for she did not hurry. But one year she did not make the journey, for she met a dragon on the road.

The dragon was long and fine and terrible, and Au-Cheu immediately knelt and touched her forehead to the road and said, "Oh, dragon, spare my life!"

The dragon only chuckled deep in his throat and said, "Woman, what do they call you?"

The dragon was long and fine and terrible.

154

Not wishing to tell her true name to the dragon, she said, "I am called Middle Woman."

"Well, Middle Woman, I will give you a choice. The first choice is to have me eat you here in the road. The second choice is to have me grant you three wishes."

Surprised, Ah-Cheu raised her head. "But of course I take the second choice. Why do you set me a problem with such an easy solution?"

"It is more amusing," said the dragon, "to watch human beings destroy themselves than to overpower them quickly."

"But how can three wishes destroy me?"

"Make a wish, and see."

Ah-Cheu thought of many things she might wish for, but was soon ashamed of her greed. "I wish," she finally said, having decided to ask for only what she truly needed, "for my husband's farm to always produce plenty for all my family to eat."

"It shall be done," said the dragon, and he vanished, only to reappear a moment later, smiling and licking his lips. "I have done," he said, "exactly what you asked—I have eaten all your family, and so your husband's farm, even if it produces nothing, will always produce plenty for *them* to eat."

Ah-Cheu wept and mourned and cursed herself for being a fool, for now she saw the dragon's plan. Any wish, however innocent, would be turned against her.

"Think all you like," said the dragon, "but it will do you no good. I have had lawyers draw up legal documents eight feet long, but I have found the loopholes."

Then Ah-Cheu knew what she had to ask for. "I wish for all the world to be exactly as it was one minute before I left my home to come on this journey."

The dragon looked at her in surprise. "That's all? That's all you want to wish for?"

"Yes," said Ah-Cheu. "And you must do it now."

And suddenly she found herself in her husband's house, putting on her pack and bidding good-bye to her family. Immediately she set down the pack.

"I have changed my mind," she said. "I am not going."

Everyone was shocked. Everyone was surprised. Her husband berated her for being a changeable woman. Her mother-in-law denounced her for having forgotten her duty to her sisters. Her children pouted because she had always brought them each a present from her journeys to the north and south. But Ah-Cheu was firm. She would not risk meeting the dragon again.

And when the furor died down, Ah-Cheu was far more cheerful than she had ever been before, for she knew that she had one wish left, the third wish, the unused wish. And if there were ever a time of great need, she could use it to save herself and her family.

One year there was a fire, and Ah-Cheu was outside the house, with her youngest child trapped within. Almost she used her wish, but then thought, Why use the wish, when I can use my arms? And she ducked low, and ran into the house, and saved the boy, though it singed off all her hair. And she still had her son, and she still had her wish.

One year there was a famine, and it looked like all the world would starve. Ah-Cheu almost used her wish, but then thought, Why use the wish, when I can use my feet? And she wandered up into the hills, and came back with a basket of roots and leaves, and with such food she kept her family alive until the Emperor's men came with wagons full of rice. And she still had her family, and she still had her wish.

And in another year there was a great flood, and all the homes were swept away, and as Ah-Cheu and her son's baby sat upon the roof, watching the water eat away the walls of the house, she almost used her wish to get a boat so she could escape. But then she thought, Why use the wish, when I can use my head? And she took up boards from the roof and walls, and with her skirts she tied them into a raft large enough for the baby, and setting the child upon it she swam away, pushing the raft until they reached high ground and safety. And when her son found her alive, he wept with joy, and said, "Mother Ah-Cheu, never has a son loved his mother more!"

And Ah-Cheu had her posterity, and yet still she had her wish.

And then it was time for Ah-Cheu to die, and she lay sick and frail upon a bed of honor in her son's house, and the women and children and old men of the village came to keen for her and honor her as she lay dying. "Never has there been a more fortunate woman than Ah-Cheu," they said. "Never has there been a kinder, a more generous, a more godfavored woman!" And she was content to leave the world, because she had been so happy in it.

And on her last night, as she lay alone in darkness, she heard a voice call her name.

"Middle Woman," said the voice, and she opened her eyes, and there was the dragon.

"What do you want with me?" she asked. "I'm not much of a morsel to eat now, I'm afraid."

But then she saw the dragon looked terrified, and she listened to what he had to say.

"Middle Woman," said the dragon, "you have not used your third wish."

"I never needed it."

"Oh, cruel woman! What a vengeance you take! In the long run, I never did you any harm! How can you do this to me?"

"But what am I doing?" she asked.

"If you die, with your third wish unused, then I, too, will die!" he cried. "Maybe that doesn't seem so bad to you, but dragons are usually immortal, and so you can believe me when I say my death would cut me off with most of my life unlived."

"Poor dragon," she said. "But what have I to wish for?"

"Immortality," he said. "No tricks. I'll let you live forever."

"I don't want to live forever," she said. "It would make the neighbors envious."

"Great wealth, then, for your family."

"But they have all they need right now."

"Any wish!" he cried. "Any wish, or I will die!"

And so she smiled, and reached out a frail old hand and touched his supplicating claw, and said, "Then I wish a wish, dragon. I wish that all the rest of your life should be nothing but happiness for you and everyone you meet."

The dragon looked at her in surprise, and then in relief, and then he smiled and wept for joy. He thanked her many times, and left her home rejoicing.

And that night Ah-Cheu also left her home, more subtly than the dragon, and far less likely to return, but no less merrily for all that.

THE STORM KING

JOAN D. VINGE

ILLUSTRATIONS BY
FREFF

They said that in those days the lands were cursed that
lay in the shadow of the Storm King. The peak thrust up
from the gently rolling hills and fertile farmlands like an
impossible wave cresting on the open sea, a brooding
finger probing the secrets of heaven. Once it had vomited
fire and fumes, ash and molten stone had poured from its
throat; the distant forerunners of the people who lived
beneath it now had died of its wrath. But the Earth had
spent Her fury in one final cataclysm, and now the mountain lay quiet, dark, and cold, its mouth choked with congealed stone.

And yet still the people lived in fear. No one among
them remembered having seen its summit, which was
always crowned by cloud; lightning played in the purple,
shrouding robes, and distant thunder filled the dreams of
the folk who slept below with the roaring of dragons.

For it was a dragon who had come to dwell among the
crags: that elemental focus of all storm and fire carried on
the wind, drawn to a place where the Earth's fire had died,
a place still haunted by ancient grief. And sharing the spirit
of fire, the dragon knew no law and obeyed no power

159

except its own. By day or night it would rise on furious
wings of wind and sweep over the land, inundating the
crops with rain, blasting trees with its lightning, battering
walls and tearing away rooftops; terrifying rich and poor,
man and beast, for the sheer pleasure of destruction, the
exaltation of uncontrolled power. The people had prayed
to the new gods who had replaced their worship of the
Earth to deliver them; but the new gods made Their home
in the sky, and seemed to be beyond hearing.

By now the people had made Their names into curses,
as they pried their oxcarts from the mud or looked out over
fields of broken grain and felt their bellies and their children's bellies tighten with hunger. And they would look
toward the distant peak and curse the Storm King, naming
the peak and the dragon both; but always in whispers and
mutters, for fear the wind would hear them, and bring the
dark storm sweeping down on them again.

The storm-wracked town of Wyddon and its people
looked up only briefly in their sullen shaking-off and
shoveling-out of mud as a stranger picked his way among
them. He wore the woven leather of a common soldier, his
cloak and leggings were coarse and ragged, and he walked
the planks laid down in the stinking street as though de-
termination alone kept him on his feet. A woman picking
through baskets of stunted leeks in the marketplace saw
with vague surprise that he had entered the tiny village
temple; a man putting fresh thatch on a torn-open roof saw
him come out again, propelled by the indignant, orange-
robed priest.

"If you want witchery, find yourself a witch! This is a
holy place; the gods don't meddle in vulgar magic!"

"I can see that," the stranger muttered, staggering in
ankle-deep mud. He climbed back onto the boards with

some difficulty and obvious disgust. "Maybe if they did
you'd have streets and not rivers of muck in this town." He
turned away in anger, almost stumbled over a mud-
colored girl blocking his forward progress on the
boardwalk.

"You priests should bow down to the Storm King!" the
girl postured insolently, looking toward the priest. "The
dragon can change all our lives more in one night than
your gods have done in a lifetime."

"Slut!" The priest shook his carven staff at her; its
necklace of golden bells chimed like absurd laughter.
"There's a witch for you, beggar. If you think she can teach
you to tame the dragon, then go with her!" He turned
away, disappearing into the temple. The stranger's body
jerked, as though it strained against his control, wanting to
strike at the priest's retreating back.

"You're a witch?" The stranger turned and glared down
at the bony figure standing in his way, found her studying
him back with obvious skepticism. He imagined what she
saw—a foreigner, his straight black hair whacked off like a
serf's, his clothes crawling with filth, his face grimed and
gaunt and set in a bitter grimace. He frowned more deeply.

The girl shook her head. "No. I'm just bound to her.
You have business to take up with her, I see—about the
Storm King." She smirked, expecting him to believe she
was privy to secret knowledge.

"As you doubtless overheard, yes." He shifted his
weight from one leg to the other, trying fruitlessly to ease
the pain in his back.

She shrugged, pushing her own tangled brown hair
back from her face. "Well, you'd better be able to pay for
it, or you've come a long way from Kwansai for nothing."

He started, before he realized that his coloring and his
eyes gave that much away. "I can pay." He drew his

dagger from its hidden sheath, the only weapon he had left, and the only thing of value. He let her glimpse the jeweled hilt before he pushed it back out of sight.

Her gray eyes widened briefly. "What do I call you, Prince of Thieves?" with another glance at his rags.

"Call me Your Highness," not lying, and not quite joking.

She looked up into his face again, and away. "Call me Nothing, Your Highness. Because I am nothing." She twitched a shoulder at him. "And follow me."

They passed the last houses of the village without further speech, and followed the mucky track on into the dark, dripping forest that lay at the mountain's feet. The girl stepped off the road and into the trees without warning; he followed her recklessly, half angry and half afraid that she was abandoning him. But she danced ahead of him through the pines, staying always in sight, although she was plainly impatient with his lagging pace. The dank chill of the sunless wood gnawed his aching back and swarms of stinging gnats feasted on his exposed skin; the bare-armed girl seemed as oblivious to the insects as she was to the cold.

He pushed on grimly, as he had pushed on until now, having no choice but to keep on or die. And at last his persistence was rewarded; he saw the forest rise ahead, and buried in the flank of the hillside among the trees was a mossy hut linteled by immense stones.

The girl disappeared into the hut as he entered the clearing before it. He slowed, looking around him at the clusters of carven images pushing up like unnatural growths from the spongy ground, or dangling from tree limbs. Most of the images were subtly or blatantly obscene. He averted his eyes and limped between them to the hut's entrance.

He stepped through the doorway without waiting for an invitation, to find the girl crouched by the hearth in the cramped interior, wearing the secret smile of a cat. Beside her an incredibly wrinkled, ancient woman sat on a three-legged stool. The legs were carved into shapes that made him look away again, back at the wrinkled face and the black, buried eyes that regarded him with flinty bemusement. He noticed abruptly that there was no wall behind her: the far side of the hut melted into the black volcanic stone, a natural fissure opening into the mountain's side.

"So, Your Highness, you've come all the way from Kwansai seeking the Storm King, and a way to tame its power?"

He wrapped his cloak closely about him and grimaced, the nearest thing to a smile of scorn that he could manage. "Your girl has a quick tongue. But I've come to the wrong place, it seems, for real power."

"Don't be so sure!" The old woman leaned toward him, shrill and spiteful. "You can't afford to be too sure of anything, Lassan-din. You were prince of Kwansai, you should have been king there when your father died, and overlord of these lands as well. And now you're nobody and you have no home, no friends, barely even your life. Nothing is what it seems to be . . . it never is."

Lassan-din's mouth went slack; he closed it, speechless at last. *Nothing is what it seems.* The girl called Nothing grinned up at him from the floor. He took a deep breath, shifting to ease his back again. "Then you know what I've come for, if you already know that much, witch."

The hag half-rose from her obscene stool; he glimpsed a flash of color, a brighter, finer garment hidden beneath the drab outer robe she wore—the way the inner woman still burned fiercely bright in her eyes, showing through the wasted flesh of her ancient body. "Call me no names, you

prince of beggars! I am the Earth's Own. Your puny Kwansai priests, who call my sisterhood 'witch', who destroyed
our holy places and drove us into hiding, know nothing of
power. They're fools, they don't believe in power and they
are powerless, charlatans. You know it or you wouldn't be
here!" She settled back, wheezing. "Yes, I could tell you
what you want; but suppose you tell me."

"I want what's mine! I want my kingdom." He paced
restlessly, two steps and then back. "I know of elementals,
all the old legends. My people say that dragons are storm-
bringers, born from a joining of Fire and Water and Air,
three of the four Primes of Existence. Nothing but the
Earth can defy their fury. And I know that if I can hold a
dragon in its lair with the right spells, it must give me what I
want, like the heroes of the Golden Time. I want to use its
power to take back my lands."

"You don't want much, do you?" The old woman rose
from her seat and turned her back on him, throwing a
surreptitious handful of something into the fire, making it
flare up balefully. She stirred the pot that hung from a hook
above it; spitting five times into the noxious brew as she
stirred. Lassan-din felt his empty stomach turn over. "If
you want to challenge the Storm King, you should be out
there climbing, not here holding your hand out to me."

"Damn you!" His exasperation broke loose, and his
hand wrenched her around to face him. "I need some
spell, some magic, some way to pen a dragon up. I can't do
it with my bare hands!"

She shook her head, unintimidated, and leered tooth-
lessly at him. "My power comes to me through my body,
up from the Earth Our Mother. She won't listen to a
man—especially one who would destroy her worship. Ask
your priests who worship the air to teach you their empty
prayers."

He saw the hatred rising in her, and felt it answered: The dagger was out of its hidden sheath and in his hand before he knew it, pressing the soft folds of her neck. "I don't believe you, witch. See this dagger—" quietly, deadly. "If you give me what I want, you'll have the jewels in its hilt. If you don't, you'll feel its blade cut your throat."

"All right, all right!" She strained back as the blade's tip began to bite. He let her go. She felt her neck; the girl sat perfectly still at their feet, watching. "I can give you something, a spell. I can't guarantee She'll listen. But you have enough hatred in you for ten men—and maybe that will make your man's voice loud enough to penetrate Her skin. This mountain is sacred to Her, She still listens through its ears, even if She no longer breathes here."

"Never mind the superstitious drivel. Just tell me how I can keep the dragon in without it striking me dead with its lightning. How I can fight fire with fire—"

"You don't fight fire with fire. You fight fire with water."

He stared at her; at the obviousness of it, and the absurdity—"The dragon is the creator of storm. How can mere water—?"

"A dragon is anathema. Remember that, prince who would be king. It is chaos, power uncontrolled; and power always has a price. That's the key to everything. I can teach you the spell for controlling the waters of the Earth; but you're the one who must use it."

He stayed with the women through the day, and learned as the hours passed to believe in the mysteries of the Earth. The crone spoke words that brought water fountaining up from the well outside her door while he looked on in amazement, his weariness and pain forgotten. As he watched she made a brook flow upstream; made crystal droplets beading the forest pines join in a diadem to crown

his head, and then with a word released them to run cold
and helpless as tears into the collar of his ragged tunic.

She seized the fury that rose up in him at her insolence,
and challenged him to do the same. He repeated the
ungainly, ancient spellwords defiantly, arrogantly—and
nothing happened. She scoffed, his anger grew; she jeered
and it grew stronger. He repeated the spell again, and
again, and again . . . until at last he felt the terrifying
presence of an alien power rise in his body, answering the
call of his blood. The droplets on the trees began to shiver
and commingle; he watched an eddy form in the swift clear
water of the stream—. The Earth had answered him.

His anger failed him at the unbelievable sight of his
success . . . and the power failed him too. Dazed and
strengthless, at last he knew his anger for the only emotion
with the depth or urgency to move the body of the Earth,
or even his own. But he had done the impossible—made
the Earth move to a man's bidding. He had proved his
right to be a king, proved that he could force the dragon to
serve him as well. He laughed out loud. The old woman
moaned and spat, twisting her hands that were like
gnarled roots, mumbling curses. She shuffled away toward
the woods as though she were in a trance; turned back
abruptly as she reached the trees, pointing past him at the
girl standing like a ghost in the hut's doorway. "You think
you've known the Earth; that you own Her, now. You
think you can take anything and make it yours. But you're
as empty as that one, and as powerless!" And she was
gone.

Night had fallen through the dreary wood without his
realizing it. The girl Nothing led him back into the hut,
shared a bowl of thick, strangely herbed soup and a piece
of stale bread with him. He ate gratefully but numbly, the
first warm meal he had eaten in weeks; his mind drifted
into waking dreams of banqueting until dawn in royal halls.

When he had eaten his share, wiping the bowl shamelessly with a crust, he stood and walked the few paces to the hut's furthest corner. He lay down on the hard stone by the cave mouth, wrapping his cloak around him, and closed his eyes. Sleep's darker cloak settled over him.

And then, dimly, he became aware that the girl had followed him, stood above him looking down. He opened his eyes unwillingly, to see her unbelt her tunic and pull it off, kneel down naked at his side. A piece of rock crystal, perfectly transparent, perfectly formed, hung glittering coldly against her chest. He kept his eyes open, saying nothing.

"The Old One won't be back until you're gone; the sight of a man calling on the Earth was too strong for her." Her hand moved insinuatingly along his thigh.

He rolled away from her, choking on a curse as his back hurt him sharply. "I'm tired. Let me sleep."

"I can help you. She could have told you more. I'll help you tomorrow . . . if you lie with me tonight."

He looked up at her, suddenly despairing. "Take my body, then; but it won't give you much pleasure." He pulled up the back of his tunic, baring the livid scar low on his spine. "My uncle didn't make a cripple of me—but he might as well have." When he even thought of a woman there was only pain, only rage . . . only that.

She put her hand on the scar with surprising gentleness. "I can help that too . . . for tonight." She went away, returned with a small jar of ointment and rubbed the salve slowly into his scarred back. A strange, cold heat sank through him; a sensuous tingling swept away the grinding ache that had been his only companion through these long months of exile. He let his breath out in an astonished sigh, and the girl lay down beside him, pulling at his clothes.

Her thin body was as hard and bony as a boy's, but she made him forget that. She made him forget everything, except that tonight he was free from pain and sorrow, tonight he lay with a woman who desired him, no matter what her reason. He remembered lost pleasure, lost joy, lost youth, only yesterday . . . until yesterday became tomorrow.

In the morning he woke, in pain, alone and fully clothed, aching on the hard ground. *Nothing* . . . He opened his eyes and saw her standing at the fire, stirring a kettle. *A dream—?* The cruel betrayal that was reality returned tenfold.

They ate together in a silence that was sullen on his part, and inscrutable on hers. After last night it seemed obvious to him that she was older than she looked—as obvious as the way he himself had changed from boy to old man in a span of months. And he felt an insubstantiality about her that he had not noticed before, an elusiveness that might only have been an echo of his dream. "I dreamed, last night . . ."

"I know." She climbed to her feet, cutting him off, combing her snarled hair back with her fingers. "You dream loudly." Her face was closed.

He felt a frown settle between his eyes again. "I have a long climb. I'd better get started." He pushed himself up and moved stiffly toward the doorway. The old hag still had not returned.

"Not that way," the girl said abruptly. "This way." She pointed as he turned back, toward the cleft in the rock.

He stood still. "That will take me to the dragon?"

"Only part way. But it's easier by half. I'll show you." She jerked a brand out of the fire and started into the maw of darkness.

He went after her with only a moment's uncertainty. He had lived in fear for too long; if he was afraid to follow this witch-girl into her Goddess's womb, then he would never have the courage to challenge the Storm King.

The low-ceilinged cleft angled steeply upward, a natural tube formed millennia ago by congealing lava. The girl began to climb confidently, as though she trusted some guardian power to place her hands and feet surely—a power he could not depend on as he followed her up the shaft. The dim light of day snuffed out behind him, leaving only her torch to guide them through utter blackness, over rock that was alternately rough enough to flay the skin from his hands and slick enough to give him no purchase at all. The tunnel twisted like a worm, widening, narrowing, steepening, folding back on itself in an agony of contortion. His body protested its own agony as he dragged it up handholds in a sheer rock face, twisted it, wrenched it, battered it against the unyielding stone. The acrid smoke from the girl's torch stung his eyes and clogged his lungs; but it never seemed to slow her own tireless motion, and she took no pity on his weakness. Only the knowledge of the distance he had come kept him from demanding that they turn back; he could not believe that this could possibly be an easier way than climbing the outside of the mountain. It began to seem to him that he had been climbing through this foul blackness for all of eternity, that this was another dream like his dream last night, but one that would never end.

The girl chanted softly to herself now; he could just hear her above his own labored breathing. He wondered jealously if she was drawing strength from the very stone around them, the body of the Earth. He could feel no pulse in the cold heart of the rock; and yet after yesterday he did not doubt its presence, even wondering if the Earth sapped his own strength with preternatural malevolence. *I am a man, I will be king!* he thought defiantly. And the way grew steeper, and his hands bled.

"Wait—!" He gasped out the word at last, as his feet went out from under him again and he barely saved himself from sliding back down the tunnel. "I can't go on."

The girl, crouched on a level spot above him, looked back and down at him and ground out the torch. His grunt of protest became a grunt of surprise as he saw her silhouetted against a growing gray-brightness. She disappeared from his view; the brightness dimmed and then strengthened.

He heaved himself up and over the final bend in the wormhole, into a space large enough to stand in if he had had the strength. He crawled forward hungrily into the brightness at the cave mouth, found the girl kneeling there, her face raised to the light. He welcomed the fresh air into his lungs, cold and cleansing; looked past her—and down.

They were dizzyingly high on the mountain's side, above the treeline, above a sheer unscalable face of stone. A fast-falling torrent of water roared on their left, plunging out and down the cliff-face. The sun winked at him from the cloud-wreathed heights; its angle told him they had climbed for the better part of the day. He looked over at the girl.

"You're lucky," she said, without looking back at him. Before he could even laugh at the grotesque irony of the statement she raised her hand, pointing on up the mountainside. "The Storm King sleeps—another storm is past. I saw the rainbow break this sunrise."

He felt a surge of strength and hope, absorbed the indifferent blessing of the Holy Sun. "How long will it sleep?"

"Two more days, perhaps. You won't reach its den before night. Sleep here, and climb again tomorrow."

"And then?" He looked toward her expectantly.

She shrugged.

"I paid you well," not certain in what coin, anymore. "I want a fair return! How do I pen the beast?"

Her hand tightened around the crystal pendant hanging against her tunic. She glanced back into the cave mouth. "There are many waters flowing from the heights. One of them might be diverted to fall past the entrance of its lair."

"A waterfall? I might as well hold up a rose and expect it to cower!"

"Power always has it price; as the Old One said." She looked directly at him at last. "The storm rests here in mortal form—the form of the dragon. And like all mortals, it suffers. Its strength lies in the scales that cover its skin. The rain washes them away—the storm is agony to the stormbringer. They fall like jewels, they catch the light as they fall, like a trail of rainbow. It's the only rainbow anyone here has ever seen . . . a sign of hope, because it means an end to the storm; but a curse, too, because the storm will always return, endlessly."

"Then I could have it at my mercy . . ." He heard nothing else.

"Yes. If you can make the Earth move to your will." Her voice was flat.

His hands tightened. "I have enough hate in me for that."

"And what will you demand, to ease it?" She glanced at him again, and back at the sky. "The dragon is defiling this sacred place; it should be driven out. You could become a hero to my people, if you forced the dragon to go away—a god. They need a god who can do them some good . . ."

He felt her somehow still watching him, measuring his response, even though she had looked away. "I came here to solve my problem, not yours. I want my own kingdom, not a kingdom of mud-men. I need the dragon's power—I didn't come here to drive that away."

The girl said nothing, still staring at the sky.

"It's a simple thing for you to move the waters—why haven't you driven the dragon away yourself, then?" His voice rasped in his parched throat, sharp with unrecognized guilt.

"I'm Nothing. I have no power—the Old One holds my soul." She looked down at the crystal.

"Then why won't the Old One do it?"

"She hates, too. She hates what our people have become under the new gods, your gods. That's why she won't."

"I'd think it would give her great pleasure to prove the impotence of the new gods." His mouth stretched sourly.

"She wants to die in the Earth's time, not tomorrow." The girl folded her arms, and her own mouth twisted.

He shook his head. "I don't understand that . . . why you didn't destroy our soldiers, our priests, with your magic?"

"The Earth moves slowly to our bidding, because She is eternal. An arrow is small—but it moves swiftly."

He laughed once, appreciatively. "I understand."

"There's a cairn of stones over there." She nodded back into the darkness. "Food is under it." He realized that this must have been a place of refuge for the women in times of persecution. "The rest is up to you." She turned, merging abruptly into the shadows.

"Wait!" he called, surprising himself. "You must be tired."

She shook her head, a deeper shadow against darkness.

"Stay with me—until morning." It was not quite a demand, not quite a question.

"Why?" He thought he saw her eyes catch light and reflect it back at him, like a wild thing's.

Because I had a dream. He did not say it, did not say anything else.

"Our debts have balanced." She moved slightly, and something landed on the ground at his feet: his dagger. The hilt was pockmarked with empty jewel settings; stripped clean. He leaned down to pick it up. When he straightened again she was gone.

"You need a light—!" He called after her again.

Her voice came back to him, from a great distance: "May you get what you deserve!" And then silence, except for the roaring of the falls.

He ate, wondering whether her last words were a benediction or a curse. He slept, and the dreams that came to him were filled with the roaring of dragons.

With the light of a new day he began to climb again, following the urgent river upward toward its source that lay hidden in the waiting crown of clouds. He remembered his own crown, and lost himself in memories of the past and future, hardly aware of the harsh sobbing of his breath, of flesh and sinew strained past a sane man's endurance. Once he had been the spoiled child of privilege, his father's only son—living in the world's eye, his every whim a command. Now he was as much Nothing as the witch-girl far down the mountain. But he would live the way he had again, his every wish granted, his power absolute—he *would* live that way again, if he had to climb to the gates of heaven to win back his birthright.

The hours passed, endlessly, inevitably, and all he knew was that slowly, slowly, the sky lowered above him. At last the cold, moist edge of clouds enfolded his burning body, drawing him into another world of gray mist and gray silences; black, glistening surfaces of rock; the white sound of the cataract rushing down from even higher above. Drizzling fog shrouded the distances any way he turned, and he realized that he did not know where in this layer of cloud the dragon's den lay. He had assumed that it would be obvious, he had trusted the girl to tell him all he needed to know . . . Why had he trusted her? That pagan slut— his hand gripped the rough hilt of his dagger; dropped away, trembling with fatigue. He began to climb again, keeping the sound of falling water nearby for want of any other guide. The light grew vaguer and more diffuse, until the darkness falling in the outer world penetrated the fog world and the haze of his exhaustion. He lay down at last, unable to go on, and slept beneath the shelter of an overhang of rock.

He woke stupefied by daylight. The air held a strange acridness that hurt his throat, that he could not identify. The air seemed almost to crackle; his hair ruffled, although there was no wind. He pushed himself up. He knew this feeling now: a storm was coming. A storm coming . . . a storm, here? Suddenly, fully awake, he turned on his knees, peering deeper beneath the overhang that sheltered him. And in the light of dawn he could see that it was not a simple overhang, but another opening into the mountain's side—a wider, greater one, whose depths the day could not fathom. But far down in the blackness a flickering of unnatural light showed. His hair rose in the electric breeze, he felt his skin prickle. Yes . . . yes! A small cry escaped him. He had found it! Without even knowing it, he had slept in the mouth of the dragon's lair all night. Habit brought a thanks to the gods to his lips, until he remembered—He muttered a *thank you* to the Earth beneath him before he climbed to his feet. A brilliant flash silhouetted him; a rumble like distant thunder made the ground vibrate, and he froze. Was the dragon waking—?

But there was no further disturbance, and he breathed again. Two days, the girl had told him, the dragon might sleep. And now he had reached his final trial, the penning

of the beast. Away to his right he could hear the cataract's
endless song. But would there be enough water in it to
block the dragon's exit? Would that be enough to keep it
prisoner, or would it strike him down in lightning and
thunder, and sweep his body from the heights with torrents
of rain? . . . Could he even move one droplet of water,
here and now? Or would he find that all the thousand
doubts that gnawed inside him were not only useless but
pointless?

He shook it off, moving out and down the mist-dim
slope to view the cave mouth and the river tumbling past it.
A thin stream of water already trickled down the face of the
opening, but the main flow was diverted by a folded knot
of lava. If he could twist the water's course and hold it, for
just long enough . . .

He climbed the barren face of stone at the far side of the
cave mouth until he stood above it, confronting the sinuous steel and flashing white of the thing he must move. It
seemed almost alive, and he felt weary, defeated, utterly
insignificant at the sight of it. But the mountain on which he
stood was a greater thing than even the river, and he knew
that within it lay power great enough to change the water's
course. But he was the conduit, his will must tap and bend
the force that he had felt stir in him two days ago.

He braced his legs apart, gathered strength into himself, trying to recall the feel of magic moving in him. He
recited the spell-words, the focus for the willing of
power—and felt nothing. He recited the words again,
putting all his concentration behind them. Again nothing.
The Earth lay silent and inert beneath his feet.

Anger rose in him, at the Earth's disdain, and against the
strange women who served Her—the jealous, demanding
anger that had opened him to power before. And this time
he did feel the power stir in him, sluggishly, feebly. But

there was no sign of any change in the water's course. He
threw all his conscious will toward change, *change,
change*—but still the Earth's power faltered and mocked
him. He let go of the ritual words at last, felt the tingling
promise of energy die, having burned away all his own
strength.

He sat down on the wet stone, listened to the river roar
with laughter. He had been so sure that when he got here
the force of his need would be strong enough . . . *I have
enough hate in me,* he had told the girl. But he wasn't
reaching it now. Not the real hatred that had carried him so
far beyond the limits of his strength and experience. He
began to concentrate on that hatred, and the reasons
behind it: the loss, the pain, the hardship and fear . . .

His father had been a great ruler over the lands that his
ancestors had conquered. And he had loved his queen,
Lassan-din's mother. But when she died, his unhealing
grief had turned him ruthless and iron-willed. He had
become a despot, capricious, cruel, never giving an inch of
his power to another man—even his spoiled and insecure
son. Disease had left him wasted and witless in the end.
And Lassan-din, barely come to manhood, had been helpless, unable to block his jealous uncle's treachery. He had
been attacked by his own guard as he prayed in the temple
(*In the temple*—his mouth pulled back), and maimed,
barely escaping with his life; to find that his entire world
had come to an end. He had become a hunted fugitive in
his own land, friendless, trusting no one—forced to lie and
steal and grovel to survive. He had eaten scraps thrown
out to dogs and lain on hard stones in the rain, while the
festering wound in his back kept him from any rest . . .

Reliving each day, each moment, of his suffering and
humiliation, he felt his rage and his hunger for revenge
grow hotter. The Earth hated this usurper of Her holy

place, the girl had said . . . but no more than he hated the
usurper of his throne. He climbed to his feet again, every
muscle on fire, and held out his hands. He shouted the
incantation aloud, as though it could carry all the way to his
homeland. *His homeland:* he would see it again, make it
his own again—

The power entered him as the final word left his mouth,
paralyzing every nerve, stopping even the breath in his
throat. Fear and elation were swept up together into the
maelstrom of his emotions, and power exploded like a sun
behind his eyes. But through the fiery haze that blinded
him, he could still see the water heave up from its bed—a
steely wall crowned with white, crumbling over and down
on itself. It swept toward him, a terrifying cataclysm, until
he thought that he would be drowned in the rushing flood.
But it passed him by where he stood, plunging on over the
outcropping roof of the cave below. Eddies of foam swirled
around his feet, soaking his stained leggings.

The power left him like the water's surge falling away.
He took a deep breath, and another, backing out of the
flood. His body moved sluggishly; drained, abandoned,
an empty husk. But his mind was full with triumph and
rejoicing.

The ground beneath his feet shuddered, jarring his elation, dropping him giddily back into reality. He pressed his
head with his hands as pain filled his senses, a madness
crowding out coherent thought—a pain that was not his
own.

(Water . . . !) Not a plea, but outrage and confusion, a
horror of being trapped in a flood of molten fire. *The
dragon.* He realized suddenly what had invaded his mind;
realized that he had never stopped to wonder how a storm
might communicate with a man: Not by human speech,
but by stranger, more elemental means. Water from the

fall he had created must be seeping into its lair . . . His face twisted with satisfaction. "Dragon!" He called it with his mind and his voice together.

(Who calls? Who tortures me? Who fouls my lair? Show yourself, slave!)

"Show yourself to me, Storm King! Come out of your cave and destroy me—if you can!" The wildness of his challenge was tinged with terror.

The dragon's fury filled his head until he thought that it would burst; the ground shook beneath his feet. But the rage turned to frustration and died, as though the gates of liquid iron had bottled it up with its possessor. He gulped air, holding his body together with an effort of will. The voice of the dragon pushed aside his thoughts again, trampled them underfoot; but he knew that it could not reach him, and he endured without weakening.

(Who are you, and why have you come?) He sensed a grudging resignation in the formless words, the feel of a ritual as eternal as the rain.

"I am a man who should have been a king. I've come to you, who are King of Storms, for help in regaining my own kingdom."

(You ask me for that? Your needs mean nothing, human. You were born to misery, born to crawl, born to struggle and be defeated by the powers of Air and Fire and Water. You are meaningless, you are less than nothing to me!)

Lassan-din felt the truth of his own insignificance, the weight of the dragon's disdain. "That may be," he said sourly. "But this insignificant human has penned you up with the Earth's blessing, and I have no reason to ever let you go unless you pledge me your aid."

The rage of the storm beast welled up in him again, so like his own rage; it rumbled and thundered in the hollow of the mountain. But again a profound agony broke its fury, and the raging storm subsided. He caught phantom images of stone walls lit by shifting light, the smell of water.

(If you have the strength of the Earth with you, why bother me for mine?)

"The Earth moves too slowly," *and too uncertainly,* but he did not say that. "I need a fury to match my own."

(Arrogant fool,) the voice whispered, (you have no measure of my fury.)

"Your fury can crumble walls and blast towers. You can destroy a fortress castle—and the men who defend it. I know what you can do," refusing to be cowed. "And if you swear to do it for me, I'll set you free."

(You want a castle ruined. Is that all?) A tone of false reason crept into the intruding thoughts.

"No. I also want for myself a share of your strength—protection from my enemies." He had spent half a hundred cold, sleepless nights planning these words; searching his memory for pieces of dragon-lore, trying to guess the limits of its power.

(How can I give you that? I do not share my power, unless I strike you dead with it.)

"My people say that in the Golden Times the heroes wore mail made from dragon scales, and were invincible. Can you give me that?" He asked the question directly, knowing that the dragon might evade the truth, but that it was bound by immutable natural law, and could not lie.

(I can give you that,) grudgingly. (Is that all you ask of me?)

Lassan-din hesitated. "No. One more thing." His father had taught him caution, if nothing else. "One request to be granted at some future time—a request within your power, but one you must obey."

The dragon muttered, deep within the mountainside, and Lassan-din sensed its growing distress as the water

poured into the cave. (If it is within my power, then, yes!)
Dark clouds of anger filled his mind. (Free me, and you will
have everything you ask!) *And more*—Did he hear that
last, or was it only the echoing of his own mind? (Free me,
and enter my den.)

"What I undo, I can do again." He spoke the warning
more to reassure himself than to remind the dragon. He
gathered himself mentally, knowing this time what he was
reaching toward with all his strength, made confident by
his success. And the Earth answered him once more. He
saw the river shift and heave again like a glistening serpent,
cascading back into its original bed; opening the cave
mouth to his sight, fanged and dripping. He stood alone on
the hillside, deafened by his heartbeat and the crashing
absence of the river's voice. And then, calling his own
strength back, he slid and clambered down the hillside to
the mouth of the dragon's cave.

The flickering illumination of the dragon's fire led him
deep into the maze of stone passageways, his boots slipping on the wet rock. His hair stood on end and his
fingertips tingled with static charge, the air reeked of
ozone. The light grew stronger as he rounded a final corner
of rock; blazed up, echoing and reechoing from the walls.
He shouted in protest as it pinned him like a creeping insect
against the cave wall.

The light faded gradually to a tolerable level, letting him
observe as he was observed, taking in the towering,
twisted black-tar formations of congealed magma that
walled this cavern . . . the sudden, heart-stopping vision
they enclosed. He looked on the Storm King in silence for
a time that seemed endless.

A glistening layer of cast-off scales was its bed, and he
could scarcely tell where the mound ceased and the dragon's own body began. The dragon looked nothing like
the legends described, and yet just as he had expected it to

It let its breath out upon him . . .

181

(and somehow he did not find that strange): Great mailed
claws like crystal kneaded the shifting opalescence of its
bed; its forelegs shimmered with the flexing of its muscles.
It had no hindquarters, its body tapered into the fluid coils
of a snake's form woven through the glistening pile. Immense segmented wings, as leathery as a bat's, as fragile as
a butterfly's, cloaked its monstrous strength. A long sinuous neck stretched toward him, red faceted eyes shone
with inner light from a face that was closest to a cat's face of
all the things he knew, but fiercely fanged and grotesquely
distorted. The horns of a stag sprouted from its forehead,
and foxfire danced among the spines. The dragon's size
was a thing that he could have described easily, and yet it
was somehow immeasurable, beyond his comprehension.

This was the creature he had challenged and brought to
bay with his feeble spell-casting . . . this boundless, piti-
less, infinite demon of the air. His body began to tremble,
having more sense than he did. But he *had* brought it to
bay, taken its word-bond, and it had not blasted him the
moment he entered its den. He forced his quavering voice
to carry boldly, "I'm here. Where is my armor?"

(Leave your useless garments and come forward. My
scales are my strength, lie among them and cover yourself
with them. But remember when you do that if you wear
my mail, and share my power, you may find them hard to
put off again. Do you accept that?)

"Why would I ever want to get rid of power? I accept it!
Power is the center of everything."

(But power has its price, and we do not always know
how high it will be.) The dragon stirred restlessly, remembering the price of power as the water still pooling on the
cavern's floor seeped up through its shifting bed.

Lassan-din frowned, hearing a deceit because he expected one. He stripped off his clothing without hesitation

and crossed the vast, shadow-haunted chamber to the gleaming mound. He lay down below the dragon's baleful gaze and buried himself in the cool, scintillating flecks of scale. They were damp and surprisingly light under his touch, adhering to his body like the dust rubbed from a moth's wing. When he had covered himself completely, until even his hair glistened with myriad infinitesimal lights, the dragon bent its head until the horrible mockery of a cat's face loomed above him. He cringed back as it opened its mouth, showing him row behind row of inward-turning teeth, and a glowing forge of light. It let its breath out upon him, and his sudden scream rang darkly in the chamber as lightning wrapped his unprotected body.

But the crippling lash of pain was gone as quickly as it had come, and looking at himself he found the coating of scales fused into a film of armor as supple as his own skin, and as much a part of him now. His scale-gloved hands met one another in wonder, the hands of an alien creature.

(Now come.) A great glittering wing extended, inviting him to climb. (Cling to me as your armor clings to you, and let me do your bidding and be done with it.)

He mounted the wing with elaborate caution, and at last sat astride the reptilian neck, clinging to it with an uncertainty that did not fully acknowledge its reality.

The dragon moved under him without ceremony or sign, slithering down from its dais of scales with a hiss and rumble that trembled the closed space. A wind rose around them with the movement; Lassan-din felt himself swallowed into a vortex of cold, terrifying force that took his breath away, blinding and deafening him as he was sucked out of the cave-darkness and into the outer air.

Lightning cracked and shuddered, penetrating his closed lids, splitting apart his consciousness; thunder clogged his chest, reverberating through his flesh and bones like the crashing fall of an avalanche. Rain lashed him, driving into his eyes, swallowing him whole but not dissolving or dissipating his armor of scales.

In the first wild moments of storm he had been piercingly aware of an agony that was not his own, a part of the dragon's being tied into his consciousness, while the fury of rain and storm fed back on their creator. But now there was no pain, no awareness of anything tangible; even the substantiality of the dragon's existence beneath him had faded. The elemental storm was all that existed now, he was aware only of its raw, unrelenting power surrounding him, sweeping him on to his destiny.

After an eternity lost in the storm he found his sight again, felt the dragon's rippling motion beneath his hands. The clouds parted and as his vision cleared he saw, ahead and below, the gray stone battlements of the castle fortress that had once been his . . . and was about to become his again. He shouted in half-mad exultation, feeling the dragon's surging, unconquerable strength become his own. He saw from his incredible height the tiny, terrified forms of those men who had defeated and tormented him, saw them cowering like worms before the doom descending upon them. And then the vision was torn apart again in a blinding explosion of energy, as lightning struck the stone towers again and again, and the screams of the fortress's defenders were lost in the avalanche of thunder. His own senses reeled, and he felt the dragon's solidness dissolve beneath him once more; with utter disbelief felt himself falling, like the rain . . . "No! No—!"

But his reeling senses righted abruptly, and he found himself standing solidly on his own feet, on the smoking battlements of his castle. Storm and flame and tumbled stone were all around him, but the blackened, fear-filled faces of the beaten defenders turned as one to look up at his; their arms rose, pointing, their cries reached him dimly. An arrow struck his chest, and another struck his shoulder, staggering him; but they fell away, rattling harmlessly down his scaled body to his feet. A shaft of sunlight broke the clouds, setting afire the glittering carapace of his armor. Already the storm was beginning to dissipate; above him the dragon's retreat stained the sky with a band of rainbow scales falling. The voice of the storm touched his mind a final time, (You have what you desire. May it bring you the pleasure you deserve.)

The survivors began, one by one, to fall to their knees below him.

Lassan-din had ridden out of exile on the back of the whirlwind, and his people bowed down before him, not in welcome but in awe and terror. He reclaimed his birthright and his throne, purging his realm of those who had overthrown it with vengeful thoroughness, but never able to purge himself of the memories of what they had done to him. His treacherous uncle had been killed in the dragon's attack, robbing Lassan-din of his longed-for retribution, the payment in kind for his own crippling wound. He wore his bitterness like the glittering dragonskin, and he found that like the dragonskin it could never be cast off again. His people hated and feared him for his shining alienness; hated him all the more for his attempts to secure his place as their ruler, seeing in him the living symbol of his uncle's inhumanity, and his father's. But he knew no other way to rule them; he could only go on, as his father had done before him, proving again and again to his people that there was no escaping what he had become. Not for them, not for himself.

They called him the Storm King, and he had all the power he had ever dreamed of—but it brought him no

pleasure, no ease, no escape from the knowledge that he
was hated or from the chronic pain of his maimed back. He
was both more and less than a man, but he was no longer a
man. Lying alone in his chambers between silken sheets
he dreamed now that he still slept on stones; and dreamed
the dream he had had long ago in a witch's hut, a dream
that might have been something more . . . And when he
woke he remembered the witch-girl's last words to him,
echoed by the storm's roaring—"May you get what you
deserve."

At last he left his fortress castle, where the new stone of
its mending showed whitely against the old; left his rule in
the hands of advisers cowed by threats of the dragon's
return; left his homeland again for the dreary, gray-clad
land of his exile.

He did not come to the village of Wydden as a hunted
exile this time, but as a conqueror gathering tribute from
his subject lands. No one there recognized the one in the
other, or knew why he ordered the village priest thrown
bodily out of his wretched temple into the muddy street.
But on the dreary day when Lassan-din made his way at
last into the dripping woods beneath the ancient volcanic
peak, he made the final secret journey not as a conqueror.

He came alone to the ragged hut pressed up against the
brooding mountain wall, suffering the wet and cold, like a
friendless stranger. He came upon the clearing between
the trees with an unnatural suddenness, to find a figure in
mud-stained, earth-brown robes standing by the well,
waiting, without surprise. He knew instantly that it was not
the old hag; but it took him a longer moment to realize who
it was: The girl called Nothing stood before him, dressed as
a woman now, her brown hair neatly plaited on top of her
head and bearing herself with a woman's dignity. He

stopped, throwing back the hood of his cloak to let her see his own glittering face—though he was certain she already knew him, had expected him.

She bowed to him with seeming formality. "The Storm King honors my humble shrine." Her voice was not humble in the least.

"Your shrine?" He moved forward. "Where's the old bitch?"

She folded her arms as though to ward him off. "Gone forever. As I thought you were. But I'm still here, and I serve in her place; I am Fallatha, the Earth's Own, now. And your namesake still dwells in the mountain, bringing grief to all who live in its cloud-shadow . . . I thought you'd taken all you could from us, and gained everything you wanted. Why have you come back, and come like a beggar?"

His mouth thinned. But this once he stopped the arrogant response that came too easily to his lips—remembering that he had come here the way he had, to remind himself that he must ask, and not demand. "I came because I need your help again."

"What could I possibly have to offer our great ruler? My spells are nothing compared to the storm's wrath. And you have no use for my poor body—"

He jerked at the mocking echo of his own thoughts. "Once I had, on that night we both remember—that night you gave me back the use of mine." He gambled with the words. His eyes sought the curve of her breasts, not quite hidden beneath her loose outer robe.

"It was a dream, a wish; no more. It never happened." She shook her head, her face still expressionless. But in the silence that fell between them he heard a small, uncanny sound that chilled him: Somewhere in the woods a baby was crying.

Fallatha glanced unthinkingly over her shoulder, toward
the hut, and he knew then that it was her child. She made a
move to stop him as he started past her; let him go, and
followed resignedly. He found the child inside, an infant
squalling in a blanket on a bed of fragrant pine boughs. Its
hair was midnight black, its eyes were dark, its skin dusky;
his own child, he knew with a certainty that went beyond
simply what his eyes showed him. He knelt, unwrapping
the blanket—let it drop back as he saw the baby's form. "A
girl-child," dull with disappointment.

Fallatha's eyes said that she understood the implications
of his disappointment. "Of course. I have no more use for
a boy-child than you have for this one. Had it been a male
child, I would have left it in the woods."

His head came up angrily, and her gaze slapped him
with his own scorn. He looked down again at his infant
daughter, feeling ashamed. "Then it did happen . . ." His
hands tightened by his knees. "Why?" looking up at her
again.

"Many reasons, and many you couldn't understand
. . . But one was to win my freedom from the Old One.
She stole my soul, and hid it in a tree to keep me her slave.
She might have died without telling me where it was.
Without a soul I had no center, no strength, no reality. So I
brought a new soul into myself—this one's," smiling
suddenly at the wailing baby, "and used its focus to make
her give me back my own. And then with two souls," the
smile hardened, "I took hers away. She wanders the forest
now searching for it. But she won't find it." Fallatha
touched the pendant of rock crystal that hung against her
breast; what had been ice clear before was now a deep,
smoky gray color.

Lassan-din suppressed a shudder. "But why *my* child?"
My child. His own gaze would not stay away from the baby

for long. "Surely any village lout would have been glad to do you the service."

"Because you have royal blood, you were a king's son—you are a king."

"That's not necessarily proof of good breeding." He surprised himself with his own honesty.

"But you called on the Earth, and She answered you. I have never seen Her answer a man before, or since . . . And because you were in need." Her voice softened unexpectedly. "An act of kindness begets a kind soul, they say."

"And now you hope to beget some reward for it, no doubt," He spoke the words with automatic harshness. "Greed and pity—a fitting set of god-parents, to match her real ones."

She shrugged. "You will see what you want to see, I suppose. But even a blind man could see more clearly." A frown pinched her forehead. "You've come here to me for help, Lassan-din; I didn't come to you."

He rubbed his scale-bright hands together, a motion that had become a habit long since; they clicked faintly. "Does—does the baby have a name?"

"Not yet. It is not our custom to name a child before its first year. Too often they die. Especially in these times."

He looked away from her eyes. "What will you do with—our child?" Realizing suddenly that it mattered a great deal to him.

"Keep her with me, and raise her to serve the Earth, as I do."

"If you help me again, I'll take you both back to my own lands, and give you anything you desire." He searched her face for a response.

"I desire to be left in peace with my child and my goddess." She leaned down to pick the baby up, let it seek her breast.

His inspiration crystallized: "Damn it, I'll throw my own priests out, I'll make your goddess the only one and you her high priestess!"

Her eyes brightened, and faded. "A promise easily spoken, and difficult to keep."

"What do you want, then?" He got to his feet, exasperated.

"You have a boon left with the dragon, I know. Make it leave the mountain. Send it away."

He ran his hands through his glittering hair. "No. I need it. I came here seeking help for myself, not your people."

"They're your people now—they *are* you. Help them and you help yourself! Is that so impossible for you to see?" Her own anger blazed white, incandescent with frustration.

"If you want to be rid of the dragon so much, why haven't you sent it away yourself, witch?"

"I would have." She touched the baby's tiny hand, its soft black hair. "Long ago. But until the little one no longer suckles my strength away, I lack the power to call the Earth to my purpose."

"Then you can't help me, either." His voice was flat and hopeless.

"I still have the salve that eased your back; but it won't help you now, it won't melt away your dragon's skin . . . I couldn't help your real needs, even if I had all my power."

"What do you mean?" He thrust his face at her. "Are you saying you couldn't ever undo this scaly hide of mine, that protects me from my people's hatred—and makes me a monster in their eyes? You think that's really why I've come to you? What makes you think I'd ever want to give up *my* power, my protection?" He clawed at his arms.

"It's not a man's skin that makes him a monster, or a god." Fallatha said quietly. "It's what lies beneath the skin,

behind the eyes—his actions, not his face. You've lost your
soul, as I lost mine; and only you know where to find it. . .
But perhaps it would do you good to shed that skin that
keeps you safe from hatred; and from love and joy and
mercy, all the other feelings that might pass between
human beings, between your people and their king."

"Yes! Yes, I want to be free of it, by the Holy Sun!" His
face collapsed under the weight of his despair. "I thought
my power would give me everything. But behind this
armor I'm still nothing; less than that crippled wretch you
took pity on!" He realized at last that he had come here this
time to rid himself of the same things he had come to rid
himself of—and to find—before. "I have a last boon due
me from the dragon. It made me as I am; it can unmake
me." He ran his hands down his chest, feeling the slippery,
unyielding scales hidden beneath the rich cloth of his shirt.

"You mean to seek it out again, then?"

He nodded, and his hands made fists.

She carried the baby with her to the shelf above the
crooked window, took down a small earthenware pot. She
opened it and held it close to the child's face still buried at
her breast; the baby sagged into sleep in the crook of her
arm. She turned back to his uncomprehending face. "The
little one will sleep now until I wake her. We can take the
inner way, as we did before."

"You're coming? Why?"

"You didn't ask me that before. Why ask it now?"

He wasn't sure whether it was a question or an answer.
Feeling as though not only his body but his mind was an
empty shell, he only shrugged and kept silent.

They made the nightmare climb into blackness again,
worming their way upward through the mountain's en-
trails; but this time she did not leave him where the mountain spewed them out, close under the weeping lid of the

sky. He rested the night with the mother of his only child, the two of them lying together but apart. At dawn they pushed on, Lassan-din leading now, following the river's rushing torrent upward into the past.

They came to the dragon's cave at last, gazed on it for a long while in silence, having no strength left for speech.

"Storm King!" Lassan-din gathered the rags of his voice and his concentration for a shout. "Hear me! I have come for my last request!"

There was an alien stirring inside his mind; the charge in the air and the dim flickering light deep within the cave seemed to intensify.

(So you have returned to plague me.) The voice inside his head cursed him, with the weariness of the ages. He felt the stretch and play of storm-sinews rousing; remembered suddenly, dizzily, the feel of his ride on the whirlwind. (Show yourself to me.)

They followed the winding tunnel as he had done before to an audience in the black hall radiant with the dust of rainbows. The dragon crouched on its scaly bed, its glowering ruby eye fixed on them. Lassan-din stopped, trying to keep a semblance of self-possession. Fallatha drew her robes close together at her throat and murmured something unintelligible.

(I see that this time you have the wisdom to bring your true source of power with you . . . though she has no power in her now. Why have you come to me again? Haven't I given you all that you asked for?)

"All that and more," he said heavily. "You've doubled the weight of the griefs I brought with me before."

(I?) The dragon bent its head; its horns raked them with claw-fingered shadows in the sudden, swelling brightness. (I did nothing to you. Whatever consequences you've suffered are no concern of mine.)

Lassan-din bit back a stinging retort; said, calmly, "But you remember that you owe me one final boon. You know that I've come to collect it."

(Anything within my power.) The huge cat-face bowed ill-humoredly; Lassan-din felt his skin prickle with the static energy of the moment.

"Then take away these scales you fixed on me, that make me invulnerable to everything human!" He pulled off his drab, dark cloak and the rich royal clothing of red and blue beneath it, so that his body shone like an echo of the dragon's own.

The dragon's faceted eyes regarded him without feeling. (I cannot.)

Lassan-din froze as the words out of his blackest nightmares turned him to stone. "What—what do you mean, you cannot? You did this to me—you can undo it!"

(I cannot. I can give you invulnerability, but I cannot take it away from you. I cannot make your scales dissolve and fall away with a breath any more than I can keep the rain from dissolving mine, or causing me exquisite pain. It is in the nature of power that those who wield it must suffer from it, even as their victims suffer. That is power's price—I tried to warn you. But you didn't listen . . . none of them have ever listened.) Lassan-din felt the sting of venom, and the ache of an ageless empathy.

He struggled to grasp the truth, knowing that the dragon could not lie. He swayed, as belief struck him at last like a blow. "Am I . . . am I to go through the rest of my life like this, then? Like a monster?" He rubbed his hands together, a useless, mindless washing motion.

(I only know that it is not in my power to give you freedom from yourself.) The dragon wagged its head, its face swelling with light, dazzling him. (Go away, then,) the thought struck him fiercely, (and suffer elsewhere!)

Lassan-din turned away, stumbling, like a beaten dog.
But Fallatha caught at his glittering, naked shoulder, shook
him roughly. "Your boon! It still owes you one—ask it!"

"Ask for what?" he mumbled, barely aware of her.
"There's nothing I want."

"There is! Something for your people, for your child—
even for you. Ask for it! Ask!"

He stared at her, saw her pale, pinched face straining
with suppressed urgency and desire. He saw in her eyes
the endless sunless days, the ruined crops, the sodden
fields—the mud and hunger and misery the Storm King
had brought to the lands below for three times her lifetime.
And the realization came to him that even now, when he
had lost control of his own life, he still had the power to end
this land's misery. Understanding came to him at last that
he had been given an opportunity to use his power posi-
tively, unselfishly, for the good of the people he ruled . . .
for his own good. That it meant a freer choice, and perhaps
a truer humanity, than anything he had ever done. That his
father had lost something many years ago which he had
never known was missing from his own life, until now. He
turned back into the view of the dragon's hypnotically
swaying head. "My last boon, then, is something else;
something I know to be within your power, stormbringer. I
want you to leave this mountain, leave these lands, and
never return. I want you to travel seven days on your way
before you seek a new settling place, if you ever do. Travel
as fast as you can, and as far, without taking retribution
from the lands below. That is the final thing I ask of you."

The dragon spat in blinding fury. He shut his eyes, felt
the ground shudder and roll beneath him. (You dare to
command me to leave my chosen lands? You dare?)

"I claim my right!" He shouted it, his voice breaking.
"Leave these lands alone—take your grief elsewhere and
be done with them, and me!"

They called him the Storm King, and he had all the power he had ever dreamed of.

(As you wish, then—) The Storm King swelled above them until it filled the cave-space, its eyes a garish hellshine fading into the night-blackness of storm. Lightning sheeted the closing walls, thunder rumbled through the rock, a screaming whirlwind battered them down against the cavern floor. Rain poured over them until there was no breathing space, and the Storm King roared its agony inside their skulls as it suffered for its own revenge. Lassan-din felt his senses leaving him, with the knowledge that the storm would be the last thing he ever knew, the end of the world . . .

But he woke again, to silence. He stirred sluggishly on the wet stone floor, filling his lungs again and again with clear air, filling his empty mind with the awareness that all was quiet now, that no storm raged for his destruction. He heard a moan, not his own, and coughing echoed hollowly in the silence. He raised his head, reached out in the darkness, groping, until he found her arm. "Fallatha—?"

"Alive . . . praise the Earth."

He felt her move, sitting up, dragging herself toward him. The Earth, the cave in which they lay, had endured the storm's rage with sublime indifference. They helped each other up, stumbled along the wall to the entrance tunnel, made their way out through the blackness onto the mountainside.

They stood together, clinging to each other for support and reassurance, blinking painfully in the glaring light of early evening. It took him long moments to realize that there was more light than he remembered, not less.

"Look!" Fallatha raised her arm, pointing. Water dripped in a silver line from the sleeve of her robe. "The sky! The sky—" She laughed, a sound that was almost a sob.

He looked up into the aching glare, saw patches that he took at first for blackness, until his eyes knew them finally for blue. It was still raining lightly, but the clouds were parting, the tyranny of gray was broken at last. For a moment he felt her joy as his own, a fleeting, wild triumph—until looking down, he saw his hands again, and his shimmering body still scaled, monstrous, untransformed . . . "Oh, gods—!" His fists clenched at the sound of his own curse, a useless plea to useless deities.

Fallatha turned to him, her arm still around his shoulder, her face sharing his despair. "Lassan-din. I always knew that you were a good man, even though you have done evil things . . . You have reclaimed your soul today—remember that, and remember that my people will love you for your sacrifice. The world exists beyond yourself, and you will see that how you make your way through it matters." She touched his scaled cheek hesitantly, a promise.

"But all they'll ever see is how I look! And no matter what I do from now on, when they see the mark of damnation on me, they'll only remember why they hated me." He caught her arms in a bruising grip. "Fallatha, help me, please—I'll give you anything you ask!"

She shook her head, biting her lips, "I can't, Lassan-din. No more than the dragon could. You must help yourself, change yourself—I can't do that for you."

"How? How can I rid myself of this skin, if all the magic of Earth and Sky can't do it?" He sank to his knees, feeling the rain strike the opalescent scales and trickle down —feeling it dimly, barely, as though the rain fell on someone else. Remorse and regret filled him now, as rage had filled him on this spot once before. Tears welled in his eyes and spilled over, in answer to the calling-spell of grief; ran down his face, mingling with the rain. He put up his hands, sobbing uncontrollably, unselfconsciously, as though he were the last man alive in the world, and alone forever.

And as he wept he felt a change begin in the flesh that met there, face against hands. A tingling and burning, the feel of skin sleep-deadened coming alive again. He lowered his hands wonderingly, saw the scales that covered them dissolving, the skin beneath them his own olive-brown, supple and smooth. He shouted in amazement, and wept harder, pain and joy intermingled, like the tears and rain that melted the cursed scales from his body and washed them away.

He went on weeping until he had cleansed himself in body and spirit, freed himself from the prison of his own making. And then, exhausted and uncertain, he climbed to his feet again, meeting the calm, gray gaze of the Earth's gratitude in Fallatha's eyes. He smiled and she smiled; the unexpectedness of the expression, and the sight of it, resonated in him.

Sunlight was spreading across the patchwork land far below, dressing the mountain slope in royal greens, although the rain still fell around them. He looked up almost unthinkingly, searching—found what he had not realized he sought. Fallatha followed his glance and found it with him. Her smile widened at the arching band of colors, the rainbow; not a curse any longer, or a mark of pain, but once again a promise of better days to come.

MY BONES WAXED OLD

ROBERT FRAZIER

ILLUSTRATION BY
REUBEN FOX

I
Her eyes like fire opals,
a rainbow flame blazing out of control in each,
she regards me with a grin like a piano keyboard,
enough ivory for a scrimshander's life work.

II
Her scales aren't iridescent, silver or pastel
green,
but a rusty copper like old faucet fixtures
sooted by the destruction her breath has
wrought;
our cobbled streets cindered in her wake.

III

Why have they invaded again like Normans or
Romans,
after being re-catalogued out of our memories?
Are the engines of Time in reverse?
Will St. George ride beside my Saab in full ar-
mor?

IV

In the smoke strewn dawn mist she dissects me
with stares,
her cut granite face a tiny yard from my
windshield;
as if it were her first encounter with the human
beast,
as if those broken houses were just jungle snags.

V

Before she turns, rose-thorned tail streaking my
hood,
I glimpse from her mind a thought like jagged
glass,
yet delicate with the texture of sentience:
we remain "turtle-apes," only the shells of our
armor grow.

SOLDATENMANGEL

VICTOR MILÁN

ILLUSTRATIONS BY
MICHAEL GOODWIN

The scarfaced, swarthy horseman spat through the bars
of his visor. "There's magic here, Captain."

The Captain rested gauntleted hands on his saddlebow.
His armor was black, his plume a brilliant red. "Of course
there is, Morisco," he said. "Why else would *Obrister*
Pappenheim order us to come instead of someone else?
He's too pious to admit it, but he knows his Captain
Tagenstern has skills other than sword and pistol."

"Can't you use your skills to destroy the thing, *Rittmeister?*" another asked.

He shook his head. "There's magic and there's magic.
Mine is demonomancy; this is temporal magic. I have no
power over it." His aquiline, black-bearded face settled
into pensive lines. "I've heard of only one practitioner of
time-magic, and I thought he was mythical. It appears I was
mistaken."

He looked out over the green-grassed Saxon valley.
Across it was a small and somewhat rundown castle, the
owner of which Tagenstern and his twenty-five Black Riders had been sent to bring to heel. Between the Riders and
the castle was a hill, and on that hill sat a monster.

To the side of the hill stood about fifty pikemen and
musketeers arranged into a lopsided square, apparently to
attend to any foemen who somehow managed to escape
the Creature. They were clad in green and purple, which
Tagenstern took to be the Baron's livery. It did not say
much for his taste.

There was no faulting his taste in guardian monsters,
however. The Creature was big and ugly and surrounded
with ominous debris. It was hung about with a remarkable
array of appendages. Most of them looked lethal.

"*Soldatenmangel,*" a Rider said portentously. He
crossed himself.

"What was that again, Streicher?"

"I saw a broadside the Evangelical heretics were passing
around to weaken our spirit," said the bearish man called
Streicher, whose eyebrows grew together in the middle of
his forehead. "It had a picture of a monster like that,
stuffing people into its mouth. They called it *Soldatenmangel*—the soldier-eater."

"How picturesque." Tagenstern's horse was tossing its
head nervously at the stench of the Creature, strong even
at this distance. He patted its neck soothingly. "Since
you're such an expert on the subject, suppose you tell us
how to deal with the thing."

The trooper was scandalized. "Attack it, of course! The
thing's a demon. It's our Catholic duty to destroy it at
once!"

"*Estúpido,*" Morisco muttered.

The Captain waved at the armor and white bones piled
about the Creature on its hilltop. "That seems to have
been tried before," he said, "without notable success. I
doubt we'd do much better."

"But we're under the protection of the Blessed Virgin!"
Streicher roared. "No witchcraft can hurt us. Are you with

me, Riders?" He ripped his sword from the scabbard and brandished it.

The Riders looked at him. They looked at their Captain. They looked at the Creature.

None of them moved.

In a rage, Streicher wheeled his mount and sent it lunging downslope toward the monster's hill. Morisco cursed and raised a carbine. Tagenstern pushed up the barrel. "Hold your fire."

Nostrils flaring, eyes red and rolling, Streicher's stallion charged up the hill. Its rider drove it full into the monster's flank. He gave a shout and drove his sword into the scaly side.

The Creature twitched. A scythe-shaped member dipped over its back and cut the Rider in half with a single snick. The charger went mad. It tried to flee. The monster's head moved with astonishing speed, and with a gulp of great jaws the horse disappeared. There was a crunch, a swallow, and a pleased puff of smoke from the stack with the jaunty red stripe encircling it.

"*Yallah,*" said Morisco. "I didn't know dragons breathed fire from their backs."

Tagenstern raised his visor. "You men would do well to bear in mind that the Black Captain is your commander, not the Virgin."

"Don't worry about us, Cap'n," a Rider responded in appallingly-accented German. "Streicher was a loon."

"Remember it, then. The next man to disobey me should hope the monster deals with him as well. It's more merciful than I am."

The Black Riders shuddered.

Tagenstern nudged his black. With the rest following he rode down into the valley to the foot of the monster's hill. The Creature watched them come with disparate eyes,

one big and moist and round like a frog's, the other a
many-faceted crystal orb with tiny glimmers of light inside
that danced and winked incessantly. As they approached,
the Creature raised its wings and shook them once.

A horse shrieked and reared. A stench of reptiles and
decaying meat washed over the cuirassiers in a hot rush of
wind. The Creature was pleased to see its appearance was
unnerving the intruders, if not their Captain. Its wings were
ornamental, of course, too small to lift its immense bulk,
but it felt they added a delightful *frisson* to the terror it
inspired.

Signing his men to wait below, Tagenstern rode straight
up the hill, slowly, to show his intentions were for the
moment pacific. *Remarkable,* he thought. *Not even I could
have conceived of such a thing.*

He saw a vast shape crouched atop the hillock. Along a
line from the tip of its unlovely snout to the end of its tail,
the Creature was divided in halves, one leathery and
scaled, the other burnished steel. Its mouth was wide, and
at each end showed a hint of tooth, one discolored ivory,
one metallic.

It took all his willpower to force his reluctant mount up to
stand before the being. "Good morning, monster," he
said, trying to talk and hold his breath at the same time.
"Can you speak?"

The Creature blinked twice. "Arrah," it said, then:
"Yes." Its voice was thunder, its breath brimstone.

"We have business with the master of the castle. May we
pass?"

"You may not." The earth trembled.

For a moment they regarded each other. "You are a
wizard?" the monster asked. Tagenstern performed a
mocking bow.

"I have been called that, yes."

The beast rumbled and smoked with pleasure. The casual quality of the admission convinced the Creature of its truth. The mere suspicion of wizardry was sufficient to earn one an unpleasantly warm demise at the hands of the authorities. This Captain must be a very potent sorcerer.

The dragon-id of the monster was thrilled. "Then we must have a contest," it said. "If you can pose me a problem I cannot solve, you may pass."

"A problem?"

"Just so. You see, I am bored. Utterly. I have the most stupendous intellect in all of history, and I cannot find enough to occupy it. I need diversion."

Lo, thought the Captain. "Very well," he said. "What goes on four legs in the morning, two at midday, and three in the af—"

"Man." The monster snorted, almost bowling Tagenstern from the saddle. "The riddle of the Sphinx. I have all known riddles and their answers in my memory banks. Riddles and word games are no use to me. Try again, please."

Tagenstem exhaled a trifle unsteadily. At least the thing was intrigued enough to give him another chance. Even with his powers he could not stand against the monster if it tired of the game.

He forced his mind into the past, to his youthful days at the Jesuit lyceum of La Flêche. If anything could enable him to stump the behemoth, his training for the Company should. He had been most studious, when he wasn't helling around with his classmates Grandier and that other youth, the skinny one with the mathematical bent . . .

"Aha," he said. "Compute *pi.*"

"3.1416," said the monster.

"To the hundredth decimal." His craft pleased him.

"3.14159265358979323846264338327950288419716939937510582097494459230781640628620899986

28034825342117O679," the monster replied, without an instant's hesitation. "No good. I can solve any mathematical problem in a fraction of a second. At the moment, my sole amusement comes from devising crossword puzzles with one part of my brain, and solving them with another." It sighed to shake the hill. "Unfortunately, I cannot resist the temptation to cheat."

The Captain grunted. This meant nothing to him—the idea of a Cross-Word puzzle (as he heard it) suggested some kind of Gnostic concept linking the Crucifixion with the Creation. He was busy following the hint of a trail through his memory.

That classmate of his, the mathematical one—what had his name been?—had also been interested in philosophy. Many an evening had they spent while he held forth over his cups, Grandier snoring drunkenly, Tagenstem good-naturedly listening as the young man tangled himself in twisted webs of logic and metaphysics. Even the youthful warlock had had difficulty following his arguments sometimes. If only . . .

Then, rosy-fingered, it dawned on him.

"My friend," he said with a glibness polished by years of lying in Confession, "your knowledge of things is incomparably vast. But yet—but yet, how do you know this knowledge to be *true* knowledge?"

"I do not understand." The huge eyes gleamed with interest.

"It is the soul of simplicity. You possess what you think is knowledge. But have you examined it in the cold light of philosophy?"

The Creature admitted it had not.

The Riders were growing restive behind their leader. Their mounts had long since settled into a sort of passive hysteria. He had to work fast before man or animal broke.

"Then I ask: how do you *know* anything?" His mind raced—was he following his friend's line of argument? It seemed to be working, at any rate. The fleshy half of what passed for the monster's brow was wrinkled profoundly. "Perhaps your knowledge is illusion, based on preconception and error."

"What you say may be true," said the Creature, in a voice like siege artillery. "But what am I to do?"

"Use your matchless reason! Apply the strength of your fabulous intellect. Reject all preconceptions—all that unbounded store of knowledge of past, of present, of future contained in your, uh, memory banks. Clear your mind and start afresh. Open yourself to those intuitive truths which thrust themselves upon your newly liberated . . ."

Like a tutor who perceives his pupil dozing off in the midst of conjugating a particularly troublesome Latin verb, Tagenstern let his words trail off. The monster lay utterly motionless. Its frog eye was half-lidded, and the light in its other was dim and distant. "Ahem," he said. The Creature did not respond.

Rank breath blew regularly through nostril and vented exhaust. The Captain leaned forward and rapped his knuckles upon the juncture of armor plate and hide at the tip of the nose. It rang hollowly. The monster muttered and twitched several of its members, then subsided.

The Black Riders cheered.

Tagenstern trotted down the flank of the hill. The pikemen shifted uneasily. They made no move to stop him as he headed for the castle. The Black Riders were the elite of the Holy Roman Empire, the most feared cavalry in Europe, and even with two to one odds in their favor the Baron's men were leery of tangling with them. Particularly since the Riders' leader had just defeated an invincible monster without working up a sweat. "Watch them,"

Tagenstern called to his men. "I'm off to meet this thing's creator."

The gates of the castle stood agape; with the Baron's pet horror on guard, there seemed no need to keep them secured. Two ancient sentinels stared in amazement as the black-shelled horseman spurred into the courtyard and dismounted with a thump of bootsoles on cobblestone.

One oldster came out of his fog and leveled a musket at the Captain from a distance of four feet. Tagenstern snapped down his visor. "Put that up before you hurt yourself," he said.

The old man pulled the trigger.

The serpentine plunged the smoking match into the primer. The powder in the pan sputtered and expired in a cloud of white smoke. Nothing happened. "Hold my horse," the Captain said. He left them as they stood, one obediently holding the reins of the warhorse, the other peering down the barrel of his musket.

Tagenstern made his way to the keep, mounted the steps that wound up into the tower. There was a door at the top of the stairs. He drew his sword and opened it.

At the sound of his footfall a white-bearded man whirled from a Gothic-arched window, nimble as a youth. Though he wore modern dress in the bilious shades of the household, he was quite clearly a Wizard. Scowling vigorously, he raised his arms above his head, muttered an incantation into his beard, and snapped his arms forward as if hurling a spear at the Captain. A glowing nimbus grew around his outsplayed fingers. A dazzling line of fire crept across the room. Air crackled at its passage.

Tagenstern waited until the deathbolt was a handsbreadth from his breastplate. Then he parried it with his sword, deflecting it downward so that it melted an irregular hole in the marble flooring.

The Wizard hissed in consternation. He gibbered words the Captain didn't understand and waved his arms in the air. At the far wall a small blue cloud appeared. Like thunderheads building of a summer's day it roiled and grew, and then unlike your normal cumulonimbus it began to resolve itself into a manlike form.

The Captain inclined his head. He sheathed his sword, drew from the scarlet sash around his middle a huge wheellock pistol, steel and blonde wood, chased with silver. Unconcernedly he pointed it at the appartition.

"Ha!" crowed the sorcerer. "That toy won't help you. Make an end of him, Azrafel—the barbarian damaged a priceless Roman flagstone!"

The indigo cloud had taken on solidity as well as a grotesquely gnarled shape. Its head was a boar's, its eyes purple flame—that color was a sort of leitmotiv in this castle, Tagenstern thought. The tusks in its grin, though, were white as a maiden's thigh, as were the talons at the end of its long arms, which seemed to have an extra joint apiece.

Toenails scraped the floor as the thing shuffled forward. Tagenstern took careful aim. Scrape and scrape and grin more widely, the demon drew closer. Tagenstern fired.

Flame shocked forth. The heavy ball caught the fiend in the chest, spun it half around. It staggered three steps and its head drooped to regard the violet-bleeding hole. The nightmare face lifted to stare at the cuirassier with incomprehension. Then the fire in its eyes went out and it fell to the floor. It decomposed rapidly into a stinking black mass that dissipated before the Wizard's bulging eyes.

"The carpet! A genuine Persian carpet, looted from the Holy Land by the first Baron Strumpp, and you've made my demon bleed on it!" He faced the intruder. "You have

"Make an end of him, Azrafel . . ."

magic powers, but you certainly lack refinement. Vandal. Visigoth. *Seisenaig!"*

"*I* lack refinement?" Tagenstern tipped up his bevor and slid the pistol back in his sash. "Look at yourself—green and purple?" He shook his head. "Nonetheless I greet you, Merlin Ambrosius."

"You know my name," the oldster said sourly, "but I do not know yours."

"Perhaps you do. *Rittmeister* Tagenstern, at your service."

"Tagen—*Helel ben Shahar!"* Merlin's jaw dropped.

"Or *Lucero,* in Spanish, or Daystar in your own adopted tongue," said the Captain, switching to flawless English. "No need to repeat the Latin. You're out of your sphere, friend Merlin. In this world you're a legend—a national myth of the Welsh."

The Wizard reddened. "A myth!" He knotted his fists and shook. He seemed on the verge of chewing his beard in wrath, which interested Tagenstern greatly, as he'd never actually seen anyone do it. "A myth, you say? I'll show you a myth!"

He stamped to the window. "Look, then!" he shouted. "See what this 'myth' has made!"

The Captain came up beside him. Merlin was pointing with obvious pride at the monster on its hill. Tagenstern nodded. "It's said you live backward in Time, and have a special affinity for that medium. I suspected you were the one responsible for that thing."

Merlin preened. "I brought its various components out of the past and the future and assembled them here. It is a dragon blended with the most sophisticated mechanisms of the future; its mind is half alive and half computer—half a device that can solve problems in an eyeblink it would take you until Doomsday to work out."

Tagenstern knew about that part already. "Impressive."

Merlin shrugged. "A tool," he said, which would have vexed the Creature sorely; for it believed Merlin had created it with no more in mind than Art for its own sake, proving we all have our small vanities, men and monsters alike. "I will use it to defy the future. I will undo the future I have experienced and replace it with a better one. I will preserve mankind from the horror of Tomorrow."

" 'The horror of Tomorrow?' " Tagenstern's tone was politely skeptical.

"The horror, I say!" Merlin began to pace. "The lung-searing smoke of industry, the slavery of sweatshop and factory, the rape of the good green earth, the evil worship of machines! Buchenwald, Dresden, Hiroshima—I will keep these things from happening!"

He stopped still. "The nightmare of the future is being made possible by the so-called advances of today. I will change that. I will save mankind from the evils of mechanism."

"A noble aim," Tagenstern said, drawing off his steel-backed gauntlets. His hands were long, almost delicate in appearance. "But I foresee a difficulty."

"Which is?"

"Myself. And my men."

Merlin scoffed. "Your men! What can they do to me? My monster will scatter them like sheep."

"I think not. Look more closely at your creation."

The Wizard went to the window and frowned out. "It does not move," he mumbled. He raised his voice: "You! Ho there, monster! Arise! Awaken! Consume these armored bravos."

The monster moved not so much as a wingtip.

"What have you done to him?" Merlin asked, turning. There was anguish on his narrow face. Tagenstern explained.

Merlin went white and red and hopped up and down on

one leg, and then he did chew on his beard. "You did
what?" he raged. "Befuddled my Creature with—with
damned Cartesian sophistry!"

Tagenstern smiled. "As you'd say—a tool."

The Welsh wizard uttered a terrible screech and spun
thrice widdershins in fury. He shrilled imprecations. Then
he drew himself to his full height—a head less than the
Captain's—and pointed a finger at his foe. "My magic may
not affect you," he said in doomful tones, "but your men
are not so well protected. Watch this!"

He turned and hurled a spell. From without came the
cries of frightened horses and men. Tagenstern lunged
past Merlin to look out.

What he saw made him afraid. Here was strong magic
indeed, and for the first time he doubted his chances of
coming away victorious from a contest with the ancient
mage. Out upon the greensward a dragon raised its toothy
head, and its scales were blood in the sunlight. Could the
Wizard call up terrors out of ancient myth with such facil-
ity?

No! As his men flew from the fire-breathing lizard,
Tagenstern gripped the sill and concentrated. He muttered
a few words of his own.

The dragon outlines wavered, diminished. The fleeing
Black Riders turned back and stared.

Standing on the turf was, not a dragon, but a half-grown
hound pup.

"Damn you," Merlin said.

Tagenstern sighed and turned to prop himself on the
window ledge. "You live backwards in time, my friend,"
he said, "so why didn't you know in advance how all this
would come out?"

The old man seemed to deflate. "That's one of the
damnable things about this time-line of yours," he said. "I
don't live in reverse. Or rather I *do,* from my normal

perspective. I'm passing along the timestream in the same direction as everybody else. Every second takes me farther from my goal."

"Your goal?"

"I have to get back to my own time, my own destiny. It's a long way from Saxony in 1627 to Arthurian England."

"True. But you can bring things here from other times. Why not magick yourself to where you wish to be?"

Merlin shook his head emphatically. "Too dangerous. Projection through time is chancy and uncertain. I could end up in the Devonian."

"Where's that? Wessex?"

"It's a When, not a Where." The Wizard crossed his arms. His tonguetip protruded pinkly between his lips. "How did you see through my illusion, anyway? It was a perfectly good seeming."

"I knew you could summon up dragons—but I thought it would take more than a couple of muttered canthrips to do it. You had all the time you needed to make your Creature. But not for that dragon."

"Ah." Merlin cocked his head. "Yes. It's quite difficult to produce an actual dragon, since they've never existed on this plane. On the other hand, something that has existed—or rather, *will*—may serve better. Yes, I do believe it might." He went to the window and reached into the sky.

"Blue Eagle Three, approaching last reported position Orange Army," Oberleutnant Hans-Ulrich Brückner *murmurs into his throat mike. Blue HQ's acknowledgment crackles in his ears.*

The Rhine is a leaden band below. The K-D hydrofoil passes, southbound. Banking, he sees passengers on the upper observation deck covering their ears against the banshee howl of his Phantom. He smiles.

The NATO troops designated Force Orange for the

*exercises are nearby, waiting for him to spy them out. But
there's something he must do first. He is a man in love with
his country's past. And one of Germany's monuments is
below: Marksburg, the only Rhine castle never to have
fallen.*

*"It's overcast and the light is bad. Brückner doesn't
mind. The weathered keep looks more Wagnerian under
clouds. He drops the F4F into a slats-down slow turn
around the castle. As he levels out he feels a sudden
dizziness and closes his eyes. When he opens them he
sees—*

Thunder split the sky down the middle. Tagenstern
winced reflexively, then leaned far out the window to stare
upward. A silver arrowhead was streaking away to the
east, trailing black smoke. The outcry of men and horses
was lost in the din.

"Behold the future," Merlin said smugly. "A Phantom
F4F. A fabulous machine built by our descendants to
destroy each other."

"A flying machine?"

"Exactly."

*—he sees blue sky and hills rolling gently off in all
directions. "Blue HQ, Blue HQ." His voice is ragged with
panic. "For God's sake, somebody answer!" Nobody
does. The radio gives only static. It's as if Blue HQ has
been swept from the earth.*

*Brückner's head whirls. He's blinked his eyes and found
himself over Saxony, a hundred fifty kilometers from the
Marksburg, fifty from the DDR. But that isn't the worst.*

*Below him, black and squat against the green, are
twenty-five shapes he knows too well from aerial identifica-
tion drills: the new Soviet T-72 tanks.*

This is no war game.

This is war.

"Your men cannot see it as it is, of course," Merlin said. "They can't conceive of anything like it. They see a dragon, a demon."

"Superlative sorcery. Congratulations." The Captain had to shout to make himself heard as the roar receded.

"It's based on affinities, as is all magic—yours on an affinity for Power, mine for Time. The man who rides and guides the skycraft has an affinity for the past. It created a gateway to ease his passage from his age to ours." Merlin smiled. "Naturally, he cannot assimilate what *he* sees any more than your superstitious ruffians can. His mind re-shapes what his eyes perceive into familiar images—familiar and inimical."

Silence. Brückner is alone. But not helpless. After making contact with Orange Army he was to proceed to a target range for simulated ground attacks; his Vulcan is loaded with 20-mm slugs and his wings are laden with air-to-surface missiles. Deciding, he puts the Phantom into a turn.

The demon ship came in low. A chattering cut across the clamor of its passage. Fountains of earth sprang up before it, blasting across the valley toward the cuirassiers. A horse pawed air in their path, its rider battling to control it. The earth-fountains cut them both in two. "Your phantom seems all too solid," Tagenstern said.

"Automatic cannon, more powerful than a culverin and firing hundreds of times a minute." The Wizard shook his fist. "Have at you, Sam Clemens," he yelled. "I'll show you Progress!"

The Phantom swept down again, straight for the castle. Masonry exploded from the walls. Tagenstern and the Wizard dove for the floor. The Captain found himself nose to nose with the fallen portrait of a plump, pale, slightly crosseyed man, clad in the ubiquitous green and purple.

The painting had a fat black hole in the middle of its subject's belly.

Again the Doomsday roared. This time there was no stacatto bark as the Phantom passed overhead, but a multiple *whoosh* instead. Tagenstem dragged himself to the window in time to see great flowers of flame blooming in the valley, throwing parts of men and horses into the air.

"How does it move so fast?" he asked, panting.

"A whirling fan impels air through a tube," the Wizard said. "Then—"

"Fan?"

A set of blades arranged like the spokes of a wheel," Merlin said impatiently. "They force the air into burning chambers, like bellows with a forge. The heated air expands and drives the ship like a bullet shot from a gun."

"Ahh," the Captain said. He rubbed his chin and frowned. *Like spokes of a wheel.* The Phantom was curving back for another run.

"Well," he said, rubbing cupped hands together, "I can't do anything myself about your war machine, but I can send for help."

He threw his hands forward. From between them fluttered a white dove. It hovered uncertainly, then winged away across the valley.

Merlin scowled. "There's nothing you can do, but you're tricky as Satan himself. We'll just see about your winged messenger." He crossed his arms and shut his eyes.

Serene, oblivious to the disturbance below, a hawk circled overhead. A tingling in the back of its skull, instinctual perhaps, made it turn and look back and down. Keen eyes caught the wink and flicker of white on green: a dove, choice morsel for a hungry raptor. It swooped.

The Phantom swoops toward the burning wrecks.

Brückner's thumb rests on the firing button. He is dead on target, ready to finish this.

At just short of the speed of sound the airplane's port engine sucked in the diving hawk. The Phantom canted right as broken turbine fan blades ripped its guts out. It soared over a ridge, nosed down. Yellow flame mushroomed, laced with black smoke. A rumble rolled across the hills.

Merlin stared speechless. He turned to Tagenstern so full of fury that his hair seemed to stand on end. "You conniving devil, what have you *done?*"

"Spiked his wheel for him." Tagenstern reached to his waist. "Time to end this shadow-play."

The old sorcerer's eyes widened as the Captain swung up a slender wheellock. "You've seen *Draco,*" Tagenstern said. "Now meet *Serpens.*"

""Why are you doing this? What does the future mean to you?"

"Nothing. I have my orders. I intend to carry them out."

Merlin sneered. "How very Germanic."

"I'm not a German."

The Wizard stood and stared as though fascinated by the slim muzzle of the pistol. "Why do you do it, any of it? You're a warlock. Why do you grovel in the dirt like a common peasant?"

"Perhaps it amuses me."

Merlin licked his lips. "Your bullets carry enchantment," he said. "I am not fated to die in this time and in this place. What would happen to the worldlines if you killed me?"

"Perhaps it amuses me to find out, as well." Tagenstern's voice was dry. "Fare well, enchanter."

He pulled the trigger. Toothed wheel spun against pyrites, sparked, filled the room with noise and fire and choking smoke. The explosion of the shot was met with

one greater. Tagenstern fell back, caught his spur on a fold
of carpet, clattered to the floor.

He lay a moment. A deep breath expanded his chest
within his cuirass. Nothing seemed broken. He stood.

And stared. No body lay before him. There were scorch
marks on wall and floor and a scent of sulfur in the air.
"Well, old man, it seems I've helped you on your way," he
said. The thought pleased him strangely. He raised pistol
to brow in salute, then turned to the stairs. There was work
yet to be done.

Armored horsemen rode from Castle Strumpp. They
had found the fat, ineffectual Baron—he of the bullet-
holed portrait—cowering in his dungeon, and hanged him
from a parapet. They were, after all, Black Riders, and they
had a reputation to uphold.

Other riders joined them in the valley. "The Baron's
men have run away, Captain," El Morisco said. "We could
not find one of them."

Tagenstern made a throwaway gesture. "Let them go.
Our business here is settled. But what about our own
losses?"

Tagenstern looked around. "I count only fourteen of us.
That leaves one unaccounted for."

"Oh." The Spaniard licked his lips. "Huppner, sir. After
the flying thing burned, we felt a . . . a sickness, and the
world spun around us." He looked sidelong at the Captain
as if fearful of being disbelieved.

"I can well imagine," Tagenstern said. "And then?"

"When the feeling passed Huppner and his bay were
gone, and in their place was—that." He jerked his head
toward the dormant hulk of the Creature. Perched atop its
smokestack was a peculiar beast with a mottled, leathery
brown hide. It was shaped like a bird, but it had no feath-

ers, and there was a pointed crest sweeping back from its narrow skull. Even as they watched it scratched itself beneath a parchment wing with its bony beak, uttered a dismal cry, and flapped off into the woods.

The Black Riders were too surfeited with wonder to do more than stare numbly after it. "A creature from another day," the Captain said. "Merlin said my trying to kill him might disorder our reality. Instead it caused a temporal tempest, I imagine, and that—" He gestured at the departing flyer. "—that was part of the flotsam it washed into our own age."

The half-breed shook his head. Such matters were forever beyond his comprehension. Of which he was most glad.

They rode round the foot of the hill on which the Creature lay. Its lord and creator gone from the world, it was vanishing piecemeal, bits and fragments fading from view as entropy called them home. Its metal side was streaked with rust.

"I . . . think," it mumbled through dying steel and fleshy lips as they rode by. "I think, therefore I—am . . ." Its great head drooped. The crystal eye cracked across.

"Sophistry," the Captain said.

By the fittings of the room in which he'd awakened, and the stench of sewage that seeped in through the shuttered window, the old man ascertained that he was still in the seventeenth century. Despite his destiny to serve as Arthur's ally in the wars against the Saxons, he was not above employing some choice phrases the invaders would bring with them in his passion of disappointment.

Sounds from without made him stir. He rose from the bed, went to the window and cracked the shutter. Outside was afternooning. A trio of men clad in blue, with leather boots rolled high up their thighs and rapiers thrust through their sashes, sat impatient horses in the yard.

One of them cupped gloved hands to his mouth. "!ar-rive we ere end Rochelle La of siege the Lest" he called. "!d'Artagnan haste Have" The three rode backwards out of the muddy courtyard.

The shutter went back, returning the room to semidark-ness. The old man hummed with satisfaction as he settled himself back on the bed.

He was closer to home after all.

ALAS, MY LOVE, YOU DO ME WRONG

JAMES TUCKER

ILLUSTRATIONS BY
VAL AND JOHN LAKEY

Paul Garrett was twelve years old when he discovered he hated his father.

It was the long winter that comes every third year of Solitude's elliptical orbit. Paul and his father, Gerard Garrett, were hunting. At Paul's hip were the long knife and scabbard his mother had made for his birthday. In his hand was the bow his father had carved, and on his back the quiver of arrows his father had made. He was a man now, his father had said, presenting the gifts. They walked the woods, climbed the hills, descended into hollows, stalking, stalking, quietly searching out the small animal they called deer.

"See that," Garrett whispered and he pointed to small brown pellets lying on the snowy path. He picked one up and easily crushed it between his fingers. He smelled it and then wiped his fingers on his pants. Paul stood patiently watching.

"Pick one up, son. Crush it and smell it." Paul did so. His father started walking again along the deer trail.

"They're deer droppings, son, and fresh ones too. It's important now that we walk quietly and keep our eyes and ears alert for game." They went on, the big Garrett trailed by the little one. Above them Solitude's sky was gray with clouds. It would snow during the night. Before then they would return to the research station, sanctuary for the three sole humans on the planet.

Paul's father sighted the first deer, a buck, grazing among dry leaves still clinging to a tree. Without a whisper, in certain silence he moved his hand in slow motion signal to Paul. His hand stopped and he stood like some ancient statue of the forest pointing the way to the living, breathing intruder and saying, *kill it, kill it now and place it on the altar at my feet.* Paul stood quiet and still. Almost without motion the arrow was in his bow. He drew it, aiming. The bow bent forever like the shadowed arch of some dusky rainbow. He took one silent breath, completed his aim; and the creature turned and looked into Paul's eyes. Almost it seemed to say, *yes, kill me now. I am ready. I have come and I have stood still so you can kill me swiftly with great joy and without regret. You are the hunter. You are the man.* Paul's hand began to waver in tense, nervous jerks. He let go the arrow. It was gone. He looked out at the deer. He hadn't even seen where the arrow went. A moment later the deer, too, was gone.

"Damn." said Garrett.

"I'm sorry, Dad, I—"

"I'm sorry, too. Let's get going. *Maybe* we'll spot another." Garrett moved out and his son followed. They hadn't gone fifty meters when Paul tripped on some brush, making a small noise. Garrett stopped.

"Paul, if you want to hunt you're going to have to learn to walk quietly." His face was hot with anger. They walked on. Another fifty meters, Garrett stopped and turned. "And listen, if you get another shot I don't want to hear any of this, *sorry Dad.* You know and I know how well you can shoot. There's no excuse for your missing that buck."

"I just—"

"I said there's no excuse; do you understand?"

Paul was silent.

"Yes, sir."

"Good. Now keep quiet and watch for game." Garrett turned and stepped away.

Three hours later Paul's father signaled again. It was another buck. Paul was ready. This time, he thought, this time I will kill you. He aimed and let go the arrow; but in the last instant all the hours of practice, the tedious shooting at targets on trees, all the coaching from his father, the mastered perfection, it all failed. In the last instant that his fingers gripped the arrow, he tensed and wavered. The arrow flew more than two meters to the side of its mark. In a rage Paul drew another arrow and sent it off at the buck, still standing there, mocking his efforts. The arrow struck a tree. The buck looked up at the tree and then went back to his mocking. Another arrow and another arrow and another arrow and on until none were left and, his face a shambles of grit and tears, Paul threw down the bow and ran screaming at the deer. It vanished like a phantom into the woods. When Paul quit shouting after the animal he turned and saw his father walking toward home. Ashamed and angry, Paul gathered his bow and followed his father, who would not turn back and walked so intently toward the castle that Paul could not catch him.

The box shaped building, erected almost overnight from prefabricated materials, little resembled a castle, but because it had a moat to keep away annoying animals, and a draw bridge, to the Garretts it *was* their castle.

"Shouldn't a man's home be his castle?" Garrett had once asked. They all agreed, and that was that.

The research station was a year old and was the first permanent observation post on Solitude. Gerard and

Judith Garrett found their work challenging and exciting. They studied the planet's weather and climate, and its geology, and most important to them, its life forms. The post was so new that hardly a day passed without discovering and classifying some new species. During the winter many animals were in migration, such as the deer, and so they had encountered species whose summer habitat was from a region in the north and whose winter quarters waited farther south. And as much as they enjoyed their work, they, nevertheless, looked forward to the end of the month when a ship would arrive, bringing their replacements.

Paul looked at the moat. It was frozen and useless; the bridge was down for the winter. The Garretts didn't worry. There were no dangerous animals in the area and none had migrated through it. Paul walked across the bridge and spoke to the door. It opened. He walked into the castle. It was warm, peaceful. *The Young Prince and the Young Princess* from Rimsky-Korsakoff's *Scheherazade, op. 35* was playing softly on the speaker system. It was his mother's favorite music. Its brightness offered nothing to Paul. He went sullen to his room. Later, at supper, Paul's mother tried to cheer things but there were no words between Paul and his father. When it was time for Paul to go to bed he went to kiss his father but was given instead a stern, demeaning glance. He walked away, certain his father would never love him again. In his room he considered the bow. Tomorrow, he thought.

In the night Judith Garrett came to her husband and folded the warmth of her body around him.

"You're too hard on Paul," she said.

"I love you," he said. He hesitated, "Maybe you're right."

When Paul woke he could hear his mother singing some

old Earth chant while she busied herself preparing experiments in the lab. Paul walked from his room to the kitchen. Unwashed breakfast dishes were in the sink. He went to the lab. His mother greeted him with a hug and a kiss.

"Mom, where's Dad?"

"Oh, he left hours ago," she said and went back to her instruments.

"Where did he go, Mom?" Paul stood shocked, unbelieving.

"Hunting. He took his bow and went hunting again." She looked at him and smiled, then went back again to her instruments.

"How could he do that? How could he go without me?" He was forcing back tears.

"Now, Paul, don't worry. He'll take you again. He was just up early and didn't want to wake you." She held a test tube to the table lamp. "Run get yourself some breakfast now."

Paul walked past the kitchen. He went to his room and got his bow, went outside and sat on the draw bridge, staring into the forest. After a while he could hear faintly the music of Albinoni's *Adagio* coming from within the castle. Its slow sad marching was his own, and he could feel his mind walking to the edge of the world and stepping into oblivion.

It was nearly noon when Paul's father came walking out of the woods, a bloody, stiff deer draped over his shoulders. Paul got up from the bridge and went into the castle. He went again to his room and sat silently on his bed. He wanted then to cry, to show himself how badly he was hurt and how painful he felt, but he would not. He would not because he knew that if he cried, when it was over he wouldn't hurt any longer and all would be well again, for a while, and he didn't want the false relief that tears always brought. He looked at the bow on his lap. He grabbed it at the ends and began to bend it, wanting suddenly to snap it, to break it and thereby symbolically break his father. The bow wouldn't break. Raging, he threw it under the bed. He stood then in the center of his room, breathing hard, gritting his teeth, promising to never forgive *him,* not ever.

Later his father brought him outside to watch the skinning and butchering of the deer. Paul had refused but his father insisted.

"Either you want to be a hunter or you don't. You decide. But I'll tell you some things. A hunter doesn't lose his patience because he misses a shot. A hunter doesn't cry because he's tired. A hunter doesn't refuse to learn what he must know. And as for throwing down your bow, the *weapon* is everything. A hunter never throws down his weapon. It is what makes him what he is. Without it he may become the hunted. Never forget that."

Garrett began to peel away hide with his sharp, glimmering, stainless steel knife. Paul watched the hide come away from the flesh, red and cold and white. The dead animal had lost all its beauty, all its glory, and was more dead than anything Paul could imagine. He looked at his father. The man was smiling and happy as he worked on the animal. There was some other beauty and glory reflected in his eyes. Paul could see it. What was it, he wondered. Was it the feel of the flesh? Was it the softness of the hide or the sharpness of the knife? No, thought Paul. It was none of these things and yet it was all of them. It was the cutting, the tearing, the rending apart of something that had been lovely, graceful and alive. It was going beyond the killing. It was the butchering. Standing there, twelve years old and afraid, Paul wanted it. He wanted to slice away at the dead animal. His father looked at him.

"Here," he said, handing over the knife. "You try it."

Paul stared at the knife, dim with blood, glistening with steel. His father shoved it at his hand. Paul backed away and looked at the man.

"I have my own knife," he said.

"So you do, use it." The father waited.

"No. I'll be a hunter. I will, but not with you." He walked away, toward the woods. The man watched him and said nothing.

Paul made his way down the last slope leading to the lake. He stepped through the cold, shoving at branches and dry shrubs. Eventually he walked out onto the ice and stood there, panting a little. It was warmer, it seemed, on the ice than walking through the woods. The ice was a huge vague mirror, white and pale silver. He watched the wind carry brittle leaves across its surface to the far edge of the lake, and he watched his own foggy breath disappear into the ice white day.

Across the lake he saw the deer. It was casually, calmly, mockingly walking to the edge of the lake. It stood there and began to beat on the ice with its hooves, digging a hole for water. Paul listened to the sound, the cracking again and again at the sterling ice. Then the deer's leg went in a ways.

It cracked some more at the ice and then began to drink. As it drank Paul slowly drew an imaginary arrow from an imaginary quiver and set it in his make believe bow. Oh, why, he thought, did I go off without it? A weapon is what makes the hunter. He drew the dream string and took the most perfect aim that any archer has ever taken, he knew. He paused and considered the deer. Good-bye, he thought, and let go the perfectly aimed arrow. He watched it sail silently across the lake in a gentle lazy arch. He watched it make its way to the deer's breast and heart.

And as the arrow buried itself Paul saw a night-blue

shadow descend from the woods and fall upon the deer. There was no sound. There was no thrashing or battle. One moment the deer was drinking, the next it lay beneath blue-scaled death and its bright red blood flowed onto and across the ice before it froze.

It's a dragon, thought Paul, trembling. At least it looks like pictures of dragons, unreal giant lizards breathing fire and speaking the language of men. But no smoke came from its snout and Paul was certain it spoke no language. Move, he told himself. His feet wouldn't budge. Move! Get the hell out of here! Like the blood of the deer he was frozen solid on the ice. The dragon thing continued to eat, pawing at the carcass and tearing out great chunks of flesh. Paul watched as its tail swung lazily back and forth across the ice. Paul managed to slide his feet backward, centimeters at a time. He could faintly hear the chewing and gnawing of bone. He ordered himself to run, to go. It was useless.

The tail stopped moving. The beast lifted its head from its feast, turned its face to the sky, and growled. Its growling was the ancient murmur of its species, telling all that it alone was king, that it alone was majesty. The hills and hollows echoed its message. When the growling was done and the echoes were gone the beast turned and stared directly at Paul, just as had the buck the day before. It did not move. It did not blink, its eyes great round black balls on each side of its head. It stood like a rock, a silent blue frozen breath of destruction. Paul, too, was silent, frozen. The creature slipped a large forked tongue from its mouth and the tnogue dipped down and licked the ice. Paul didn't move. The tongue licked awhile and then slid back into the mouth. The head, sparkling sapphire, went back to the corpse of the deer.

Paul turned and ran. He dodged trees, jumped logs, ran;

ran climbing out of the hollow, away from the lake. Fear and sweat and cold burned out of him and through him. He dodged a bush and leaped too late to avoid a log. He was down, his face in the snow. He sat up, snow clinging to his cheeks, and turned for the first time. He had come a hundred meters easily, and below and across the lake, the thing was still eating at the deer. Paul stood, less frightened, brushed the snow from his face and clothes, and started home again. After a while his running became a trot. By the time he reached the station, home, the castle, he was walking. He stopped on the bridge and looked back into the woods. He stood there and wondered what it had been. A dragon, he told himself.

Inside, he found his parents sitting at supper.

"Paul, where have you been?" his mother asked. He stared at her and didn't know what to say.

"*Answer* your mother when she's talking to you!" his father yelled. What's wrong, Paul wondered. Why are they so upset?

"I, I went hiking, down to the lake, I—"

"You've been out *too* long. For that, young *man,* you can skip the supper you're late for. Go to your room." His father went back to eating. Paul stared at him and then turned to his mother who seemed helpless. The man looked up.

"I said, go to your room!" His father's face was red. *Something's* wrong. What is wrong?

"Dad—" His father stood up and his hands went to his belt buckle. Paul turned without another word and fled to his room. He started to slam the door, thought better of it, and closed it quietly.

Later, while he was lying in bed, staring at the ceiling, he could hear his father shouting, and could feel his mother quietly standing by.

"How can they do it!" he demanded, and Paul could feel his mother shrinking.

"An *extra* year in this Godforsaken hole! They *can't!* God, Judith! Tell me they can't! Tell me they can't!" Judith was silent.

"It's criminal! It's not possible! I'll *kill* the bastards!" It was as though Judith wasn't there. Garrett went on and on, decrying the injustice. Finally he stopped, and there began a long silence.

Paul got out of bed and walked from his room. The castle living room was dark but he could see them on the floor. They were naked and their bodies were wrestling urgently. He could hear their heavy breathing, and their sweat made their bodies smack and crackle as they moved. He wanted to go to his mother, to pull his father's hands away from her, to pull him off her body. But he stood and watched and listened, and finally they held still and Paul's mother began to whisper words Paul couldn't hear. He stared at them a while longer and then went back to his room and to his bed.

Later he heard them walking about. There was a faint knock at his door.

"Come in."

"Hi. Thought you might be hungry." She set a tray with sandwiches, milk, and cookies on the bed. "Your father's upset tonight, Paul."

"What's wrong, Mom? What's going on?"

"Paul, we got word today that we won't be leaving Solitude next month. It'll be another year before the ship gets here." Paul looked confused.

"Why? Why are they doing that?"

"Don't worry. We'll be all right. I'm sure it's just scheduling problems. Don't worry." She came close and gave him a hug and a kiss. "Eat your supper and then get some sleep. Okay?"

"Sure, Mom." She started to leave. "Mom?"

"Yes, dear."

"What about Dad?"

"Don't worry about your father. He's all right. And he doesn't mean to hurt you. Anger is just his way."

"Sure. Good-night, Mom."

"Night, son."

'After he had eaten and climbed into bed, Paul lay in the darkness and remembered the lake and the deer and the creature.

"I'm not a little boy any longer," he told the dark. He rolled over and reached under the bed. His hand gripped the hard smooth wood and he brought the bow out and laid it against his chest. Tomorrow, he thought, I will prove it. He drifted to sleep with visions of his arrow piercing the cold blue scales.

Paul left the castle before dawn while his parents were still sleeping. He headed for the lake. When he got there the first light was reflecting off the ice and cast a strange low rainbow on the lake. He crossed to where the deer had been killed. The hole it had made was frozen over. Everywhere there was frozen blood and bones. Paul glanced around the bank in search of tracks. They were easy to spot. The beast's trailing tail left an easy path for him to follow. There was only one trail leading from the lake and Paul reasoned the animal, the dragon, must have left the same way it came. He reached behind his back to check the security of his quiver. All well, he set out on the trail. The hunt began.

By noon he had crossed the crest of five hills. The trail had taken him nearly due east of the lake. At the bottom of the third hollow the trail divided. Paul took what looked like the fresher trail. It headed north. Four hours, and many hills, hollows, and windings later, he was back at the lake. The creature had returned for water. Already its water hole was frozen. Paul walked onto the ice and kicked the frozen hole with his boot. The ice cracked. He knelt and took his knife from its scabbard. He used it to pick at the ice. A few minutes later he was lying on his belly and scooping water into his mouth. He swallowed quickly, the water cold and sudden and perfect in his throat. He was pushing himself up when the shadow fell from behind him onto the ice. Paul rolled istantly, his hand at his knife, the eight inch blade flashing, an agent of death. The shadow moved.

"What are you doing there, boy?"

Paul looked at his father, relaxed, began breathing again.

"I'm hunting. And I'm not a *boy*. Not any longer. I'm a *man*. I'll prove it if you'll just leave me alone. I don't need your help." He started to get up; his father tripped him and he fell.

"Having trouble standing on your own feet, little boy?" Garrett smiled. "Well, maybe you don't need my help, but for today it's time to get back. It'll be dark soon." He reached out and grabbed Paul's arm, hauling him up. Paul retrieved his bow from the ice and walked over to the bank. He pointed, indicating the trail.

"That's what I've been hunting," he said, never smiling once, trying and trying for the seriousness that would cause his father to take him seriously. The man walked to the bank and his eyes followed the trail into the woods.

"What is it?" he asked the boy, his eyes never leaving the trail as it wound between the trees and became obscure only a few meters away. Paul hesitated.

"What is it, I said."

"A dragon," Paul said. His father looked at him.

"A *what?*"

"It's some kind of large lizard-like creature. It looks like a dragon, like the pictures we have of dragons, anyway."

"You made this trail, Paul, don't joke with me." He playfully cuffed at the boy, but Paul ducked and Garrett's hand only waved through the air. Paul didn't feel like playing.

"It's not a joke. Over there. I saw it kill a deer yesterday. Look at the bones."

Garrett walked over and examined the bones. He looked at Paul, and then again at the bones. He saw the old trail winding into the woods.

"It was large, larger than *you*. It has blue scales, and when it was eating it growled like angry live gravel and it had a tongue nearly as long as my arm." Garrett wondered. There were no reports of any large reptilian species in this climate. Still, the surveys were far from complete, such animals could exist. This could be the first signs of a migration.

"Why didn't you tell me about this yesterday, Paul?"

"I—"

"Be quiet." Garrett cut him off, remembering well why the boy hadn't.

"I'm going to kill it, Dad."

"You're going home with me now. I'll see to this thing, this *dragon* of yours, tomorrow."

"No!"

The man turned on the boy. "What's that?"

"I said no!" Paul was yelling and standing stiff with his arms stiff at his sides.

"Listen, son. We're going home. What do *you* know? What are you doing out here anyway? You're not a man, son. You're a silly little boy who's gone off without sense enough to tell the people who care about him where he's going. And you're *no hunter*. Any fool could have followed that trail. Just as any fool could lie face down with his back to it. Just like any fool did. What if it had been that animal instead of me that walked up on you while you were drinking?"

Paul stood silent, shivering.

"Let's go."

"No!"

Garrett walked up to his son and glared at him. Without warning he struck, slapping the boy's face. Paul spun and fell.

"Let's go," Garrett said again, unsmiling. "Now!"

Paul scrambled to his feet, rubbing his face, trying to erase the heat of the slap. They walked away together with long hard hot steps that spoke their anger and exasperation with each other.

Descending the last hill before the castle, Paul mumbled.

"What's that?" his father asked.

"I said I *hate* you." They walked on. Garrett said nothing. The silence of the evening was broken only by their feet cutting through the snow. They were about a hundred meters from home when Paul first heard the growling. He stopped.

"Come on, boy."

"Listen, Dad. Listen."

Garrett stopped. There was only the sound of shadow and sunset. No wind. No birds. The solemnity of nothing. Then from the castle came the heart of the deep, the cold broken-ice sound of growling.

"That's it, Dad. That's how it growled yesterday, when it was eating the deer." Garrett paused in thought, then broke into a run. Paul followed.

They found her remains on the draw bridge. The monster was gone and all that was left of their wife and mother was a mass of scrambled blood and bones and flesh. Garrett screamed and cursed. Paul stood motionless, his eyes filled with the sight that had been his mother.

Darkness began to fill the hollow. Paul got down on his knees and wrapped his arms around his head. He tried to shut out his father's screams, tried to turn away from the man's wild dance as he dashed in and out of the woods cursing the monster, the castle, space research, and Paul. But Paul kept watching, could not take his eyes off his father's stomping, cursing, spitting, damning, until at last the man fell down in the snow and layed there moaning.

Paul turned away from his father. Numb, he walked into the castle. He came back and on his hands and knees went about gathering the strewn bones and flesh. He put them into a plastic bag, sealed it, took them into the castle and left the bag on the kitchen table. He walked into the living room. His father was there. His face was pale and wet with melted snow. He held his rifle and was shoving bullets into its loading magazine.

"What are you doing, Dad?" Paul watched, bewildered. Garrett looked at his son and moved for the door.

"I'm gonna get that thing, tonight!"

"*Dad!*" Garrett was gone. Paul wondered what to do. He tooked at the kitchen door. Everything inside him exploded. Tears he didn't know were there washed down his face. He walked out the door and watched his father, rifle and heat lamp in hand, walking into the woods, illuminating and warming the night. He walked onto the bridge and his foot kicked something. He looked down. It was his bow. He picked it up out of the muck of blood. He looked at the woods. He could still see the light from his father's lamp. He looked at the bow, the blood, the light. He reached behind his back. The quiver of arrows was still secure. He moved out. I'm going to kill it, Mom, he thought. Not Dad. *He* never loved you as much as I did. I'm going to kill it, Mom. I swear. He headed after the light. Damn you, he thought, thinking not of the creature but of his father.

In the castle the sound system came on automatically at 1830 hours. Through the open door of the castle the world Solitude listened reverently to Handel's *Messiah* performed by the Arcturus Capitol Symphony and the Mormon Tabernacle Choir.

Paul followed his father from the dark. *Here,* he thought, I'll have the advantage. *I'll* have the first shot. It will be my arrow that takes it, not *his*. He watched his father following the trail leading away from the station, heading to the lake. Neither Paul nor Garrett knew how fast the thing, the dragon, moved, but leaving a trail like it did it was only a matter of time before they caught it, and then killed it. Paul could easily see his father's face and he knew that killing the dragon was all that mattered to the man. It was all there was and all there ever would be, and Paul hated him more because of it.

The light moved away and Paul followed, farther and farther into night and woods and the certainty that the hunt would not stop until the wild blue scaled dragon was dead at their feet and Judith was avenged. By my arrow, thought Paul. *Then,* they could celebrate. *Then* they could grieve.

In the night, with the heat lamp lighting their way, there were no colors but black and white. Paul, stalking his father, who in turn stalked the dragon, stopped. He stood in the center of night. His father moved away. It was like waking from a dream. What was real and what was imagined? Had it happened? Is Mom back there, butchered, slaughtered, gone forever, he wondered. Is there some dragon-thing ahead with Dad chasing it? He looked at his hands. They were knuckle hard and clamped the long and deadly bow. He stared at it, held it to the dwindling light. The bow became the only reality, the sureness of all things, living and dead. Paul then understood the nature of truth. It is death, he thought, and moved out after the light.

Paul grinned, secure, knowing he would be the one, *never* his father. In his mind he could see the dragon, scales sparkling, and he imagined again and again drawing the bow string and letting fly the arrow that would prove his love to his mother and that would mock his father's manhood. He's old, thought the boy, and I'll tell him so. I'll tell him how much I hate him and how worthless he is that he has a son who hates him and a wife that is dead because he could not protect her.

He saw his father stumble and slide on his knees out onto the ice of the lake. Garrett came to a halt. Paul stepped behind a tree and leaned into a dead branch.

Crack.

The sound of breaking wood shocked the boy and the father. Garrett held high the light. Nothing. Nothing. He fired into the abyss of darkness. Nothing. You can't kill me like you killed her, thought Paul. Garrett got to his feet. Paul watched him study the trail. It ended at the lake's edge. Where had it gone, wondered the man. Where had it gone, wondered the boy. Garrett raised the lamp as high as he could and looked out across the ice, black and glistening in the artificial light. There was nothing. The man started walking the circumference of the shore, searching. The boy stepped onto the ice, and watched, waiting.

Garrett circled half the lake. He came to the deer bones, went a little farther and stopped. There was nothing. He sat down on a large rock protruding from the ice. Paul watched him put the lamp at his feet. The lamp immediately began to melt at the frozen lake. Garrett didn't mind. Paul watched, waiting, waiting.

You're here, thought Garrett. He stared into the light, taking in its warmth, bathing himself in light.

Paul walked to the center of the lake and stopped. Who's the hunter, he wanted to call. What kind of fool sits at a light so that he can become the victim of his own quarry? Any fool, he thought. Just as any fool has. I'll tell him what a fool he is. He saw his father stand behind the light and bend slowly to pick it up. The man's shadow leaped huge from behind him and buried the hill beside the lake in blackness that only ended when it reached the sky and the stars. His father held the lamp between them, and Paul could see the rifle cradled in his arm. His father turned and the shadow on the hill danced, then grew larger.

Paul saw the dragon first. In an instant an arrow was in his bow and drawn. The dragon came out of the shadow and stood on the ice, facing Garrett. The lamp fell to the ice. Garrett brought the rifle to his shoulder. The monster lunged.

"No!" Paul screamed and took aim. "Dad, run!"

Paul let sail the arrow. He heard it strike, solid. The dragon paused. Paul saw his father lying on the ice, the arrow in his chest. Then the dragon was on the body, feeding, and its blue scales sparkled in the light of the lamp.

Paul could not move. He watched the dragon. He wanted to draw another arrow. He wanted to kill the thing. He could not move. The beast gnawed, gnawed and tore and swallowed. And then it lifted its head to the stars, and growled. The growling was its voice of victory, its claim to freedom, its statement of self and purity. The growl was its anthem to the dead it devoured. Hearing it again, Paul was released, released and hating and ready to kill. Destroy the growl, he thought, the growl that meant the dragon was finishing his mother, the growl that meant it was filling itself on his father. Destroy it. He took an arrow from the quiver and it was long and lean and straight in his bow. He pulled smooth and certain, drawing the kiss of death. He focused his aim on the dragon, and the dragon turned. Just as it had the day before, just as the deer had done, it looked directly into his eyes. Paul tensed, his aim wavered, he let go the arrow and it flew past the dragon and into the waiting dark. A moment later the heat lamp melted through the ice and fell into the lake. The only light remaining was the ghostly glow from the lake bottom and the twinkling of the stars. Paul turned and ran. And ran. And ran.

He was blisters and sweat when he topped the hill overlooking the castle. Far in the distance he could see a light coming from the door. He walked, too far gone for running any longer, down the hill, into the hollow, hoping to be caught. Not a man, he thought, a nothing. I loved no one. I hated my father and killed him. But it was an accident. Was it? Sure. Was it? I killed him. That's all that matters. And if I had truly loved my mother she would be alive now. Mindless, he still held the bow and walked stumbling and slipping between the trees. *I ought to be the dead one, not them. Why couldn't it have been me? Oh, please God, bring them back and let it be me.* On and on he went, down and down into the hollow, slowing for the dragon, knowing it would catch him, that it must. He was alone, he knew, and it was too much. Remembering the night before when his mother brought him supper, and had hugged and kissed him, he began again to cry. And when he could cry no more he discovered that indeed the weeping had made nothing better.

He stepped out of the woods into the clearing that surrounded the castle. The door to the castle was open and light from within fell upon the bridge and lit the clearing. The wind began to stir and it was getting colder. He walked

"I'll kill you now," he told them.

toward the castle, stepped onto the bridge and it creaked.
He stopped, turned back to the woods, giving the monster
one last chance to catch and destroy him. He did not want
to be home, did not want to face its emptiness, the same
emptiness that he knew was everywhere. He turned again
to the castle and listened, realizing for the first time that
music was coming from the sound system, *Greensleeves.*
He began to sing the words, tears again falling from his
eyes.

Alas my love, you do me wrong
He sat down on the bridge and leaned against his bow.
To cast me off, discourteously.
He stared into the soft, inviting light of the castle.
And I have loved you so long,
A shadow moved inside. He stopped singing.

"Mother!" He was up, running at the door. The shadow
filled the doorway.

The dragon walked out of the castle and onto the bridge.
They both stopped, less than ten meters apart. Paul faced
it.

It was beautiful, half silouetted in the light of the door. Its
scales shimmered like blue scalpels against the night.
Greensleeves was all my joy, thought Paul, the music still
playing. He wasn't afraid against such beauty, and he held
still not from fear but from awe. The monster waited for its
eyes to adjust again to the dark. It bowed its head and
licked the ice in the moat. Paul watched, fascinated. It
began licking his mother's blood. He reached for an arrow.
His quiver was empty. Too late, he considered his sudden
motion.

The dragon rushed him. Paul dived. His shoulder
slammed into the ice of the moat, and he slid. Stopped.
Held still for death. *Kill me now,* he thought, waiting for the
pain, waiting. But the only pain that came was the ache

and swelling in his shoulder. He looked up. The dragon was gone. Where, Paul asked himself. Why am I alive? Lying in shadow, ice, and guilt, the answer came, he heard the growling.

Paul got to his feet. The dragon was standing at the edge of the clearing. It was darker there but Paul could see the other dragon coming out of the woods. They were growling and pawing at each other. Are they going to fight, Paul wondered. The dragon from the woods began to push and climb at the other. And then Paul knew what was happening. They were mating. He saw the long slender organ slide under the female and into her body. They growled another moment, wrestling slowly, and then they froze, the growls became murmurs until in silence they were transfixed together by their own greatest desire.

Paul climbed from the moat and walked toward the creatures. They must have seen him, but they remained rigid. Like many similar species, they entered a strange comatose state while mating. Paul circled them, amazed that they were so completely shut off from the world. He stared into their eyes, large black pools. He smiled. The music still played, *And who but my Lady Greensleeves.* Watching them in their moment of glory he remembered the night before and the last time he had seen his parents together.

"I'll kill you now," he told them.

They didn't move.

"I'll carve out those great dark eyes." He climbed the dragons and straddled the neck of the male. Still they didn't move. He held the handle of his knife and slipped the blade from its scabbard. The music played. The wind was cool but Paul didn't notice his own shivering. He held the knife to the light. It gleamed, and he remembered his father skinning the deer. He listened to the music, and he remembered his mother singing. He felt good as he slowly sunk the blade into the male's eye and began to carve. Beneath the eye, he supposed, was the brain.

Greensleeves was my delight, he thought, cutting, slicing. Still they did not move.

The first bit of morning sun lit the castle and the hollow. Paul sat on the edge of the bridge, looking across the clearing at the beasts, their tongues swollen in their mouths. They were no longer beautiful. They were only dead.

I'm a *man* now, thought Paul. I have killed them. He looked at the dragons and was glad. He was the hunter. He thought of his father, his bones scattered on the lake. He thought of his mother, her remains in a plastic bag in the kitchen. He got to his feet. He walked across the bridge. The sun was up and it burned at his back. He went into the castle. Behind him he could hear growls coming from the hills and hollows. A large migration, he thought.

FEAR OF FLY

LYNN MIMS

ILLUSTRATIONS BY
RON MILLER

There was a fresh layer of slime on the walls.

Prince Bon (Bonny to his many friends) walked down the middle of the narrow hall, his arms drawn in to avoid the greenish stuff. They'd never had trouble with slime in the dungeons before; he wondered what sort of thrill his old bag of a stepmother got out of it. She spent a lot of time down here. He sighed, wondering why she had summoned him. He'd stayed out of her way as much as possible.

A figure wrapped in silken veils jumped into the hallway ahead of him and gestured him on. Despite the draperies, he had no trouble recognizing his stepmother: no one else had the shape of a block of granite or the grace of a staggering workhorse. He followed her to a barred wooden door and into the room behind it. And there he froze, staring.

Most of the chamber was curtained off with flaming red brocade: *So that's what happened to Father's favorite bedspread,* he thought. The only furniture he could see was a scattering of gaudy pillows, a mirror, a wooden chest . . . and a bed. He had the queasy feeling he knew why she had called him.

The mirror caught his attention briefly as the door closed behind him. He'd been heading for the stables when he received his stepmother's note; on his way to start another of the trips he made about the kingdom periodically. The tall, wiry figure in the mirror looked back at him wistfully, then jerked around as silk brushed the back of his neck. With a muffled curse Bon turned to face his adversary.

She sidled up to him coyly, the yellow veil slipping enough to reveal her sloping forehead and tiny blue eyes. What he could see of her was even harder and less appealing than usual.

"Welcome, dear boy," she husked. "I thought it was time we grew better acquainted . . . after all, I've been here six months now and you've been gone so much of the time. I want to get to know you." She laid a massive hand on his forearm.

I was afraid you might, he thought. *Why do you think I've been traveling?*

"Madam, this is completely irregular—" he began.

"But it could be so much fun," she crooned. There was something wrong with her voice, too: it was harsher, deeper than normal. He tried to pull away but the hand on his arm clamped down like a nutcracker. "And I've been so lonely," she added.

"You're my stepmother!" he sputtered.

"So?" She leaned against him; he caught a whiff of raw silk, sweat and formaldehyde. "Believe me, honey, six months with your father is like 60 years with any other man. Besides, I only married him so I could get to you."

"What?"

"And the kingdom, of course." She loosened the veil so it would fall if she shook her head, turned him to face her. "It's a very nice little place . . . and you're such a good-looking jock. Why fight?" She shook her head, tilted her face and waited . . .

Silence, while Bon tried to to find his voice. He found it. "What's that on your lip?"

The tiny blue eyes snapped open. Abruptly her expression changed as she got a look at herself in the mirror. "Damn!" she muttered, shoved Bon aside and ran behind the curtain. He picked himself up and followed.

She paid no attention to him, bent as she was over a spiderweb of tubes and beakers. Everywhere he looked were bubblings and oozings; the smell was enough to choke him. He put a hand nervously to his dagger.

She looked up at him with annoyance. "Dammit, I must have gotten the hormones mixed up. I should have known better than to use a man's recipe."

"Recipe?"

"I was trying to brew a love potion," she said irritably, "and it probably works—for men." She smoothed the faint dark mustache on her upper lip thoughtfully, then smiled. "Well, I suppose there are advantages. I can sing the bass line now in the Gregorian chants."

"If that's what you want," Bon said. She grinned.

"Among other things. I'll just have to keep working until I come up with something that'll affect you."

"I don't think Father would like that," Bon said slowly. Her grin twisted.

"And how will he ever find out? You were going to take a little trip, you might as well keep going. You don't think I'd let you tell him, do you?"

"I don't think you'll have any choice," he replied with more confidence than he felt, and drew his dagger. He stepped forward—

He thought he recognized his prison as soon as he woke. His stepmother chuckled at his look of dismay. "I thought this would be a good place to put you, dear.

Hardly anyone comes this way. And I've set a guard few men will face."

She's a witch, he thought. "What sort of guard? An ogre—or are you going to do it yourself?"

Her smile was a bit patronizing. "Actually, I'm into insects. Go take a look at him, dear."

Reluctantly Bon moved to the only window. As he'd suspected he was in the topmost level of a tower. There were a number of such places in that part of the world, erected by various evildoers. Naturally she'd know them all.

He was studying the ground beneath him when a flash of indigo caught his attention. A second later he leaped back from the window with a yelp as eyes the size of his head peered in at him. The hum of huge wings filled the room.

His stepmother had a maternal look. "Such a lovely creature," she said. "Dragons are in such short supply these days—louts like you keep killing them off. But I think this will do just as well. Don't you?"

Bon didn't answer. He was staring at the thing outside.

It was at least fifteen feet long, but that wasn't what made his stomach knot. Neither did the four glassy wings that droned as the monster hovered. Or its metallic blue scales or even the enormous, crystalline eyes. No, what froze him was quite simple:

It had a man tucked ito its six legs, held tightly to its slender body, and its serrated, pincer-like mandibles were ripping ito his neck . . . it had severed his spinal cord with one ragged bite. It was a noisy eater. Bon gulped as it rose out of sight.

"Don't worry, dear, it was just a tax collector," his stepmother rumbled. "My pet eats everything, of course. He's the largest dragonfly I've ever bred. He'll keep you safe enough. Unless—" she leered, "you'd prefer to come back with me right now—"

He shook his head wordlessly. "Very well," she said. "I'll be back."

She vanished in a puff of damp green smoke.

After a couple of abortive escape attempts Bon tried to settle into a routine. It wasn't a happy one. His only pastimes were crafts and watching the dragonfly attack other princes, who'd heard the local enchanted tower had a new inhabitant and assumed it had to be female. He was almost glad none of them ever reached the base of the tower; he would have had a hard time explaining. But he never had to try, for the dragonfly was eternally hungry and it had no trouble scooping up an attacker—horse, armor and all.

Now and then his stepmother would drop in to renew her offer. He grew desperate, but never *that* desperate, so after a while she'd puff out again and leave him to his brooding. Sometimes he wondered if Fate wasn't grinning at his predicament, and if it would ever end.

Though he didn't know it, help was on its way.

"It ate my horse," the exhausted young knight was saying at the back of the tavern. He'd collected a crowd in the hour since he'd first staggered in. One of his listeners, a young mercenary, tossed a coin to the inn-keeper and bought him another beer. He gulped it down at once.

"It dived on me from the tower," he continued. "The sun shone off its wings like gold fire! And those jaws! It knocked me off my horse and then it picked him up and—and carried him to the top of the tower." He paused. "I walked back. I never want to see anything like it again."

"But what was it?" someone asked. "A dragon?"

The knight looked down into the empty mug. "It—" he began, choked himself off. It came out in a rush. "It was a dragonfly!"

The man who'd asked him burst into jeering laughter. "You expect us to believe a story like that?"

"Let him speak," the mercenary said quietly. "I want to hear more about this. Just where is the tower?"

"On the border of Oxbow, due west of here." He shrugged. "There must be something in there worth guarding; I don't understand why Prince Bon hasn't looked into it. After all it's in his father's kingdom. But nobody's seen him lately."

"Gee, that's too bad," the mercenary said thoughtfully. She pushed away from the table and stood. The knight started.

"What are you going to do?"

She blinked. "I think I'll take a walk."

Her name was James, her profession wanderer. Her father, a diminutive scholar at the University of Oxbow, had wanted a son and decided to do the best he could with what he had. By the time she dropped out of school James had an abiding interest in two things: combat and entomology.

She had her problems. Damsels in distress were even more distressed when rescued by a sword-swinging female; and the men who were attracted to her (she was delectably feminine beneath her armor) were put off by her thirty-four inch longsword—aptly named Mankiller.

So she took to the road. She never lacked work. Jealous husbands found her the ideal chaperone for traveling ladies of rank. And the castle that sheltered her experienced a drastic drop in the vermin population as she experimented with pesticides and traps. She had just finished such a job when she met the unfortunate knight, and started packing.

Two weeks and fifty miles later she trudged over a hill and got her first look at the tower. The dragonfly was sunning on the pinnacle; she stared up at it and nearly dropped the 'Killer. "Hot damn," she said.

She hung around a few days to observe its habits. One other would-be hero showed up: an old man in patch-work armor, riding a swaybacked nag. He charged the tower and the dragonfly swept him up. Apparently, though, the old man and his horse were too tough and stringy: the fly dropped them. Luckily the man landed on his head. No one else came near. Word had gotten around.

James decided to move closer. The dragonfly hunted before dawn each day to supplement its diet; they weren't sending princes like they used to. It had been reduced to hunting alligators in the nearest swamp. So James watched it leave, its scales glimmering in the late moon-light.

She circled the tower searching for a door, but the only opening was the prince's window. She cursed.

The sound brought Bon to the window. He saw the dark figure below and knew what was needed. Being bright, he had prepared for this: one of his hobbies was macrame. He lowered his thirty-five-foot plant hanger to the visitor.

When he saw the projections on his rescuer's armor he nearly let go. James grinned and climbed faster.

She climbed over the edge at last and stood. "I thought you might be up here. But why haven't you tried to climb out?"

"I have. Mom put an alarm in the casement; the fly comes every time."

"Hot damn!" she said.

"Then we'll have to get rid of it." James began to empty her pack. "I've got a plan . . . is it male?"

"Male? Yes. Mom said it was," Bon said. "Why?"

"Because I did a little research on dragonfly pheromon back at the University," she said, mixing the contents of five vials. "Once he gets a whiff of this that dragonfly isn't going to pay any more attention to you."

"You're going to poison it?" Bon looked doubtful.

"No. Just hike up his sex drive. With any luck he'll go looking for a mate . . . we'll have to wait for him to get back. This works best at close range."

They waited nervously for dawn. Bon wasn't at all sure James' plan would work and frankly, neither was she. But it was all she could think of.

The rising sun showed them the dragonfly returning. Quickly James picked up the vial of pheromone and stood by the window with it. The prince took a deep breath. Their lives depended on the next few minutes . . .

It may have been inspired timing or simply lousy luck that caused his stepmother to pop in just then. In any case, a hand pulled James around just as she was uncapping the bottle. She found herself looking at the burly figure of the stepmother, who'd been so incensed she'd forgotten to shave. There was only one thing James could do and she did it. She dashed the pheromone over the other woman's new leather jacket and pulled away. She and Bon flung themselves against Mom's back and shoved her through the window. They leaned out of it to watch.

The pheromone worked perfectly. The dragonfly, convinced a giant-sized mate was nearby, dived to intercept the reeking stepmother. It misjudged its angle of descent and slammed into the wall, but James doubted it ever noticed. With his legs still wrapped around the object of his affection the dragonfly fluttered brokenly to the ground. She and the prince watched for nearly half an hour . . .

James turned away at last. "At least it died happy," she said. Bon grinned crookedly.

"So did she."

There was great rejoicing. When the two had finished rejoicing they put on their clothes and left the tower. Bon took James to his father's palace, where the relieved monarch appointed her Chief Biologist and they all tried to live happily ever after . . .

Well, at least they tried.

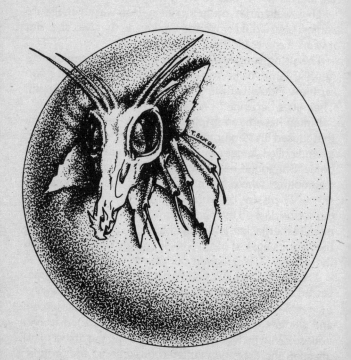

THOUGH ALL THE
MOUNTAINS LIE
BETWEEN

JEFFREY CARVER

ILLUSTRATIONS BY
JANNY WURTS

. . . In those days before the founding of the
Guild, riggers lived with constant insecurity.
Shrewd masters controlled them—often with
subtle means, but controlled them nevertheless;
and riggers then rarely supported one another
against abusive masters. But if they suffered in
the normal world, they found freedom in the net,
in the dream by which they steered their ships,
which their masters could never hope to share.
The lucky rigger found a way to carry that freedom out of the net, to the other side of life . . .

Jona'Jon'—*Gazing Into
Yesteryear,* for ages 7-11

The starship moved quietly through the Flux, though its
motion was invisible from the bridge, where Jael stood
facing Mogurn. Only instruments told her of the ship's
motion; she would see it for herself, more clearly, when
she entered the rigger-net. She waited anxiously.

Mogurn's eyes were dark and stern. With his hands folded across his heavy chest, he studied her with those eyes, kept her frozen. "Alright, Jael," he said, releasing her from his gaze at last. He glanced one final time over the thicket of instrumentation in the nose of the bridge, and then he indicated the rigger-station with a tilt of his head. "Go ahead and take the net," he said. "Don't tire yourself." With that he turned away, his robelike tunic spinning in folds, and he strode from the bridge. The door darkened to opacity behind him, leaving Jael alone in the ship's small control cell.

He doesn't trust me, she thought nervously, staring after Mogurn. Well, I don't care. She turned and made another brief inspection of the console, even though Mogurn had already done that with her, and then she climbed into the rigger-station, a couch recessed in a tight alcove on the starboard side of the bridge. She stretched out and relaxed gradually, staring at several mirrored monitors overhead as she tried to forget about Mogurn and think instead of the ship, of the Flux. She shut her eyes and let her neck settle against the neural contacts in the couch.

Her senses darkened and exploded outward into the rigger-net, outward from the ship, into the Flux. Into the streams of space. Jael opened her eyes to a vast and clear purplish sky; she floated like a seed high over a strangely glowing blue- and green-mottled landscape. The net glittered faintly around her, binding her to the invisible ghost of a spaceship which it was her duty to guide. She spread her arms, and in the net her arms billowed outward as great wings, filling with a rising updraft of wind. Jael (and the ship) rose, soaring.

The landscape beneath her was an odd matrix of color, reflecting her mood. It was her own image, painted by her mind on the flowing canvas of the Flux, on the currents which carried her and her ship through the curved passageways of space among the stars, bypassing the endless lightyears of normal space. The currents and tides of the Flux were objectively real, but it was her imagination, her thoughts and fantasies transmuted through the rigger-net, which detailed the realm through which she navigated.

Her feelings were quiet, now, and she flew silently through empty skies, daydreaming. She felt mildly depressed, neither happy nor actively unhappy, and she flew slowly, not even attempting to seek out faster wind currents. Hours went by, and she was content to float, to drift. Occasionally the landscape below shimmered and flared in response to tremors within her, aches which she kept unnamed. Certain longings she preferred not to allow expression; but whether she willed it or not, the landscape flared—now more and now less, sometimes with unfocused green fire and sapphire sparkles and sometimes with tiny billowing bloody plumes. The ache was always there within her and the landscape always responded to it.

She wished she could change the image somehow, drift away and leave the ache behind.

The com-signal chimed softly in her consciousness, and Mogurn's voice broke into her solitude. *Jael, what's wrong? The feedback out here looks poor.*

The landscape turned to brimstone and filled the sky with burning haze. She tried to control it, to cover her anger. *Nothing's wrong,* she answered. *Everything's fine.*

Are you sure? Mogurn's voice was low, disapproving. She envisioned him on the bridge, squinting anxiously, leering at her still form in the rigger-station. His voice was bodiless in the net, but physically he must be very near. She countered an urge to avoid him by retreating to the extremities of the net.

I'm fine, she said. The image was disintegrating, creating a potentially dangerous condition. She drew more energy into the net, trying to stabilize the image.

I'm depending on you, said Mogurn.

Jael didn't bother to answer. She thought hard a moment, searching her imagination, and then she focused on the angry horizon. The colors bled, and crimson sunset swelled over mountains to the northwest. Mountains . . .

The route through those mountains was actually the most direct to their destination, Lexis; but it was more dangerous, by all reports, than the skirting route Mogurn had ordered. Still, he had not absolutely forbidden her to fly in the mountains, and after all she was the rigger—she chose the images and the streams of the Flux to ride. Ultimately the choice was hers. The net sparkled as she grew excited—at the thought of danger, at the prospect of quickening the flight. She knew she shouldn't.

Abruptly she transformed herself into a mountain eagle, and she caught a new current and soared northwest, pulse racing, net glittering like diamonds in the Flux.

Sunset ahead. Twilight. Mountains jagged and black against a maroon sky, deepening into evening.

She scanned ahead with the edges of her mind. Would there be dragons? Riggers in the ports boasted of dueling with dragons along the Aeregian mountain routes. It seemed that there was a special quality of the Flux in this corridor which demanded mountain imagery and, sometimes, dragons. Many riggers believed the dragons to be living inhabitants of the Flux; others said they were just especially compelling images. Either way, it sounded dangerous; it sounded glorious.

A sense of quiet anticipation settled around her as she winged toward the mountains. She rather hoped that dragons might appear, to ease her loneliness.

The com-signal chimed again, chilling her pleasure. What now?

Isn't it time you came out? asked a bodiless Mogurn.

They were flying very low. Mountain landscape rushed by . . .

Is it? she replied, shivering in a sudden crosswind.

Six hours, Jael.

Six hours? she repeated, stalling.

What's wrong, Jael?

It may not be safe right now.

Not safe? Why not?

She spread her wings to catch a warm updraft. *Because*—and she hesitated, then said—*there may be dragons.*

His eyes squinted furiously, in her imagination. *Dragons? Dragons? The mountain route?*

Jael beat her wings furiously. *Yes.*

Find a stretch of safe passage. And then you come out and see me, Jael. His voice touched her like ice, and she stopped pumping. His anger made her tremble.

Yes, Mogurn, she answered, and the world grew cold with fear and loneliness. She did not want to face him, but she had no choice. Not if she wanted to receive the pallisp tonight.

Banking left, she flew parallel to the still-distant range, where she thought she could safely leave the net. But she stalled, gliding, watching the ominous peaks to her right, wishing that the fear and the loneliness would somehow subside. Finally she reluctantly set the stabilizers, the starship's sea-anchor in the Flux; and she set the alarms. Her senses melted back into her body as she withdrew from the net, and she opened her eyes, blinking, and looked around the rigger-cell and the bridge. Gloomy. Lonely. Nothing but instruments to greet her. She preferred it that way.

She climbed uneasily from the pilot-station and stretched. Her stomach said hunger, and her limbs said weariness. But Mogurn had said come immediately. Sighing, she left the bridge and went to Mogurn's cabin door;

the ship was only a small floater, and the compartments were tightly clustered, so it was a matter of a few steps. She pressed the signal fearfully. The door paled and she stepped inside.

Mogurn was seated facing her, smoking. When she entered, he rose and gestured for her to sit. She slid onto a narrow bench-seat; above and behind her an expensive crystal tapestry covered half of one wall. Mogurn exhaled sharp-scented smoke and frowned, studying the end of his long, tubular smoking pipe. "Jael, why did you disobey me?" he said.

Jael shivered, certain now that he would deny her the pallisp. "I meant no disobedience—" she stammered, which was at least half true. He'd not forbidden her to rig through the mountains; he'd only made it clear that he disapproved of that route, that in fact perhaps he was afraid of the mountains, or of the dragons.

Mogurn stepped closer, hovering over her, alternately blocking and exposing the light panel behind him. Jael squinted nervously. "Did I not say that I preferred the longer route, Jael? Was there some special circumstance you haven't told me of, some need to take the more perilous course?"

Was that fear in his voice? No; he was the master. Jael bit her lip. "I—was having trouble—the other way. But this way—I think the stories are just stories. Dragons! They can't be real."

"What is 'real' to a rigger?" Mogurn asked sharply. "What is in the Flux, or what is in the mind? Either can destroy us."

Jael nodded mutely.

"And, drunken sods though most of those riggers may be, one should never laugh at a rigger legend, should one?"

"No."

"Now, are we still close enough to our original course to turn back?" He exhaled another cloud of smoke, which drifted past her face to be sucked into the ventilators. She opened her mouth to reply in the affirmative, but something stuck in her throat. She shook her head. "We can't avoid the mountain?" he growled, and she shook her head again. Mogurn stared at her, smoking. After a long moment, he turned away.

When he turned back, he held a small, gleaming cylinder with a dull grey sphere attached to one end. "All right, Jael. It is time for your pallisp," he said. His eyes showed no kindness, but his words nevertheless sent a thrill of relief down Jael's back. Unhappiness and loneliness welled up out of her soul in anticipation.

At Mogurn's gesture, she bent forward and pushed her hair up from the back of her neck. Mogurn stood close beside her and lowered the pallisp until the grey ball touched the base of her skull. She felt the touch, cool, and then a warmth seeped into her from the touch, a warmth which encircled the ugly, waiting feelings of alienation, of fear, of anger, and which closed around those feelings like flowing blood, heating and soothing and transforming the emotions, stripping and softening shells of defense and filling her with love, with companionship . . .

The wave turned cold. Jael swayed with dizziness as a tide of paranoia rushed over her. The pallisp was gone. She sat up, blinking wildly, struggling to hold back tears. As Mogurn spoke, she could hardly see him through blurred eyes. "That's all for tonight, Jael. You must understand what obedience means, even for a rigger." Jael trembled, desperate with pain and frustration. Finally she steadied herself. Mogurn said, nodding, "Now, Jael, help me with my augmentor—and then you may retire."

. Though dying to scream, she obeyed. Mogurn reclined and she fitted the synaptic augmentor to his head and adjusted the controls; and when Mogurn was reduced to a silent figure fluttering his hands or pawing himself with a blind-eyed grin, Jael backed away and fled to her cabin. The pallisp—lord how she wanted it, needed it to take the lonely bitterness from her soul and turn it into something warm, and she would almost kill for it, but only Mogurn knew how to use it and so she needed Mogurn, too. She stalked the tiny deck space of her cabin, brooding, and then she tossed and writhed violently in the sleep-field, unable to rest. Unable to stop thinking.

Unable to stop remembering.

Remembering . . . Dap, and the night and the dream-link. Dap had been gentle and yet willful, telling her of the intimacies to be shared by riggers with the help of the dreamlink machine. And she had been young then—she was young now—and she had been seduced by his earnestness, his offer of friendship. Even now she could see his eyes, dark and earnest under silver brows, as he told her, "We'll be looking right into one another, and our souls will link . . ."

. . . They drove in a groundcar from the rigger hall to a cottage retreat where the dreamlink machine was located. They glided over the roadway in a gorgeous pink sunset. Jael steeled herself as they stopped, as they walked up to the retreat—a real house, not a multiplex—but Dap touched her arm, smiling. The gesture lent her enough strength to overcome her doubt and her suspicion; and she entered the house with Dap, moving about touching walls and banisters with nervous curiosity. In a small back living room, the dreamlink machine, a specialized type of synaptic augmentor, was set up—a half-silvered hemisphere which projected a golden glow when Dap turned it on. "We'll just let the field coalesce for a few minutes," he said. "Sit down and relax." He gestured to paired-off seats just at the fringes of the golden field.

"What's going to happen? How will I know?" Jael asked nervously, thinking to herself, he's your cousin good old Dap and why are you worried, he knows what he's doing. Dap smiled at her question and leaned forward to touch her hand gently. His eyes twinkled, and she thought he was amused by her naivete, and perhaps being just a bit flirtatious.

"You'll know," he said. "It's gentle." He settled into his seat, looking relaxed but eager, and Jael realized she was worrying about nothing, after all. Nothing.

They talked idly, this and that about riggers and family, and Jael nearly forgot about the intensifying golden field in the room. Dap laughed, his eyes seeking hers, as he talked about his last flight—a three-system hop, fast and exciting, played in the net as skipping-stone islands in a tropic sea. It was a teamwork freighter flight with another rigger, and he hinted at the intimacy which underlay the teamwork. "It was the best part of the trip," he said, his eyes still seeking hers, holding her eyes a little longer than she wished them held. "She's left. Out just the other day on a long haul. But I wouldn't give up that experience for anything."

Something in Jael choked silently, but she tried to contain it, to not betray her envy. There was a warmth around her, though, a suffused glow that somehow made it seem less important to hide her feelings. There was a gentle feeling of release in her thoughts, and suddenly as she looked at Dap, she no longer heard his words alone, but saw visions directly from his mind, across the widening dreamlink. She saw the woman he'd rigged with, the flights of fancy across space, the sly querying interest he felt now toward her.

Feelings stirred in her heart which she couldn't control, and before she was aware of what was happening, thoughts and images rushed up out of her mind like a fountain, and spilled glittering into space, into the dreamlink: glimpses of her half-brother steeling himself against their uncaring father, unable even to reach to his sister. Jael herself at her father's closed door, suffering and wanting and needing. Rigging an occasional flight alone, too lonely to dare to seek companions. The images rushed out, and so too did her anguish. Before she could stop herself, she'd released it all, glimpses of herself that she'd never meant to let any person see.

In the dizzying energy of the dreamlink, the openness suddenly wrenched, tore—as Dap betrayed his dismay, that someone could release such staggering need. Betrayed his revulsion. Dap, who'd promised understanding. Without a word Dap closed himself from the dreamlink, faded in the glow which now was a suffocating shield around a Jael who fumed with self-loathing and hurt. Dap no longer would look at her, and as she cried mutely in pain, he rose and left without her, left her there alone and desperate in the dreamlink field.

She made herself her own last audience: she let her pain dance in the field like threads of fire, tightening around her like a noose, choking her, and no one here to help—there never was, neither Dap nor her father—they forgot their promises and closed the door, one just like the other. She wanted to kill them both, and she was going to kill herself with this hate if she didn't do something to—

—control it—

—bottle it—

—which she did, wrapping it tightly around her finger and corking it back inside. And then when she was safe, while she was still sane, she turned off the dreamlink

augmentor. And she returned to the hall where the riggers
mobbed and brooded, looking for assignments. And a few
days later she found Mogurn—

—who offered her a job. And the pallisp.

She started out of a brooding daze. Sleep was impossible. But insomnia was better than the cruelty of dreams.
She thought constantly of the pallisp, which alone could
soothe her anxieties and fears. A sophisticated electrostim,
the pallisp was illegal except in the hands of a psych-med; it
was terrifying addictive, just as Mogurn's synaptic augmentor was addictive. But the pallisp was Jael's only
release. Except for the net.

She could go to the net now, she realized. There she
could let her feelings go—shape them and play them out in
images. It was perilous to let dark feelings loose in the net,
but was it any better to keep them corked until they
exploded? Mogurn would be furious if she went to the net
now, while he was under his bliss-wire. But if she didn't do
something, she would go crazy.

Leaving her cabin, she crept to the bridge. She climbed
into the rigger-cell. The neural contacts touched her neck
and head.

Her senses, electrified, sprang into the net. Into the Flux.
The ship floated as a balloon-borne gondola in a nighttime
sky, riding downrange winds. Jael let the breeze soothe
her, and then she changed altitude, seeking higher
crosswinds to take her to the mountains. The gondola
swayed as she found the airstream she wanted. She set her
sights upon the approaching range. A full, creamy moon
sank slowly toward jagged black peaks, which looked like
sullen teeth against the horizon. Backlighted by the moon,
a blunt-nosed mass of clouds was moving out of the mountains toward her. Spooky. She liked it: darkness and gloom

and eerily lighted clouds which looked like moving glaciers, or like bold angry pincers reaching out to shred the balloon . . .

The bag abruptly disintegrated. She caught at the air with her hands. For a moment she tumbled earthward, flailing, and then she controlled her panic and remade the image. The ghostly net shimmered and became a varnished glider, whispering downward through the air with her perched astraddle the fuselage. She leveled out, thinking: Take care! A rigger had to be careful of her images; dangerous thoughts could become real and could smash the ship into splinters, to drift forever in the currents of this strange reality, the Flux.

She let the wind soothe her face, let her feelings swirl ahead of her in the sky, in the emptiness between her and the clouds. They could hurt no one there. Time passed and she drew closer to the range.

The dragons stormed out of the clouds in random formation, like gulls out of a rain squall.

Jael stared into the moonlit night in astonishment. Dragons! Dreadful winged shapes, still distant, wheeled before the clouds. Sparks of red flame flickered. She could scarcely believe it; dragons weren't real—they were something from primal dreams, from legend, from racial fears and magical desires. But they were here in the sky right now, and she hadn't summoned them from her imagination—at least, she didn't think she had. Could they be real? Creatures which lived here in the Flux? Coolly nervous, she controlled the glider tightly.

The dragons grew in the moonlight. They soared and circled far off her wingtips. Three dragons broke from the others and spiraled in closer. She caught sharp glimpses of them as they swooped past her. One flew so close that its scales looked like polished pewter in the moonlight, throwing light back in subtly altered form, grey but not grey, as though banked fires lay beneath the surface of the scales. The dragon's head was rough carved and tipped with flaring, glowing nostrils, and its wings were serrated and broad, not narrow as Jael had pictured dragons' wings to be. Its eyes glinted. Another swept across her path, and then for a moment she lost sight, until she saw the three orbiting at a distance, as though she and her glider were hovering still in the air.

She held her course. What did one do when met by dragons? The old riggers talked in the bars of dueling—but what did that mean? These dragons looked capable of ruthless battle. Jael knew nothing of dueling and did not want to know. She wished she had come another way.

Are you afraid? she heard.

She looked around, frightened, thinking that Mogurn had awakened and was taunting her in the net as punishment. But the voice was not Mogurn's voice.

You are afraid, said the voice. *Shall we kill you now, as a kindness?*

With a start she realized that a dragon was speaking. She peered into the night and spotted a dragon alongside her whose eyes gleamed, betraying him in the night. The dragon edged closer. *What do you want?* she said hotly, fearfully.

The dragon's eyes flickered as it passed. The other two dragons retreated to join the rest, and the one remaining banked close by her, its eyes glowing brightly green. Turbulence buffeted Jael, and she fought to control the glider. *What are you doing?* she cried. *What do you want?*

Does that mean "No"? inquired the dragon, exhaling a cloud of sparks. It circled her. *You prefer to die in battle?*

What do you mean? Jael asked indignantly. *Who are you, anyway? What do you want—and how dare you speak to me that way?* She hunched low, pulled the net in around the edges.

Child! said the dragon. *One question at a time! You want to know who I am, and then—*

You haven't answered that yet!

Nor shall I. But you should not have given me so many questions not to answer. Do you think it's easy? Do you think you're the only rigger to come crashing through here looking for a fight?

Then it's true! You dragons are real!

The dragon sighed or snarled. *I never meant to tell you that! Duel, rigger!* It flipped in mid-air and bore down upon her, sparkling in the moonlight. It grew larger, larger . . .

Jael screamed. The glider shuddered. The dragon thundered and raked her with fire as it passed. *What are you doing?* she shrieked. Her skin sizzled, and flames crackled along the wings of her glider. Quickly she changed the image to a fireproof alloy glider. A flurry of snow cooled her skin and quenched the flood of energy in the net.

The dragon approached again, flapping its wings slowly. It eyed her suspiciously. *Your reactions were slow,* it said and moved off.

Jael looked after the dragon in astonishment. Suddenly it turned and streaked toward her in another attack.

Jael froze. She tried to make herself small. The dragon grew with terrifying speed. *Stop it!* she screamed.

Peeling off in surprise, the dragon circled warily. In the moonlit clouds, the other dragons looked like small dots, wheeling and cavorting. *All right,* said the dragon testily. *If you didn't want to duel, why did you come here?*

Jael was dizzy with confusion, fear, and anxiety. *I didn't expect you to try and kill me!*

What did you expect?

I don't know.

The dragon sighed impatiently and leveled off. He spoke in what seemed a mockingly measured and conciliatory tone. *Well all right, then. Do you want to talk instead? I can see you're distressed, irritable—and who can blame you? I feel the same way myself sometimes. You want to just fly along and maybe chat lightheartedly? I promise not to try to kill you.*

Jael eyed him suspiciously. *Can we?*

Sure. The dragon tipped his head and winked. Jael nodded, but she felt uneasy. She decided to change her image; she became a winged pony and beat against the wind. *Very nice,* said the dragon, falling in beside her.

She did not answer. The night was changing, the clouds closing in. A moonbeam broke through the clouds to show mist swirling about a black and jagged mountain slope. *Do you know where we're going?* asked Jael.

Yes, said the dragon craftily—and suddenly it slide-slipped and seized her in its talons. Jael's breath went out with a gasp. The dragon lowered its head, jaws gaping, as though intending to rend her with its teeth. Its hot breath washed back over her. Jael squirmed, twisted, and managed to roll forward just enough to kick with her hind legs. Her hooves caught the dragon squarely in the stomach and it wheezed, releasing her. Jael tumbled, beating frantically with her wings but losing altitude, headfirst, through the clouds. She glimpsed horrible sawtoothed slopes rushing to meet her. Frantic, she transformed herself to a hawk, warped her wings sharply, and pulled herself out of the dive. She spiraled back upward, squinting to evade the dragon.

Well done, the dragon said grudgingly, right behind her.

In a panic she looped up fast and came down behind it. She dogged its tail angrily, and warily. *Liar!* she shouted.

You promised and you lied! Is that a dragon's kind of honor?

Of course.

What? she screamed. *Do you all lie?*

What the dragon did next she could hardly believe. One moment it was in front of her, and the next it was above her, and then behind, and it curled its wing around her like a net and scooped her earthward. She trembled and fluttered, a frightened bird, as they plummeted. The dragon lurched to a landing on a black outcropping of rock. It craned its neck to sniff her with smoldering nostrils and peer at her with green eyes. She puffed up her feathers and stared back. *You lied, and now you're going to kill me!* she squeaked.

The dragon seemed puzzled. *Of course I lied. Didn't they tell you before they sent you to duel?*

No one sent me! Jael cried. *I just came.* She choked in the dragon's breath. *Would you mind letting me have some air?*

Hissing, the dragon opened its wing. *I think you'd better show yourself as you really are,* the creature warned.

The world was wreathed in fog, but the night air revived Jael somewhat. *All right,* she muttered. Concentrating, she transformed herself back to Jael, a human girl, in the nexus of a ghostly neural-sensory net. Haloing the net was a shimmering ethereal spaceship.

Impressive, acknowledged the dragon. *I just wanted to see you, though, not your spaceship.*

She made the spaceship disappear. She stood lonely and frightened and cold before the dragon. *My name is Jael,* she said.

The dragon reared its head back and shrieked in dismay. Its cry reverberated through the mountains. *I did not ask your name!* it wailed. *Why have you given me your name? Now I am obligated to give you my own name, and then I shall not be able to duel with you!* It blew a great gout of fire into the night and screeched and scratched at the rock in distress.

I don't want to know!

I suppose you may call me Highwing. I am the Sire of the four fastest—

You are a braggart, said Jael coldly. The dragon whuffled into silence. It shifted position awkwardly; the crag was crowded with the two of them. *I only want to be on with my flight,* Jael said. *You aren't helping me much.*

You didn't come here to duel with us? the dragon asked, in a wounded tone. Jael wondered if she really had hurt his feelings. Highwing watched her thoughtfully. *You are upset about something,* he observed. *And not just about me. Do you want to talk about it?*

No.

I have given you my name. You can trust me.

You? After you lied and tried to kill me?

That was when we were dueling. Before you knew my name. It was expected.

Not by me.

Uncomfortable silence followed. Highwing cleared his throat steamily. Some of the clouds broke and stars appeared over the mountains. Jael stared at them longingly.

Another voice broke the silence. *What's going on?*

Highwing peered around in confusion.

I'm flying, Mogurn, answered Jael.

Come out of the net at once, ordered Mogurn's bodiless, furious voice.

I can't. There are dragons. Jael glanced at Highwing. *Please don't argue,* she thought. *It's both of our lives.*

I'm disappointed in you. You get yourself out of trouble, and then you come and see me. Mogurn broke the link.

Highwing's dragon eyes glowed over his snout. *I see,* he

said. *You must answer to someone on your spaceship. But you don't like it. Am I right?* His gaze bore into Jael. *Little Jael,* he said, *perhaps you had better come with me for a while. Perhaps I can help.*

She glared at him, startled by the suggestion. *Why? Never!*

I am your servant now, Jael, because we have exchanged our names, and you really must come with me. It is our duty to help each other if we can. The dragon sounded utterly earnest.

Why should I trust you? she shouted, stamping.

I am all you have at the moment, answered the dragon mildly.

Irrationally, Jael felt her anger subsiding. Some part of her wanted to go with this dragon—even though he'd tried to kill her. She squinted at him—at his huge unblinking eyes, at his great knobbed and finely scaled head. Certainly he had nothing to fear, and no need of tricking her. *I suppose,* she said cautiously, *you're going to promise not to hurt me. And I should believe that.*

No one can promise not to hurt, little one, said Highwing.

Jael was startled. The answer seemed honest. And at the moment what choice did she have? *Not that I believe you,* she said, *but what did you have in mind?*

Climb onto my back. The dragon crouched low, and after a long hesitation Jael climbed up and perched astraddle his back, just in front of his wings. She held onto his neck. *Hold tight,* he said, and unlimbered his wings and sprang into the night air.

Jael clung, dizzy with confused emotions, with relief and fear. The wind whispered at her, and the movements of the dragon's powerful musculature soothed her. Instinctively she stroked his silken-hard scales. *I like to be scratched behind the ears,* the dragon remarked as he flew.

Abruptly she stopped. *Too bad,* she said coldly.

Highwing chuckled and banked so that she could see the landscape below. They were flying very low. Mountain landscape rushed by, jutting rock and dark ravines. He banked the other way, descending. She clung breathlessly. A valley spread open in the night. *Where are we going?* she shouted. The dragon belched a flame in answer.

They slowed and passed through a veil of mist. She felt a curious shifting, or twisting, of her time sense. Stars seemed to sparkle inside the veil, and she glimpsed dark stone walls sliding by. The veil shimmered and vanished, and in clear night air they glided into a fairyland valley. Highwing followed a trail of glittering dust strewn in mid-air, and below them, soft lights swung in the boughs of trees. Gossamer strands crisscrossed overhead, forming a continuing arch under which the dragon flew, barely fluttering his wings. *How do you like it?* he asked proudly.

Jael stared about in puzzled fascination. To the left, a waterfall spilled into a starlit pool, where several odd-looking creatures watered. *It's pretty,* she said, *but what are we doing here?*

Highwing craned his neck to look back at her. *Little one,* he said. *I wish I could remember your name. What was it?*

Jael, she said stiffly. Then she saw the twinkle in his eye. She flushed at the teasing, feeling—what?—anger? Perhaps—but despite herself she felt a trickle of warmth.

Little Jael, the dragon said.

Quit calling me "little"! Now that did make her mad.

Dear me, said the dargon. *Don't you know? I call you that as a measure of our friendship, little Jael.*

We have no friendship.

You say that now, large Jael. But we have come for you to see otherwise.

"I'm depending on you," said Mogurn.

Jael hiked herself up to look the dragon squarely in the eye. *Hah!* she said. And then her gaze locked with the dragon's, and she seemed to fall into the depths of those glowing eyes, down a twisting spiraling pathway to the edge of another consciousness: a mind watching hers, almost as in the dreamlink field. But the consciousness she touched here seemed far deeper than any she'd encountered before, and she sensed that it was kinder, and that it observed her with interest but without malice or displeasure at what it saw. Catching reflected images of herself, she realized suddenly that the other saw beneath her surface, deep within her thoughts. She shivered, and her shiver resonated down the pathway and reflected back in a sympathetic chord. Astonished, she pulled free of the link, of the dragon's gaze, and she sat back blinking.

The dragon counted itself her friend and companion. He did.

But that was impossible.

What was she to do, then? She closed her eyes and thought. She stretched her senses back through the rigger-net; she felt the ship, the flux-pile energizing the net, holding her here in the reality of the Flux. Should she pull clear now, face Mogurn and explain her folly, suffer his wrath in hopes of forgivness, in hopes of the pallisp, the dear pallisp? And then return, to modify the image if she could? But . . . Mogurn was very angry. He would never give her the pallisp now.

She could stay. Highwing had said he would bring her through, that he would help her.

She opened her eyes and said, *Well,* the dragon's nostrils smoked inquiringly. *This doesn't mean anything—but shouldn't we be moving on?*

The dragon turned to face forward again. *As you say, diminutive one.* Jael glowered, but before she could speak, Highwing added, *Look!*

The scenery ahead was different, starker and yet more magical—faceted angular rock faces, gleaming faintly, towering high, and here and there among the faces dim alcoves and caves. Jael felt a strange premonition. In those caves lurked dragon magic. She clung to Highwing in wondering apprehension. As the dragon wheeled slowly, picking his way through a maze of vaguely gleaming passageways, Jael again felt that curious twisting of time, as though each turn moved her backward or forward through years, or stretched seconds to infinity. Soon she felt quite disoriented.

Presently the dragon came to a landing before the entrance to a small cave. *Well,* he said.

Well, what? Jael rose up and peered in. The cave interior was gloomy, lighted by a single moonbeam piercing the ceiling. An enormous spiderweb spanned the back of the cave, shimmering in the moonbeam. The web seemed almost alive. There was a sparkling of light across its strands, and then a vertical rippling of cold fire. Jael watched, puzzled. The web danced with ghostly quicksilver, and suddenly stilled, and Jael found herself looking through a living window.

At Mogurn.

It was Mogurn at the spaceport, not on the ship. The background slowly fell into focus: the rigger dispatcher room in port. This was Mogurn the businessman; Mogurn the merchant, the thief. Mogurn the trader in illegal and immoral goods. He was talking with someone—a spaceport crew steward. Hanging onto Highwing's neck, Jael strained forward to pick up words from the window, but she could hear nothing. Both men smiled meanly at something Mogurn said, and the steward turned and pointed. A female rigger stood in profile, beyond them.

Jael trembled, recognizing herself half a year ago. She looked meek, frightened, lonely. Mogurn leaned toward

the steward, grinning, and withdrew from his hip pouch—
just far enough for the steward to see—the probe of the
pallisp. The steward nodded, winking. They touched
hands in farewell, and something twinkled between their
fingers as they did so. Then Mogurn strode toward the
rigger, Jael, standing bewildered in the lobby. And Jael,
her stomach knotting, watched the younger Jael turn,
startled at a sudden sensation of warmth, of companionship. Watched herself meet Mogurn, watched herself accept work—and watched herself surrender to the pallisp.

Jael's stomach fought back as for the first time she really
saw the uncaring anticipation on Mogurn's face as he
enslaved her with the pallisp. And for the first time she
admitted to the rush of hatred which shook her when she
thought of the man. Humiliation and anger rushed up in a
torrent.

The dragon stirred as she wrestled with her emotions,
trying to corral them, and she heard him say, *Shall I burn
him for you, Jael?*

Yes! she cried, blinking tears, not even knowing what
she was saying. *Yes! Burn him!*

Highwing lifted his head and breathed fire. His breath
was a blowtorch, a leaping flame which engulfed the
cave. The ghostly Jael vanished, and the ghostly Mogurn
whirled in surprise—and screamed once before he died in
the incinerating fury of the dragon's fire. Jael gagged at the
dying sound of the scream, at the sight of the man dying in
hellfire at her command. And when it was over, and the
smoke cleared from the gutted cave which had held the
image of the man she hated, she felt a sudden and enormous rush—of catharsis—of cleansed emotions. Of exhaustion.

She scarcely noticed as the dragon carried her away
from that place. Her thoughts were blurred, confused.
Time strained and slipped by.

Gradually she regained both her strength and her wits as the dragon flew through the stark-walled and misty vale. *You took that from my own mind, didn't you?* she asked softly, stroking his scales to regain the feel.

What? he answered idly. He banked to the right and turned into a bowl-shaped dell and landed abruptly. Jael stared, frowning. The dell was a small, wooded place, in fading twilight. As darkness filled in, hundreds of gnatlike fireflies appeared, darting and corkscrewing through the glade like so many fiery atoms. Hundreds more joined them, and more still, until a cloud of whirling sparks filled a space beneath several of the largest trees. Jael was about to speak, to say *Stop—no more,* when the whirling sparks coalesced and from their midst emerged a man. Dap.

Jael's breath stopped. Dap looked as always, handsome and gentle, but—and this astonished Jael, who'd witnessed this scene before, but had never noticed—he was also frightened, anxious, putting forth a brave expression which hardly disguised his terrible insecurity. The sunglow of the dreamlink field came over him (and over an invisible Jael) and as the augmentor worked its magic on him, his discomfort became yet more evident. Images of Jael's memories danced about him like tiny sunbursts: her father opaquing doors as he retired with his women and boys, some not much older than Jael; her brother (before the groundcar accident that took his life, as he ran from his insane mother) wincing with the pain he never allowed out, though it tore him apart; her father ignoring, shutting out their pain, teaching them how to make walls but never windows.

All this Dap caught, in the swirl of memories among the fantasies, desperately lonely fantasies, rigger fantasies which Jael let free in the dreamlink. "Is all this true?" he asked, frightened at the enormity of her pain. And Jael remembered her answer well. "Only fantasies," she had lied, even as she tried to sweep them away, to hide them. As Jael watched Dap draw back from the unseen Jael here, she recalled the agony she'd felt, the abandonment. But the expression on Dap's face was fear, shame for his own needs and wants in the face of his helpless inadequacy. As she tried to cover, so did he. As she was frightened, so was he.

As he turned now to flee, Jael heard Highwing's voice, softly: *Shall I?* The dragon drew a deep breath.

No! she cried, startled. *Don't hurt him—don't burn him! I didn't know—I never realized!* Dap had fled out of fear, out of hurt. Perhaps even cowardice—but not hatred.

Highwing sighed, and the image and the cloud of sparks dissipated. *Did you remember it that way?* the dragon asked, rumbling.

No, said Jael. *No, I*—and she fell mute, remembering the abandonment she'd felt, thinking that Dap hated her, and remembering how she'd vowed never to let anyone touch her that way again.

Well, then, Jael—look up.

Reluctantly she lifted her gaze. For a moment she couldn't see what Highwing wanted her to look at, and then—in a sheltered aerie high above the glade—she saw a man.

Who is that? she asked, though a suspicion grew in the pit of her stomach.

Don't you know? Without waiting for an answer, the dragon sprang aloft and carried her to a perch near the aerie, where she could look across and see for herself. It was her father. He was a cold-eyed, stiff-limbed man, exactly as she remembered him. He gazed outward, apparently expecting a caller, but the angle of his stance suggested retreat, as though he refused to leave the shelter of the aerie. His eyes stared, his mouth curled with distaste,

as when he'd wondered aloud why he'd saddled himself
with two former wives, a son, and a daughter.

Kill him, Jael said softly, anger and loathing rising out of
her heart. *Burn him.* The dragon did not immediately
obey, and for a moment her anger flew at Highwing. *I hate
him, I say—burn him!* And then she knew why the dragon
hesitated. Not because he disapproved—but because her
father was already two years dead, at the hands of a
jealous lover. What point to burn him now? She cursed
futilely, squinting at this man who was so hopelessly cold,
so desperately alone, who had turned two wives against
him and taught a son and a daughter how not to feel. *All
right, Highwing—never mind. Maybe he suffered enough.
I doubt it, but maybe he did. Now let's get out of here.*

The man vanished into the aerie as Highwing turned.
He leaped, and they were airborne. *Little one—*

Let's get out of this place, dragon! Jael answered darkly,
her mood blighted by anger. The dragon vented smoke
from his nostrils in sympathy. That angered her further,
and she struck his hardened scales with her fists. *Take me
out of this valley and let me finish my journey in peace.*

The dragon circled higher. He was silent for a time
before speaking. *As you will, Jael. But when I take you out
of these mountains, we will be near the place where I must
leave you—and you will be near your destination. There I
shall have to say good-bye to you.*

Too many images burned brightly in Jael's mind for her
to respond to the dragon's sadness. As if she were concerned anyway. It was the damned dragon who had
brought her here, pushed her nose in those memories,
made them hurt—although, true, he had burned Mogurn
to a crisp for her, in image if not reality.

Jael clung silently to the dragon as he beat his wings to
gain altitude, as the lights of the valley fell away behind

them. Images flashed brightly through her mind: her brother desperately gathering his dignity, unable to share his hurt even with his sister; Dap and the other riggers struggling with their own loneliness and fear; a rigger named Mariel who once treated her kindly; Mogurn in oblivion with the synaptic augmentor. She shook as feelings replayed in her mind faster than she could react to them, as memories of anger and pain and loneliness and frustration and hatred spawned a cyclone in her soul. Memories of a father who had loved no one, least of all himself. She scarcely saw the mountain peaks passing, dark and grim in the night, or clouds which muffled them and opened again, or the stars which gleamed like diamonds and then stretched peculiarly into lines . . . in response to the sensation of speed . . . in response to her fatigue in the rigger net.

In the faint roar of wind, she finally raised herself on Highwing's neck, understanding that she was exhausted, that she had been flying in the net for too many hours. *Where are we?* she asked, her voice straining.

On the way to where you wanted to go, said the dragon.

If I went away—to sleep—could you stay with my ship until I return? The net sparkled, off color. She didn't even know why she'd asked that, but she felt a jab of pain, of loneliness. She didn't quite want to leave him.

I will be here, answered the dragon.

Sighing, Jael gathered her senses, materialized an image of the ship which was bound to her through the net, just a ghostly nose of the ship extending out of nothingness into the Flux, and she set the stabilizers astraddle Highwing. *I'll see you in a while, then,* she offered.

A plume of smoke. *Yes.*

Jael withdrew. Her senses darkened—and rekindled back in her own body. She climbed out of the rigger-cell and stood, weary, in the gloom of the bridge. She stretched once. Then she stole into the galley and ate ravenously, expecting an angry Mogurn to burst in at any moment. When she finished, and Mogurn had not appeared, she crept to his door and signaled. No answer. She paled the door and peered in. Mogurn was under the synaptic augmentor, his eyes rolled up into his head, a grimace stretching his mouth. His chest rose and fell slowly; otherwise he lay still. He hadn't been able to wait for Jael to help him.

Jael frowned, thinking reflexively of the pallisp, and then realizing that she didn't really need it just now. She could live without it while she slept. Turning, she went to her own cabin and fell almost instantly into deep sleep.

She blinked; her dreams fled. Mogurn's voice startled her a second time, growling, "Are you being paid to sleep?" The anger in his voice was sharp, too sharp. She turned to look at him, standing just inside her door, and she pictured him cremated by dragon fire. "Make yourself ready and come see me in the galley," he ordered. Then he vanished.

Jael roused herself worriedly. Mogurn sounded unwell, perhaps unstable. Could that be a result of a synaptic overdose? She'd have to be careful—best to get back into the net quickly. And—strangely!—she was terribly anxious about Highwing. A queer ache settled in her chest when she thought of the dragon; it reminded her of the longing she felt for the pallisp. Or used to feel. At the moment, she didn't want the pallisp; she wanted to be with Highwing.

Head spinning, she went to the galley. Mogurn was eating, and under his baleful eye she dialed something for herself. As she began to eat, he spoke sharply. "Twice you've disobeyed. And you entered the net without permission, and put us in trouble with dragons. Are we clear of dragons now?" His voice sounded strained.

Jael swallowed. Highwing, burn him! she thought, wishing that the dragon could be here to obey. She chose her words cautiously. "We could still have trouble." Mogurn's eyes flashed. "But we are nearing the final current to Lexis. I should return to the net at once."

The shipowner squinted, his facial muscles tense. "You don't like me much, do you?" he said tightly. "You never did. But you like your pallisp well enough, don't you? And there is no man who can wield the pallisp for you as I do."

Jael held her gaze rigid, meeting his. I do not need a pallisp, she thought . . . not any longer. Nevertheless, she trembled under Mogurn's gaze. "There will be no more mistakes, Jael. No disobedience. No pallisp—until you have removed this ship from danger." Mogurn smiled queerly, triumphantly, and crossed his arms.

What a pathetic man, Jael thought—however cruel. What weapon did he hold over her now? She still feared him physically, yes, but—"I do not need your pallisp," she said aloud. Her throat constricted. "And now I must—"

"You *stay* until I command you to *leave!*" shouted Mogurn furiously.

An alarm on the bridge quailed, signaling changes in the Flux. Mogurn started, jerked his head around. "Go!" he said bitterly.

Jael hurried. If Highwing had left her . . .

When her senses sparked outward into the net, she found herself astride the dragon, flying in clear winds over low mountains. She trembled with relief. Two suns, pink and orange, were setting before her. The sky overhead was a sea of liquid crystal, and she knew at once that she was bound upward for that sea. Greetings, small one, sighed the dragon, snorting fire.

Jael hugged his neck, wanting to cry. Highwing, she said softly, did you call me?

The dragon pumped his wings slowly. *I wanted you to return,* he said. *I don't know if I called you or not.*

I knew it was time to come. Are we—are we almost at the end?

Of my range, yes, Jael. Dragons do not go beyond these foothills. I am zigzagging to go more slowly, but we are almost at the end. Do you wish me to fly straight?

No—please no. Oh, Highwing, can't you come further with me? Or can't we go back? Even as she spoke, Jael knew that it was impossible. She had a ship to bring in, and even Mogurn was her responsibility. The currents of the Flux were inexorable; dragons could fly against them, perhaps, but Jael and her ship could not.

Sometimes friends must part, said the dragon softly.

And I made you leave, said Jael, half to herself, *when all along you were trying to help me. Just as you promised.* She was ashamed; tears wet her cheeks. *What will I do, Highwing? What will I do now?*

You will find others—and I will still be here, thinking of you.

Jael trembled and wept, and after a long time her tears dried. How could she dispel the terrible loneliness she felt already closing in upon her? The pallisp came to mind, and she turned it away. The price for that was too high, the comfort too short. No, Highwing's advice was best. However difficult, it was better than settling for the likes of Mogurn and the pallisp. Better than shelled-in emptiness.

Things will be different. Things will be better, she said, as though to the wind. But not without pain.

Highwing heard her and answered. *It will be different for me, too, little Jael. Never again will I duel a rigger without thinking of you. You, who have my name—and I yours.*

They flew in silence for a few moments. The lowest of the low mountains came into sight. *Highwing,* Jael said, *if I fly this way again, shall I see you?*

The dragon breathed fire. *I shall be looking for you, little Jael, and so will other dragons. Cry, "Friend of Highwing!" and I will hear you, though all the mountains lie between us.*

Jael trembled with emotion. *Then let us fly high, now, and part in the sun,* she said, urging him toward the sky.

The dragon complied at once, soaring high toward the inverted lake of sunset crystal above their heads. Jael leaned with him into the wind, feeling it sting her cheeks and toss her hair, feeling the glowing radiance of the celestial ocean overhead filling her eyes and her soul. The two suns were setting now, but they threw their radiance in fuller color than ever into the sky. Channels opened in the clouds, and light poured through in great rays, washing over the dragon and Jael, and they flew up one of the beams, into the crystal sea, where colors shifted brightly and the currents of the Flux moved in streams and gossamer strands. And here, she knew, Highwing would leave her, for this was not a dragon's realm.

Highwing shivered, and she thought she heard echoes of weeping, and he blew a great cloud of smoke and sparks and a single brilliant, billowing flame. Jael caressed his neck one last time, and then extended her hands into space and turned them into great webs touching the streamers of light. *Farewell, Highwing,* she cried softly.

Farewell, Jael, said the dragon, and he wheeled and suddenly Jael was no longer astride him but in flight on her own, rigger once more. Highwing banked and circled around her, his eyes flashing, and he issued a long, thin stream of smoke in final farewell, and then he banked sharply and plummeted.

Jael looked after him, holding her tears, as he dwindled toward his own world. *Friend of Highwing!* she cried after him, and her voice reverberated gently down the sunbeams, and perhaps she was only imagining but she thought she heard his laugh echoing in the distance below. And then she set her sights ahead and knew that the tears would flow and dry, for a while, and she looked in the shifting sky for the currents that would carry her to her destination star system, to the end of this voyage, to normal space. And she thought of how she would tell Mogurn that she was leaving his employ, and his pallisp, and she laughed and cried and turned her thoughts back to the sky.

Until I return, Highwing, she thought, and she saw the streamer she wanted and caught it in her webbed hand, and with her the ship rose high and fast into the current.

The maid of the quest appeared in the entrance.

THE LADY OF THE PURPLE FOREST

ALLAN BRUTON

ILLUSTRATIONS BY
GEORGE BARR

The knight was terrified.

His shield bore a heart, red on blue, with the bend sinister in sable over all, a device myriads of enemies had cause to fear, but Sir Gerhart Ravenlock could not put down his own fear. Nevertheless, he guided his destrier into the clearing, as honor and life demanded.

Ahead was a large cave, unmistakably a dragon's lair: the trampled grass in front, the bones, animal and human, piled in a heap to one side, were sufficient to prove that. Gerhart noticed that the bones were very bleached. He saw bits and pieces of the dragon's hoard in the entrance —a golden candlestick, a silver tray and silver tableware, a few coins and some jewelry. There were no recent tales of dragons among the Mountains of the Moon. This one must have just awoke from the long hibernation of the dragon-kin. They could sleep a century, he knew, if they wished.

He rode to a point a few yards before the cave, centered himself exactly, and drew a deep breath. "Come forth, foul worm, and meet thy nemesis!"

For awhile nothing happened, though he made no move to enter the cave. Experience and legend both had taught him that it was safer to accost the Devil in Hell than

291

to enter a sleeping dragon's cave. The problem was to get the beast awake, while staying alive during the process. He was inhaling for another shout when he heard footsteps, sandals shifting heaped coins, picking their way over candelabra and jeweled chalices.

Gerhart lowered his lance as the maid of the quest appeared in the entrance. The knight knew she was the lady, for she was beautiful, and she fit this day of adventure as well as he.

"Fair lady, is your captor in residence?"

She placed her hand on the cave wall, leaned against it, and inspected him coolly. Suddenly she smiled. "No, but I think he will be here again. Are you come to rescue me?"

Gerhart relaxed, hung his shield on his saddle, stepped his lance. "Yes, if you are a lady in distress. You look quite comfortable! Might I ask your name?"

She laughed and walked out of the cave. "I suppose I am, for he will not let me leave, though he treats me very well. I am Lady Arlis of the Purple Forest. Master Ferasand told me that he would not be back for some time after noon. Would you like refreshment? You must have ridden long. But who are you, sir knight? I see that you are of the House of Oldburg, but your wicked stripe confounds me. And who wears a *white* plume in all this land?"

He came to earth heavily in his armor, leaned his lance against his saddle. While looking skyward he said, "I am called Gerhart Ravenlock, and I am of the House of Oldburg, though my father must needs leap through the boudoir window to get me there." He removed his helm, grinned at the plume, then at her. "The white is my flag of truce to God, lady, that he take pity on me. And yes, bread and wine would be welcome."

Ravenlock, indeed, she thought, as she tried to keep her eyes from widening. If only half the tales were true, she was now confronting one of the ten best knights in all the Holy Alliance. His hair fell around his face, framing dark eyes above a mouth held firm against the smiles crowding behind. She saw him still keeping a wary eye upward, one hand near his huge broadsword. "You shall eat with me, but not if you trust not my words. He will give you fair warning. I know him."

Again he grinned. "Perhaps. Though if you are wrong you lose only a possible emancipator, while I lose my life. But you are the lady, I shall relax." And he tethered his horse and removed his swordbelt. The lady returned to the cave, emerged again with a golden tray bearing bread and meat, fruit and wine.

They sat on the dragon's lawn and Gerhart ate while reflecting that she was utterly graceful in all that she did. He found himself hungrier than he had thought, and applied himself to his meal. She ate and drank sparingly, watching him.

At last, hunger and thirst satisfied, he leaned back on his elbows and looked across at her. She had long since finished eating, and was lounging on the lawn, turning a goblet round and round in her hands. She looked inquiringly at him. "Lady Arlis, how did you come to get captured? The Purple Wood is a long journey from the Mountains of the Moon."

Looking into her cup, she said, "Because I am foolish, Sir Gerhart, if you must know, and because a man's long journey is but an afternoon's amble for a dragon. But I live within the woods, and seldom venture out, for I love them—the trees, the brooks and birds. But one day, a clear day—a dragon's day, just as this is a dragon's day—I felt too full of life. I saddled my horse, and we went riding through the grasslands, leaving the trees behind. Thus it was easy for Master Ferasand to catch me." She looked at him. "It was only seven days ago. How did you know I was here?"

Watching her fingers twist the goblet, he said, "Because I also was foolish. I heard adventure calling me. Truly. The day fair shouted that a lady in need was near me as I traversed the way between the mountains. I did not know it was you, but I knew you had to be here."

"You could have ignored the call."

"Nay, lady, I could not. Ferasand is your captor's name now?"

A fleeting look of puzzlement crossed her face at the "now" but she only said, "Ferasand al-Kelakh. He tells me he has slept for sixty-seven years, and woke to an adventurous day, rather like yourself."

"Yes, that would be so." He smiled, though not at her. His eyes looked toward Elor, the mountain rising behind the dragoncave, but she thought he saw nothing of it, and wondered at the flash of sadness that swept over him, almost too fast to detect. Then he chanced to look up, and froze.

Only for an instant, then he was on his feet. Seconds later his helm covered his head, and his sword and shield were in his hands. He glanced at her, still lying by the remains of their picnic, and barked, "Get into the cave! Fast! Please." His manner brooked no argument and she ran inside, crouching down behind a heap of golden coins. Gerhart was scanning the sky.

She looked up, saw the angular shape of a dragon far above, circling. From a seemingly infinite distance, she could hear a long drawn hissing snarl. She recognized Ferasand, her captor, and this errant knight's new-found enemy. She heard a deep hiss and snap, as the dragon roared flame. Gerhart was motionless, sword in hand, shield raised, his eyes following the giant beast. Time seemed to stand still as the dragon circled once, twice.

Suddenly the great wings folded, the dragon dived. The very air seemed to scream, tortured, as the monster body sliced through it. The great jaws gaped open as the dragon hurtled toward the knight. Flame shot out, and engulfed the man. The grasses were blackened. Close over the man shot the dragon, soaring up once again. The smoke dissipated as Ferasand came around for another pass. Shocked, Arlis saw a streak of blood along the dragon's underside. Sir Gerhart was once again visible, his shield blackened but his sword point red. He swung the blade over his head in triumph, ecstasy, and insult. She knew that the two had shouted to each other but nothing registered as she crouched under the overhanging lip of the cave, shaken, immobile.

Suddenly she was aware of herself, running to be between the two as Ferasand dove in again. Hearing returned, and smell—the air whistling—around Gerhart's sword and Ferasand's wings—the grass smoke stinging. She was shouting, "Stop! Stop! Why must you fight?"

Gerhart's sword arm dropped, along with his jaw. The dragon staggered in the air, coming to a shaky landing before her. The two antagonists looked at her, at each other, in bafflement. Ferasand found voice first. "By the far side of the misty Mountains of the Moon, can such things be?" He spoke to Gerhart, not to her. The knight stared at her for another moment, then spoke to the dragon.

"We must pause, and educate the lady."

The lady, looking from one to the other, felt as if she were becoming moonstruck. What she had expected she could not have said, but it was not what she had got. She felt numb as Gerhart led her to an unsinged area of lawn, sat her down. He and Ferasand sat before her, bafflement evident still. "What is wrong?" she asked. "You look as if the earth has fallen from under you."

"Nay, lady." It was Ferasand, who possessed a soft, sibilant voice quite at odds with his appearance. "We look as if the earth has fallen from under you. How can you not know why we fight?"

"There is no reason!" She almost screamed, and felt tears start down from her eyes. "I have a liking for both of you, both of you are good in your way, and why must you battle?"

Ferasand turned his mighty head to Gerhart. "Sir knight, you are the poet. Perhaps you have words."

Gerhart smiled, a trifle sadly. "Perhaps." He turned to Lady Arlis. "Sweet lady, life is not reason alone, not mind and logical sequence and nothing besides, not cold frozen thought constructed in symmetrical shapes and lines. Life is a multitude and includes the strange, the wonderful—and the moonstruck and irrational. We two are what we are—dragon and knight—and so must fight to the death for you."

She shook her head, her hair flying in disarray. "No, not so. You are not just knight or dragon, you can choose not to fight."

Gerhart looked to Ferasand, who said, "Lady, we can. But life is also a game—and we must follow the rules as laid down or what point to play at all? We choose what we are, we must take the consequences whatever they may be—we cannot take only what we desire, or why run the race at all?"

She did not capitulate, and argued further. But the two did not take back what they had said. After a time, Gerhart looked at the sun and ended the debate. "Master Ferasand, our business must be concluded soon. Lady, we *must* battle. Please go to the cave."

She looked to the dragon, but he only nodded his ponderous head. Still uncomprehending but acquiescent, she walked to the cave, and sat down to watch the end. Ferasand leaped into the air. She saw again the smear of blood along his underside as he circled. Gerhart again donned his helm, slung his shield on his arm, lifted his sword. After a time the dragon dived.

The sun was touching the hills before the battle ended. Lady Arlis lost count of the number of times the dragon dived or flamed, of the times she felt certain the man had been burned or clawed to his death. Gerhart's armor was presently ripped in many places and reddened with blood—his and that of the dragon. The lawn became burnt all across and there were several fires smoldering on the forest verge. Once, when a chance wind blew the air clear of smoke, she saw that Gerhart's beard was completely singed away. However, his sword was red from point to guard, and Ferasand was also covered with blood. They were both very tired, the dragon lurching unsteadily through the air, the knight moving slowly under the weight of his mail.

The pattern of combat was steady. The dragon would circle, suddenly dive, trying to catch the knight from an unguarded angle, or before he could dodge, while the knight would try to avoid the fire by dodging and take the talons on his shield while wielding his sword. Many stratagems were tried and none succeeded entirely. Once Ferasand came straight in, surging upward at the last instant, tempting a cut to his belly while his barbed tail swept under him to knock Gerhart senseless, or at least off his feet. But the knight jumped aside and slashed a barb off the sweeping tail. Another time the knight leaned into the flames splashing off his shield, hoping to use the smoke and glare as a cover for a decapitating blow. The dragon twisted in midair, however, and almost knocked the sword flying with a swipe of one great claw.

The sun was almost below the horizon, and the clearing was lit mostly by burning trees, when the dragon was finally unable to hold the air any longer. He alighted, about thirty yards from the knight. His panting breath seemed to slip almost softly around the sounds from the crackling fires clinging to the skeletal trees. Gerhart slouched visibly, and his sword no longer arose except when absolutely necessary. It was clear to the lady that neither would be able to battle much longer.

Slowly Ferasand crept toward the motionless knight. Once he flamed, but lacked the strength to do so again. Just out of sword reach, the dragon paused. Choppily, stopping for breath after each word, he said, "Sir Gerhart, you are the most mighty man that I can remember. You will have a great ballad one day."

Also panting, Gerhart replied, "And you are the greatest dragon of all tales told, Master Ferasand."

With that the dragon advanced, rearing up, his front talons reaching. With a last surge of speed, the knight took two steps forward, his sword flashing for the throat. The dragon tried to lower his head and bat the sword away but his weariness was too great, and the blade went home. The reaching claws met behind Gerhart's back, and the dragon's long neck fell over them.

Slowly, slowly, the knight climbed from under the body and went to stand in front of the fallen dragon. Arlis was there before him, heedless of the ashes and the blood. Her hand touched the great head, and Gerhart noticed a little life in the yellow eyes, almost closed.

"Farewell, fair lady." The voice was almost ridden under by the hiss of the flames roundabout. "Protect her well, sir knight. You have earned much honor this day."

Gerhart gave salute, replied, "I shall sing your tale greatly, master dragon; you shall be remembered long among men."

Arlis was there before him, heedless of the ashes and the blood.

"Thank you. And now, I ask your last favor." The eyes closed.

Gently moving the sobbing lady away from the dragon's head, Gerhart took his dagger, aimed carefully, and plunged it through one eye into the brain behind. The body gave one convulsive shudder and was still. The knight stood also still for a moment, then retrieved his sword. Lady Arlis was standing in the same place to which he had moved her a moment before, tears rolling down her face, her body still. He took her arm and began to walk out of the burning clearing.

After a few steps she came out of her daze, jerking him to a halt. "Wait, wait. Should we not do more for him?"

Gerhart gently urged her on, toward the last unburning part of the forest verge. "Nay, lady, we need not. Ferasand will do all that is necessary." They reached the trees and turned. The heat from the fires around was mixing her tears with perspiration, he saw, and her dress was a much darker red in places. On the blackened lawn Ferasand's corpse seemed to glow. Then, it was a flaming mass, a searing bright flame that turned the fires around pale. In an instant he was gone, but for a rising mass of glowing smoke and gas. His body his pyre, and nothing was left behind.

The knight and the lady went on into the forest.

He walked her as far as he could still put one foot in front of the other, far enough that the dying fires behind them were out of sight and the smell of smoke was no longer omnipresent. Just before he felt he would lose his senses he stumbled onto a natural lean-to, formed by a fallen forest giant. He hollowed out a space for them among the broken and twisted branches, and they crawled in, exhausted emotionally as well as physically. Both were asleep in seconds.

Gerhart's destrier wandered to them the next morning and they spent the day riding through the forest to the grassland. They were silent. Arlis sat behind him, her forehead against his back. Grieving? Recovering from the shock of battle? He did not know, but respected her mood and left it alone.

At long last the day ended with them in the grassy hills of the Eastern March. They made a rude camp in a small copse of lindens. Their crackling fire threw the scene into a surrealistic relief—the overhanging trees, the distant bulk of Gerhart's destrier cropping grass, saddle and weapons and bushes and shrub. Arlis stared long into the twisting flames after the scanty meal—Gerhart had carried few supplies—seeming to attempt to wrest something from the smoke and glow. Gerhart, wondering yet what troubled her, was still loathe to ask, for her pensiveness was such to command respect. He watched the play of orange and shadow across her face, the glints in her eyes, and bided his time.

The fire was burnt to a dim glow and the night chill was creeping into them when she stirred. "Build up the fire, please. It grows cold yet sleep is not near me now. Perhaps you could tell me of some of your adventures. You must have had many in your years of errantry." No longer was she a young woman rescued from a dire fate, but the Lady Baron of the Purple Forest.

Willing to talk of adventure at any time, he obeyed, and once again the fire cast flickering shadows and lights about the camp. "What would you like to hear, lady?"

"Tell me of your greatest adventure."

He smiled. "The greatest adventure is always the one of the present, lady, but even if it were not so, it would be this one."

"We will get to this one later. The next greatest, then."

"That would be leading the charge at Asfodel, where we broke the heathen army. Do you wish a story of battle this eve?"

"A knight's adventures turn always to violence, Sir Gerhart. Tell me the story of Asfodel."

"Let me think—" He pulled out his pipe and filled and lit it as he collected his thoughts. Blowing an enormous smoke ring, at which she almost laughed, for it haloed her for an instant, he told her the story of Asfodel.

Knights marched through the firelight, harryings and slayings winding among the flames. Her eyes were sharp upon him, and she seemed to try to glimpse his soul as he spoke. The steady gaze caused him some unease, but that was covered by the glow he always felt when remembering his deeds at Asfodel. He told her of the king's displeasure when he, Gerhart, had left the royal service after the campaign, then he fell silent.

His pipe had gone out sometime during the tale and he sat about rekindling it. The lady was silent with him for a time, seemingly in thought. Then she said, "Why did you do it, sir knight?"

"Do which, bright lady?"

"Leave the king."

"It was because of a decision I made when my father knighted me, my lady. I decided that I should walk alone and not to any man's orders. I would answer to myself and God and no one else."

"Would you not swear yourself to your lady, as to God?"

He smiled back at her. "Bright lady, knights errant have no ladies, for if they love adventure, they can love no lady."

"And if they love no lady there shall someday be no knights, not so?"

"Perhaps, but my father had no lady."

This brought a laugh, then she answered, "Then you walk where your father walked?"

A look of surprise came over his face, and he laughed heartily. "Well spoken, lady, you have spitted me on my own sword."

They watched the fire for a time, each satisfied in his own way at their talk. Then she spoke again. "Perhaps I read the tale wrongly, but you seemed to know each other."

"Ferasand, lady? Of course we had never met, but we knew each other. Did you not? You called him 'Master.'"

"Is that a title? He introduced himself so."

"It is a title. While you were in his care, did you note the many golden coins inscribed with a rampant dragon?"

"Yes, but I thought nothing of them."

"Those coins belong to a tale of greatness. Have you not heard of the great dragon who laid the entire Eastern March under tribute seventy years ago?"

"Yes." She looked puzzled for a moment. "That was Ferasand?"

"Indeed he was, though he had a different name then. He was the only dragon ever to live under the Mountains of the Moon. He came out of the east one day as a scourging flame, burning all in his path. A round dozen of the greatest knights of the Holy Alter perished before him. The king gathered a mighty army and led it into the Corridor against him, only to have it broken by this one dragon. My father told me that his father, a most redoubtable knight, was slain in this battle.

"After this, the Duke of the March sent an emissary to the dragon, asking if he wished to produce a wasteland or if he loved gold more. When the dragon replied that gold was much more to be desired than blackened hillsides and burning villages, the Duke offered him tribute, which was paid for fifteen years. Then the dragon disappeared.

"While he was receiving the gold they called him Master of the March, and he was considered the greatest dragon that ever tales told. Those dragon coins you saw in Ferasand's cave were struck in recognition of that."

"Why did he go to sleep?"

"How could he not? It was his supreme hour of greatness; nothing more lay before him that he could do. I think he hoped to wake up in a new world, to find new adventures. That is probably why he took you, to stimulate new adventures."

"Adventure. He spoke of it, you speak of it. I saw the gleam in your eyes as you told me of Asfodel, but I do not understand it."

"It is as he told you—life is a game to be played by the rules as they are written. Perhaps it is not the best game, yet it is not a bad one, and we both played it heartily. There is no reason for a knight to seek adventure, nor for a dragon to snatch maidens or burn villages and be what he is, except that the game demands it of us, and we give it willingly.

"He knew, I think, that he would die when he saw my shield. True knight and foul dragon, you know."

She started, as he had intended. "And are you a true knight, Sir Gerhart? What of your bend sinister?"

He laughed. "*I* can never know, lady, can never be sure. Yet so the tales say, I hear."

She sighed, and her eyes left him for the fire, again in embers. For a time she watched the glowing coals, as if she would wrest whatever she sought from the low flame. Then she stirred again. "I know not if you speak truly, Sir Gerhart, but I see that you believe what you say. Since Ferasand did likewise, I suppose I should not grieve over this."

"If you wish. Yet grieve if you would. Indeed, he was the Master, and now he is gone."

Incredibly, she smiled. "To be sure. And I think I shall ask a price of you for your deed."

Gerhart's heart jumped. One never knew what a lady would ask of a knight. "What might that be, lady?"

"All in good time, sir knight. And now, to bed."

They continued, riding through the March, over the Rolldazzle River, into the green hills of Moralia, taking weeks for the distance Ferasand had flown in a night and a morning. Gerhart bought another horse with some of his gold, and they rode together through the forests, past the seldom farms, across the winding rivers. They sang many songs those days, and told many tales, he of great deeds and stirring adventures, and she of the ways and life of the Purple Forest.

Their camps were merry—they stayed seldom in inns or castles, for that land was little settled, and those who do live there are often dark and glowering—and Gerhart felt the lady was healed in soul from her captivity and later battle. She kept her secret which involved him, which caused her much amused satisfaction. He wondered, and worried, at what new duty would be laid upon him. She owed him favor, but she was a lady and he a knight, and he would have to make whatever quest she sent him on. He sometimes asked what she was hiding, but always she answered as she had before: "All in good time, sir knight." The late summer had imperceptibly advanced into fall before they came to the Purple Forest.

Occasionally there were encounters. Just after they left the March, in fact, a dragon swooped low over them as they rode one bright afternoon, hissing and smoking. Gerhart looked up once—and rode on. He did not put Arlis off the horse, or even draw his sword, indicating an almost insane contempt. When the dragon swooped once more the knight shouted, "I slew Master Ferasand just one week ago. Seek you the same fate?" And the dragon staggered in the air, and left them in peace.

After that the news seemed to fly ahead of them, that the Master of the March was gone forever. It happened that no knight met on the road cared to challenge Gerhart when he saw Gerhart's shield, for the shadow of the Master still lay over the kingdom, after those many years. Several of the greatest knights of the Holy Alter passed them by, stopping only for the giving of compliments, and awe. This was more honor than Sir Gerhart had ever expected for such a deed. It surprised him, and after a time began to bring chagrin; for where was a knight in all the land from whom he could gain honor after this greatest of all deeds? What was he to do next? For Lady Arlis, the honor given to her rescuer brought high satisfaction, and she often smiled in anticipation, which also brought Gerhart unease.

Finally, they arrived at the house of the Lady of the Purple Forest.

The Purple Forest is a land of rather glowing mystery.

It lies north of the king's city of Serolo, just before one comes to the Northern March of the Holy Alliance. It is not a large wood, but is instantly known, for the trees in summer have a purple cast found nowhere else. There are a few farms carved from the trees but most of its people are foresters. Once each year the trees are tapped for their sap, from which comes an astounding clear wine. In the midst of the wood lies the house of the lord of the Purple Forest.

The great lords of the land have their towered and barbicanned castles, with high walls on rocky hills or rising from made ground in marshes and lakes, and the kings and dukes their palaces within their walled cities. Even the poorest country baron will have a keep with a stone wall around it. Yet the house of the Lord of the Purple forest is nothing like these, but just a house. It is a large house, but of wood; there is no wall, for the men of the forest live by and with their bows, and they are the wall around the lord's home. There he lives, and is much more a leader, than a lord.

Here came Sir Gerhart and Lady Arlis one evening as the sunlight was fast reddening toward night. Word of them had preceeded their arrival, and the household and many of those living nearby were waiting in the yard. When he and Arlis came out of the trees the crowd cheered and rushed loudly forward. Gerhart saw that these people did not bow to their lady, but hugged and kissed her. He himself had his hand shook, his back slapped, his face kissed, and a wineglass pressed into his hand.

Fires were lit and tables set up and in a short time there was a picnic-banquet in progress. The lady sat by one of the fires in a simple chair and he stood in the place of honor on her right hand. Through the long evening those present came to welcome her back and she presented them to her rescuer. She seemed to know everything about all her people.

During a pause in the procession he commented that they seemed certainly to love her. She corrected him: "They are not my people. We are our people. But they do seem overly happy."

He laughed at that. "Who would not be happy to have a young and beautiful lady, just returned from a dragon's den?"

Which gave her opportunity to smile and ask, "Who indeed?"

There was much drinking and eating, then musical instruments were produced and the singing and dancing began. Gerhart sang a ballad, and caused a sensation. He danced, and caused another.

Arlis laughed as he returned to her side. "Well, sir knight, and now there are twice dozen girls yearning to fling themselves at your feet!"

He pulled her to her feet, and whirled her off them. "And you?'

Afterward toasts were given, to Arlis, to her rescuer, to the trees, the wine, the ladies, to each star above.

He was given a room in the house, and escorted there by a score of worshipful boys and twice that number of love-struck girls. Alone, he watched the yard under his window for a time, as the banquet was dismantled. Introspecting, he noticed that he felt rather peaceful and happy, even more so than on the long ride just finished. The Purple Forest seemed to encourage such feelings. After a time the people were all gone home and the house was silent. He reflected that he and the lady were now alone in this house, for servants in the Purple Forest lived in their own homes, and wondered. In no other place in all the lands he knew would a lady's honor be credible in this situation. Here, it seemed, a lady was thought capable of minding herself, not needing guards.

Though at peace with himself he found himself wakeful. He dressed once more and left his room to wander. After a time he found the stairway leading up to the watchtower and climbed to its top. The tower looked over the forest below and, in the bright moonlight, he could see very far—almost to the misty top of the westernmost Mountain of the Moon. So he leaned against the railing and thought of his most recent adventure, and wondered what now he would do.

The night was moving toward dawn when Lady Arlis found him there.

He had heard the soft footfalls on the steps below, so turned to greet her as she emerged onto the floor of the tower.

"Well, sir knight, are my beds so hard?"

Feeling light hearted, or perhaps the wine still held him, he replied, "Nay, lady, just thoughts of you."

She moved to the railing, looked over the forest. "And what thoughts of me, sir knight, to lead you here? You could have had the thoughts, and the presence as well, had you come to me."

He made no answer to that but a smile, and they watched the slowly lightening horizon for a time. At last she turned to him. "What shall you do now, Gerhart, when you have once more tired of peace?"

Gerhart watched the sky until he could see just the barest tip of Mantos, western rampart of the Mountains of the Moon, and finally said, "I know not, lady."

And so she surprised him again, for she put her arm around him, kissed his cheek, and said, "I do. "

He looked at her then, smiling merrily at his flushing face and blinking eyes. "You do?"

Still smiling, she stepped away, walked to the opposite railing, watched him for a time with laughter crowding her face. He noted that she was in white this morning, the dress V-necked and off the shoulder, flaring below a golden belt, with gilded shoes. Her hair was shining in the moonlight and dawn, not bound but straight and flowing to her waist. A red rose, bright against her white dress and pale skin, sat saucily between her breasts.

But she had always been beautiful to him. What stopped his tongue was that she was in wedding costume. He stared at her while his mind raced. Finally, weakly, he said, "Lady, surely you are teasing me."

"Nay, Gerhart, I am not. Let us reason together."

Weakly, he said, "Lady, surely you are teasing me."

"If you wish, but I am more afraid of your reason than any sword, for you are much the sharper."

He gained a laugh at that. "Perhaps. Then I shall propound the catechism, and you chop the logic, and we shall see what we shall see."

He could not help smiling, and suddenly they were laughing together. "Lead on, then, sweet lady."

"Ferasand in part sought oblivion, for there was no higher adventure left him, not so?"

"Most likely, fair lady."

"And this past adventure has been the most high of all your deeds, again not so?"

"Most certainly, dear maid."

"And there is no greater deed for you to do, sir knight?"

"Again, most likely, sweet interrogator."

"So there is nothing further for you to do, dear knight errant?"

"Indubitably, oh chatelaine mine hostess."

"Therefore, for your peace of mind, the adventure should never end. And is that not so?"

"Adventures always end but you are right, sweet lady."

Now she paused. "What, have you exhausted your variations?"

"Oh, Lady of the Forest, the best ones should be repeated—not so?"

Another laugh. "Look in your purse, Gerhart."

He blinked. Slowly he took out the one golden coin left to him from his previous escapade, the only one not spent in getting her home. He looked at it, somewhat surprised since he had forgotten it. "Ah, yes, so once I told you, did I not, that one never brings treasure away from an adventure, that it is always lost. So it is not yet over, is it? Still going on." His voice was low, bemused. "Knights errant rarely marry because they seldom die old, or in bed. Yet a sign is a symbol is a prophecy, as the saying goes, though one wonders what will happen after the peace of repose is gone and the wanderlust strikes again. But there are adventures and adventures—to adventure through a soul as through the world . . ."

He was debating with himself now. She listened, wondering but not really in doubt as to the outcome. He was thinking, of life as he had known it, of life and loves, of love. And—what had she meant, that night by the camp among the lindens, that a knight's adventures tended always to violence? He had not asked, and he did not know. And what was there among the purple trees that could produce a lady so free, and one which could love a dragon so fell? He could not say, and if he rode on he would never know. He looked at her, smiling, waiting, one last vagrant moonbeam shining in her eyes. He was returned from the greatest adventure of all tales told, he had thought with regret, but here she stood in the gloried dawn, warm mysteriousness that said the story should never end, that her soul was infinite space for his wanderlust did he win or lose. And what knight worried of defeat? He suddenly flipped the coin into the air, returned it to his bag. "You have chopped a fair logic, Arlis, unanswerable and true. But I have not a bride price for your hand."

The lady recognized the rear guard action of a good soldier. "Ah, but you do, if you insist upon giving one." He looked a question and she continued. "What would be thought of me, Sir Gerhart Ravenlock, should the greatest knight of the Holy Alter give over adventure for my hand?"

His eyes widened in surprise, and a slow brightening came over his face, and his lips twitched. Then he said, "So, for a reputation and one gold royal, a satin hand . . ." He leaned upon his elbows and looked at the sky for a last moment, then came to her forever. " 'Twere best done quickly?"

She seemed to fly toward him. The rose was crushed and her hair was mussed but neither noticed.

And thus it was the adventure did not end and they, of course, lived happily, ever after.

I am Dragon.

A DRAGON IN THE MAN

KEVIN CHRISTENSEN

ILLUSTRATION BY
JANET AULISIO

I am dragon.

The blade penetrates the chamber in my breast. I writhe and roar as if I am to die.

The lenses of the man-shaped mailed figure record the participant visual for branch F, track sixteen.

Off to the right, other cameras record the full scene for those who will be waiting in line for a turn on the Dragon's Cavern darkride.

"All right, that's good," Cassandra called. "Sechin, park that thing and take a break." She stood at a safe distance, and I felt her straining to be polite. And well she should. Last time she berated me for a performance, I ate her.

I got up, plucked the sword from my breast and handed it to the mailed telefactor. Then I flew the short distance to the stocks beside the set, poked my head and limbs into the holes, and flicked at the lock with my tail. Then I shifted my awareness to the day's wardrobe.

I brought Danseur today. Cassandra wore her Hitchcock. There is really no point. She wears them all the same. Once she managed to make my dragon look like a man in a funny suit. How she raged when I ate her. Not only did

315

she neglect to shift out until she had passed out from the pain, but the Wertmuller was her favorite.

I sat a moment to adjust to the new perspectives, and lack of tail and wings. I also checked silently for any signs of tampering. Cassandra is an imaginative sort, and is likely to seek some further revenge. The fine I had to pay was worth it though. She still looks small to me, even from this perspective.

The break in filming looked to be a general one. The technical crews, production people, and directors sorted themselves into cliques for brews and smoke. Tanya moved the telefactor to the starting point, and shut it down. I saw someone helping her from the exoskel tactile transceiver assembly she uses to control the telefactor's motions. The cavern set is designed to restrict a rube's motions, and simplify the recording process to a manageable level. The final effect of matching the rube's course and actions to the dragon responses is nigh indistinguishable from participant reality.

Tanya always takes the time for a token conversation. She moves gracefully in the low-g at the production level of the habitat, considering the adjustment she must make after being encased in a one-g simulation. I can't shake the impression that her motivation is totally professional. After asking my impression of her moves, she inquired after the expectation of seeing me at the party this evening. Though I made no firm answer, she said she'd pick me up.

Cassandra called for everyone to get back to work. I sat Danseur comfortably and shifted back to the dragon. In a ride like this one, there are certain points in each encounter that will result in branchings. Between crucial points it makes little difference what a rube does; he is given visual and tactile feedback according to his own moves. At a branching, we act out various possible consequences.

The mailed figure stumbles over a stalactite and I grip the writhing figure in my jaws.

Tanya had never come by my house before. I discovered that she has a habit of entering without knocking. I was wearing Zulu.

"Sechin?"

I nodded.

"Are you ready?"

"I'm deciding who to wear." I gestured to the booths which nourished my wardrobe.

"How many do you have?"

"Only these six." I gestured to the five opaque doors, and Zulu's opened booth. The blank brained bodies were fed and exercised when hot in use, as was my real self.

"Which is the real you?" She had seen Danseur, Zulu, Abdul, and blandman. But neither Aphrodite, nor myself. I was reluctant to show her Aphrodite, not sure why I had purchased her. So I stepped into Zulu's booth, shifted to myself, and stepped out.

Tanya drew her hand quickly to her mouth, then relaxed and tried to smile. "This must be why you are the best."

I turned around completely for her. Then I dropped to all fours, flicked out my long tongue, swished my tail, then rose from the floor with a beat of my leathery wings.

I am human, but genetically altered and given cyborg capacity to transmit my awareness. My neck is thirty centimeters long and very flexible. My arms and legs are articulated so I can walk on all fours as easily as upright. A dragonman.

After hovering briefly, I dropped to the floor and did my human impression.

"My parents were showbiz people. They forsaw the market for these attributes."

"You've done well," Tanya said.

"I can imagine them discussing it. How to insure Sechin's well-being? Well, we could make him a freak."

"Were there many altered people when you grew up?"

"Lots more cyborgs than genetics." I stepped toward the booth. "And not many of them either."

"I may yet go cyborg. If the ride franchises well."

I selected Danseur. We walked down through the sand and cypress around my house, and on to a fliverport. Then we took the flight across the habitat interior, making a Coriolis curve toward the party.

Once at the party, Tanya wandered off to chat with the more talkative types. I drifted among the gathered dancers, diners, gamers, and high-headers. I can usually find a sofa in the fringes. I prefer to think of parties as a trip to a zoo. I detach myself from the tempo and amuse myself with voyeurism. A glitter-boy started to pal up to me. Wearing Danseur turned out to be a mistake. From the corner of my eye, I noticed a man winding his way across the floor with two flaming skewers. The glitter-boy asked me if I really ate Cassandra. I had seen Cassandra here, wearing Merian C. Cooper. I've often wondered what she really looks like.

I felt a terrible pain in my side. The glitter-boy screamed in a high soprano. I jerked and turned to rise. A skewer hung from my ribs, and flames began licking over my clothing. The man swung the other skewer at my head. I tried to block it, and lost my hand. He struck towards me again, and I shifted home. The last sight I knew from those eyes was his face. Zulu.

I stepped from blandman's booth, panting. I flicked on the light, and stepped over to check. Zulu's booth was empty. I heard a tone from the visiterminal. It was Tanya calling from the party to see if I was okay.

I asked what had happened to Danseur and Zulu. She said Danseur was a horrid mess, cut and burned. Zulu collapsed after carving me. She said that Sepol had been contacted. I told her Zulu was mine and I was coming back for him. I stepped back into the booth and shifted.

As I rose the glitter-boy started screaming again. Someone soon quieted him. Tanya approached me hesitantly. Next to her Cassandra gave a ghosted smile.

"It is I, Sechin Hanna."

Someone had put a cover over Danseur. I lifted it.

"Please don't," Tanya said. She held back paled.

"Cassandra, come look," I said. "You've done at least as well as I."

"Don't slander me Sechin."

"Who else shall I accuse? Now that you've had your fun, perhaps you'll tell us how you broke my band."

"I'm not as petty as you like to think," she replied. "As far as I'm concerned the matter is finished. You paid. In cash."

"You had it done." I plucked one of the skewers from the corpse. At that moment, the Sepols walked in. One of them scowled at me. "You worried about fingerprints?" I handed the skewer over.

We were all on a first name basis after the prior incident. I formally accused Cassandra. They were half-inclined to agree, but found no evidence of any tampering with my wardrobe coding. After they finished I varied all the bands, and increased my securing.

Work went well the next day. The hostility was appropriate to the theme. After I parked the dragon, and fed him, I headed straight home. Tanya ran up beside me and asked if I'd gotten any word on who might have intruded on my wardrobe.

"I don't often have visitors."

"Why would I?" She started laughing. Then she saw my look. Perhaps she also reflected on my viciousness today. "I'm your friend," she protested.

"Define friend. I can teach you. Cassandra can pay you."

"Sechin, please."

"Sechin, please," I mocked. She left.

Mirrorshift gathered light from the habitat as I walked home. I live nearly parallel to the set, so there is little inertial change. At times I wished I could as myself, dragonman, free in the dark sky. But children might go into weeks of hysterical nightmares, so they forbid me. Perhaps when a few more people have moved to the larger structures. Already much of this habitat is left to grow wild.

My home is a kidney-shaped coral swelling in the cypress and sand forest in this area. A slow motion waterfall flows over the top and into a pool I rarely use.

Inside I parked Abdul and stepped out as blandman. He seems to possess the best sense of taste, so I habitually use him for eating, even if I've no appetite. Across the room, I saw Abdul flashing his white teeth. He had pulled a long dagger from the heraldic set over the hearth.

"Cassandra!" I stepped back. Abdul crouched and moved forward. I looked to the v.t. The screen was shattered. I retreated into the booth as Abdul rushed me. I stepped from behind Abdul as Zulu. He turned, but I got across the room, and pulled the broadsword from the wall.

"Stay bitch." I held the heavy weapon in two hands. "Die again, and leave me alone."

Abdul pushed a chair in front of me, and ran across to dragonman's booth.

"No!" I threw the blade and lunged. The edge ran

across Abdul's back, leaving a red slash, and making him fumble with the door.

I grabbed him and pulled him away as the door opened. "Leave me alone." He jerked his head back violently into my nose, breaking it. I got my leg between his, and tripped him as I fell back. I heard the clatter of the dagger. We rolled and struggled. Then I struggled alone. Abdul had gone limp. I stood and turned.

The heavy broadsword fell in Aphrodite's grip. The blade crashed through my collar bone, crushed into my ribs and my lungs filled with blood. "I'll kill you," I gurgled, and fell.

I came out as dragonman. Aphrodite was pale. She released the sword and fled outside. I skittered across the room on all fours.

She fell under one of the cypress trees near the pond. I flew and hovered over her. She was vegetable. I heard noise inside.

I flew back to the door to see Abdul pulling the sword from Zulu's chest. I hissed. He looked up and ran through the door on the other side, carrying the stained blade. I flew over the house and above him as he ran. "I'll give you nightmares," I hissed.

Abdul fled into a copse of trees. I flitted around it and over it, shouting curses, insults, and threats. I found a stone. Then I flew up and landed atop one of the trees and crept silently down. Abdul held the sword easily in one hand. His back glistened wetly. I tossed the stone. Abdul glided silently towards the sound.

I dropped atop him, clutching the sword hand with my taloned feet and grabbing his throat with my hands. "See it through Cassandra," I hissed. "You'll need the practice." Abdul went limp.

I cursed and released him. I took up the sword and flew up to make my way to her quarters.

A great shadow fell over me. I snaked my neck to see the dragon above me, dropping. I cried out involuntarily, manuvered and twisted and thrust up at the heart. The sword slid into the chamber.

"No," I whimpered. I flew back. The dragon closed the distance easily and a whoosh of fire scorched over my back. The flesh of my wings withered and tore. I fell to the sand. The dragon hovered over me. I landed in a burnt and scarred heap. The dragon landed beside me. The shadow loomed over me. I looked up to see the jaws descending, shimmering heat. I screamed. The terrible jaws lifted me, fangs penetrated flesh and crushed bone, and a fire surged up and over into horrible agony on and on and on . . . and I fled into my mind's last chambers and wept in darkness like a womb.

Without knowing in whose tender arms I rested I begged forgiveness and wept. Perhaps hatred is a way of hiding truth. In the horror of pain, the bitterness had fled from my mind, and I learned wonders.

I felt myself as blandman. Sechin Hanna. I was not in soul dragonman. I had known once, but had somehow forgotten. My parents forced cyborging into the dragon-man awareness from a very young age.

It had not been Cassandra, nor could it had been. She wore them all the same. I had assumed her hatred, edited out her forgiveness.

I felt the arms to be Aphrodite's, but did not know who she was to weep over me and caress me. "Tanya?" I asked. "Do you hate me so much?"

Before the being within Aphrodite denies this identity, I know I am wrong. Still, I want to flee from the truth.

"From within," she says mournfully. "I couldn't live in the dark, so very dark and deepening always. Like a storm seething always."

In its absence, purged by fire and fear, I knew what storm she referred to.

"I'm insane," I whispered.

"Could we expect otherwise?"

"Do you hate me so much?" I asked.

She shook her head. She let me go and stepped to the booth.

"No." I said, understanding some. I rose and walked to see light pouring through from dawn mirrorshift.

"Look," I whispered. "So lovely."

The room remained silent.

I walked over to the booth. When had I purchased this one? She had purchased me.

"Stay with me." I whispered. The room was quiet and lonely.

"Please." There was no sound or feeling.

"Stay with me."

Her eyes opened and glistened with the morning.

A PLAGUE OF BUTTERFLIES

ORSON SCOTT CARD

ILLUSTRATIONS BY
DON MAITZ

The butterflies awoke him. Amasa felt them before he saw them, the faint pressure of hundreds of half-dozens of feet, weighting his rough wool sheet so that he dreamed of a shower of warm snow. Then he opened his eyes and there they were, in the shaft of sunlight like a hundred stained-glass windows, on the floor like a carpet woven by an inspired lunatic, delicately in the air like leaves falling upward in a wind.

At last, he said silently.

He watched them awhile, then gently lifted his covers. The butterflies arose with the blanket. Carefully he swung his feet to the floor; they eddied away from his footfall, then swarmed back to cover him. He waded through them like the shallow water on the edge of the sea, endlessly charging and then retreating quickly. He who fights and runs away, lives to fight another day. You have come to me at last, he said, and then he shuddered, for this was the change in his life that he had waited for, and now he wasn't sure he wanted it after all.

They swarmed around him all morning as he prepared for his journey. His last journey, he knew, the last of many. He had begun his life in wealth, on the verge of power, in

Sennabris, the greatest of the oil-burning cities of the coast. He had grown up watching the vast ships slide into and out of the quays to void their bowels into the sink of the city. When his first journey began, he did not follow the tankers out to sea. Instead, he took what seemed the cleaner way, inland.

He lived in splendor in the hanging city of Besara on the cliffs of Carmel; he worked for a time as a governor in Kafr Katnei on the plain of Esdraelon until the Megiddo War; he built the Ladder of Ekdippa through solid rock, where a thousand men died in the building and it was considered a cheap price.

And in every journey he mislaid something. His taste for luxury stayed in Besara; his love of power was sated and forgotten in Kafr Katnei; his desire to build for the ages was shed like a cloak in Ekdippa; and at last he had found himself here, in a desperately poor dirt farm on the edge of the Desert of Machaerus, with a tractor that had to be bribed to work and harvests barely large enough to pay for food for himself and petrol for the machines. He hadn't even enough to pay for light in the darkness, and sunset ended every day with imperturbable night. Yet even here, he knew that there was one more journey, for he had not yet lost everything: still when he worked in the fields he would reach down and press his fingers into the soil; still he would bathe his feet in the rush of water from the muddy ditch; still he would sit for hours in the heat of the afternoon and watch the grain standing bright gold and motionless as rock, drinking sun and expelling it as dry, hard grain. This last love, the love of life itself—it, too, would have to leave, Amasa knew, before his life would have completed its course and he would have consent to die.

The butterflies, they called him.

He carefully oiled the tractor and put it into its shed.

He closed the headgate of the ditch and shoveled earth into place behind it, so that in the spring the water would not flow onto his fallow fields and be wasted.

He filled a bottle with water and put it into his scrip, which he slung over his shoulder. This is all I take, he said. And even that felt like more of a burden than he wanted to bear.

The butterflies swarmed around him, and tried to draw him off toward the road into the desert, but he did not go at once. He looked at his fields, stubbled after the harvest. Just beyond them was the tumble of weeds that throve in the dregs of water that his grain had not used. And beyond the weeds was the Desert of Machaerus, the place where those who love water die. The ground was stone: rocky outcroppings, gravel; even the soil was sand. And yet there were ruins there. Wooden skeletons of buildings that had once housed farmers. Some people thought that this was a sign that the desert was growing, pushing in to take over formerly habitable land, but Amasa knew better. Rather the wooden ruins were the last remnants of the woeful Sebasti, those wandering people who, like the weeds at the end of the field, lived on the dregs of life. Once there had been a slight surplus of water flowing down the canals. The Sebasti heard about it in hours; in days they had come in their ramshackle trucks; in weeks they had built their scrappy buildings and plowed their stony fields, and for that year they had a harvest because that year the ditches ran a few inches deeper than usual. The next year the ditches were back to normal, and in a few hours one night the houses were stripped, the trucks were loaded, and the Sebasti were gone.

I am a Sebastit, too, Amasa thought. I have taken my life from an unwilling desert; I give it back to the sand when I am through.

Come, said the butterflies alighting on his face. Come,

they said, fanning him and fluttering off toward the Hierusalem road.

Don't get pushy, Amasa answered, feeling stubborn. But all the same he surrendered, and followed them out into the land of the dead.

* * *

The only breeze was the wind on his face as he walked, and the heat drew water from him as if from a copious well. He took water from his bottle only a mouthful at a time, but it was going too quickly even at that rate.

Worse, though: his guides were leaving him. Now that he was on the road to Hierusalem, they apparently had other errands to run. He first noticed their numbers diminishing about noon, and by three there were only a few hundred butterflies left. As long as he watched a particular butterfly, it stayed; but when he looked away for a moment, it was gone. At last he set his gaze on one butterfly and did not look away at all, just watched and watched. Soon it was the last one left, and he knew that it, too, wanted to leave. But Amasa would have none of that. If I can come at your bidding, he said silently, you can stay at mine. And so he walked until the sun was ruddy in the west. He did not drink; he did not study his road; and the butterfly stayed. It was a little victory. I rule you with my eyes.

"You might as well stop here, friend."

Startled to hear a human voice on this desolate road, Amasa looked up, knowing in that moment that his last butterfly was lost. He was ready to hate the man who spoke.

"I say, friend, since you're going nowhere anyway, you might as well stop."

It was an old-looking man, black from sunlight and naked. He sat in the lee of a large stone, where the sun's northern tilt would keep him in shadow all day.

"If I wanted conversation," Amasa said, "I would have brought a friend."

"If you think those butterflies are your friends, you're an ass."

Amasa was surprised that the man knew about the butterflies.

"Oh, I know more than you think," said the man. "I lived at Hierusalem, you know. And now I'm the sentinel of the Hierusalem Road."

"No one leaves Hierusalem," said Amasa.

"I did," the old man said. "And now I sit on the road and teach travelers the keys that will let them in. Few of them pay me much attention, but if you don't do as I say, you'll never reach Hierusalem, and your bones will join a very large collection that the sun and wind gradually turn back into sand."

"I'll follow the road where it leads," Amasa said. "I don't need any directions."

"Oh, yes, you'd rather follow the dead guidance of the makers of the road than trust a living man."

Amasa regarded him for a moment. "Tell me, then."

"Give me all your water."

Amasa laughed—a feeble enough sound, coming through splitting lips that he dared not move more than necessary.

"It's the first key to entering Hierusalem." The old man shrugged. "I see that you don't believe me. But it's true. A man with water or food can't get into the city. You see, the city is hidden. If you had miraculous eyes, stranger, you could see the city even now. It's not far off. But the city is forever hidden from a man who is not desperate. The city can only be found by those who are very near to death. Unfortunately, if you once pass the entrance to the city without seeing it because you had water with you, then you can wander on as long as you like, you can run out of water and cry out in a whisper for the city to unveil itself to you, but it will avail you nothing. The entrance, once passed, can never be found again. You see, you have to know the taste of death in your mouth before Hierusalem will open to you."

"Its sounds," Amasa said, "like religion. I've done religion."

"Religion? What is religion in a world with a dragon at its heart?"

Amasa hesitated. A part of him, the rational part, told him to ignore the man and pass on. But the rational part of him had long since become weak. In his definition of man, "featherless biped" held more truth than "rational animal." Besides, his head ached, his feet throbbed, his lips stung. He handed his bottle of water to the old man, and then for good measure gave him his scrip as well.

"Nothing in there you want to keep?" asked the old man, surprised.

"I'll spend the night."

The old man nodded.

They slept in the darkness until the moon rose in the east, bright with its thin promise of a sunrise only a few hours away. It was Amasa who awoke. His stirring roused the old man.

"Already?" he asked. "In such a hurry?"

"Tell me about Hierusalem."

"What do you want, friend? History? Myth? Current events? The price of public transportation?"

"Why is the city hidden?"

"So it can't be found."

"Then why is there a key for some to enter?"

"So it *can* be found. Must you ask such puerile questions?"

"Who built the city?"

"Men."

"Why did they build it?"

"To keep man alive on this world."

Amasa nodded at the first answer that hinted at significance. "And what enemy is it, then, that Hierusalem means to keep out?"

"Oh, my friend, you don't understand. Hierusalem was built to keep the enemy in. The old Hierusalem, the new Hierusalem, built to contain the dragon at the heart of the world."

A story-telling voice was on the old man now, and Amasa lay back on the sand and listened as the moon rose higher at his left hand.

"Men came here in ships across the void of the night," the old man said.

Amasa sighed.

"Oh, you know all that?"

"Don't be an ass. Tell me about Hierusalem."

"Did your books or your teachers tell you that this world was not unpopulated when our forefathers came?"

"Tell me your story, old man, but tell it plain. No myth, no magic. The truth."

"What a simple faith you have," the old man said. "The truth. Here's the truth, much good may it do you. This world was filled with forest, and in the forest were beings who mated with the trees, and drew their strength from the trees. They became very treelike."

"One would suppose."

"Our forefathers came, and the beings who dwelt among the trees smelt death in the fires of the ships. They did things—things that looked like magic to our ancestors, things that looked like miracles. These beings, these dragons who hid among the leaves of the trees, they had science we know little of. But one science we had that they had never learned, for they had no use for it. We knew how to defoliate a forest.''

"So the trees were killed.''

"All the forests of the world now have grown up since that time. Some places, where the forest had not been lush, were able to recover, and we live in those lands now. But here, in the Desert of Machaera—this was climax forest, trees so tall and dense that no underbrush could grow at all. When the leaves died, there was nothing to hold the soil, and it was washed onto the plain of Esdraelon. Which is why that plain is so fertile, and why nothing but sand survives here.''

"Hierusalem.''

"At first Hierusalem was built as an outpost for students to learn about the dragons, pathetic little brown woody creatures who knew death when they saw it, and died of despair by the thousands. Only a few survived among the rocks, where we couldn't reach them. Then Hierusalem became a city of pleasure, far from any other place, where sins could be committed that God could not see.''

"I said truth.''

"I say listen. One day the few remaining students of the science of the dragons wandered among the rocks, and there found that the dragons were not all dead. One was left, a tough little creature that lived among the grey rocks. But it had changed. It was not woody brown now. It was grey as stone, with stony outcroppings. They brought it back to study it. And in only a few hours it escaped. They never recaptured it. But the murders began, every night a murder. And every murder was of a couple who were coupling, neatly vivisected in the act. Within a year the pleasure seekers were gone, and Hierusalem had changed again.''

"To what it is now."

"What little of the science of the dragons they had learned, they used to seal the city as it is now sealed. They devoted it to holiness, to beauty, to faith—and the murders stopped. Yet the dragon was not gone. It was glimpsed now and then, grey on the stone buildings of the city, like a moving gargoyle. So they kept their city closed to keep the dragon from escaping to the rest of the world, where men were not holy and would compel the dragon to kill again."

"So Hierusalem is dedicated to keeping the world safe for sin."

"Safe from retribution. Giving the world time to repent."

"The world is doing little in that direction."

"But some are. And the butterflies are calling the repentant out of the world, and bringing them to me."

Amasa sat in silence as the sun rose behind his back. It had not fully passed the mountains of the east before it started to burn him.

"Here," said the old man, "are the laws of Hierusalem:

"Once you see the city, don't step back or you will lose it.

"Don't look down into holes that glow red in the streets, or your eyes will fall out and your skin will slide off you as you walk along, and your bones will crumble into dust before you fully die.

"The man who breaks a butterfly will live forever.

"Do not stare at a small grey shadow that moves along the granite walls of the palace of the King and Queen, or he will learn the way to your bed.

"The Road to Dalmanutha leads to the sign you seek. Never find it."

Then the old man smiled.

"Why are you smiling?" asked Amasa.

"Because you're such a holy man, Saint Amasa, and Hierusalem is waiting for you to come."

"What's your name, old man?"

The old man cocked his head. "Contemplation."

"That's not a name."

He smiled again. "I'm not a man."

For a moment Amasa believed him, and reached out to see if he was real. But his finger met the old man's flesh, and it did not crumble.

"You have so much faith," said the old man again. "You cast away your scrip because you valued nothing that it contained. What do you value?"

In answer, Amasa removed all his clothing and cast it at the old man's feet.

* * *

He remembers that once he had another name, but he cannot remember what it was. His name now is Gray, and he lives among the stones, which are also grey. Sometimes he forgets where stone leaves off and he begins. Sometimes, when he has been motionless for hours, he has to search for his toes that spread in a fan, each holding to stone so firmly that when at last he moves them, he is surprised at where they were. Gray is motionless all day, and motionless all night. But in the hours before and after the sun, then he moves, skittering sure and rapid as a spider among the hewn stones of the palace walls, stopping only to drink in the fly-strewn standing water that remains from the last storm.

These days, however, he must move more slowly, more clumsily than he used to, for his stamen has at last grown huge, and it drags painfully along the vertical stones, and now and then he steps on it. It has been this way for weeks. Worse every day, and Gray feels it as a constant pain that he must ease, must ease, must ease; but in his small mind he does not know what easement there might be. So far as he knows, there are no others of his kind; in all his life he has met no other climber of walls, no other hanger from stone ceilings. He remembers that once he sought out couplers in the night, but he cannot remember what he did with them. Now he again finds himself drawn to windows, searching for easement, though not sure at all, holding in his mind no image of what he hopes to see in the dark rooms within the palace. It is dusk, and Gray is hunting, and is not sure whether he will find mate or prey.

*   *   *

I have passed the gate of Hierusalem, thought Amasa, and I was not near enough to death. Or worse, sometimes he thought, there is no Hierusalem, and I have come this way in vain. Yet this last fear was not a fear at all, for he did not think of it with despair. He thought of it with hope, and looked for death as the welcome end of his journey, looked for death which comes with its tongue thick in its mouth, death which waits in caves during the cool of the day and hunts for prey in the last and first light, death which is made of dust. Amasa watched for death to come in a wind that would carry him away, in a stone that would catch his foot in midstep and crumble him into a pile of bone on the road.

And then in a single footfall Amasa saw it all. The sun was framed, not by a haze of white light, but by thick and heavy clouds. The orchards were also heavy, and dripped with recent rain. Bees hummed around his head. And now he could see the city rising, green and grey and monumental just beyond the trees; all around him was the sound of running water. Not the tentative water that struggled to stay alive in the thirsty dirt of the irrigation ditch, but the lusty sound of water that is superfluous, water that can be tossed in the air as fountains and no one thinks to gather up the drops.

And then in a single footfall Amasa saw it all.

For a moment he was so surprised that he thought he must step backward, just one step, and see if it wouldn't all disappear, for Amasa did not come upon this gradually, and he doubted that it was real. But he remembered the first warning of the old man, and he didn't take that backward step. Hierusalem was a miracle, and in this place he would test no miracles.

The ground was resilient under his feet, mossy where the path ran over stone, grassy where the stones made way for earth. He drank at an untended stream that ran pure and overhung with flowers. And then he passed through a small gate in a terraced wall, climbed stairs, found another gate, and another, each more graceful than the last. The first gate was rusty and hard to open; the second was overgrown with climbing roses. But each gate was better tended than the last, and he kept expecting to find someone working a garden or picnicking, for surely someone must be passing often through the better-kept gates. Finally he reached to open a gate and it opened before he could touch it.

It was a man in the dirty brown robe of a pilgrim. He seemed startled to see Amasa. He immediately enfolded his arms around something and turned away. Amasa tried to see—yes, it was a baby. But the infant's hands dripped with fresh blood, it was obviously blood, and Amasa looked back at the pilgrim to see if this was a murderer who had opened the gate for him.

"It's not what you think," the palmer said quickly. "I found the babe, and he has no one to take care of him."

"But the blood."

"He was the child of pleasure-seekers, and the prophecy was fulfilled, for he was washing his hands in the blood of his father's belly." Then the pilgrim got a hopeful look. "There is an enemy who must be fought. You wouldn't—"

A passing butterfly caught the pilgrim's eye. The fluttering wings circled Amasa's head only once, but that was
sign enough.

"It is you," the pilgrim said.

"Do I know you?"

"To think that it will be in my time."

"*What* will be?"

"The slaying of the dragon." The pilgrim ducked his
head and, freeing one arm by perching the child precari-
ously on the other, he held the gate open for Amasa to
enter. "God has surely called you."

Amasa stepped inside, puzzled at what the pilgrim
thought he was, and what his coming portended. Behind
him he could hear the pilgrim mutter, "It is time. It is time."

It was the last gate. He was in the city, passing between
the walled gardens of monasteries and nunneries, down
streets lined with shrines and shops, temples and houses,
gardens and dunghills. It was green to the point of blind-
ness, alive and holy and smelly and choked with business
wherever it wasn't thick with meditation. What am I here
for? Amasa wondered. Why did the butterflies call?

He did not look down into the red-glowing holes in the
middles of streets. And when he passed the grey labyrinth
of the palace, he did not look up to try to find a shadow
sliding by. He would live by the laws of the place, and
perhaps his journey would end here.

*   *   *

The Queen of Hierusalem was lonely. For a month she
had been lost in the palace. She had strayed into a never-
used portion of the labyrinth, where no one had lived for
generations, and now, search as she might, she could find
only rooms that were deeper and deeper in dust.

The servants, of course, knew exactly where she was,
and some of them grumbled at having to come into a place

of such filth, full of such unstylish old furniture, in order to
care for her. It did not occur to *them* that she was lost—
they only thought she was exploring. It would never do for
her to admit her perplexity to them. It was the Queen's
business to know what she was doing. She couldn't very
well ask a servant, "Oh, by the way, while you're fetching
my supper, would you mind mentioning to me where I
am?" So she remained lost, and the perpetual dust irri-
tated all her allergies.

The Queen was immensely fat, too, which complicated
things. Walking was a great labor to her, so that once she
found a room with a bed that looked sturdy enough to hold
her for a few nights, she stayed until the bed threatened to
give way. Her progress through the unused rooms, then,
was not in a great expedition, but rather in fits and starts.
On one morning she would arise miserable from the bed's
increasing incapacity to hold her, eat her vast breakfast
while the servants looked on to catch the dribbles, and
then, instead of calling for singers or someone to read, she
would order four servants to stand her up, point her in the
direction she chose, and taxi her to a good, running start.

"That door," she cried again and again, and the servants would propel her in that direction, while her legs
trotted underneath her, trying to keep up with her body.
And in the new room she could not stop to contemplate:
she must take it all in on the run, with just a few mad
glances, then decide whether to try to stay or go on. "On,"
she usually cried, and the servants took her through the
gradual curves and maneuvers necessary to reach whatever door was most capacious.

On the day that Amasa arrived in Hierusalem, the
Queen found a room with a vast bed, once used by some
ancient rake of a prince to hold a dozen paramours at
once, and the Queen cried out, "This is it, this is the right

place, stop, we'll stay!" and the servants sighed in relief and began to sweep, to clean, and to make the place livable.

Her steward unctuously asked her, "What do you want to wear to the King's Invocation?"

"I will not go," she said. How could she? She did not know how to get to the hall where the ritual would be held. "I choose to be absent this once. There'll be another one in seven years." The steward bowed and left on his errand, while the Queen envied him his sense of direction and miserably wished that she could go home to her own rooms. She hadn't been to a party in a month, and now that she was so far from the kitchens the food was almost cold by the time she was served the private dinners she had to be content with. Damn her husband's ancestors for building all these rooms anyway.

* * *

Amasa slept by a dunghill because it was warmer there, naked as he was; and in the morning, without leaving the dunghill, he found work. He was wakened by the servants of a great Bishop, stablemen who had the week's manure to leave for the farmers to collect. They said nothing to him, except to look with disapproval at his nakedness, but set to work, emptying small wheelbarrows, then raking up the dung to make a neater pile. Amasa saw how fastidiously they avoided touching the dung; he had no such scruples. He took an idle rake, stepped into the midst of the manure, and raked the hill higher and faster than the delicate stablemen could manage on their own. He worked with such a will that the Stablemaster took him aside at the end of the task.

"Want work?"

"Why not?" Amasa answered.

The Stablemaster glanced pointed at Amasa's un-clothed body. "Are you fasting?"

Amasa shook his head. "I just left my clothing on the road."

"You should be more careful with your belongings. I can give you livery, but it comes out of your wages for a year."

Amasa shrugged. He had no use for wages.

The work was mindless and hard, but Amasa delighted in it. The variety was endless. Because he didn't mind it, they kept him shoveling more manure than his fair share, but the shoveling of manure was like a drone, a background for bright rhinestones of childish delight: morning prayers, when the Bishop in his silver gown in-toned the powerful words while the servants stood in the courtyard clumsily aping his signs; running through the street behind the Bishop's carriage shouting "Huzzah, huzzah!" while the Bishop scattered coins for the pedes-trians; standing watch over the carriage, which meant drinking and hearing stories and songs with the other servants; or going inside to do attendance on the Bishop at the great occasions of this or that church or embassy or noble house, delighting in the elaborate costumes that so cleverly managed to adhere to the sumptuary laws while being as ostentatious and lewd as possible. It was grand, God approved of it all, and even discreet prurience and titillation were a face of the coin of worship and ecstacy.

But years at the desert's edge had taught Amasa to value things that the other servants never noticed. He did not have to measure his drinking water. The servants splashed each other in the bathhouse. He could piss on the ground and no little animals came to sniff at the puddle, no dying insects lit on it to drink.

They called Hierusalem a city of stone and fire, but

Amasa knew it was a city of life and water, worth more than all the gold that was forever changing hands.

The other stablemen accepted Amasa well enough, but a distance always remained. He had come naked, from outside; he had no fear of uncleanliness before the Lord; and something else: Amasa had known the taste of death in his mouth and it had not been unwelcome. Now he accepted as they came the pleasures of a stableman's life. But he did not need them, and knew he could not hide that from his fellows.

One day the Prior told the Steward, and the Steward the Stablemaster, and the Stablemaster told Amasa and the other stablemen to wash carefully three times, each time with soap. The old-timers knew what it meant, and told them all: It was the King's Invocation that came but once in seven years, and the Bishop would bring them all to stand in attendance, clean and fine in their livery, while he took part in the solemn ordinances. They would have perfume in their hair. And they would see the King and Queen.

"Is she beautiful?" Amasa asked, surprised at the awe in the voices of these irreverent men when they spoke of her.

And they laughed and compared the Queen to a mountain, to a planet, to a moon.

But then a butterfly alighted on the head of an old woman, and suddenly all laughter stopped. "The butterfly," they all whispered. The woman's eyes went blank, and she began to speak:

"The Queen is beautiful, Saint Amasa, to those who have the eyes to see it."

The servants whispered: See, the butterfly speaks to the new one, who came naked.

"Of all the holy men to come out of the world, Saint Amasa, of all the wise and weary souls, you are wisest, you are weariest, you are most holy."

Amasa trembled at the voice of the butterfly. In memory he suddenly loomed over the crevice of Ekdippa, and it was leaping up to take him.

"We brought you here to save her, save her, save her," said the old woman, looking straight into Amasa's eyes.

Amasa shook his head. "I'm through with quests," he said.

And foam came to the old woman's mouth, wax oozed from her ears, her nose ran with mucus, her eyes overflowed with sparkling tears.

Amasa reached out to the butterfly perched on her head, the fragile butterfly that was wracking the old woman so, and he took it in his hand. Took it in his right hand, folded the wings closed with his left, and then broke the butterfly as crisply as a stick. The sound of it rang metallically in the air. There was no ichor from the butterfly, for it was made of something tough as metal, brittle as plastic, and electricity danced between the halves of the butterfly for a moment and then was still.

The old woman fell to the ground. Carefully the other servants cleaned her face and carried her away to sleep until she awakened. They did not speak to Amasa, except the Stablemaster, who looked at him oddly and asked, "Why would you want to live forever?"

Amasa shrugged. There was no use explaining that he wanted to ease the old woman's agony, and so killed it at its cause. Besides, Amasa was distracted, for now there was something buzzing in the base of his brain. The whirr of switches, infinitely small, going left or right; gates going open and closed; poles going positive and negative. Now and then a vision would flash into his mind, so quickly that he could not frame or recognize it. Now I see the world through butterfly's eyes. Now the vast mind of Hierusalem's machinery sees the world through mine.

* * *

Gray waits by this window: it is the one. He does not wonder how he knows. He only knows that he was made for this moment, that his life's need is all within this window, he must not stray to hunt for food because his great stamen is dewing with desire and in the night it will be satisfied.

So he waits by the window, and the sun is going; the sky is grey, but still he waits, and at last the lights have gone from the sky and all is silent within. He moves in the darkness until his long fingers find the edge of the stone. Then he pulls himself inside, and when his stamen scrapes painfully against the stone, immense between his legs, he only thinks: ease for you, ease for you.

His object is a great mountain that lies breathing upon a sea of sheets. She breathes in quick gasps, for her chest is large and heavy and hard to lift. He thinks nothing of that, but only creeps along the wall until he is above her head. He stares quizzically at the fat face; but it holds no interest for him. What interests Gray is the space at her shoulders where the sheets and blankets and quilts fall open like a tent door. For some reason it looks like the leaves of a tree to him, and he drops onto the bed and scurries into the shelter.

Ah, it is not stone! He can hardly move for the bouncing, his fingers and toes find no certain purchase, yet there is this that forces him on: his stamen tingles with extruding pollen, and he knows he cannot pause just because the ground is uncertain.

He proceeds along the tunnel, the sweating body to one side, the tent of sheets above and to the other side. He explores; he crawls clumsily over a vast branch; and at last he knows what he has been looking for. It is time, oh, time, for here is the blossom of a great flower, pistil lush for him.

He leaps. He fastens to her body as he has always fastened
to the limbs of the great wife trees, to the stone. He plunges
stamen into pistil and dusts the walls with pollen. It is all he
lived for, and when it is done, in only moments when the
pollen is shed at last, he dies and drops to the sheets.

* * *

The Queen's dreams were frenzied. Because her waking
life was wrapped and closed, because her bulk forced an
economy of movement, in her sleep she was bold, untir-
ing. Sometimes she dreamed of great chases on a horse
across broken country. Sometimes she dreamed of flying.
Tonight she dreamed of love, and it was also athletic and
unbound. Yet in the moment of ecstasy there was a face
that peered at her, and hands that tore her lover away from
her, and she was afraid of the man who stared at the end of
her dream.

Still, she woke trembling from the memory of love, only
wistfully allowing herself to recall, bit by bit, where she
really was. That she was lost in the palace, that she was as
ungainly as a diseased tree with boles and knots of fat, that
she was profoundly unhappy, that a strange man disturbed her dreams.

And then, as she moved slightly, she felt something cold
and faintly dry between her legs. She dared not move
again, for fear of what it was.

Seeing that she was awake, a servant bowed beside her.
"Would you like your breakfast?"

"Help me," she whispered. "I want to get up."

The servant was surprised, but summoned the others.
As they rolled her from the bed, she felt it again, and as
soon as she was erect she ordered them to throw back the
sheets.

And there he lay, flaccid, empty, grey as a deflated

stone. The servants gasped, but they did not understand what the Queen instantly understood. Her dreams were too real last night, and the great appendage on the dead body fit too well the memory of her phantom lover. This small monster did not come as a parasite, to drain her; it came to give, not to receive.

She did not scream. She only knew that she had to run from there, had to escape. So she began to move, unsupported, and to her own surprise she did not fall. Her legs, propelled and strengthened by her revulsion, stayed under her, held her up. She did not know where she was going, only that she must go. She ran. And it was not until she had passed through a dozen rooms, a trail of servants chasing after her, that she realized it was not the corpse of her monstrous paramour she fled from, but rather what he left in her, for even as she ran she could feel something move within her womb, could feel something writhing, and she must, she must be rid of it.

As she ran, she felt herself grow lighter, felt her body melting under the flesh, felt her heaps and mounds erode away in an inward storm, sculpting her into a woman's shape again. The vast skin that had contained her belly began to slap awkwardly, loosely against her thighs as she ran. The servants caught up with her, reached out to support her, and plunged their hands into a body that was melting away. They said nothing; it was not for them to say. They only took hold of the loosening folds and held and ran.

And suddenly through her fear the Queen saw a pattern of furniture, a lintel, a carpet, a window, and she knew where she was. She had accidently stumbled upon a familiar wing of the palace, and now she had purpose, she had direction, she would go where help and strength were waiting. To the throne room, to her husband, where the king was surely holding his Invocation. The servants caught up with her at last; now they bore her up. "To my husband," she said, and they assured her and petted her and carried her. The thing within her leaped for joy: its time was coming quickly.

* * *

Amasa could not watch the ceremonies. From the moment he entered the Hall of Heaven all he could see were the butterflies. They hovered in the dome that was painted like the midsummernight sky, blotting out the tiny stars with their wings; they rested high on painted pillars; camouflaged except when they fanned their graceful wings. He saw them where to others they were far too peripheral to be seen, for in the base of his brain the gates opened and closed, the poles reversed, always in the same rhythm that drove the butterflies' flight and rest. Save the Queen, they said. We brought you here to save the Queen. It throbbed behind his eyes, and he could hardly see.

Could hardly see, until the Queen came into the room, and then he could see all too clearly. There was a hush, the ceremonies stopped, and all gazes were drawn to the door where she stood, an undulant mass of flesh with a woman's face, her eyes vulnerable and wide with fright and trust. The servants' arms reached far into the folds of skin, finding God-knew-what grip there: Amasa only knew that her face was exquisite. Hers was the face of all women, the hope in her eyes the answer to the hope of all men. "My husband!" she cried out, but at the moment she called she was not looking at the King. She was looking at Amasa.

She is looking at me, he thought in horror. She is all the beauty of Besara, she is the power of Kafr Katnei, she is the abyss of Ekdippa, she is all that I have loved and left behind. I do not want to desire them again.

The King cried out impatiently, "Good God, woman!"

And the Queen reached out her arms toward the man on the throne, gurgled in agony and surprise, and then shuddered like a wood fence in a wind.

What is it, asked a thousand whispers. What's wrong with the Queen?

She stepped backward.

There on the floor lay a baby, a little grey girlchild, naked and wrinkled and spotted with blood. Her eyes were open. She sat up and looked around, reached down and took the placenta in her hands and bit the cord, severing it.

The butterflies swarmed around her, and Amasa knew what he was meant to do. As you snapped the butterfly, they said to him, you must break this child. We are Hierusalem, and we were built for this epiphany, to greet this child and slay her at her birth. For this we found the man most holy in the world, for this we brought him here, for you alone have power over her.

I cannot kill a child, Amasa thought. Or did not think, for it was not said in words but in a shudder of revulsion in him, a resistance at the core of what in him was most himself.

This is no child, the city said. Do you think the dragons have surrendered just because we stole their trees? The dragons have simply changed to fit a new mate; they mean to rule the world again. And the gates and poles of the city impelled him, and Amasa decided a thousand times to obey, to step a dozen paces forward and take the child in his arms and break it. And as many times he heard himself cry out, I cannot kill a child! And the cry was echoed by his voice as he whispered, "No."

Why am I standing in the middle of the Hall of Heaven, he asked himself. Why is the Queen staring at me with horror in her eyes? Does she recognize me? Yes, she does, and she is afraid of me. Because I mean to kill her child. Because I cannot kill her child.

The grey shadow had come in from the wall.

As Amasa hesitated, tearing himself, the grey infant looked at the King. "Daddy," she said, and then she stood and walked with gathering certainty toward the throne. With such dexterous fingers the child picked at her ear. Now. Now, said the butterflies.

Yes, said Amasa. No.

"My daughter!" the King cried out. "At last an heir! The answer to my Invocation before the prayer was done— and such a brilliant child!"

The King stepped down from his throne, reached to the child and tossed her high into the air. The girl laughed and tumbled down again. Once more the King tossed her in delight. This time, however, she did not come down.

She hovered in the air over the King's head, and everyone gasped. The child fixed her gaze on her mother, the mountainous body from which she had been disgorged, and she spat. The spittle shone in the air like a diamond, then sailed across the room and struck the Queen on her breast, where it sizzled. The butterflies suddenly turned black in midair, shriveled, dropped to the ground with infinitesimal thumps that only Amasa could hear. The gates all closed within his mind, and he was all himself again; but too late, the moment was passed, the child had come into her power, and the Queen could not be saved.

The King shouted, "Kill the monster!" But the words still hung in the air when the child urinated on the King from above. He erupted in flame, and there was no doubt now who ruled in the palace. The grey shadow had come in from the walls.

She looked at Amasa, and smiled. "Because you were the holiest," she said, "I brought you here."

* * *

Amasa tried to flee the city. He did not know the way. He passed a palmer who knelt at a fountain that flowed from virgin stone, and asked, "How can I leave Hierusalem?"

"No one leaves," the palmer said in surprise. As Amasa went on, he saw the palmer bend to continue scrubbing at a baby's hands. Amasa tried to steer by the patterns of the stars, but no matter which direction he ran, the roads all bent toward one road, and that road led to a single gate. And in the gate the child waited for him. Only she was no longer a child. Her slate-grey body was heavy-breasted now, and she smiled at Amasa and took him in her arms, refused to be denied. "I am Dalmanutha," she whispered, "and you are following my road. I am Acrasia, and I will teach you joy."

She took him to a bower on the palace grounds, and taught him the agony of bliss. Every time she mated with him, she conceived, and in hours a child was born. He watched each one come to adulthood in hours, watched them go out into the city and affix themselves each to a human, some man, some woman, or some child. "Where one forest is gone," Dalmanutha whispered to him, "another will rise to take its place."

In vain he looked for butterflies.

"Gone, all gone, Amasa," Acrasia said. "They were all the wisdom that you learned from my ancestors, but they were not enough, for you hadn't the heart to kill a dragon that was as beautiful as man." And she *was* beautiful, and every day and every night she came to him and conceived again and again, telling him of the day not long from now when she would unlock the seals of the gates of Hierusalem and send her bright angels out into the forest of man to dwell in the trees and mate with them again.

More than once he tried to kill himself. But she only laughed at him as he lay with bloodless gashes in his neck, with lungs collapsed, with poison foul-tasting in his mouth. "You can't die, my Saint Amasa," she said. "Father of Angels, you can't die. For you broke a wise, a cruel, a kind and gentle butterfly."

MORE SCIENCE FICTION FROM BART